SHADOW OF BETRAYAL

SHADOW KNIGHTS
BOOK 4

MICHAEL WEBB

CONTENTS

ALSO BY MICHAEL WEBB

The Shadow Knights Series:
Prequel Novella - Shadow Knights: Origine
The Shadow Knights Trilogy
#1 - The Last Shadow Knight
#2 - Rise of the Shadow
#3 - Shadow of Destiny
Shadow Knights Generations
#4 - Shadow of Betrayal
#5 - Shadow of Sacrifice (coming 2024)
#6 - Shadow of Hope (coming 2024)

Treasure Hunters Alliance:
#1 - Fortress of the Lost Amulet
#2 - Legend of the Golden City

Get a FREE prequel novella to the Shadow Knights series - Shadow Knights: Origine - by signing up for my mailing list at www.subscribepage.com/michaelwebbnovels or scan this QR code

STORY SUMMARY

Did you forget what happened in the last book? I've got you covered!

Go to michaelwebbnovels.com/book-summaries to get short summaries of each of the previous books in the series.

Land of Terrenor
North Sea
Bryveld
Nortris
Neraverre River
Daratill
Norshewa
Korob Mountains
Rydland
Gap of Thaeder
Kyrd Forest
Molyaigh
Westfale Ocean
Karad
Tarendu
Feldor
Naice
Bromhill
Tienne
Kandis
Felaverre River
Felting
Rynor
Felaverre River
Lorranis
Terraverre River
Straith Mountains
Tarving
Palenting
Isle of Paratill
Tarphan
Portris
Searis
Marris
Gulf of Tartis
Palthi Mountains
N
Parathan Ocean

PART I

FAMILY

1

LORRANIS

Wind tugged at the edge of his cloak as Veron Stormbridge leaned into the darkness. Cold seeped through the seams in his clothes, but he pushed the discomfort away. Gripping the stone edge of the tower, the mortar pressed against his fingertips. One foot rested on the ledge while the other dangled far above the ground. He scanned the area below as he waited. Ready to protect. Prepared to kill.

Quiet two-story shops along the edge of the square wallowed in a blanket of fog. Streets split the buildings, connecting the open area to the rest of the city. Behind him, the Felavorre River poured into the Westfale Ocean. The arc of a bridge jumped out of the fog, leading over the river to the other half of the port city of Lorranis. Along the ocean side of the square, waves lapped against a stone pier, cresting white from the glow of the moon. The salty tang of fish tickled his nose.

The square itself was quiet. Vendor carts stood empty, and benches sat open. Veron only spotted one lone couple through the fog, sitting in the shadows, locked in a tight embrace.

At the center of the square, a body lay on a bench, covered

by a cloak. He grinned as the figure extended a hand with an open palm—*ready*. Veron returned the gesture. His gaze jumped to the edge of the square, next to the pier. Shrouded in fog, a pile of crates stared back at him. Nothing moved. Veron squinted, keeping his arm out, but there was no response. "Come on," he whispered. "Where are you?"

His grip on the stone shook as the tower rang with a hollow boom. Once. Twice. Three chimes. *It should be time.* Veron pulled himself back through the window.

"Did you see anything?" Mason Danby whispered, stepping from the shadows of the bell tower, and taking his hands off from over his ears. His hood was up, and the black Shadow Knights cloak wrapped around him.

Darkness covered them except for the lantern tucked in the corner. A shade obscured it, allowing only slivers of light to peek through the edges. In the tower, narrow openings served as windows, but visibility was limited, the light from the moon barely penetrating the space.

"Nothing yet," Veron replied.

"What about the others?"

Veron's forehead wrinkled. "I'm sure they'll be ready." He hesitated before adding, "It's too dark to tell behind the crates."

"Do you want me to go down and make sure she's there?" Mason's eyebrows lifted. "I could hold the position with her."

"Just because you have a crush on her doesn't mean we adjust our plan."

Mason's eyes widened.

"Oh, you thought I hadn't noticed?" Veron asked.

"I—uh . . ." Mason stuttered. "I . . ."

Veron laughed, resting his hand on the twenty-year-old's shoulder. "It's all right. Just stay focused on your job."

Mason nodded then turned to look out a window slit. His boot scraped on the floor when his body tensed.

"What is it?" Veron moved to another window. A tall figure

strode across the square, hastening toward the pier. "They're here."

Peering through another window confirmed a second person. The two shadowy figures met on the pier and huddled together in conversation.

"Now it's only a matter of time," Veron said. "You check the river approach; I'll watch the north. They should arrive soon."

Silence filled the tower as they peered through openings on each side. Veron watched the street ahead and scanned the square. Nothing moved. A gust of wind puffed through the bell tower, rippling the end of their cloaks.

"How many do you expect?" Mason whispered from his post.

"No more than two."

"Um . . ." Adjusting feet scraped from the far window.

"What is it?" Veron glanced Mason's way. Visible lines wrinkled the younger man's forehead. "What's the matter?"

"There are *twelve* men coming."

"What?" Veron rushed across the tower and leaned out the window. Between the buildings, a crowd of men moved as one. Swords either hung from their waist or filled their hands. Two men held torches, dashing any pretense of secrecy while they strode up the middle of the street.

Veron ran to the opposite side and stretched the lantern out the window. He flashed the shade—two long flashes and two short—*all hands needed.* After repeating the sign three times, he set the lantern down and leaned back out, holding onto the stone while his body dangled.

The person on the bench shifted. The glint of a sword peeked from under the cloak, and they lifted to a partially sitting position. Veron looked back at the crates, straining his eyes. His chest rose and fell several times. *Nothing.*

"What if she's not there?" Mason asked from inside the tower. "Can Chelci handle them all?"

"She'll be there." Veron's voice wavered, the wind blowing it away. He continued to watch. "But even if she's not . . ." He couldn't voice the rest of his thought.

His heart pounded, the thudding filling his ears. Raucous laughter and jeers snapped his attention to the right side of the square. *They're here.*

The men with torches passed the body on the bench, not stopping to inspect. A shout issued from the gang, and they spread out. The two figures on the pier turned their heads and stepped away from each other. They glanced around frantically, but there was nowhere to go.

The figure on the bench stood, the black cloak over their shoulders draping to the ground. A hood kept the face shrouded.

Veron looked toward the crates. "Come on," he muttered to himself. "Where are you?"

"She's not there." Mason's words echoed his thoughts. "Will Chelci abort?"

Veron shook his head as he watched her. Hooded and in shadow, she approached the men from behind.

"Weatherford!" one gang member yelled as the group stepped onto the pier. "The Black Lanterns warned you there would be consequences. Now you will pay with your life!"

Swords gleamed as the remaining men pulled their weapons. Chelci drew closer, the men oblivious to her presence.

"What can we do?" Mason asked, his voice wavering.

Veron's grip on the stone window was the only thing keeping him up. He dropped his gaze. The hard stones of the square lay far below. A warm tingle hummed deep inside him —the origine waiting to be used.

"You're not thinking about—" Mason stopped when Veron released his hand.

Wind whipped his hair. His cloak trailed above him as he

fell, the edges of the black fabric snapping around his head. When he was a body length off the ground, he pulled from the origine. Power flooded into his limbs. His sight focused, and his hearing sharpened.

He crouched when he hit, allowing the strength in his knees and legs to absorb the force. Stones crumbled beneath his feet where his boots punched into the hard ground. Veron looked up. A loud cracking sound echoed off the far walls of the square, but the men ahead paid no attention to him. Chelci had arrived. Veron became lost in his wife's movements, forgetting his purpose.

Chelci's sword sang through the air as she spun and twirled. Men fell around her, grabbing their wounds and shrieking in pain. The gang gave up on their original targets and focused on her, moving into defensive positions. She continued to attack, dropping more of them. The air around her shimmered. Her cloak billowed. A faint whistle could be heard from the speed with which she moved.

She can do it. She can do it.

When a few men remained, her movements slowed, her shoulders slumping as she sucked in air. Veron paled. The remaining attackers smirked as they closed in. A large brute with a dark beard stepped forward and cocked his sword.

No!

Snapping into action, Veron raced forward. His body hummed, using everything he had stored. He pulled Farrathan from over his shoulder, the ruby in its hilt catching the moonlight. He moved with such speed that the gang of men ahead looked frozen in time.

The space across the square seemed to grow farther with every step. Veron put all he had into his run, desperate to reach Chelci. The man's nearly frozen sword crept forward as Veron raced against it. He stepped onto the pier when the weapon remained a hair away from her chest. With a roar, Veron exploded into the midst of the group, swinging his weapon at the extended blade. The man's sword exploded into pieces, shattering the night with the crash of metal. Jagged shards embedded in the stomachs and faces of the remaining two members of the gang.

Veron spun back to the bearded man, who held nothing but a broken hilt. He didn't even have time to look toward Veron before Farrathan struck him in the chest.

Bodies covered the pier. Some still moaned and writhed, but most were motionless, waiting for the rest to join them in eternal sleep. Blood ran through the wooden slats to drip into the salty water below.

Veron turned to Chelci. "Are you all right?" he asked, puffing. He placed a hand on her arm and checked her body for injuries. "That was too close."

"I'm fine. Why are you here?" she asked, her hands on her knees as she sucked in breaths. She turned to the square. "Where is she?"

Veron's jaw tightened. From the base of the bell tower, Mason ran toward them. Veron raised his hand and pointed, indicating for him to check behind the crates.

"I don't know," he said, turning back to Chelci.

She closed her eyes and exhaled a deep breath, her shoulders falling along with her chin.

"Um . . . thank you," a man on the pier said, shuffling to approach while maintaining space from the dying men. "Are you . . . shadow knights?"

"Yes, Lord Weatherford, we are," Veron confirmed. "We heard of the plot on your life, and we came to protect you."

The lord's eyes grew, and his mouth dropped. "You're Veron Stormbridge!"

Veron dipped his head.

"You killed Edmund Bale and saved our kingdom! Thank

you for what you did." He gestured to include Chelci. "Thank you both for what you do, still."

"Don't mention it," Veron said. "You're trying to do good things here in Lorranis. I'm sorry you had to deal with these guys." He turned to the other man. "You're the treasurer's assistant, correct?"

The man nodded, shaking. "They said if we didn't reverse the new tax edict, there would be consequences. I never expected this, though."

Veron kneeled next to one of the unmoving bodies.

"Taxes are tricky," Chelci said. "Sometimes they create hardships, but in this case, it only upset the greedy ones, like the men of the Black Lanterns. Keep at it, Lord Weatherford."

The lord ducked his head in a respectful bow. "Of course."

Veron stood, holding a leather sack that jingled.

"Is that their purse?"

Veron nodded. He opened the tie and rummaged through the bag, coins clinking. After tying the sack again, he tossed it to Weatherford. "See that this is used to help the victims of the Black Lanterns' oppression."

"It will be done," Weatherford said.

Jogging steps turned Veron's head. Mason approached.

"She's not there," the younger knight said.

"Who's not there?" the assistant asked.

Veron frowned and looked at Chelci. Her mouth made a tight line. "No one," Veron said, turning back to Weatherford. "It's for us to deal with. Now, we must go."

Veron led the way, with Chelci and Mason close behind. Their cloaks trailed them as they hurried across the square into the dark city.

VERON GRIPPED the stone wall with the tips of his fingers. His feet found only the slightest hint of purchase. Despite the minuscule size of the ledges, he made his way upward, the warmth of the origine simmering inside him. He glanced down as he approached the third-floor window. The shadowy ground of the alley waited below him. Holding on to the wall with one hand, he used the other to pull the window open. The casement emitted only the slightest rattle, then he slipped inside.

The sparse room contained a bed and a desk with a chair. A cold candle sat on the desk, and a body lay in the bed. The ruffled, brown hair of a man peeked out from the covers.

Veron cleared his throat, but the man didn't stir. He stepped closer and tried again, louder.

The covers moved. The sleeping man adjusted his head, and his eyes peeked open. With a start, he jumped to a sitting position and brought his hand to his chest. "What is this! Oh, Veron. Curse you for scaring me like that!"

Veron's mouth curled up at the edge. "Sorry about that, Griff."

"I wish you would meet during the day and come to the door like a normal person." He pressed his hand against his chest as he breathed out. Once collected, he threw the covers back and stood. "Any luck?"

"Yes. Thank you for the lead. The Black Lanterns were there —twelve of them."

Griff Batterston's eyes widened. "Twelve! I'm so sorry. I didn't realize they'd send so many! Were you all right?"

Veron nodded. "We managed." He pulled the handful of coins he had stashed in his pocket and dropped them into the man's hand. "Pay your team."

"I will. What happened to the Lanterns?"

"They won't bother Lorranis for a while."

Griff lowered his head and nodded. "Good riddance. Thank you, Veron. I don't know what we'd do without you. Let me know if there's ever anything I can do for you."

Veron angled his body toward the still-open window. He

stopped moving as an idea came to him. "Actually, I do need help."

Griff straightened and leaned toward him.

"Are there any gambling halls around here that would be open right now?"

Griff's eyebrows lowered. "I never took you for a gambling man."

"And you would be right. Still . . . are there any?"

Griff nodded. "Yes, there's a place nearby."

Veron exhaled, his mouth forming a tight line. "Where?"

2

———

THE TARTIS PIT

Raucous laughter sounded around the tavern, but Lia tuned out the distraction. She stared ahead. The sailor in front of her looked back, chewing on a splinter of wood. Long, stringy hair fell down his face, obscuring one eye. His rough beard contained foam from his last gulp of ale. His gaze tore away from hers to check his cards, as if they could have changed since the last dozen times he'd looked. On the table between them, a pile of coins lay ready for someone to claim them. Lia drummed her fingers on the table, waiting for the man to decide.

On either side, grimy men watched. A skinny sailor named Barley had a patch over his right eye and an oily beard. His pile of coins dwindled. The other man, Zarid, was shirtless and showed off scores of tattoos across his chest, some covered by his long, red beard. When he opened his mouth, gaping holes showed where half of his teeth were missing.

Around her, the gambling den exhibited more of its gritty display. Dim lanterns flickered along the walls. Tables of men filled the room, drinking, smoking pipes, and holding on to barely dressed women. One man twirled a knife in one hand while downing a drink with the other. Unable to escape the presence of the nearby sea, a salty taste filled the air along with a strong smell of damp sweat and sour ale.

Lia raised her mug and took a long drink of ale, setting it back empty on the table with a thunk. A dull buzz filled her head, silencing the pain of the past that had been creeping through her mind all night—the memories that seemed to haunt her on every mission.

"Are you going to play or not, Mudge?" she asked the stringy-haired man, her voice barely cutting through the din of the room.

A scowl grew on the man's face. After a moment, his nose curled, and he threw his cards down on the table. "I'm out," he grumbled.

Lia grinned. She discarded her hand and raked in the pile of coins.

A barmaid arrived with a full mug of ale and a raised eyebrow. Lia nodded and accepted the drink, taking a large swallow. The cool, foamy liquid poured down her throat, punctuated by her lips smacking with a satisfied "ahh."

Mudge grabbed her cards and flipped them over. *A star prince, two moon jesters, and a diamond baron.*

"Hey, you can't—"

"I knew it!" he shouted. "You had nothing."

"Did you?" she taunted, wiping the foam off her mouth with her sleeve. "Did you, really?"

He scowled back.

"You didn't pay to see those."

"I don't care," Mudge grumbled. "You show up here, a stranger, and dare to take our money." He looked at the other two men at the table. "Should we kick her out?"

The other men shrugged. Barley spoke up. "I don't mind having her here. She's much better to look at than you two."

Zarid flashed a toothy grin. "Yeah. I'm having fun picturing her in a short dress instead of that black cloak."

Lia's chair jumped back as she leaped to her feet, pulling Zarid up with a fist full of his beard. The man teetered on his feet as his own chair fell back against the floor.

"You say something like that again and my fist is going to knock out every one of your remaining teeth. Am I clear?"

The men at the table and the others nearby hushed.

Despite the threat, the bare-chested man grinned back, taunting her. "Yes, very clear."

Lia's mouth turned down. She pulled a dagger from a sheath tucked into her belt and held the tip to his neck. "Or maybe I'll need to find other ways to get my point across?"

Zarid's smile faltered. "It's clear," he repeated.

Lia released the man's beard and put up her dagger. She pulled her chair back and sat, her brown hair bouncing with the motion.

"If you like action, perhaps you'd be interested in the tartis pit," Mudge said, tossing his head toward the back corner of the room while monitoring her pile of coins. A wry smile grew on his face.

Lia followed his nod with her eyes. While most of the tavern was filled with tables, ale, and gambling men, the back corner contained a doorway that peeked into a different scene. Through the opening, a wall of men's backs faced her. They shouted and cheered, pumping their fists while looking down as if a spectacle played out on the ground before them.

"Mudge," Barley said. "Come on. She doesn't—"

"I'm not saying she should participate. I just thought she might like the action."

"What is it?" Lia asked.

"That's where the bravest men of Lorranis go," Mudge said.

"It's also the best place to earn some coins, if that's what interests you," Zarid added.

She lifted her mug and drank while she thought. After a pause, she collected the coins on the table in front of her. "Sure. I'll check it out."

Mudge and Zarid chuckled as she stood. She put the money she had won in the pocket of her cloak and left the table, drinking as she walked. The buzz from the ale made the room spin as she crossed it. Conversations muddled in her head.

As she passed through the corner doorway, a large bald man stepped in front of her. He scowled at her with crossed arms that were as thick as her legs. "No girls allowed back here."

Lia narrowed her eyes. "It's a good thing I'm a woman, then."

The bald man laughed. "How old are you?"

"Twenty-one," she lied, hoping the years of exaggeration were believable.

The man pursed his lips but didn't reply.

"What is this back here?" she asked, nodding over his shoulder. She strained her neck, trying to look past the wall of men.

"The tartis pit is where men come to prove themselves and everyone bets on how they'll do. The house takes five percent and pays out based on odds. If you pick the right people, you can make some money."

"How much can you make?"

The man chuckled. "That depends on how much you want to risk. The challengers are the ones who really make the money. They get half of the house cut."

A cheer erupted from the onlookers, afflicting her with a fresh wave of dizziness. Lia raised on her toes to see, but the bald man held his arm out to block her.

"Looks like Corrus just got his cut."

"What do the challengers do?" Lia asked.

"Gunden!"

The shout came through the doorway from across the tavern. Lia turned. Still at his seat, Mudge raised a hand. "Let her by. She's got money to spare."

Lia turned back to the man addressed as Gunden with a raised eyebrow.

"Fine. We're closing soon anyway," the bald man said. He pointed to a desk in the corner where men gathered. "That's where you make bets. Have at it."

Gunden stepped away, but Lia grabbed his tunic. "And what if I want to be a challenger?" she asked.

He raised both eyebrows then erupted into laughter. As his laughter settled, he pointed to a man stretching by the wall. Muscles rippled down the man's exposed arms. He leaned his head from side-to-side, veins bulging from his thick neck. "Why don't you watch Perciun over there first? Then . . . if you still want to take part, let me know."

Gunden moved aside, and Lia stepped forward. A man with shaggy black hair and a thick beard made his way out through the wall of spectators. Splotches darkened his shirt where sweat made the fabric cling to his broad chest. He held a burlap bag extended at an arm's length. A bony man with glasses and a yellow tunic arrived, took the bag, and disappeared. The sweating man's chest sank as he exhaled.

"Nice job, Corrus," large-armed Perciun said, clapping him on the shoulder while holding his own limp burlap bag.

"Last call for bets!" a man shouted from the table in the corner. A few more men scurried to him, setting coins down while he wrote their names in a ledger.

After another minute of muddled conversations and drunken laughter, Perciun stepped through the crowd. A cheer rose from the onlookers. The challenger waved his massive hand then dropped below Lia's sight.

She tried to peer between the bodies of the crowd, but the wall was too tight, and she was a full head shorter than most of the men. She caught glimpses of a pit. Through a gap between two men, Perciun's head came into view as he walked into the middle of a sunken chamber with what looked like a sandy floor.

"I'm betting on you, Perciun!" a man shouted from the crowd. "Don't let me down!"

"What does he have to do?" Lia asked a bow-backed man with crooked teeth next to her.

He sneered and chuckled but didn't answer.

A hush fell over the onlookers, and Lia turned to the pit, unable to catch little more than glimpses. The challenger spun below, and for a long moment, everyone was silent. Finally, gasps echoed around the ring.

What is it? Perciun focused on something she couldn't see.

A roar from the crowd and a round of clapping indicated something had happened, but the tension remained. After another moment, a wave of cheers filled the space again.

Amidst the cheers, Lia ducked and squeezed between rows of legs. Men jumped aside when they noticed her, and soon she found herself standing in a front-row position. Her feet toed the edge of a pit with no railing to hold her back. With nothing to block her view, her eyes widened. A dizzy spell from the ale made her waver.

Smooth rock walls dropped a body's length to a large sandy floor. At the edge of the floor, multiple mouse-sized holes, obscured by mounds of sand, disappeared into the walls. In the center of the pit, Perciun stood with his knees bent. His right hand held the sack, no longer limp but moving with an undulating rhythm. His left arm extended forward, and his eyes locked straight ahead. Coiled on the sand, the green-and-black checkered pattern on a snake's back made Lia's mouth drop. The serpent held its head off the ground where it puffed into a hood shape, swaying side-to-side. Its tongue flicked in and out while Perciun circled it.

A tartis viper! The serpent from the southern kingdom was the deadliest snake in Terrenor. The venom worked so quickly it was said that a victim could die before they even realized they were bitten.

She pulled from her well of power, using a bit of origine to flush the effects of the alcohol from her system. Her vision grew crisp, and her legs firmed.

With a hiss, the snake lunged. Perciun spun out of the way and reached behind the animal's head, clamping his hand around its body. The tail wriggled, whipping against the man's leg, but he held tight. His other hand allowed the sack to open, and he placed the snake inside, tail first. After he closed it again, he spun around, his eyes raking over the sand.

"One more, Perciun!" a spectator shouted.

Sweat dripped down the man's neck. He turned again, searching.

Lia scanned the floor of the pit but saw nothing. *It should be easy to see, right?*

Sand ruffled at the challenger's feet, but he stood as still as stone. *That's odd,* Lia thought. *Why would the sand be—*

A viper exploded from the floor, its head rising next to Perciun's leg with fangs bared. The man's head jerked, but the rest of his body was too slow. The serpent sank its teeth into the bare flesh of his calf.

Gasps erupted from the onlookers. Perciun's scream filled the pit and the rest of the tavern. He attempted to grab the snake, but it had already released his leg and slithered a safe distance away. After two lumbering steps, he fell forward, his face smacking into the sand.

Most of the men around the ring of the pit erupted with shock and disappointment, but a few celebrated, dancing their way to the betting table. Two bony men wearing yellow descended the ladder, carrying sticks and yellow rags. One ran for the burlap sack that had fallen free from Perciun's grip. The sack wriggled on the sand, and the head of two snakes peeked out of the widening opening.

"Back in, you!" the man shouted, waving a yellow rag at the opening. The serpents recoiled at the brightly colored fabric. When they retreated, he snatched the bag.

The other worker backed the loose snake into a wall, shaking a yellow rag of his own. Having nowhere else to go, the snake darted into the nearest mouse hole.

The man with the bag moved to a different hole in the wall. He upended it, allowing three vipers to fall from the sack. The snakes hissed and lunged toward him, but he was ready with his stick and rag. He held up the fabric and prodded them toward the hole in the wall with the stick. Soon, all three disappeared.

Lia studied the crowd and spotted Gunden's thick arms at the betting table. He was counting a stack of coins when she arrived.

Lia drained her mug then set it on the table with alacrity. "I want to be a challenger."

Gunden stopped mid-count and raised his head. He chuckled then glanced to either side before settling his eyes back on her. "You're joking, right?"

"No. You said challengers can earn a lot of money."

"Yeah," he pointed toward the pit while scoffing. "Did you see that?"

Lia looked where he pointed. The two men in yellow raised Perciun's lifeless body out of the pit. Onlookers parted, allowing them to pass.

"Yeah, I saw that. His reflexes were poor."

"And you think yours are better?"

"I do."

Gunden narrowed his eyes as he stared back. Around the pit, the crowd dispersed. He shook his head then shrugged.

"Fine. What happens is on you." He raised an arm and caught the attention of a man in yellow. "Give her a sack."

Lia's pulse jumped. She glanced at the pit, the hole beckoning to her. "Can I bet on myself?"

A man in yellow arrived and handed her a burlap bag as Gunden answered. "Sure, but at half odds and only to win. If you bet against yourself, we don't give the money to your dead body."

She swallowed the lump in her throat.

Gunden raised his voice. "Don't leave yet, men! We have one more challenger."

The shuffling crowd stopped and glanced their way.

"What's your name?" Gunden whispered.

"Lia."

"Lia . . . the Savage will enter the pit."

Lia raised an eyebrow at the nickname. The crowd chuckled and muttered while returning to their places.

"Place your bets now. Odds are—" He glanced at her and ran his eyes up and down her body. "Four to one . . . against."

Lia was the first one to the gambling table, but many others lined up behind her. "Six argen, four tid . . . to win."

The worker at the table raised an eyebrow. He jotted down her name and wager then took the coins without speaking.

A man behind her pushed her out of the way. "Three argen . . . to lose."

Lia glanced at the man. He sported a thick beard and dark brown hair that fell across his eyes.

He looked back at her and shrugged.

She held back a laugh. *If he only knew.*

Lia headed to the pit, then stood for a few minutes while men bet on her. She caught curious glances as she scanned the crowd, but most looked away when they saw her noticing them.

A man with stringy hair and a rough beard watched from across the ring. *Mudge.* A faint smirk appeared on his face as he shook his head. His lips mouthed the word, "fool," but she couldn't hear over the din of the room.

"You're up, Savage," Gunden said from behind her. "To win, you must capture all four snakes and not get bitten."

Lia tightened her grip on the sack and stepped to the edge of the pit. The crowd hushed as she took one last look around. The faces that stared back held a mixture of pity, interest, and greed. She grasped the edge of a ladder and lowered herself rung-by-rung until her feet touched the floor.

Sand squished under her boots as she walked to the center of the pit. The burlap bag felt rough in her hand. A stench of decay replaced the salty air above, and her nose wrinkled. She watched the holes around the perimeter of the pit, expecting snake heads to emerge at any moment. Only shadows stared back. A dull rumble of conversation reached her ears from above, but she tuned it out.

She pushed away a trickle of fear. *I can do this.* She wriggled her toes and fingers. Her arms and legs were ready to react. A warm, tingling sensation simmered in her gut. The origine was ready to be used.

A gasp from the crowd sounded above her. She spun and saw the source of worry. A diamond-shaped head poked out of a hole with a tongue flicking. *There you are.* The snake slithered out, allowing its full body to enter the arena. The green-and-black pattern across its back contrasted with the sand. Its body undulated, crossing toward her. She crouched, holding the bag ready when the serpent's body began to sink. It continued moving, but the colorful pattern disappeared beneath the sand. The head was the last part to hide. The sand continued to move, but soon, even that stopped.

Lia gulped. *How can I catch it when*—Another head poked from a different hole. As it emerged, a hiss turned her around. A third snake was already on the sand, with the fourth poking its head out of another hole. The third coiled its body, puffed its head into a hooded shape, and lifted itself as high as her waist. She moved closer to it while spinning to keep a watch on the others. The one under the sand was nowhere to be found while the other two continued slithering into the ring. She approached the coiled one, well within striking distance.

The muttering from the crowd grew into a rumble. She tried to block it out to focus on the danger before her. A hiss from the coiled viper commanded her attention. She held a hand ready. Her knees were bent. The power waiting inside her begged to be used. She watched for it to strike, ready to pivot and grab it. The serpent swayed back and forth but didn't move for her. *Why is it not striking?* A wild thought came to her. *If it was smart, it could distract me while—*

A disturbance of the air tingled her senses. She pulled from the origine, and time seemed to freeze. The swaying snake stopped. The noise from the crowd grew distorted. Lia spun. Her eyes widened as she found a tartis viper stretched out with most of its body leaping through the air to strike her in the back of her leg. While not frozen, the moving serpent was slow enough to allow her to react.

She took the burlap sack and opened it where the animal lunged. When she released the power, time sped up. The snake struck into the bottom of the sack, its fangs extending through the coarse fabric. Drops of venom splattered on the sand.

Lia closed the bag while the crowd roared. *One down, three to go.* She ignored the spectators and turned back to the other serpents. The last one to emerge had left its hole and coiled just out of reach. Her eyes jumped between the two visible animals. One flicked its tongue while the other hissed. They both swayed in matching rhythms.

Where is that other one? She backed away from the two she could see and turned to take in the rest of the pit. Watching the sand, she stepped across the ground. Nothing gave away its location. Chanting voices called for her attention, but she tuned them out.

She used the origine to heighten her hearing, focusing on the sand. A tingle in her gut warmed her. Rustling grains reached her ears, but nothing visibly shifted. She clenched her teeth. *Where are you?* She padded across the mounds, glancing behind to make sure the other vipers weren't making a move.

A rustle caught her eye, and she froze. A wave of motion disturbed the grains, moving in a wavy pattern toward her. She backed up, but the hidden snake drew closer. Her heart thudded. Suddenly, the motion stopped. Her stomach dropped as hissing sounded from either side. She swiveled her head to see two coiled serpents, well within striking range.

Frozen, she sensed motion beneath her. The origine rushed into her, filling her body with impossible strength and speed. She crouched and rolled, flinging sand into the air as her back flipped over the ground. The spot where she had stood exploded, and the head of a viper rose. The coiled snakes struck simultaneously, springing forward with fangs bared.

Lia struck out, grabbing the snake rising from the sand just behind its head. Continuing the motion, she snatched the next one, caught between her index and middle finger. While the final viper remained frozen, she pulled the bodies of the two in her hand and whipped their tails through the air, knocking the last serpent to the sand. Before it could recover, Lia scooped it up between her middle and ring finger. Finally, she released her hold on the origine.

The vipers writhed with vigor. Their three tails thrashed against her arm, body, and legs, but she gripped tightly, straining against the flailing bodies. Gasps, shouts, and applause boomed above her. She set down the bag and threaded the whipping tails into the opening. Finally, she dropped the heads and cinched the sack closed.

Lia threw her arms up in celebration. Her chest heaved as

she sucked in air to recover from the heavy use of energy. She looked up and took in the scene. Men stared down, roaring with applause. She spun, waving to the crowd while they cheered her victory. Her eyes met Gunden's. The bald man shook his head while his lips curled into a grin. He clapped.

Suddenly, his hands faltered and his eyebrows narrowed. Lia's smile weakened. Gasps reached her from every direction. Before she turned, a sharp pain racked her body. It was as if a knife plunged into her leg and twisted. She screamed and fell to the ground while turning.

A tartis viper released its hold on her leg. Its green-and-black hood puffed up, and it swayed, staring into her eyes. Half of the serpent rested on the sand, while the rest of its body poked through a hole torn in the bag's bottom.

Moving like lightning, Lia smacked the snake in the side of its head, sending it flying across the pit to thump into the smooth wall. She dropped the bag and fell to all fours, closing her eyes. Pain grew in her leg, spreading up the limb toward the rest of her body.

She tapped into her remaining energy. The warm flood of power rushed through her. She willed the healing power of her body to attack the toxin. Her leg shuddered, and her arms trembled. She fought the convulsing that threatened to distract her while beads of sweat formed on her face. Her leg prickled. She pulled as deeply as she could from her well of energy.

The searing pain subsided. She glanced at her calf. A yellow substance oozed from the puncture site. Soon, it was gone, and a black scab formed over the pair of holes where the fangs had entered her leg.

A deep breath helped her settle. She closed her eyes and focused. The trembling stopped, and she rose to her feet. Dizzy from exhaustion, she steadied herself against the wall, continuing to suck in lungsful of air.

The cheering crowd no longer cheered. The spectators' mouths gaped, their bodies frozen.

Lia offered a half-hearted laugh and a weak smile. She raised a hand. "I'm all right."

Several of the men took a step away from the lip of the pit, their jaws continuing to hang limp.

Lia spun, searching for someone to celebrate with her. Gunden looked aghast, his head shaking like before but with a different meaning. Zarid's and Mudge's heads poked through the crowd, but their wide eyes confirmed their fear.

Beside Mudge, the crowd shuffled aside, and Lia's heart sank. A tall man with shaggy brown hair and a beard approached the edge of the pit, his black cloak hanging to the floor. He looked down. The hard look of his eyes and his set jaw showed a mixture of disappointment and anger.

"Lia," the man said in an even but stern voice, "come out of there."

Lia dropped her head. Her feet felt rooted in place. She glanced at the side of the pit, but her body wouldn't move.

"Lia," he repeated.

"Yes, Father," she mumbled before turning to the ladder. "I'm coming."

3

———

A TENSE RETURN

Veron's body rose and fell with the slow gait of the horse's walk. His head ached. He touched his forehead with his free hand, feeling the deep, furrowed lines.

"You're brooding," Chelci said at his side.

Veron glanced at her, forcing his forehead to relax. Chelci's long brown hair draped across her shoulders. She wore a gray tunic with sleeves to her wrists and an orange tie around her waist. Her brown riding pants frayed at the ends where boots tucked into her horse's stirrups.

"I'm fine," he replied.

She cocked her head before turning to glance over her shoulder. Veron followed her gaze.

Mason rode just behind them, his grin reflecting a positivity Veron didn't feel. The younger knight was eager to please, but Veron wasn't in the mood.

Past Mason, Lia Stormbridge sat on her horse and scowled. The animal she rode followed the one in front of it, but Lia averted her eyes to watch the trees they passed. Her cloak was gone, leaving her riding in a set of black-on-black tunic and pants. If Veron ignored her ever-present frown, her build and straight-brown hair made her the spitting image of her mother when she was younger.

"Talk with her," Chelci urged. "She needs to hear from you, and ignoring it won't make it any better."

He nodded, his horse continuing at a steady pace.

Chelci's raised eyebrow caught his attention. Veron sighed. He pulled on the reins, bringing his horse to the side of the trail. Mason nodded as he passed.

Veron nudged his mount to proceed when Lia arrived. He rode next to her, but she kept her eyes in the opposite direction. The clopping of hooves on dirt helped smooth out the awkward moment. He cleared his throat. "Lia?"

Her torso stiffened, but she didn't answer.

"We need to speak about last night."

"Why?" she began, "So you can yell at me?"

His blood heated. "I'm not going to—" He stopped with a huff.

Ahead, Chelci turned, motioning for him to calm.

"I care about you," Veron said with forced composure. "And I care about our knights. What you did put your mother in danger. I *should* yell at you."

"Pff. She wasn't in danger."

"She was!"

Lia flinched.

I've got to keep myself under control, Veron thought. He exhaled. "Chelci was outnumbered, and you were supposed to be there with her. There were *twelve* men!"

"You train us to fight like that. Shovel stance with short breaks—attack them two at a time, right? She's fine, isn't she?"

"That's not the point! It was your job to be with her. She was *not* all right. She almost died! I had to rescue her."

Lia turned, her scowl remaining. "See. You were there. Why did I need to be? She's fine."

Veron's blood raged. After a long moment, he forced a calm voice. "Lia, she's your mother."

A slight wince registered on her face, but she didn't reply.

"You can't go to those gambling halls."

"Why not?"

"You're only sixteen, and you're a shadow knight! You can't —It's just not—" He groaned in frustration. "We must have discipline and order. We had a job to do, but you were off losing all your money."

She scoffed. "They said I lost because I was bitten, but it wasn't fair. It was their stupid bag that had a hole in it. I should have won."

"It doesn't matter, Lia!" Veron yelled. "It's our job to maintain the freedom of Terrenor and fight oppression and injustice. When you go out, you represent us. I don't want to do it, but there's no way around it. There must be a punishment."

Lia's eyes narrowed. "You're going to punish me?"

"One week of Tribulation."

Lia groaned. "It's not fair! You pick on me because I'm your daughter."

"You represent the Knights, and you represent our family. Maybe if you did a better job of either, I wouldn't *have* to pick on you."

"There it is!" She threw her hands up in the air. "I'm an embarrassment to you. Sorry I'm not the *perfect* daughter that you can parade around the city."

"That's not it!" Veron cried in frustration. "You have to be there for your team, Lia! We were there for a purpose, and you let your team down."

"No one ever asked me if I wanted to be on a team!" Lia shouted back. "I never got to decide."

"You—" Veron stopped, speechless. He leaned back in his saddle. "I thought you—" He looked ahead to Chelci, but his wife's stiff torso faced forward.

Before he could form his thoughts, Lia kicked her heels, sending her horse into a canter. She hurried past the others and kicked up dust as she hurried around the bend on the narrow road ahead.

His mind still reeling, Veron trotted ahead, passing Mason.

"Sir," the younger knight said, "Do you want me to go after her? Maybe I could talk to—"

"Stay out of this, Mason," Veron huffed.

"I'll speak with her when we make camp tonight," Chelci said when Veron arrived next to her.

"Were you like this when you were young?"

She nodded. "When I was young . . . yes."

"What happened? Did you grow out of it?"

"It was my time in Nasco—living with Nevi and Russell after I'd run away from my parents. I softened while I was there."

"But, we're not like your parents—or at least your mother—are we?"

She shook her head. "I don't think so. It must be something else." She paused and turned to look at him. "One week of Tribulation, huh?"

Veron winced. "Yeah. We have to do something."

"I agree with you, but—" She whistled. "She's going to be a bear."

"I can't figure out whether to act as the Shadow Master or as a parent. I feel like I need to be both, but I don't think I'm doing either right. And I lose my temper at the drop of a hat. I never used to be like that."

Chelci laughed. "You have a teenage daughter. That's why. I feel it too. We need to be patient with her and understand how she's feeling. Remind yourself of the things you love about her."

Veron thought for a moment. "Her passion. Her spirit. She's incredibly smart and skilled at everything she does. If only she would—"

Chelci held up a hand. "Stop there. Leave off the rest."

Veron nodded, a smile forming. "I love her *so* much, which is why I care. It's the reason I get worked up."

"I know. Me, too."

They rode in silence, settling into the rhythm of the horses' steps. A group of birds chirped around them. The steady flow of the Felavorre River gurgled through the trees.

"Sir?" Mason said.

Veron angled back. "Yes?"

With the path wider, Mason kicked into a trot to come alongside. "What exactly did we do back there in Lorranis?"

"The Black Lanterns have been a plague on the city for years," Veron replied. "They run the Barrow District along the waterfront."

Mason's eyes widened.

"That's right—thieves, murderers, everything bad you might imagine comes from that district."

"Why were they after that guy?"

"Lord Weatherford is a good man. He issued a new tax on borrellroot trading."

"And they didn't like that?"

"They sell borrell spice."

Mason gasped.

"The drug's only a few years old, but men and women addicted to the spice already fill the Barrow District. That's why they kill and steal—to pay for their fix."

"So, the tax eats into their profits?"

"Well, yes, but it's not the tax they were upset about, it was what it was for. Weatherford was going to use the money to fund a recovery program. He wants to help the people living there to recover from their addiction and move out of the area. Our contacts learned about their plan to assassinate him, which is why we came."

Mason rode awhile, staring ahead. "So, the money you found on them . . ."

"Spice profits. Taken from desperate, hurting people."

"We could have used that money, couldn't we have? For the Knights? We don't seem to have a great deal to spare."

Veron shrugged. "We need little. We're funded by the four kingdoms, and that's enough. Plus, those coins are better served helping the exploited people they were taken from."

"*If* Weatherford uses them for that. How do you know he will?"

"I don't. It's up to him to do what's right; all I can do is trust that he will. Either way, it's out of my control."

The curious younger knight seemed to have run out of questions, and the three settled into a quiet ride. The day progressed, causing their shadows to lengthen.

After cresting a short rise, Everwood Ford came into view. Crossing the calm and narrow tributary on horseback was easy. The location marked a full day's ride from Lorranis.

"What if she's not here?" Chelci asked.

Veron didn't answer, the same question running through his own mind.

His horse entered the water without breaking stride. Cold drops kicked up, invigorating him after the long day of riding. When they arrived at the far side, his neck craned to see above the bank. The sun was just setting and a dim, orange light blanketed the area. His shoulders relaxed when he spotted Lia's caramel colored horse, Ginger, tied up to a tree.

"She's here," he said over his shoulder. Veron pulled up to a halt, dismounted, then tied his horse to the same limb. Chelci and Mason dismounted behind him.

Lia emerged from behind a tree, moving toward a circle cleared of leaves and sticks. She glanced at the arriving trio and made eye contact with Veron before turning away. The scowl she wore earlier remained. An armful of wood rested in her arms, which she tossed onto a small pile. A pair of limp rabbits lay next to the sticks.

Lia dusted off her arms and grabbed a bundle of blankets strapped to the side of her horse. "I gathered wood, and you can help yourselves to the rabbits. I'm not hungry." Without making eye contact, she carried her bundle and walked farther into the woods. "I'm sleeping on my own tonight."

"Lia, wait!" Chelci called.

After their daughter disappeared behind a tree, Chelci turned to Veron with a thin smile and raised eyebrows. "At least she stopped," she said.

Veron nodded. "And she caught us food."

Chelci rested a hand on his arm. "Let's give her some time. Maybe we can try talking again tomorrow."

Lia didn't talk the next day or the two after that, despite both Veron's and Chelci's attempts to engage with her. By the time they arrived back in Felting, they had given up trying.

The four shadow knights led their horses by the reins as they walked down Rampart Way. On the left, Felting Castle towered above the city. Memories rushed through Veron's head of his time there: meeting King Wesley when he was only a slave and becoming one of his advisors, seeing the king assassinated, Chelci's father—Darcius—being selected as the next ruler.

Felting held many memories for him, his most meaningful happening in the time since he overthrew Bale: marrying Chelci, rebuilding the Shadow Knights Academy, and Lia's birth.

With his hood up, Veron looked ahead where Lia walked, leading her horse. Her pulled-back, brown hair bounced off her shoulders. She was the spitting image of Chelci back when Veron and she first met. A reluctant smile curled his lips. *She has her same spirit, but I wish she would find her kindness.*

A plain, unpainted wooden door with *Palace Guard Training* scrawled on it drew nearer as they walked. The wall of the building had cracks and chips of stone missing. The unkempt exterior of the Shadow Knights base served as an effective front to prevent the citizens of Felting from knowing what happened behind the walls. The neighbors assumed it was a training ground for future palace guards.

Lia's feet angled toward the front door.

"Lia," Veron scolded. When she looked at him, he nodded toward the ramshackle house farther down the street.

Lia sighed but plodded in that direction.

"You may think it's over-cautious," he whispered, "but anytime you arrive with us—in the day especially—take the—"

"I know." She cut him off, disdain dripping from her words. "You're too famous, so we take the secret entrance."

The disguised entrance hid in a run-down, old house. Its roof had partially collapsed. The furniture had long been destroyed. The bedroom in the back contained nothing but splinters of an old chair and a heavy metal panel—a panel only someone with use of the origine would be able to lift. The dreary, stone tunnel beneath ran below four other buildings to connect to the Shadow Knights center. With Chelci's and Veron's potential to be recognized, arriving through the alternate entrance in daylight could keep a casual observer from putting things together.

Mason gathered the reins from each of them and continued ahead, leading the animals toward the stables while Lia ducked through the door of the nearby building.

Veron turned to face Chelci, his practiced eyes scanning the street for any signs of tails while he held the door open. He nodded over his shoulder and touched Chelci's arm. "I'm going to go ask him for advice."

Chelci nodded with a weak smile, her hood bouncing. "Sure. Tell him I said hello." She rested her hand on his hip and stretched up to give him a kiss.

Veron let the door close, then continued down the path.

Mason walked ahead, leading the four horses. The young knight would make sure they were watered and fed at the nearby stables before coming back to the training center. The boy was young and filled with promise. Always ready to please, he did anything that was asked of him. When Mason turned down a street on the right, Veron kept straight.

A hilly area rose on the left after the buildings ended. Stone markers stuck out of the ground, dotting the hill. Veron ascended a packed dirt path between the stones. Near the top of the hill, he turned right, walking five markers down the row. He slowed and lowered his hood when he approached.

The faded writing on the marker noted *William Stormbridge - Father, Friend, and Servant of Terrenor. Died so that others could live.* Grass grew over the seventeen-year-old grave.

In the years following his father's death, Veron often came to ask for advice. While the conversations about getting married and training shadow knights were one-sided, they helped him sort through his thoughts. Over the years, his visits became less frequent.

"Father, it's me." He looked around the hill of graves. He was alone. "Sorry, it's been a while. I've meant to come by more, but life has been busy. I could use some help with Lia. She's sixteen now. I know—it's crazy. I wish you could have met her." A smile tweaked the corner of his mouth. "She's strong and learns quickly. She has *some* of her mother's kindness in her, which shows when we least expect it. But, often, she's moody and contrary. She gets angry at us—me in particular. She won't listen and abandons her responsibilities. She acts like she doesn't want to be in the Knights."

He paused to feel the wind whistle up the hill, pulling at his clothes. He laughed. "I know it seems silly to ask you for parenting advice, but I don't know what to do. We didn't have a lot of time together, but I wonder what you would do. How can I get her to listen—to want to do what's right?"

Veron looked back down the hill. Rampart Way connected shops and homes together. The Shadow Knights Academy stood out in the distance from the surrounding buildings while Felting Castle rose to the sky behind it.

"She may not want to do what I want her to do. Maybe I need to listen to her more," Veron said, turning back to the grave. He sighed, his shoulders drooping. "I've tried to make her into what I think she should be. Maybe I need to give her room to be herself. I'm just not sure I like what being herself may look like.

"Despite our issues with Lia, the Knights are doing well. Missions seem to come less frequently. King Darcius has things running smoothly in Feldor, and with Norshewa at peace, Terrenor has seen its longest stretch of calm in hundreds of years. Tarphan has some unrest, but overall, things are good.

"Still, we train. The knights are young, but skilled and disciplined. We *have* gotten away from the secrecy the Shadow Knights maintained for years. Word got out after we returned from defeating Bale. The attention is regrettable, but"—he shrugged—"it's working out. I think you'd be proud of the team we have."

A gentle breeze blew up the hill, ruffling his clothes and blowing his hair. A smile tugged at his face at the thought of his father's pride, as if William communicated through the wind.

"Chelci says hello, by the way."

Talioth stood at the mouth of the cave, staring into the verdant bowl of green. On all sides of the high-mountain valley, snow-capped spires rose to the sky, blocking them from the outside world. A plume from a thermal vent caught his eye as it puffed a round of steam into the air, keeping the chilly air at bay.

Footsteps sounded behind him. He turned as Valdok approached. Dim crystals set into the walls of the cave gave a faint glow, barely illuminating his fellow marked one. In the comforting warmth of the caves, his tunic hung loose, the black stain on his neck standing out.

"It's getting almost too dim to see," Valdok said.

Talioth's mouth fixed in a tight line. He glanced at the pendant hanging around his neck and lifted the red crystal. Its usual glow was almost gone.

"Balakolt is even worse today," Talioth said.

"The cough?"

He nodded. "It's back."

Valdok frowned. "I-I'm sorry."

Talioth took a deep breath then let it out slowly. "It's time. Gather the others. We need to find a new source."

"Yes, sir," Valdok said with a quick nod.

Talioth looked back at the peaks. He touched his neck absently, running his finger along the thick scab that had been there for years. "It's time we head down the mountain."

4

SHORTCUTS

The bag of sand weighed down Lia's shoulder, bouncing in time with her shuffling feet. Her right arm slung over the sack, the metal bracelet around her wrist pressing into her skin. Sweat matted her hair. Her breath fogged as she huffed. The sun had only just risen over Felting, and the chill of the early suether morning had yet to be driven off.

Bridgette ran at the front of the pack, step-for-step with their trainer, Dayna. The sandbag looked to weigh as much as Bridgette did, but somehow, she kept up. Mason and Shawn came next. Mason was nice—a little too nice. His crush on Lia was obvious. She didn't mind, but also didn't share the sentiment. Shawn was quiet. A hard worker, he kept to himself. Lia and Danik brought up the rear of the group.

Danik Bannister was her closest friend in the Knights. Older by a few years, his dirty-blond hair never looked out of place, even after a run. His blue eyes always held a twinkle when they looked at her. Although she often found herself in trouble, Danik seemed to be with her every time. His strength and speed were some of the best in the group, powered by his strong legs and athleticism. He only ran in the back of the pack because she was there.

Lia's breath labored more than usual. She struggled to keep up. The casual looks on the other knights' faces caused her to grind her teeth. She glanced at her sandbag—twice the size of anyone else's. *Stupid Tribulation. A full week of extra work.*

"I would probably have collapsed by now if I had to carry that thing," Danik said.

The hard line of her mouth softened. "You *have* carried this before, and you've been fine. You get in trouble more than I do."

"I'm not as good as you, though," Danik said. "None of us are. Your father—yeah, he still is, but I don't imagine that will last long."

"You'd never know it from any of the others. They treat me like I'm a screw up."

"I'm serious, Lia. You've got talent."

She smiled at the compliment then looked at the bracelet around her wrist. *If only I didn't have this on. I could show them all.*

The running group entered Turba Square. Vendors set up carts in the growing light, but no shoppers had arrived yet. A statue on a plinth in the middle of the space stared down at the runners. The figure held a sword high while a cloak fell down his back. *Veron Stormbridge—Deliverer of Freedom.* Lia scoffed and turned her face away as they continued to pound the stone with their feet.

"So, are you gonna tell me what happened in Lorranis?" Danik asked as they exited the square.

"How do you know something happened?"

"Veron and Chelci have been in a foul mood since you returned." He nodded ahead to where Mason ran. "And Suck-Up over there will only say 'she did the best she could,' but I don't know what that means."

Lia stifled a laugh. "It wasn't a big deal. We had four knights to do a simple job. They didn't need me."

"So, what? You ditched them?"

"I went to find a card game. A tall drink and taking some poor suckers' money was more fun than sitting on the cold stone behind a stack of crates."

"You win any money?"

She shook her head. "I should have, but they cheated me."

"Well, I'm glad you're back," Danik said. "It wasn't any fun while you were gone. Dayna drilled us relentlessly, saying 'we need to be ready,' as if someone's about to attack the facility."

"That's ridiculous. No one is attacking us."

"I know. Plus, we're ready. What more preparation does she want?"

"Lia! Danik! You're dragging," Dayna shouted from the front of the line, angling her body backward as she continued to run. "You need to be faster. Tribulation isn't an excuse to be lazy. Pick up the pace!"

"Ugh, she drives me crazy," Lia muttered.

"You and me, both," Danik confirmed.

Lia shifted the sandbag on her shoulder. "I'll show her fast."

"What are you gonna do?"

Lia pulled the bracelet off her wrist and tucked it in her pocket. It felt as if a heavy blanket lifted off her. Her legs felt lighter and her heartbeat steadied. She pulled from the well of energy deep inside her, sending strength to her legs and oxygen to her lungs.

"See you at the finish," she whispered to Danik.

In a few quick steps, she passed Mason and Shawn.

"Hey, Lia," Mason puffed.

She ignored him and closed in on the remaining runners. Bridgette jerked her head to the side as Lia passed. Dayna stared when she came alongside.

"That's more like it," the trainer said. "Don't burn yourself out with that heavy bag. Pace your speed so you can—"

Lia surged ahead, stopping Dayna mid-sentence. The tingle of origine flooded through her body, easing her fatigue and fueling her body. The bag felt light on her shoulder. She looked ahead as she ran. Her long strides sped faster and faster. The buildings they passed became a blur.

At the next turn, she glanced back. Her running crew remained far behind. She laughed as she turned the corner. "That will show her," she muttered.

Lia settled into a fast jog for the rest of the route, making sure to not burn too much energy. The pride in passing the others would turn into embarrassment if she ended up collapsed on the street and they passed her back. The trickle of power she used gave her just enough to fend off the fatigue and keep her moving despite the heavy burden.

She slowed to a walk as she entered the Shadow Knights Academy. The older knights sparred in the courtyard. Her father and Gavin faced off with a pair of quarterstaffs. Salina sparred with Bradley using spears. And Ruby and Chelci engaged in a fierce match with swords. They all stopped and stared as Lia walked to the equipment room and tossed her bag in a pile.

Free from her burden, she slipped the metal band around her wrist before anyone could notice it was missing. In a rush, exhaustion crashed over her. She leaned against the wall of the equipment room and bent over with her hands on her knees. Her breath came in gasps, her lungs aching for relief. Her legs felt weak. While she panted, a smile came to her face. "Who's the one dragging now?" she muttered with a smirk.

After a couple of minutes, the other runners arrived, their heavy breathing announcing their presence. Lia had mostly recovered and stood straight, taking care to not show any weakness.

"There you are," she said with a smug grin. "I thought maybe you'd gotten lost."

Dayna glared as she passed but said nothing.

"Nice run, Lia," Mason said, sucking in air while he tried to recover. "That was impressive."

Once he passed, Lia leaned closer to whisper to Danik, "Maybe if he wasn't so busy staring at me, he could run faster, too."

Danik covered his mouth with his hand, but his laugh lines peeked out.

"Grab practice swords," Dayna said. "Mason and Shawn, pair off. And Lia and Danik. Bridgette, you rotate in. I'll be back."

The instructor walked away toward her father, the dirt of the courtyard crunching under her feet. Lia's stomach swirled, but she pushed the feeling aside as she turned to the equipment room.

Various weapons and gear filled the armory: swords, daggers, staffs, bows, arrows, axes, spears. The weapons hung on the walls and filled the shelves. Lia knew them all. In the center of the wall of swords, a ruby stared at her from the hilt of a blade. Farrathan was the sword passed down from Talon Shadow, the founder of the Shadow Knights. Many knights had borne it over the years, but now it belonged to her father.

The young knights grabbed wooden swords from a barrel. She hated the clunky, unbalanced weapons and preferred to use real steel. The grimy handles and the dents along the wooden edge showed their use.

Danik moved to one side of the courtyard and waited for her to approach. "You gonna keep your training bracelet on this time?" he asked with a raised eyebrow.

"What are you talking about?" she smirked, showing off her wrist where the band encircled her arm. "We're training. Of course I will."

"I just want to make sure. People are watching, and I can't have you beating me too badly."

With a wry grin, Danik lifted his weapon and moved into snake stance. Lia countered by dropping into horn. They stared at each other for a moment before Danik moved.

His step forward came with an overhead blow. Lia stepped into it, deflecting his swing to the side and kneeing him in the ribs.

"Oof!" Danik stumbled but raised his weapon. He came again.

Lia ducked, his blade missing her. She laughed as she tapped him on the side with her sword. "Come on, Danik. You can do better than this."

"Maybe he should take off his bracelet." The voice behind Lia made her jump. "Would that make it more fair?"

She spun. Veron stood before her with Dayna just behind him. His fitted brown tunic rippled in the breeze, which tousled his shaggy hair.

"I think so, Father," Lia replied with a laugh. "Maybe then he could beat me."

Veron did not laugh. "I hear you've been taking shortcuts during training."

"What?" she cried in feigned outrage. She looked at Dayna whose hard face revealed nothing. "I'm training like everyone else."

"It's not just like everyone else when you use an advantage."

"But I'm not."

Veron raised an eyebrow. "Did you take off your bracelet while on your training run?"

Her eyes flitted to Dayna before looking back at her father. "No."

"Really?"

She didn't answer.

"You train to get better, and you can't get better if you cheat."

"I didn't cheat!"

The other knights had stopped their practicing and watched the argument.

"Why does it matter? I'm already better than all of you!" Her chest rose and fell as she stared around the courtyard.

Most sets of eyes opened wide, but Veron's were soft, turning to the dirt. He took in a deep breath then slowly exhaled, whispering, "Passion . . . Spirit . . . Skill," in a calm and steady cadence. After a pause, his eyes raised to her. "We all train. Number five of the Shadow Knights' code—*No matter how skilled or wise you are, there is always someone better, so have the attitude of a learner.*"

"What about number eight? *Never allow your abilities to be known?* Do you remind your statue in Turba Square about that one? Or do you tell it to all your *fans* when they see you around the city?"

Breaths sucked in around the courtyard, and Veron's mouth formed a hard line. "I never asked for that," he said. "Besides, the bracelets aren't only for your training, Lia. They're to keep us safe. If you run through the city using the origine, you will attract attention and could be identified as a shadow knight. What if someone were to follow you here?" Veron motioned to the surrounding facility. "We work hard to keep this location a secret."

She scoffed. "Like that matters. No one's lining up to attack us."

"They might if they knew where we were."

"If the rest of the knights could keep up with me, it wouldn't matter either way."

"So you don't think you have any more you can improve?"

Lia opened her mouth and then closed it again.

"Knights!" Veron called into the courtyard. "Group attack."

Lia's stomach clenched. Her heart pounded as ten elite warriors abandoned their previous sparring sessions, spread out, and approached her.

Chelci was the only one who stayed back. Her mother stood by the wall, setting her sword point down into the dirt. Her face wrinkled. *What is that?* Lia wondered. *Regret? Disappointment?*

Lia bent her knees and lowered her sword tip, angled forward to the dirt. Shovel position appeared deceptively open and allowed for quick counter strikes.

"The bracelet stays on," Veron said.

Lia swallowed, sensing the cold metal around her wrist. She scanned the faces. None were menacing. They were the same people she'd grown up with. Bridgette held a goofy grin as if she had no clue what was happening. Mason wore a look of apology but had his sword at the ready. Danik's mouth turned up at the corner while his weapon rested against his shoulder. *He's enjoying this.*

Lia tightened the grip on her sword, the wood grain of the hilt creaking. Her head moved on a swivel as she waited for the first to move. *Two at a time. Strike fast. Take breaks.*

Dayna attacked first, with Shawn just behind. Lia brought her sword up, flinging dirt into the air. She blocked Dayna's blow and stepped in, spinning away from Shawn's slow attempt. A knee to his gut sent him reeling while her own sword thumped into Dayna's side. She didn't allow herself a moment to celebrate. More came at her.

The courtyard became a twirling jumble of bodies and weapons. Lia parried and struck, ducking and dodging as the knights came at her. Her breath grew rapid. Dust kicked up from the flurry of steps filled her mouth. Two at a time, her friends bowed out after their brief attempts to reach her.

Mason's effort was half-hearted. She tapped him on the back to finish him rather than giving him the bruise she could have. Danik tried his best. He laughed as he attacked, but his strikes were easy to parry. Her kick to his chest knocked him flat on his back.

Veron was the final attacker. The others held their bruised bodies and sulked at a distance. Her father crouched, his staff held at a diagonal. His own metal bracelet peeked out from under the sleeve of his tunic.

Lia abandoned shovel stance and moved into plow. With her sword held hip-high, angled up, she was prepared for a strike from either end of his staff. She watched his eyes rather than his hands. Although he had seemed angry with her, there was a softness in his face. An almost imperceptible flinch caused her to move. She brought down her sword while taking a step back. His strike was quick, but she was ready for it. A loud wooden clack filled the courtyard.

Her father surged forward. Her arm danced, parrying the rapid attack from both ends of his staff. She spun to get away, but his weapon blocked her retreat. Her jump backward allowed the end of the staff to swing a hand's breadth from her chest.

Her eyes lit. *There's my chance!* She lunged, trying to reach his unprotected side. Her movement was quick, but Veron's was quicker. The opposite end of his staff crashed into her wooden blade. The force knocked the grip loose. She gasped as the weapon fell and thumped on the dirt. A pressure grew under her chin. She focused on the end of the staff against her neck while her father held the weapon firm.

Her breath heaved as she stood still. A tight lump formed in her throat. The other knights watched, but no one cheered. She scowled, then batted the end of the staff away. "What are you trying to prove, huh? That you're better than me?"

Veron's head jerked. He stepped back with a deep furrow in his brow. "No . . . I—"

"Is that what a Shadow Master does?"

Veron's lips moved, but he couldn't articulate a response.

"Is that what a *father* does?"

"Lia, no. You misunderstand. I only wanted—"

"Stop it!" she yelled as she stormed across the dirt. The knights parted as she left the courtyard.

5

———

THE FELAVORRE RIVER

Lia rubbed her nails against the top of the wall, staring absently over the city. Against the western horizon, the sun had faded to a faint orange over the forested hills. Candles in windows and lanterns in streets created glowing pockets of light in the otherwise dark city.

A deep breath in filled her lungs with crisp air. She savored the sensation until a whiff of garbage tainted her senses and wrinkled her nose.

The door to the Shadow Knights Academy opened below the wall where she posted, and laughter spilled onto the street. Six indiscernible heads turned toward Fetzer's Tavern, talking and joking as they prepared to relax for the evening.

They have fun while I stay on guard duty, she grumbled.

Lia chewed her lower lip while the knights faded down the street. A light in a window caught her attention.

The Merryweather family lived in an upstairs flat, across the street from the Shadow Knights. The father, Johann, ran a cobbler shop nearby on Castlewood Street. Debra, the mother, stayed home, cooking and caring for their two children, Anna and Nathan.

A wistful smile formed on Lia's face as she watched through the glowing window. The family sat at their table, talking, despite the likely meager supply of food on their plates having run out. Johann leaned forward and said something, causing the children to burst into laughter.

Lia sighed. The family never had much, but they always seemed happy. *A friendly dinner with the family. I wonder what that would be like.* Her hand twitched. She sniffed, attempting to ignore the jealousy that festered. She couldn't remember the last time Veron, Chelci, and she had a family meal together. Someone was always out saving the kingdom or preparing for a mission. When they did eat, it was shared with the rest of the knights.

Debra pushed back her chair to stand and Johann jumped up. He took the dishes from her hands and nudged her away from the kitchen while he proceeded to clean up.

While the children brought over their dishes, Nathan bumped the table and dropped his plate. Lia couldn't hear a crash, but the heads in the room jerked in his direction. The young boy covered his eyes and hung his head. Lia heard a faint cry.

The father dropped to the boy's height and spoke softly to him. At first Nathan only nodded, but then a smile crept back on his face. Finally, Johann wrapped the boy in his arms then kissed the top of his head.

A muffled bark accompanied their dog, Wolf, propping his front paws on the counter. His head leaned forward, and his tongue lapped at the air beside the plates, unable to reach them.

Lia grinned. The pet always put a smile on her face. Every time they met in the street, his tail wagged so hard his body shook. She always stopped to say hello.

Johann took the plate and brought it down to the floor.

Wolf's tail violently swung back and forth while he lapped at any scraps that remained on the plate. Johann rubbed his back.

A warm feeling rushed through Lia. The contentment and love their family displayed comforted her.

Debra appeared in the window and glanced into the street.

No, don't do it.

She pulled the curtains closed.

Lia sighed. Watching their family was the solitary joy she found during night watch. Now, nothing but hours of boredom stretched before her.

Her thoughts turned to Veron and the memory of him embarrassing her in front of everyone during training. Her stomach turned.

Why can't he just love me for who I am?

The dark city stared back, but no answers came.

"Lia, what do you think?"

Lia jerked to attention and scanned the room. Bridgette, Danik, Mason, and Shawn all sat, watching her. At the front of the room, Gavin, the oldest knight besides her parents, stood looking at her. His deep-umber skin stood in sharp contrast to the white tunic he wore.

"I'm sorry. What was the question?" Her mind felt muddled from the endless buckets of water she had to haul and the extra sword forms she alone had to practice.

Gavin sighed, his long, black beard bouncing as his chin fell. He ran a hand over his shaved head. "Bridgette, what about you?"

The blonde student lifted her chin. "Edmund Bale trying to take over Norshewa."

Gavin pointed at her. "Great example. The lower three kingdoms were at peace, but Bale's greed led him to conquer them all, which he would have done had Veron and Chelci not stopped him."

Lia squirmed in her seat. The constant praise of her parents always made her uncomfortable. An ever-present expectation to live up to their standards weighed on her.

"What else?" Gavin asked. "What's an example from farther back where greed led a group of people down a dark path?"

"How about King Vitrion?" Mason said.

"What about him?"

"That was . . . three hundred years ago. Norshewa ruled all of Terrenor."

"Yes, they were known as Norshand then. What was dark about that time?"

Mason screwed up his face. "Um, people were sick and dying. Norshand made them give some sort of offerings, I think."

"That's right," Gavin confirmed, "at the offerdoms scattered around the land."

"People were killed if they didn't give enough, but it only made those in power even richer. It wasn't until Talon Shadow formed the Shadow Knights and stopped him that things got better."

"Good," Gavin nodded before scanning the group. "It's important we understand these actions from our past so we can learn from them. What else?"

"Who defines what's dark?" Danik asked.

"What do you mean?" Gavin asked.

"You ask about examples where people turned down a dark path, but . . . isn't the path only dark depending on which direction you're looking at it from?"

Gavin chuckled. "Yes, you're correct. Bale didn't see his actions as having dark consequences. To him, it was good. But he was the oppressor, the one displaying greed. I'm asking from the perspective of the oppressed."

"I guess in that case, we should mention Talon Shadow as well," Lia said.

Gavin's forehead pinched. "What do you mean?"

Lia glanced at the confused faces of the other knights in the room before continuing. "He showed greed and tried to oppress others."

The room was quiet for a long moment until Gavin broke the silence. "Sure, it's possible he may have had conflicting motives when he killed Vitrion, but the results of his actions were positive for most others."

"I'm not talking about freeing the kingdoms from Norshand," Lia clarified. "I mean embracing the devion."

A gasp escaped Gavin's mouth. The teacher's eyes jumped to the other young knights, but their faces only held confusion. "We're not talking about that," he blurted.

"Why not?"

"What's the devion?" Bridgette asked, her head cocked.

Gavin shook his head.

Danik turned to Lia. "What is it? Why can't we talk about it?"

Lia opened her mouth.

"Enough!" Gavin shouted, making the others jump. "Lia, you are not to speak about that." He leaned his head toward her and spoke quieter. "And your parents will hear about this."

Her face grew red as the eyes of the room bore down on her.

The door to the room opened, and Dayna entered. "You about finished?"

Gavin paused, then nodded. "Close enough. You can have them."

Dayna clapped her hands. "Get changed, all of you. It's time for some training laps. We're swimming the river."

· · ·

THE MUSTY SCENT of the Felavorre River filled the air as they turned onto Perlian Street. Lia walked with Danik at the back of the line. The docks and the warehouses surrounding them lined the street ahead. A vague disquiet filled her at the sight of the docks. Dredged memories crept through her mind. She took a deep breath to settle her nerves. *No . . . that was a long time ago. This is fine.*

"I bet it's gonna be a rough one today," Danik muttered. "Dayna has that masochistic look about her."

Lia stifled a laugh.

Walking slower, heading in the same direction, young Nathan Merryweather stayed on the right side of the path while the group passed him. Long brown hair partly covered his eyes, hiding a thin layer of dirt. A broad grin covered his face, and his feet seemed to skip along. Both hands cupped together in front of his chest, pressing so hard they were white at the joints.

"Nathan," Lia greeted, slowing as she passed. "Good morning."

The boy jerked to the side, swerving his hands even farther away. When his eyes met Lia's, he relaxed, but worry lines still etched his forehead.

"Do you recognize me? I live across the street. My name's Lia."

He nodded but didn't speak. No longer extended away, his cupped hands remained clenched.

She pointed at his hands. "What are you up to, today?"

"It's my sister's birthday," he said after a pause. He uncovered his top hand to reveal a small collection of copper coins. His smile returned. "I've been saving to buy her a loaf of sweet bread from the bakery up there."

Lia's heart swelled. "That's really kind of you."

Danik tugged at Lia's sleeve. "Come on." He pointed up the street. "We're falling behind."

She kept her attention on Nathan. "I'll bet your sister really appreciates that. She's lucky to have a little brother like you." Lia's stomach clenched as she heard her own words. *Little brother.* Dark memories she tried to keep away returned. Her pulse quickened.

The boy nodded. "My birthday is coming up this Week-term. My parents are going to take me out to a tavern for dinner. We never get to do that."

Lia chuckled, pushing away the moment of anxiety. "That sounds like fun." She glanced ahead, then resumed walking. "Enjoy the bread, if your sister lets you have some."

After a moment of quick walking, Lia and Danik caught up with the others at the end of a dock.

Dayna removed her outer clothes first, revealing a tighter swimming garment underneath. The other knights followed suit. "Today's workout is five laps—"

Groans from the group caused their trainer to pause.

"Don't make me change it to six. Five laps from the docks to the mill. Bracelets stay *on!*"

Lia squirmed under the glare from the instructor.

"The river looks slow today, so it should be easy," Dayna said before walking to Lia. "Let me see your arm."

Lia paused from unbuttoning her outer tunic. She held out her arm, and Dayna turned the clasp on the side of her bracelet. The metal object tightened on her wrist.

"Just making sure."

"Five laps, huh? You're not going to make me tie weights around my waist while I swim?" Lia asked with a smug grin.

Dayna mirrored the grin. "It's seven for you."

Lia's smile dropped as the instructor returned to the edge of the dock.

Danik cringed in her direction.

She huffed, then resumed undressing as Dayna, Bridgette, and the boys dove into the river.

A whistle turned her head. Five men sat on crates at the edge of the dock. Their loose clothing, tan skin, and bare feet suggested a life lived on the water.

"Hey, pretty thing," a man with crooked teeth and a scar across his cheek said, lewd laughter issuing from the others. The man's nostrils were stained red, a sign of sniffing borrell spice.

Lia pressed her hands against her legs, wishing the fabric of her swimming clothes stretched farther down her calves.

An older bald man with a gray beard stood and walked forward. "You going for a swim? That's a nice outfit you've got there. You need some help with it?"

"Lia, ignore them. Let's go," Danik called from the edge of the dock, the only other knight remaining. He stood shirtless, wearing his half-length bathing trousers. Lia glanced downriver. The other trainees, heads down and arms pulling through the water, had already begun their swims.

"Ignore us!" the bald man roared, turning to his crew, who stood and approached. "Do you hear him, guys? How rude!" He toed up, face-to-face with Danik. "We were only talking with the young lady, and you had to butt in."

"We're going for a swim," Danik said, his voice wavering. "Lia, come on."

"Going for a swim, are you?" the bald man said.

A shove against his chest caused Danik to flail. His body teetered at the edge of the dock before he fell backward and splashed into the water. The five men laughed before turning to Lia.

She swallowed hard, her head on a swivel while the men formed a circle around her.

"That's better," the bald man said, a lecherous grin on his face. "Now it's just us. My name's Xander. I've got a ship moored nearby. Why don't you come hang out with us? We've got plenty to drink, and you don't have to get all wet."

"No thanks," Lia said, looking past Xander's broad shoulders while trying to push past the ring of men.

"Whoa," Xander said, his eerie voice quieting after pushing her back into the center. "No one said you could leave."

"Lia!" Danik called from where a ladder was fixed to the side of the dock. One sailor propped a foot on the top rung and glanced down, pointing a short sword over the edge. Danik's hand stopped on the second-to-top rung while water dripped into the river below. "Get out of my way," he warned in a half-hearted attempt to get the man to move.

"Let me go," Lia said, spinning to monitor them all. She attempted to loosen the clasp on her bracelet, but the tight fastener argued with her fingers.

Xander took a dagger from a sheath and twirled it in his fingers. He stared at her with his appraising eyes narrowed.

With her fists clenched at her sides, she sucked in measured breaths, glaring with as much intensity as she could muster. "Try it," she whispered. Her heart pounded.

The sailors paused, and Xander's eye twitched. The river lapping against the dock posts was the only sound audible over the whistle of the wind.

After a long moment, the man with the scar on his cheek nodded back toward the road. "Come on, Xander," he said. "I'm hungry. Let's go and find some food."

The men slunk toward the road, leaving one at a time. Xander held Lia's gaze while stepping backward. When he neared the end of the dock, he sheathed his knife and turned toward the road.

"Here we go," one of the men said.

The sailor's words only registered when Lia spotted the boy, Nathan, heading back up the road with his loaf of bread in his arms. The boy's oblivious smile cut through her heart as she watched the sailors approach.

No!

The man with the scar grabbed the loaf from Nathan's hands.

"Hey!" the boy yelled in a high-pitched protest. With his eyes and arm reaching for the bread, he missed Xander's arrival.

The bald man shoved Nathan to the side. The boy tripped over his own legs and fell hard into the nearest building. The group of sailors laughed as he struggled to get back on his feet. The man with the scar held the bread out as if displaying a medal he'd earned to the others.

Without hesitation, Lia's legs pumped, propelling her toward the street as fast as she could run. A faint protest from Danik registered somewhere behind her, but she ignored it. She had eyes only for the sailors.

Her shoulder slammed into Xander's side at full speed, the crack of his ribs reverberating through her body. The bald man yelled and folded in a heap.

The other sailors froze, looking stunned. The man with the bread set it on a nearby ledge while the standing men surrounded Lia.

"Get her," Xander groaned from where he writhed on the ground.

Lia spun, her fast feet knocking the legs out from under the man with the scarred cheek. A fist directed toward her side found air as she deflected a man's arm. She clamped the man's forearm between hers and spun, the torque yanking him sideways. A loud crack filled the air, and the man screamed, his arm jerking unnaturally.

"You're gonna regret that!" another sailor yelled.

A dull thud reverberated in her head as an unseen fist slammed into her jaw. Lia's vision flashed white, and her ears rang. She stumbled backward, tottering with a metallic taste filling her mouth.

She saw the next attack in time: an elbow flying toward her

face. Lia leaned her head backward, the appendage passing in front of her. She grabbed the man's extended arm and pulled him to the ground. His body thudded on the stone pavers.

The next man pulled a dagger from a sheath at his hip. He waved it before him, circling around Lia. "Who do you think you are, you—"

Lia kicked, and her foot found its mark. The knife flew into the air. The man yelled and clenched his hand. While he watched the spinning weapon, her next kick met his chest. The man's arms flailed as he stumbled diagonally onto the dock. The wooden boards ran out before his steps did, and he splashed into the river.

The man with the scar was upright again. Lia turned to him, the hum in her head settling. The sailor backed away and alternated glances between her and Danik, who had finally arrived at the end of the dock. The other sailors made their way back to their feet, holding injured limbs and groaning. Lia feigned an advance, prompting the men to shrink back. She smirked as they ran down the road, tripping over their own feet to get away.

"You okay?" Danik asked as the men disappeared.

Lia pressed gingerly against her jaw, wincing at the tender site. "Yeah, I think so."

Nathan had been hiding, pressed against the wall. He didn't look away from Lia as he lunged forward, picked up the loaf, and ran in the opposite direction from the sailors without uttering a word.

Lia laughed. "A *thanks* would have been nice," she muttered.

Danik hit her playfully on the shoulder. "Nice job."

Lia blushed. "Thanks." She stretched her jaw in a circular motion then glanced down the river. The other knights grew smaller as they swam. "You think that exercise will get me out of swimming?"

Danik exploded with a single loud laugh. "Good luck convincing Dayna of that."

Lia nodded. "It's hot anyway. The water will feel good. Let's go."

6

———

THE LUMBERYARD

The axe bit into the side of the log, sending chips of parthe wood into Raiyn's face. Blinking them away, his hacking continued. He scored the log along the side up to the line of chalk, changing directions every few swings.

His shoulder groaned from the repetitive movement, but after a season of steady work, it was much better than when he had begun, a few weeks into the previous wiether. Processing lumber wasn't what he wanted to do with his life, but he and his mother needed the money.

After knocking off a bulging knot near the edge, he ran a hand down the side, feeling for bumps and nicks. He smiled when he reached the end. The long piece of wood had transformed from a round trunk to the square beam before him. His log was complete.

Setting the axe down on the table next to his workstation, Raiyn placed his hands on his hips and arched his back. His muscles reveled in the momentary break. The tendons in his hands celebrated when he clenched then stretched them.

While he took a moment to rest, he scanned the lumberyard. Six other men worked on logs like the one he had just finished. The logs suspended across trestles, raised off the ground around hip height. On the ground, finished, square beams formed a large pile, which other teams of men worked at sawing into planks.

Just past the yard, the Gulf of Tartis reflected the sun as it dipped toward the horizon. At the edge of Searis, the Goss Lumber Mill was the principal supplier of parthe wood for the kingdom of Tarphan. They exported some of the wood to Feldor and Rynor, but the cost of shipping made the wood found only in the southern climate a luxury few in the farther kingdoms could afford.

"Looks good, Raiyn," a dark-skinned giant of a man said. Kip Chilton was the closest thing Raiyn had to a friend at the lumberyard.

"Thanks. Yours looks good, too. You're almost done."

"The twins begged to come to work with me today. Can you imagine what a mess that would be?"

A smile crept over Raiyn's face as he pictured two five year-olds running around grabbing saws and axes while their father chased them. "Maybe they could have helped. I'm sure Cara would have welcomed having them out of her hair."

Kip laughed. "I bet she would."

"Raiyn, you finished?" Hubert Deans approached, stopping at one end of the log.

The lumberyard supervisor was older by twenty years and made of muscle, built from a lifetime of hard work. The loose front of his tunic showed a barrel chest covered in a thick layer of dark hair.

Kip returned to his own work.

Raiyn dragged his hand along the smooth surface as he walked to the opposite side. "Yeah, all set."

He cupped his hands under the end and lifted with his legs. The weight of the log strained his muscles. He took short, shuffling steps across the sandy dirt, matching Hubert to carry the beam to the pile of others. With a grunt, he dropped his end on the ground as his supervisor did the same.

"Nice work. This one looks good," Hubert said.

"Thank you." With the log completed, a wave of exhaustion washed over him. He rested his hands on his knees and took deep breaths.

Hubert retrieved a ledger from a nearby table and made a mark. "This makes . . . thirteen today?"

"That's right," he panted, unable to hold back the smile.

The supervisor whistled. "For as young as you are, I still don't see how you do it." He nodded to the other workers. "Lewis over there is only finishing up his eleventh, and he's been doing this for years."

Raiyn glanced at the shorter man working on the last side of his log. The scowl on Lewis's face was hidden behind his thick beard while he took a moment to rest. The older man rolled his shoulder and shook out his arm before turning his attention back to his work.

Raiyn straightened and turned back to his supervisor. "I guess I just have that youthful energy. I like to push through until a log is done, then I take a moment to rest when it's finished."

"Well, you're lucky we pay per log completed."

A weak smile crossed his face. "Yeah, well, my mother can't work, so we need the money."

"How's she doing?"

Raiyn pursed his lips and glanced back toward the city. Pale, sun-bleached buildings seemed to grow from the ocean, spreading up the hill to where they faded into the greenery of the trees and mountains that jutted up along the coast to the south. On the water, built on a rocky promontory that jutted into the sea, the castle of Searis towered over the city. On the opposite side of the city, he and his mother lived amid sandy streets in a messy jumble of buildings.

"Her sickness seems to get worse every week. We've tried a couple of doctors, but they just tell her to rest. So, she's resting, but nothing seems to improve."

"And your father . . . ?"

Thunder rumbled in the distance from the dark clouds arriving over the sea. Raiyn shook his head but didn't put his embittered thoughts into words.

"You know . . . I have a doctor we used when my father grew ill—Doctor Dalby on Baytrail Street. No one else knew what to do, but he figured it out. He prescribed some elixir we'd never heard of. It wasn't cheap, but it healed him right up. You want me to send him by?"

Raiyn swallowed hard. He pressed a hand against his empty pocket, wishing for a better paying job.

Raiyn shook his head. "Thanks for the offer. We'll be all right, though."

Footsteps drew near, and both their heads turned to find Raymond Goss approaching. Hubert stood straighter and pressed his tunic flat with his hand.

"Mr. Goss, sir. How can I help you?"

The owner of the lumber company gave a curt nod to Raiyn as he stood between the men. He plopped a stack of documents on the flat log and turned to the supervisor, angling his back to Raiyn.

"We're in a spot, Hubert. We took out the loan last season to expand the yard and harvest the southern wood."

"Yes, sir. Production has been strong with the new hires. It was a great decision." The supervisor smiled.

"These documents prove otherwise," Goss said with an edge to his voice.

Raiyn and Hubert both leaned in closer to see the papers.

Notice of loan adjustment: As Goss Lumber has grown delinquent on their payments, the Bank of Tartis will adjust the rates and double the weekly required remittance as per your signed loan agreement. Until such time as . . . Raiyn couldn't read any farther as Mr. Goss blocked the rest of his view.

"What does it say, Sir?" Hubert asked. "I'm sorry, but I can't read."

Goss sighed.

"We're lumber workers," Hubert added. "None of us here can. If we could, we wouldn't be working at a lumberyard!"

Raiyn's stomach twisted. He heard his mother's voice in his head. *Don't let them know who you are or what you can do. Your life depends on it.* He clamped his teeth tight to keep from revealing too much.

"What it says," Goss began, "is that our payments to the bank are behind."

Hubert's face screwed up. "Why is that?"

Goss hit the pile of lumber with his hand. "Because of this. We're too productive."

"How is that a bad thing, sir?"

"We're producing lumber—plenty of it. But we're not selling enough. Now the bank wants us to pay double to catch up, but we don't have the money."

"What do we do? How do we get the money to pay?"

Goss stood straighter. "We have fourteen employees averaging one tid five pintid per week. Over a thirty-week season, that's a lot of money."

Six sol three argen, Raiyn thought, having run the numbers in his head.

"It's around twelve sol," Goss said.

Raiyn stifled a laugh at the owner's error, thankful the man faced the other direction.

"To pay our bills, we need to cut wages, and to do that, we cut workers."

The men with saws and axes standing nearby came to a halt and turned in their direction.

"Let them know." Goss lowered his voice. "Six must go. Half wages for the rest."

Raiyn's heart dropped.

Goss grabbed the papers and walked away toward the office in the corner of the yard. Hubert ran his hand over the back of his neck and stared at the ground. The twelve men in the yard all gathered around the pile of lumber.

"What'd he say, Hubert?" someone asked.

Lewis got in the supervisor's face, his long beard almost touching the other man. "Half pay? And you're sacking six of us?"

Hubert held his hands up and stepped back. His feet kicked into the pile of wood. He had nowhere to go. "Guys, I'm sorry. You heard Mr. Goss just like I did."

The first worker pressed in closer. "How are you going to choose?"

"Seniority, right?" Lewis said. "That's only fair, let the newer ones go."

Kip stood next to Raiyn. Both of their foreheads wrinkled.

"It sounds like whoever stays will have to take half pay," Hubert said. "So, do any of you want to volunteer to leave?"

Raiyn clenched his jaw. *Half pay would be bad enough, but being out of work . . . ?* None of the men volunteered.

"All right. In that case . . ." Hubert scanned the group. The men stood tall and puffed out their chests. Several lifted their chins.

"Who's leaving?" Lewis asked, his eyes narrowed.

Hubert swallowed. His voice wavered as he spoke. "Vaughn, Alfred, Billy, Brent, Kip, and . . ." He met Raiyn's eyes, but his head turned. "And Lewis."

The six men exploded with insults—some meant for

Hubert, others for Goss, and the ones from Lewis spewed at Raiyn.

"I'm sorry, guys," Hubert said. "See the bookkeeper to get whatever last payment they'll give. "

Raiyn looked at the ground while the men vented their frustration. Before long, the angry ex-workers stormed off, heading toward the office to collect whatever portion they could of a final payment.

Kip Chilton was the only worker who remained behind. A tear formed at the corner of his eye. "Sir."

Hubert waved his hand. "I'm sorry, Kip. You're one of the newer guys, and your production is not—"

"No, it's fine," Kip interrupted. "I wouldn't beg. I just wanted to say thank you . . . for giving me the chance you did."

"I know you have a family. You're a good worker, and you'll find something. I'm sure of it."

Kip nodded. He clapped Hubert on the arm then turned to Raiyn. "Good luck, kid."

Raiyn nodded in thanks as Kip followed the other men toward the office.

"Thanks, Hubert," Raiyn muttered after Kip had left.

The older man pointed at his chest. "Those men had more experience than you. Keep producing so I don't regret keeping you."

Cold drops fell from the sky as Raiyn made his way home. The stone became slick. Sand gathered in rivulets of wet slurry along the sides of the path. His hair soon grew soaked, and he brushed the water off his forehead. He felt his pocket. The metallic clink of coins reached his ears, but the weight was less than he was used to.

How are we supposed to get what we need with this?

Passing a bakery, the smell of freshly baked bread taunted

him. He stopped under an awning and stared at the rows of loaves, thankful for the reprieve from the rain. A sign listing the price as three pintid made him frown.

We still need to pay the overdue rent plus the food we bought on loan last week. For this week's food, that leaves . . . Raiyn's gut clenched. *It leaves nothing.* The pulse in his neck throbbed. His stomach growled, desperate to be filled.

The baker helped a man at the counter. They were deep in conversation as Raiyn entered the shop and creeped toward the displayed bread. A loaf with a light-brown crust sat before him. Steam rose off the top. He shifted his eyes to check on the baker —*still distracted.*

Raiyn flexed his abs, willing his body to have the speed it needed. A faint tingle filled him, warmth in his gut. He grabbed the loaf and sprinted out of the shop. He moved so quickly that the baker and his customer appeared to be frozen in time.

When Raiyn hit the street, he turned up the closest alley, pumping his legs as fast as they could go and sending eruptions of water in every direction. The expected fatigue arrived after a moment, and a distant cry of a baker's outrage reached his ears. Soon, despite his urgent attempt, he could move no faster than a brisk walk. His lungs sucked in air. He tried to keep his shoulders up as he willed his body to move as fast as possible. The momentary burst of energy was gone.

A smile tugged at his face, tempered by a flutter of guilt. He pictured the baker looking around the shop for him, but the effort wouldn't matter. Raiyn was long gone.

7

A NEW OPPORTUNITY

The rusty hinges creaked when Raiyn opened the front door to their house, the familiar odor of decay wafting out. Drops of water leaking through the roof plunked on the floor, welcoming him home. He lifted the knob as he closed the crooked door behind him—the only way to get it settled back in its frame.

"Mother?" Raiyn called, running a hand through his wet hair to knock off the water. He passed through an open doorway and found his mother laying on her bed, propped up on a pillow against the headboard.

Catina's eyes were closed, but her body rustled and her lids blinked open. "Raiyn, you're back."

"I'm sorry. I didn't mean to wake you."

"That's all right. I was only napping." Catina's chest heaved, and she devolved into a fit of coughing.

Raiyn winced.

When his mother pulled her hand away from her mouth, a tinge of red glistened on her skin.

"Mother!" He set the damp loaf of bread on a table. After

grabbing a stained rag, he sat on the side of her bed and handed it to her.

She dabbed around her mouth and wiped off her hands. "It's all right. Only a little blood. It's been like that all day."

Raiyn's eyes drifted to the small table next to her bed, where two rags, stained red in multiple areas, collected.

"That bread smells good," she said, nodding toward the loaf. "I think it will be just what I need. I guess you got paid today?"

Raiyn swallowed. "I . . . uh . . . Yeah, I did."

"Remember, we owe last week's rent plus this one. Also, we need to pay back Mr. Woolstencroft for the food we borrowed."

"Yeah, I know."

"How did your lumber production end up this week?"

His voice wavered. "Uh, it was good. Thirteen logs today."

Catina sighed, her shoulders relaxing. Her cheeks dimpled as a broad smile grew on her face. "I'm so proud of you, Raiyn. And I'm relieved."

I can't let her know about the half wages. She has enough already to worry about.

He rose and grabbed a knife from the other room before returning to the bread. "Do you think Mr. Woolstencroft could spot us again?" he asked as he sliced a chunk off the end of the loaf.

Catina's forehead creased. "He wasn't too happy about it and insisted it was a one-time thing. Why do you ask?"

"You're right. No, it's fine." Raiyn sat back on the bed and handed a piece of bread to his mother. "I was thinking it could be nice to use some money to get you medicine."

"Oh, Raiyn, I don't need medicine." Another fit of coughing took over her. He looked away as she wiped the edges of her mouth again. "We already know I just need some rest. This bread will help my stomach—maybe some soup tomorrow. I'll be good in no time." She took a meager bite of the bread.

Raiyn sat, looking down at his hands for a long moment. "Mother?" He looked up.

She swallowed her bite and her eyebrows raised. "Yes?"

"What do you think about me trying to get a better job?"

Catina's eyes grew wide and she inhaled. "No!"

"But, Mother, I work all day and barely make any money. We live in this"—he paused to wave his hand around the room—"*hovel*, and I can't even pay our bills or provide food."

"I'll be better soon, and then I can return to doing laundry." She smiled. "Remember when you were little, and we used to hang the laundry together on that roof?"

He chuckled. "That old warehouse we lived in? Yeah." He sighed, images of happier times running through his head. "It had all those lines to drape clothes from. I remember running through the rows of laundry, trying to hide. But you always found me."

"That's because you giggled every time."

They both rested in the silent memories for a long moment until Raiyn's nostalgic smile faded. "What if you don't get better?" His mother didn't answer. "What if you can't? I can read, Mother. I know about finance and economics. You've taught me since I could walk, but you won't let me use it! Why can't I try?"

"You know why." Catina's words left the room silent. Water dripping in the other room was all he could hear.

"Mother, we need help."

"We have each other."

"But it's not enough!" His voice trembled. Tears formed at the corners of his eyes as his chest tightened. "I can't do this. The money isn't enough. I can't take care of you."

She rested her hand on his and spoke in a kind voice. "We'll make it through this, Raiyn. You have to believe. Besides, where would we go for help?"

"I don't know," Raiyn said. "Your parents are dead. We don't know anyone because you won't let us, and Father is—"

Her hand jerked away from his. "Don't you speak of him!"

Raiyn took a deep breath. "I'm sorry. I know." A thick moment of silence rested in the room.

"Thank you for the bread," Catina said. "Now, let me rest. I'm sure I'll feel better tomorrow."

Raiyn nodded, then rose. He pulled the threadbare blanket up to her chin as she settled onto her pillow. Pausing at the doorway, he glanced back. A peaceful look rested on her face.

Rest well, Mother. I'll figure something out.

RAIYN LEFT the rented flat in the morning before his mother woke. The sun only peeked over the buildings, but people already bustled through the streets. The rain from the previous evening had stopped, but a muggy thickness remained. He caught a whiff of his clothes, grimy and still covered in wood shavings. Rips at the hem of his tunic flapped in the breeze that swirled up the alley.

His feet felt heavier than normal as he followed the familiar route to the lumberyard. The knowledge that the upcoming work he was about to perform would only receive a half wage weighed on him.

Turning onto Greenbury Street, a sign caught his attention at Westerpoint Bank. *Wanted: entry-level accountant, must have experience with loan amortization, starting pay six tid per week.*

Raiyn stopped, resulting in a man colliding into him from behind.

"I'm so sorry," Raiyn said, raising his hand in apology. The man only mumbled in response as he continued on. Raiyn turned back to the bank.

Six tid per week! That could change everything!

His mother's words of warning came back. His jaw

clenched. *We can't live like we are. Mother doesn't realize how bad it is.* With great effort, he took a step toward the bank. Soon his hand was on the door handle, and he pulled.

A bell rang as he entered. The office was bright, with large windows that allowed sunlight to fill the room. Scattered bookshelves covered wooden walls painted white. Three clerks bustled behind a counter, filling out papers and filing documents. Two desks faced them on the opposite side of the room where a man and a woman pored over papers.

"Can I help you?"

Raiyn jumped and turned to the sound of the voice. A gray-haired man who looked close to sixty stood next to the door with his fingertips pressed together. A stringy eyebrow arched in question.

"Yes. I'm sorry. You caught me by surprise."

Neither the man nor the eyebrow moved.

Raiyn motioned toward the door. "I saw the sign about the accountant job. I would like to apply."

The man's eyes squinted. Continuing his silence, the man looked up and down at Raiyn's clothes. His nose wrinkled. "I'm sorry, but we're wrapping up interviews today. You're too late."

Raiyn's forehead wrinkled. "So . . . you're still interviewing today?" He flashed a smile. "That's great, because I'm here today! I will be a great worker. You'll see."

"Saul, who's this?" a man asked as he approached. "Who are you, kid? What are you doing here?"

The hair on Raiyn's neck prickled. *I'm not a kid.*

The new man looked ten years younger than Saul. A potbelly proved he spent few nights wanting for food.

"Good morning, Reginald," Saul said. "This . . . boy inquired about the accountant position. I told him he was too late."

Raiyn looked to Reginald with eagerness in his eyes, hoping the new arrival would give him a chance.

The heavyset man glanced up and down while frowning.

He shook his head. "Saul is right. We've had plenty of applicants, and we're wrapping up today." He shooed Raiyn away with his hand. "Go on and get out of here."

Raiyn hung his head and dragged his feet as he walked toward the door.

"Speaking of applicants, who's first today?" Reginald asked.

Raiyn set his hand on the door.

"Someone named Crabtree at nine," Saul's aged voice replied. "I've not met him yet. A clerk signed him up."

Raiyn took a step into the street and allowed the door to close behind him. He glanced up at the clock in the street. *Fifteen minutes until nine.*

He continued up the street. Through the break in the buildings, he saw the lumberyard ahead with stacks of wood ready to work. He sighed. *I wish I were Crabtree. If only they'd given me a chance. I'm sure I could—*

Raiyn stopped. Again, a man bumped into him from behind. "I'm so sorry!"

The man muttered a curse and walked around him.

Raiyn looked back at the bank. Men and women passed by in the street in front of it. A grin formed on his face. *Maybe I can get lucky.*

He patted his pockets and removed a rag tinged with faded pink and brown stains. *Good. Now only if I could . . .* He looked around the street and stopped when he found it—Searis Apothecary.

LEANING against the wall across the street from the bank, Raiyn's head swiveled back and forth. A crying kid pulled on his mother's dress as they traveled up the street. An older man carried a basket piled with fabric. A girl a few years younger than Raiyn ambled up the road, her eyes giving away her intent to pick pockets.

A man in a suit approached down the street with his eyes set on the bank. Raiyn's heart sped. He came off the wall and took a few steps in the man's direction.

"Crabtree?" Raiyn said, loud enough to be heard, but not so much to draw attention.

The man continued walking without missing a beat. He arrived at the door to the bank and entered.

I guess that wasn't him. He looked up at the clock. *Five minutes left.*

He resumed his position against the wall and continued to wait. Minutes passed with no likely candidates.

With a minute to go, a well-dressed woman approached from the opposite direction. Her cleaned and pressed skirt hung to her ankles, and her sharp tunic gave off a professional presence.

Could that be her? He hesitated, remaining by the wall while the woman approached the bank.

Her hand reached out to grasp the handle.

"Crabtree!" he shouted.

Several heads of other people turned in his direction, but the woman's did not. The door opened, and a friendly greeting from someone inside wafted out. The woman waved into the room as the door closed behind her.

Raiyn bit his lip. Lingering by the wall, his head jerked back and forth. *Did I miss him?* No one seemed dressed for an inter-view. No one approached the bank. He glanced at the clock. *Three minutes after.* He looked down the street toward the lumberyard. *I'm already late. I should—*

The moment he saw the man, Raiyn knew it was him. The young fellow hurrying up the street wore a stiff hat pulled low on his head. A sharp brown suit hugged his body as only an expensive tailored outfit could. His brown shoes reflected the early morning rays of the sun on the shiny polished leather.

Raiyn came off the wall and intercepted the young man

when he was a few steps from the bank. He held up his arm, stopping him in his tracks.

"Crabtree, you're late," Raiyn said, standing erect and extending his chin.

The young man's brow furrowed. He glanced between Raiyn and the door to the bank.

"For your interview," Raiyn continued. "You were supposed to be here at nine."

"Yes—uh," He glanced up and down, taking in Raiyn's clothing. "I'm sorry. I, uh—"

"Saul and Reginald asked me to let you know they are no longer interested in your application. At Westerpoint Bank, punctuality is paramount. We cannot hire someone who we can't trust to arrive on time. Be off with you." Raiyn motioned back in the direction Crabtree had come.

The young man's face fell. After another glance at the bank, he nodded and lowered his head before he turned and trudged in the opposite direction.

A twinge of regret pulled at Raiyn as he watched the young man leave. He shook the feeling off and followed.

The number of people on the street gave Raiyn pause as he trailed the young man. The mental clock in his head ticked away the seconds, the tardiness increasing his stress. Soon, the man turned down an alley and Raiyn's heart jumped. He picked up the pace.

The alley was narrow, a shadowy passage between two buildings that led to a street paralleling Greenbury. Crabtree was the only person in sight.

Raiyn pulled the rag from his pocket, the damp center wet against his fingers. Quick hands at the apothecary's shop had given him a sample of etheylanin onto his rag. A pungent odor filled the air, but he moved too quickly for it to affect him. With no one to see, Raiyn tapped into the power waiting inside him and closed the distance between him and Crabtree.

The man cried out, but the damp rag covered his mouth. Raiyn held his breath, but the sharp tang of the chemicals made his eyes water. After a brief struggle, Crabtree's body went limp and slumped to the ground. His chest still rose and fell, but he was out.

"Sorry, Crabtree," he whispered. "But I need this more than you do."

Raiyn tossed the rag away, then glanced behind him to make sure he was alone. Content that the act had gone unnoticed, he hastened to take off the man's shoes.

8

WESTERPOINT BANK

The suit fit well. The pants were short, but standing, no one could tell. A trough of water helped him rinse off his hands and face and slick his hair back. The professional clothing helped him appear ready for an interview. *I just hope they don't recognize me.* Raiyn looked at the clock in the street. *Nine-fourteen.* He pulled the hat low on his head, then grabbed the handle to the bank door. The bell rang over his head as he entered.

Saul had been speaking with the woman at the desk. He glanced at the door, looking agitated, and when Raiyn entered, he took a step in that direction.

Raiyn moved first. He stepped with purpose toward the old man and extended his hand. "You must be Saul. I'm Crabtree, here for my nine-fifteen interview."

Saul narrowed his eyes but didn't shake. "Crabtree?"

Raiyn nodded with a smile, hoping the low hat and new clothes would be enough to disguise him. He kept his arm extended as beads of sweat popped onto his forehead.

"Your interview was at nine sharp. You're late."

Raiyn made a show of narrowing his brows. "I remember

being told nine-fifteen. I even asked the clerk a second time—" He looked around the office. "I don't see them here today, but they assured me it was now. I'm sorry if there was a mistake. I don't want to get anyone in trouble."

Saul's questioning look morphed into a sickly smile. He reached out to shake the extended hand. "Very well. You're here now, so let's talk. Please, come with me."

The other workers at the bank barely glanced at him as he walked across the wooden floor, following the banker. The new outfit did its job.

"Take a seat." Saul motioned to a chair at a small table. He passed a piece of paper and a pen to Raiyn. "You have ten minutes to complete this."

Raiyn flipped the sheet over, noticing mathematical problems on both sides. Addition, averages, division, tracking financial ledgers. His mother had given him similar work ever since he was young. Saul walked away, and Raiyn smiled as he went to work.

He jotted down numbers, using the paper for his calculations. He answered the problems one at a time, making quick work of the math.

"Three minutes left," Saul said as he returned a while later. "Don't feel like you need to get to them all. Most people only get through around half of the—"

Raiyn lifted the paper and held it out. "I'm finished."

"Really?" Saul accepted the work and scanned down the sheet. After a moment, he flipped it over and mumbled, "Hmph. Not bad. Come back to speak with our manager."

Saul led him into a back office where Reginald Lumsden sat in a dark leather chair. A second chair rested empty across a desk. "Sir, this is Crabtree," Saul said, extending the sheet Raiyn had filled out.

Reginald stood, lifting his hefty body by using his hands on the sides of his chair to leverage himself up. They exchanged handshakes and the man took the paper.

"There was a mix-up with the scheduling, but I told him we could still hold the interview."

"Thank you." Reginald scanned down the sheet. "I can take it from here."

Saul backed out through the door.

"Was this done within the time limit?" Reginald asked.

Saul stopped, having pulled the door partly closed. "Yes, sir —with minutes to spare."

The manager's eyes widened as he continued staring at the sheet. He motioned to the empty chair. "So . . . Crabtree. What's your first name?"

"Raiyn, sir."

"Raiyn Crabtree. It's good to meet you. I'm Reginald Lumsden, bank manager. I have some questions I like to go through with potential employees to get to know you. First off, why do you want this accountant position?"

Raiyn swallowed. *So my mother doesn't die. So we can have food to eat.* "I've trained all my life for a position like this—math, economics, finance. I had just spoken with my mother about finding a full-time job, and running into your sign struck me as the perfect timing. I love working with numbers and keeping things straight. This job would be perfect. I guarantee you'll be glad you hired me."

Reginald held a reserved smile. "What training?"

"I'm sorry?"

"You say you've trained all your life. In what way?"

"My mother taught me since I was young."

Reginald's head inclined forward as if he waited for something more.

"And . . . then I went to King's Academy in Felting," he lied, "which I graduated from last year."

Reginald's eyebrow raised. "King's Academy. Impressive. Do you have your graduation papers?"

His stomach dropped. He patted his suit. "I'm sorry I didn't think to bring them." An awkward moment of silence followed. "But I can! When I'm hired, I'll bring them if you like."

"Very well." The manager nodded before leaning back in his chair. "Here's a scenario for you, Raiyn. Imagine a woman comes into the bank. She tells a sob story about how her husband just died, she had all her money stolen, and she needs a loan to get back on her feet. What would you do with her?"

"Is that a scenario I might run into as an accountant?"

"We see it at least once a week at the bank. I'd like to know how you would respond." The manager tilted his head back and looked down his nose.

Raiyn fidgeted in his seat. *Is he a man who values compassion or the bottom line?*

A knock rapped before the door to the office opened and a clerk poked his head in. The young worker jumped when he saw Raiyn sitting there. "I'm so sorry, sir. I didn't realize you were in a meeting."

"What is it, Simon?" Reginald barked.

"Um . . . the other clerks wondered if—with the Festival of the Sea coming in two weeks. We know the office is closed, but we—they wondered if they would earn their regular weekly pay."

The manager's mouth formed a hard line. "You're wondering if you earn pay . . . for a day of work when you don't work. Is that right?"

The clerk shifted his feet. "They wanted me to ask."

A thick silence filled the room. Raiyn looked between the two men until the clerk took a step backward.

"I'll, uh . . ." The clerk swallowed hard. ". . . let them know they shouldn't expect anything." He pulled the door behind him. "Sorry to disturb you."

Reginald's smile returned. "I apologize for that intrusion. Back to the question . . ."

Raiyn flashed a smile of his own. *At least now I know where he stands on compassion.*

"I don't mind," Raiyn said. "Well, this is a bank, not a charity ward, right?"

Reginald chuckled.

"If the woman wants a loan, we should treat her like any other customer regardless of her personal issues. I imagine we would require proof of income, collateral, or at least a strong recommendation of character—preferably all of those. If we were to approve her, the interest rate should follow the risk. Without a strong guarantee of her making her payments, the rate we charge should be higher. Either way, it's not our job to make up for her life situations. If she had things stolen, she should go to the city constable's office."

The manager's smile grew. He nodded. "I have a word problem for you." He slid a sheet of paper and a pen across the desk. "Use those if you like."

Raiyn picked up the pen and waited for instructions.

"I would like for you to *estimate* how long it would take to move enough stones from the quarry at Uberforth to build an *average-sized* castle in Searis."

Raiyn's brows pinched together. "I'm sorry . . . this interview is for an accounting position, right?"

The manager laughed. "Yes, it is. I like to test your reasoning skills. Imagine you have eight workers and only one average-sized cart with two rydannor to pull it. How would you estimate the time? Talk me through your thought process and explain any assumptions you make."

Raiyn blinked several times. He looked at the pen, then down at the blank paper. "How many stones are in an average castle?"

"You tell me."

Raiyn gave a nervous chuckle. "All right." He touched the pen to the paper and paused for a moment. After his mind whirled, he scribbled. "I'm going to picture a plain, square-shaped castle that might be . . . twenty blocks high and . . . two hundred blocks long down each side. The walls could be five layers thick. The interior is going to be open courtyard and rooms made of wood, so the number of blocks we'll need will be—" He paused while he jotted numbers on the sheet. "Twenty thousand along each wall, times four walls makes eighty thousand blocks."

The manager nodded and leaned forward.

"An average cart can hold around," his eyes looked up and to the side as he pictured carts he'd seen, "four layers of . . . five by four makes . . . eighty blocks per trip. So we will need . . . One thousand trips."

"All right," Reginald said, "so how long would that take?"

"Uberforth is a five-hour journey by cart at the slow speed of a rydannor. The workers would need an hour to load and an hour to unload. That would make one day per trip."

"So . . . one thousand days?" the manager suggested.

Raiyn shook his head. "Labor laws say workers must have off for Weekterm, so we'd only get five days of labor in a six days in a week. That would make—" He wrote some more. "Two hundred weeks . . . or . . . three years and twenty weeks."

A reserved grin formed on the manager's face. "Impressive. So you—"

"But if the goal is efficiency, the approach is wrong," Raiyn interrupted.

Reginald's jaw hung open. "How so?"

"The limiting factor is the cart trip. Eight workers is great, but they're wasting time while the cart travels between locations. It would be better to cut two of the workers and use that money for another cart team. Keep two men at each end, with the other two as drivers. The loading and unloading time would take longer, but all the workers would keep busy. Instead of one load per day, you'd average . . . one and three quarters. That would take . . . a hundred and . . . fifteen weeks—just shy of two years."

Reginald leaned back in his chair with a broad grin. "That may be the best answer I've ever heard to that question."

RAIYN FELT good when he left the interview. He thought they seemed impressed and liked him, but he didn't know how the other applicants fared. They had promised to let him know soon, using his conveniently updated address. Meanwhile, he had to keep working.

As much as he wanted to keep it, he took the suit back to the *actual* Crabtree, who remained passed out in the alley where he left him. Raiyn changed back into his regular clothes and hurried off to the lumberyard.

He was over an hour late by the time he arrived. Hubert was furious, and it took some creative excuses about his mother needing his help to smooth things over. All day, his mind was on the accountant job, but even with the late start and distraction, he still polished off eleven logs.

RAIYN ROLLED HIS ARM, stretching out the tendons as he trudged up the street back to his home. The setting sun cast a gloom over the narrow street still awaiting the lamplighters.

When he arrived at his stoop, a white envelope tucked in the door caught his attention. He mounted the steps in two jumps and pulled the object out. Neat handwriting spelled *Crabtree* across the front. His heart jumped. Raiyn tore open the envelope and extracted the folded paper inside.

· · ·

Raiyn Crabtree,

Thank you for your interest in joining Westerpoint Bank. We enjoyed meeting with you and are delighted to offer you an accountant position. Please arrive Halfday at eight o'clock sharp to begin your training.

Sincerely,

Reginald Lumsden
Bank Manager

Raiyn gasped. He grinned and shouted. *We can have food, medicine, proper clothing!*

He pulled open the front door with a jaunty flourish and bounded inside. "Mother!"

As soon as he called out, his stomach turned. *She won't like this.* His steps slowed as he passed through the room to the doorway leading to hers.

"What is it?" her weak voice replied.

Raiyn entered her bedroom. A pile of rags sat on her bedside table, the one on top sporting a fresh shade of red. He tucked the letter into his pocket. "I'm home."

She frowned. "What's going on?"

He pursed his lips and shook his head. "Um, nothing. Just letting you know I'm home."

"You were going to say something. What was it?"

His mouth opened, but he froze. He touched the letter in his pocket.

"What was that letter?"

Raiyn sighed. He pulled the paper out. "They cut my wages at the lumberyard."

"What?" Her forehead creased.

Raiyn nodded. "They're having trouble. They can't afford

full wages . . . But it's gonna be all right." One side of his mouth curled up. "How would you like to have medicine to get better, and maybe some proper food for a change?"

Catina tilted her head, her eyes widening. "What did you do?"

He stared at the paper. "I got a job. It's an entry-level position. I'm going to be an accountant."

"What?" Her shout filled the room before it turned into a round of coughing.

"It's going to be fine. They know nothing about me. They think my name is Crabtree. I'll go to work, do my job, and bring home money."

"You don't understand, Raiyn. It's too dangerous! I told you not to do this!"

"I have to, Mother! We can't pay our bills anymore, and you're *not* getting better!"

"No!" She flung the sheets back and swung her feet over the side. "Listen to me!"

Raiyn held out his hands. "Take it easy. You don't need to get riled up."

Catina stood, keeping one hand on the mattress for support. "Your father left us in this place, and now we have limits on what we can do! You need to—"

She lurched forward, clutching her chest.

"Mother?"

Her arm against the bed weakened and she fell to the floor. Her knees pounded against the wood. Raiyn rushed to her side as a spasm of coughs took over her body. Deep, throaty hacks loosened fluid inside of her as she coughed on all fours. Blood dappled the wood.

Raiyn rested his hand on her back, but there was nothing he could do. He gasped when a spatter of black mixed with the red on the floor. A surge of panic raced through him. He tried to breathe but found his own lungs struggling to operate. With a trembling hand, he reached for a dirty rag. He dabbed at her mouth after she rolled onto her back.

"It's going to be all right, Mother." His weak voice shook. "Take it easy."

The coughing had ended, and her eyes closed.

He watched her chest, waiting for any sign of life. His shoulders relaxed when she managed a breath. With gentle arms, he scooped up her emaciated body, placed her back on the bed, then pulled the sheets up. She muttered something he couldn't make out.

His desperate mind thought of nothing but Hubert's doctor. *I'm not sure what else to do.*

9

THE APOTHECARY

"She's through there," Raiyn said, pointing to his mother's room while he closed the door behind Doctor Dalby.

After his mother's collapse, he wasted no time running through the city to find the doctor Hubert had recommended. He didn't inquire about cost and decided to deal with that when it was time.

Raiyn cleared the rags off the table, allowing Dalby to set his bag down. Catina's eyes remained closed. She mumbled as her head turned from side to side.

"How long has she been like this?" the doctor asked.

"She's been in bed for weeks—probably seven. Tonight is the worst it's been."

The doctor lifted her eyelids to inspect, but still she didn't respond.

"How long has she had the black phlegm?"

"Today is the first I've seen it."

Dalby used prods and inspection glasses to check in her mouth and ears. He felt for her pulse on her wrist. Raiyn paced the room while the doctor worked.

"We've had two doctors come by before," Raiyn said after being silent as long as he could. "They've both said it was nothing and that she just needed to rest. But it keeps getting worse."

"This isn't nothing, that's for sure." Dalby lowered a listening device and turned to Raiyn. "She has a deep infection—one that rest or common tinctures can't fix."

Raiyn felt dizzy. He sat at the end of the bed to keep from fainting.

"I only know of one thing strong enough to help—barkleaf elixir."

Raiyn leaned forward. "What's that?"

"Barkleaf fungus comes from the woods of Tarphan, but few apothecaries know how to make the elixir." The doctor scanned the room before settling back on Raiyn. "And it's not cheap."

Raiyn swallowed hard. "How much?"

"She needs an ounce—maybe two. That will cost at least an argen."

Raiyn froze, his eyes wide.

"That's ten tid," the doctor added.

"I know what an argen is," Raiyn snapped before catching himself. "I'm sorry. You're just trying to help. Thank you."

"I can't sell you the elixir, but most apothecaries will have at least a small amount, even if they had to buy it elsewhere."

Raiyn nodded, staring down at the dried blood on the floor. "How much for the visit?" His heart pounded in his chest as he looked up at the doctor.

The man's eyes held a softness. "How much can you spare?"

A tear pooled at the corner of Raiyn's eye. He wiped it away and shook his head. "We don't have anything. I'm sorry."

Dalby's shoulders fell. He placed his instruments back in his bag.

"I start a new job tomorrow as an accountant!" Raiyn added.

"I'll be making good money. Can we settle up after my first payment?"

The doctor nodded as he stood. "Sure. You know where to find me."

Raiyn escorted the man to the front door and let him out.

"Maybe you can get an advance from your new job for the medicine. She's going to need that elixir soon, otherwise—" The man stopped. Each instant that passed added more weight to Raiyn's invisible burden. "Well . . . the sooner the better."

After closing the door, Raiyn returned to his mother's side. She looked troubled in her sleep, her chest rising and falling in shallow bursts. He paced the room, chewing the tips of his fingers.

"Son," Catina said. Her raspy voice sent a chill down Raiyn's spine.

"Yes?"

"Don't worry about the medicine."

Raiyn sat on the side of her bed. "You're not getting better. You need it."

She coughed again—weak. "I wish I could heal like you do." Her eyes drifted to the far wall.

Raiyn followed her gaze, noticing the leather pouch on the shelf where it had rested for as long as they'd lived there. "Maybe you can."

His pulse sped as he thought of what the pouch contained and what it could mean. He readied to stand until her hand rested on his.

She shook her head. "I tried for years. It won't work. I think this is it for me."

His jaw quivered as he sat again. "Don't say that, Mother."

"Raiyn," she waited until his eyes met hers, "I'm sorry I couldn't give you a better life."

"What are you talking about? I—" He stopped as cold fear choked him.

"You've been limited because of . . . of everything. I wish it could have been different." She winced and brought her hand to her chest. After several deep breaths, she patted his hand. "Let me rest. It's late."

After blowing out the candle on the table, he left her room. His own bed called to him, but he couldn't bring himself to lie down. His heart ached. *I have to do something.* He turned to the front door and opened it to the moonlit street beyond.

RAIYN PASSED the apothecary's shop once, allowing himself only a fleeting glance. Windows separated the street from the small shop, where rows of bottles lined a wall behind a counter. When he arrived at the corner past the shop, he stopped, glancing down each of the streets. They were clear.

Westerpoint Bank stood on the cross street, watching him— judging him. *I wish I had a week or two,* he thought. *Then I could have some actual money.*

He turned away from the bank and tried the front door to the shop. Locked, as he expected. He pulled hard on the knob, but the door didn't budge. A rock caught his attention on the street, and he scooped to pick it up. The grit of sand and dirt rubbed against his hand. Soon, he stood back in front of the glass window with a knot in his stomach.

How easy will it be for them to trace this back to me? If they ask Dalby, would he turn me in? He rubbed the rock under his thumb. *Even if they do find out it was me, it will be too late to stop her from taking the medicine.*

His mouth formed a determined line. A glance to either side confirmed he was still alone. Sweat formed on his brow. Taking a few steps away from the window, he reared his arm back and threw the rock. The object collided into the window, splintering the glass into a hundred pieces. The shattering sound filled the street and Raiyn panicked. His feet angled to run but then he stopped. The bottles in the shop stared back at him through the cleared pane. He pictured his mother in her bed, clenched his jaw, and moved to the window.

Jagged pieces remained in the frame. He kicked out the glass his leg could reach, then pulled out the rest. When it seemed clear enough, he ducked through the opening.

Glass crunched under his boots as he scanned the shop. Candles covered a table with cooking oils and spices against the far wall. A hallway led back into the darkness, but Raiyn's interest lay in the colorful bottles along the wall. He wasted no time leaping over the counter to inspect them.

Sage, antispurn petals, borrell bark, turnfoil root . . . The glow from the moonlight in the street barely allowed him to read the labels. *Where is the barkleaf elixir?*

A faint thump sounded above him. He glanced up and imagined the wooden planks in the ceiling vibrating. *I need to hurry!*

The top shelf held smaller bottles, which he couldn't identify. He pulled a stepping stool up and climbed on top to give him a better view. *Baltam powder, toadgrass extract . . .* He reached for the back of the shelf and pulled a small bottle forward. The label was dim, and he had to angle it toward the light. His heart raced when the glow revealed the contents —*barkleaf elixir.*

"What are you doing?" a voice shouted.

Raiyn flinched and nearly lost his balance. A man held a candle in the entrance to the room from the back hallway. He wore a robe while wisps of gray hair fell down over his face.

"You're gonna pay for that!"

"I-I'm sorry," Raiyn stammered, his pulse pounding in his ears. "It's my mother." He jumped down from the stool and ran to the hole in the window.

The man shouted at him. The crunching of glass grew closer, but Raiyn only paid attention to navigating his way through the jagged window. A sharp tear on his arm caused him to cry out, but he continued through the window. When his feet hit the street, he ran, using his speed to put distance between himself and the shop.

After turning down several alleys, Raiyn stopped. He bent over and set his hands on his knees as his chest heaved. A red gash along his arm caused him to wince. Blood dripped from it, falling to the stone floor of the alley.

He closed his eyes, focusing his energy into thoughts about his arm. A tingle started in his gut and spread to his limb. When he opened his eyes, the band of red scabbed as he watched, turning into a tight line of dark red until the tingle was gone.

With a gasp, Raiyn fell to the street. His legs didn't want to hold him anymore. His pulse pounded and lungs gasped for air. The use of his power to heal left him utterly exhausted. The silhouette of the buildings above him wavered as his vision blurred. He could no longer keep his eyelids open and soon passed out.

A FAINT TUG at his body registered in Raiyn's mind, fighting away the darkness. Through much effort, he blinked open his eyes to the slanted daylight of morning. A man bent over his body, rummaging through the pockets of his cloak.

"Hey!" Raiyn shouted, rolling up to a sitting position.

The man, with greasy hair and a scraggly beard, jumped back and muttered as he scurried down the alley to get away.

Raiyn's body ached as he stood. His back and legs groaned with sore muscles, protesting the movement. He studied the dried blood along his arm. The line of the scab—fainter than the night before—reminded him of what had happened.

The bottle! His eyes opened wide.

He patted his pockets but found nothing. He spun,

searching the street, but no small bottles appeared. *Did that man—* He stopped when he pressed against his chest pocket. His shoulders relaxed. He reached into the pocket and pulled out a small glass bottle. Black lettering on a white label brought a smile to his face. *Barkleaf Elixir.* His mind jumped back to his home. *Mother!*

Raiyn hurried up the alley to the main street at the end, unsure where he had run to in the night. The familiar butcher shop he passed every day confirmed he was only a street away from home.

A clock on the wall of a building caught his attention and caused the blood to drain from his face. *Seven thirty-two! I need to clean up and get to the bank!*

He hurried up the street. His legs and body ached, sore from using all his energy the night before and passing out on the rough stones of the alley. The next side alley led to the door of their flat. He grinned as he opened it and shut it behind him. He hurried through to the next room.

"Mother, you won't believe what—"

Catina lay in bed. Her head hung to the side with her jaw drooping open. One eye cracked while the other was shut. Her chest didn't move.

"Mother?"

She didn't stir.

Raiyn ran to her side and placed his hands on her upper arms. "Are you all right?" He lifted her head upright. "I've got the elixir the doctor mentioned. It's gonna—"

Her head fell to the side again. Her chest remained motionless.

"No. This can't—" His voice cracked with emotion. He pulled out the elixir and unscrewed the tiny stopper. "Here. This will help."

He tilted her head back and tipped the bottle into her open mouth. His hand shook as the blue liquid poured out. Some fell into her mouth while a few drops spilled, staining her shirt. Once most of the bottle's contents was in her mouth, he held her jaw closed.

"Swallow this." He sniffed. Tears formed at the corners of his eyes. "You'll feel better soon."

When he released her jaw, blue liquid dripped out.

"Mother?" Tears ran freely. Raiyn buried his face into the sheets of the bed as thick sobs filled the room. His medicine was too late. His mother was dead.

A gut-wrenching pain twisted in his stomach. His chest ached. Minutes passed with Raiyn staring at nothing. When his tears dried, he wiped his eyes and blinked to clear his vision. *What do I do now?*

The job at the bank nagged at him, but his body lacked the motivation to move. *Surely, they'll understand why I'm not there.* He pictured Reginald and Saul and frowned. *They may not understand.*

Raiyn stood, extending his hand to the wall for balance. His mind pleaded with him to change into cleaner clothes and wash his hands and face, but his lifeless steps still carried him out the door.

The street felt foreign, filled with the muffled chatter of the city. He followed the route he knew without thinking. He bumped into people but continued forward, tottering on numb legs. His mind warred between telling him to go back to his mother and to not be late for work.

He passed under a clock in the street. *Three minutes after eight. Not ideal, but close enough.* The bank loomed at the end of the road. Saul stood outside of the doors, looking in each direction.

Raiyn picked up his pace. As he passed the apothecary's shop, his head turned. The broken window was just as he'd left it, and inside the shop, the owner spoke with a constable. Raiyn wanted to duck or hide, but all he could do was stare at the gray-haired man. The apothecary stopped mid-sentence and looked back. The old man's eyes narrowed, but Raiyn continued in a daze toward the bank.

When he entered the cross street, Raiyn raised a hand. Saul's eyes focused on him. It took the banker a moment, but recognition reflected on his face before he cocked his head in question. *I wish I had taken the time to clean up,* Raiyn thought.

"That's him!"

The muddled voice from the apothecary bounced around in Raiyn's head for a moment before he made the connection. Rough arms pulled his hands behind his back when he was only a few steps from the bank. Metal cuffs clinked, slapping around his wrists. Instantly, the faint power he felt simmering inside dissipated. He gasped at the loss of sensation.

Saul's face hardened. He lifted his chin. "You're that kid who wanted an interview. How did—? What did you do to Crabtree?"

"He's the one from my shop!" the apothecary shouted, pointing at him and glaring. "He broke my window then stole some of my medicine."

Raiyn had trouble piecing the statements together in his addled mind. He stared vacantly, not bothering to argue. He pulled at the cuffs, but the source of strength and speed he could always rely on was gone—as if the restraints took it away.

"It's the dungeon for you, boy," the constable said, pulling him down the street.

Raiyn glanced over his shoulder to see the bank grow smaller behind him. The manager, Reginald, joined Saul. Both men shook their heads with arms crossed.

10

THE TOWN OF PIRYD

"Cecil! It's time for chores!"

Cecil Gregson shrank against the wall, trying to not laugh. His mother's steps crunched on the dirt in the other room. He steadied his breathing, trying not to give himself away while strands of blond hair fell across his eyes. After a moment, the sound grew fainter, and he glanced around the corner. His mother faced away with her hands on her hips. He ran on his tiptoes out the open door.

A smile broke on his face as he inhaled the fresh air and took in the surrounding mountains. He jogged through the village, passing the handful of houses and shops. An open window to another house beckoned him. He grabbed the edge of the frame and poked his head inside. A boy his age sat, shelling peas into a bowl on his lap. His dog, Maggie, sat next to him, watching with her tongue hanging out and a grin on her face.

"Joey," he whispered.

The boy turned, creases at the corners of his mouth replacing his glum expression. Maggie cocked her head.

"Let's play."

Joey lifted the bowl for emphasis. "My mother wants me to finish these peas."

"You can do it later. Come on."

Joey glanced around. Appearing content with the lack of another presence, he set the bowl on the table and got up. When he exited the house, both boys laughed and took off at a run, with Maggie following, stride for stride.

The fountain in the center of the village bubbled water, brought through an underground spring from the mountains above. Next to the fountain, the three-story village tower watched over the couple dozen buildings that made up Piryd.

"Hello there, Cecil! Hi, Joey!" an older man by the fountain said with a wave. "Where are you two running off to?"

"Heading to the woods," Cecil replied, not breaking stride.

The man raised an eyebrow. "You're not running away from your chores again, are you?"

"Of course not, Mr. Boyland."

Cecil and Joey left the man behind and ran up the slope, disappearing into the trees at the edge of the village. Cecil paused at the trunk of their favorite climbing tree and squatted down on a knee.

"Hey, Maggie!" He scratched under the dog's chin, sending her tail wagging so hard it thumped into the trunk. She panted with a smile while her mottled-brown hair rippled in waves.

"Race you up!" Joey said, leaping to grab the lowest branch.

"Hey! That's not fair!" Cecil gave Maggie one last pet, then jumped for a limb on the opposite side to catch up with his taller and stronger friend.

Both boys clambered limb-over-limb as they scurried up to the highest boughs of the tree. The edge of a stick scraped Cecil's knee, but he kept going. As the limbs narrowed, the two boys converged on the same spot.

"Beat you!" Joey shouted, stepping a foot into the V-shaped

split of the trunk that marked the highest place they could climb.

"Because you started first," Cecil grumbled, stopping at the branch below.

Both boys took deep breaths as they looked out through the nearly bare limbs. Buds of leaves had just begun to sprout, so the view was clear in every direction. Down the slope, the village of Piryd rolled along the hillside. Far below, the Relavorre River flowed through Rynor, making its way to the sea. The city of Kandis was barely visible in the east where the land met the shimmer of the Parathan Ocean.

To the west, the Straith Mountains towered above them. Capped with snow, the peaks jutted in angles and jagged cliffs.

"Do you think we'll ever be able to explore over the mountains?" Cecil asked.

Joey scoffed. "Like our mothers would ever let us do that."

"Well, it's not like we have to *ask* permission."

"I guess, but—" Joey glanced up the slope and whistled. "But it's a ways up there."

Wisps of white blew off a peak far in the distance. Cecil sighed, looking at the pass that snaked its way between the spires. "I'd love to reach the top of the ridge and look down at Feldor. I wonder what it's like there."

"Feldor?"

"Yeah. Are the people like us? What do they eat? What sort of jobs do they do?"

Joey paused for a moment. "Do you think you'll be a miner like your father?"

Cecil shrugged. "Maybe. There's good money in baltham."

Joey broke the end of a small branch. "If you live."

His friend's bitter tone caught Cecil by surprise, but he understood where it came from. One of his only memories of Joey's father was of the man waving goodbye as Cecil and Joey chased chickens in his friend's yard. That was six years before —the day of the mine collapse.

"I know it's dangerous," Cecil said, "but . . . accidents are rare."

Joey sniffed. "Yeah, I know."

Cecil looked back up into the mountains, his smile returning. "I'd rather raise sheep. Can you imagine it? Going out for days at a time. Driving the herd to find untouched high pastures. Sleeping at the top of cliffs."

"Aric says monsters live in the mountains."

"And you believe your brother?"

"It's not just him. I've heard it from others—my mother, even."

A faint unease tickled at Cecil's gut. "I've heard it too, but I don't think anyone's ever *seen* a monster. I think they're stories adults tell, so we don't wander off."

"None of the other shepherds travel past Goddard's Ridge."

"Which is ridiculous," Cecil said. "You can *see* all the grass past it."

Joey shrugged. "I don't know. If the adults are not going there, it's probably for a reason."

A commotion sounded in the village, drawing both boys' heads.

"Who are you?" an agitated voice carried through the trees, coming from the village. A woman's scream tore through the air.

"Hey! Let her go!" someone yelled.

"What's that?" Cecil whispered.

"I can't see," Joey said, leaning forward. He held onto a limb, straining forward until he shook his head, then descended. "Come on. Let's go to the tower."

Cecil followed, scrambling down the tree and dropping to the dirt, his knees bending as he hit. Joey led the way. He ran down the short slope, leaving the trees around the back of the tower.

The square, wooden structure consisted of steps that spun up the three floors. The tower tripled in purpose as a lookout, a central point to hang a clock, and a focal point to identify the village from farther down the mountain. Cecil panted as he and Joey emerged onto the upper platform. They moved to the short wall that served as a railing and leaned out.

A dozen people gathered close to the tower's base. Up the slope, six men and three women stood in a line. One man held a woman from the village with a dagger pinned to her throat.

"Mrs. Parkins," Joey whispered, his mouth agape.

The strangers wore gray cloaks and dark boots laced high up their legs. Each person wore a necklace ending in a dull red object. Cecil's stomach turned.

"Who are they?" Cecil asked. "Where did they come from?" He glanced up the slope, imagining another village somewhere higher up.

"I don't know," Joey breathed.

Each of the nine strangers bore a black stain at the base of their neck that peeked out from their clothing. Cecil extended a finger. "What's that on their necks?"

Joey leaned forward and squinted. "It looks like a black mark."

"That's odd."

Swords hung at each of their hips, but other than the dagger held to Mrs. Parkins, none of the newcomers moved to their weapons.

"I said, let her go!" a villager shouted—Mr. Parkins.

Other men and women continued to gather, creating a large crowd. Maggie walked up, joining the crowd with the hair on her back crested in an upside-down V shape. She growled then unleashed two fierce barks.

From the group with the black marks, a man stepped

forward. His long, gray hair fell down both sides of his face. He stroked his thick beard as he scanned the crowd. "My name is Talioth, and we require your men." The man spoke calmly, but his voice projected across the village.

"What do you mean?" James Tarrington asked. "For what?"

"That's not your concern."

"I'd say it *is* my concern." Mr. Parkins pointed a sword at the man holding his wife. "Let her go, then we'll talk."

Talioth took another step forward. "If you refuse to cooperate, we will kill her."

Cecil and Joey gasped. The villagers muttered and glanced at each other.

"You aren't going to do that," Mr. Parkins said, his voice wavering despite its attempt at sounding strong.

"And why is that?"

"Because there are sixty-two of us living in this village," Tarrington said, "and there are nine of you. If you kill her, every one of you is going to die."

Men in the crowd raised their bows, arrows at the ready. Swords and clubs materialized in the hands of the villagers.

Talioth turned to the man holding Mrs. Parkins and nodded. Without hesitation, the dagger slid across the woman's throat.

Cecil gripped the railing while the village exploded. Shouts filled the air as Mrs. Parkins' body fell limp to the ground. Panic ensued. Women shrieked, scooping up screaming children and scattering. Maggie's ferocious barks filled the air. Several people appeared frozen in shock. Bows loosed, but the arrows never arrived. The men and women in gray dodged the projectiles heading for them. Talioth's hand blurred as it moved, catching the arrows in mid-flight. He dropped them to the ground as the stunned crowd gaped.

Mr. Parkins yelled, brandishing a sword as he charged. Talioth stood with a quizzical look. Parkins swung his weapon, but the gray-haired man ducked at the last second. He pulled his own sword from its sheath, stabbing it into the villager's chest in one movement.

Cecil's heart pounded. His eyes bugged. *How did he do that?*

"Look what you all made me do!" Talioth projected to the rest of the crowd. "I don't want to kill you men. You must come with us if you wish to remain alive."

Cecil scanned the crowd. "Father!" he gasped, panting and backing away from the railing.

Titus Gregson towered above the other villagers, his strength exceeding them all. He ran through the panicked crowd toward the strangers, with a pickaxe slung over his shoulder. His broad shoulders lumbered forward as the frenzied crowd parted before him.

"I'm sure your father will be all right." Joey said.

Cecil grabbed the railing again, clutching it with sweaty palms.

"I'm going closer." Joey dashed off the rail.

"Are you crazy? Don't—" Cecil spun, but his friend was gone. Stomping feet descending wooden steps told what happened. He looked over the square-shaped drop and saw the other boy scurrying to the ground. "Joey!"

His friend exited the tower. Cecil made it back to the railing as Joey sprinted past the fountain to join the crowd.

"Get him, Titus!" Tarrington shouted.

Cecil's father continued forward. He lowered the pickaxe from his shoulder and held it with both hands. He stared, locking eyes with Talioth for a long moment. Titus moved. He stepped forward and hefted the axe above his head. Talioth didn't even flinch as the heavy metal object hurtled toward his head. When the sharp pick was about to collide with the man's skull, his hand jerked up and grabbed onto the metal.

What in the world? Cecil thought, his heart pounding. The

pickaxe stopped in midair. Titus strained on the handle, but the tool didn't budge.

After a brief chuckle, the man with the black mark grasped the axe with his other hand and snapped off the pick head as if it were a dry twig. Titus backed up. Talioth grabbed either end of the heavy, iron object and bent it. A creaking sound filled the air as the pick groaned, folding in half.

That's impossible!

Two other black-marked men sprung to Titus' side and clasped his ankles in chains.

Cecil tried to breathe, but his lungs struggled to work. His arms shook while his father struggled against the shackles.

Maggie raced forward, snarling and barking. Talioth cocked his head as the dog lunged at him. A lightning-fast backhand smacked across the animal's snout, and her yelp pierced the air. She tumbled into the dirt. After quickly scrambling to her feet, she jogged away, keeping the intruders at a distance.

With the village champion in chains, any hope remaining dissipated. The crowd scattered. The other eight strangers sprang into action while Talioth called out orders.

Screams filled the air. Villagers ran in every direction, but the men and women in gray cloaks were too fast. Women and children fell by the sword, and men were bound with chains connecting their feet.

Cecil's pulse raced at the screaming and death happening below him. He scanned the carnage for the yellow dress his mother wore that day but couldn't find it.

"Bring the strongest sixteen."

Cecil ducked, keeping an eye peeking over the railing. Just below the tower, Talioth stood with two of his men near the fountain. He scooped a hand into the water and took a drink from it as if nothing happened around him.

"Men or women, whoever looks the healthiest," the leader clarified. "Kill the rest and burn the village."

Cecil covered his mouth to keep from crying out. *This can't be happening. Who are these people?* A smoky, thick scent filled his nose and made his eyes water.

He propped himself on the railing. Flames licked the bases of nearby houses, growing to take them over. Two of the invaders with torches walked between buildings, touching the flames to the dry wood.

Cecil's eyes watered. He coughed, taking in a lungful of smoke. *Where is that—?* He turned and froze. Black smoke poured up through the stairwell to the tower. He ran to it and looked down the opening. Flames covered the stairs, growing higher by the second. He backed away. At the railing, he looked out, searching for anything that could symbolize hope, but flames crept up the exterior of the tower as well. No trees were close enough to jump to. *Maybe someone will rescue me. Maybe—*

His mind stopped. His jaw quivered. A woman in a yellow dress lay across the ground on the far side of the fountain. A stain of red blossomed over her chest. She didn't move. *Mother!* His arms shook. Tears begged to form, but the adrenaline of the moment pushed them away.

Cecil ran to each side of the tower, monitoring the stairwell where flames had breached the floor. Each side burned, the flames creeping higher every second. Smoke singed his lungs, sending him into a coughing fit. *I would have liked to have been a shepherd,* he thought. *I would have enjoyed exploring over the mountains.*

Groaning filled the air. Cecil glanced around him. The tower seemed to sway. At first, it was a slight movement, but it quickly escalated. With white knuckles holding on to the closest railing, Cecil fell along with the burning wood as the tower collapsed. He closed his eyes, clenching them tight as the burning tower toppled.

11

STUDYING

Veron turned the page and smoothed it down. The fragile paper required care and a delicate hand. A candle on the small table next to him cast a flickering light over his book. Bookshelves lined two of the walls. Six shelves high, running the length of the room, the books could keep anyone occupied for years.

Against the short wall, a fireplace popped as simmering flames added heat and light to the Shadow Knights' study. A blanket of warmth filled the room. Chelci occupied the chair opposite Veron, her head buried in a book of her own. To the side, Gavin sat in silence, staring into the flames.

Veron's book was titled *Dawn of the Era of Justice*. He had borrowed it from the King's Library in the castle. Common citizens didn't have access to the ancient collection of books, but King Darcius let Veron and Chelci in whenever they liked.

Veron's eyes crossed as he scanned the pages filled with names of unfamiliar kings, lords, and battles.

"Anything?" Chelci asked.

Veron looked up. His wife raised her eyebrows. A loose strand of brown hair fell across her face, glowing in the firelight. She blew out of the side of her mouth. The hair fluttered but resettled across her nose, blocking her view even further. They both laughed.

"No, nothing," Veron said. He closed the book with a thump. "Just early history. The Shadow Knights don't come around for another two hundred years from where this leaves off." He nodded at her book. "What do you have?"

Chelci lifted the cover. "*Advanced Metallurgy*. Not the most exciting. And nothing indicating how it could stop the origine."

Veron sighed. "We should check the King's Library again. Is it too late?"

"No, it's barely dark," she closed her book and smiled, "and I'd love to see my father!"

"Gavin, you want us to look for anything for you?" Veron asked.

The other knight shook his head, continuing to stare at the hearth.

"We should ask Lia," Chelci said, standing. "She may want to see her grandfather."

"I, uh . . ." Gavin started, drawing their attention. "I'd been meaning to tell you something."

Veron's gut twisted at his tone. "What is it?"

"A few days ago, she brought up the devion in training."

Veron inhaled sharply, his breath catching. "What?"

Gavin nodded. "In front of the other trainees, too."

"She knows better than to do that," Chelci said.

Veron stood. "What did she say?"

"We were talking about greed and oppression, and she mentioned Talon Shadow."

Veron groaned. "I told her that in confidence. I don't want all the young knights to be afraid."

"I cut off the conversation. She didn't have a chance to say more."

"I think we'll need to tell them," Chelci said.

"I guess so." Veron rubbed his chin. "I just wish . . . I'm not sure what I wish."

"You wish . . . If they don't know about it, then they'll never have to deal with it?" Gavin said.

"Yeah, I guess."

"In reality though," Chelci added, "we need to talk about it so they can know *how* to deal with it."

Veron sighed. "All right. We'll tell them. It's not like we have a choice now, anyway."

Chelci and Veron left the study and walked down the hall. Passing the common room, Veron spied his daughter playing cards with Danik, Mason, and Bridgette. He poked his head through the door.

"Lia?"

She looked up, her eyes narrowing when she saw him.

"We're heading to the castle. Are you interested in coming?"

She scoffed. "Why would I want to do that?"

Veron's jaw tightened. "We're going to the library. I thought you may want to say hello to your grandfather."

The crease in her brow softened. She glanced at the cards in her hand before she looked back. "I'll stay here."

"Are you sure?" Veron asked. "How are you doing with your herbology and natural medicine research?"

Lia pursed her lips and drew a card from the stack in front of her. "I'm fine," she said after a pause.

"Will you be ready to present your training assignment?"

"It's short and sweet." She held her hand up as if declaring something to the room. "Poisons are bad."

Veron frowned and inclined his head forward as the other young knights at the table muffled their laughter.

"Sorry," Lia cleared her throat, her shoulders dropping in a rare sign of guilt. "I'm teasing. Yes, I'm ready. I'll talk through all the poisons in Terrenor—how to spot them and how to cure them."

"Good." Veron glanced at Chelci and paused for a moment before looking back. "Well . . . if you change your mind, come and catch up."

A LIGHT DRIZZLE fell as they walked the short distance up the street. After a few minutes, the castle entrance loomed. A grand staircase rose from the street to an enormous set of closed doors. Torches burned under a portico on either side of the doors, backlighting two royal guards standing at attention.

"Halt! Who goes there?" a guard called out, drops of water rolling off the front of his hat.

"Sorry for the late hour," Veron began. "We wanted to—"

"Veron and Chelci Stormbridge!" the guard interrupted when they were close enough to be recognized under their hoods. "I'm so sorry. I didn't recognize you at first." He grabbed the circular ring on the door and pulled. "The Shadow Knights are welcome here any time."

Veron pulled at his shirt, his clothes feeling awkward.

"Thank you," Chelci replied as they approached the open doorway. "And thank you for being here. You do our kingdom a great service."

"Here. Let me get you a lantern." One of the guards said, following them inside. He grabbed a metal lantern tucked against the wall and used a torch to light it.

Veron accepted the light source and nodded his head. "Thank you." He brushed the water off his clothes, and they both lowered their hoods.

The halls of the castle were deserted. A few lanterns lit each corridor, casting long shadows wherever they traveled. Guards posted along the way merely nodded, allowing the knights to continue.

After ascending several flights of stairs, Chelci led the way. "I hope he's not in bed yet," she said.

Light spilled into the dark hallway through the open door to the king's study. The lone guard outside nodded at their presence.

The room appeared empty. Several lanterns rested on stands, giving the room a welcoming feel. Stuffed leather chairs and couches filled the space. Thick rugs covered the stone floor, and paintings of the Feldorian countryside adorned the walls. A desk with stacks of papers and books sat in the center of the chamber.

"Father?" Chelci said, stepping into the room.

Darcius Marlow's head popped up from behind the desk with an eyebrow raised. His face melted into a smile and his arms opened wide. "Chelci! Welcome!"

The King of Feldor stepped around the oversized desk and wrapped his daughter in a hug. After a long squeeze, he turned to Veron and gave him the same treatment.

"What were you doing back there? Hiding from us?" Chelci asked.

He laughed. "My desk has a wobble to it." He pushed down on one side of the desk, causing the piece of furniture to tilt. "I thought I had it fixed but . . ."

"You are the King of Feldor, you know," Veron said. "You can have someone take care of that for you."

Darcius waved a hand, dismissing the idea. "I know, but . . . I enjoy it. How's my granddaughter doing?" He glanced behind them. "She didn't come?"

Veron pursed his lips and glanced at Chelci.

"She wasn't feeling up to it tonight," she said.

"We've been having some trouble with her," Veron added. "I'd love some advice, if you don't mind."

The king's smile grew, creating creases around his eyes. "Not at all. Please, sit." He motioned to the furniture.

Veron joined Chelci on a couch while Darcius settled into a chair.

"What's causing you trouble?" the king asked.

Veron looked at Chelci, pausing before he began. He sighed. "She won't listen. Whatever we want her to do, it seems like she wants to do the opposite."

A laugh escaped the king's mouth before he covered it with his hand. "I'm sorry," Darcius said. "It's not funny. It just sounds familiar." He glanced at his daughter, raising his eyebrows. "Go on."

Chelci jumped in. "She takes shortcuts during training. She doesn't seem to care about the overall vision of the Shadow Knights."

"It's setting a bad precedent for the others," Veron said. "We have to discipline her like we would any knight, but that makes her pull away even more."

"Does she ever say why she acts that way?" Darcius asked.

Veron sighed. "She says we've never asked her what she wanted."

"Have you?"

The king's question stopped Veron. "Um . . . I mean—" He looked at Chelci. "I don't—I guess not."

"This is our family," Chelci said with a puzzled look on her face. "Being a shadow knight is what we do."

"But she may not want to," the king said.

Neither Veron nor Chelci answered.

Darcius leaned back in his chair. "It sounds like she wants to make some of her own decisions—be in charge of her actions. Veron, you grew up on the streets. So, you see the life you're trying to give her and assume she's going to want that, but she may not. You both *wanted* to be shadow knights, but she never got a choice. She may want to be a normal person. Or at a minimum, she may just want the chance to decide."

Veron nodded, leaning forward with his elbows resting on his knees. "Yeah, maybe so." He looked at his wife. "We could try that."

"So, did you just come here for advice?" Darcius asked.

"Actually, no," Chelci said. "We wanted to search through the library again."

"Ah! Of course. Still looking for something on that *pure connection* you found?"

Veron glanced over his shoulder to make sure the room was empty. While the Knights were no longer as secretive as they once were, he hoped to maintain as much mystery about their abilities as possible. "I'm about ready to give up," he said. "I found it that once, fighting Bale, but not even a trace since then."

"And I've been researching the metal band limitation," Chelci said.

The king nodded. "To find why it limits your power?"

"Yes, but even more to find out why *he* is the only one able to work through it."

Darcius looked at Veron. "Still, none of the others can do it?"

Veron shook his head. "We're not sure why."

"Interesting." After a pause, the king looked at both of them. "How have you two been?"

Veron's mouth turned up at the edges. He looked at Chelci and reached for her hand, intertwining their fingers. "We've been good."

"The Shadow Knights Academy keeps us busy," Chelci said, "but at least we're doing it together."

"Do you ever think you'll have—" The king cut himself off. "I'm sorry. Never mind. It's not my business."

Chelci's arm grew tense. "Another child?" she asked.

Veron held his breath.

"We don't think it's going to happen at this point. Not after —" Her voice wavered.

Veron squeezed her hand. "We're no longer trying for it. It's been painful, and we're hoping to avoid that." Moisture pooled at the corner of his eye.

The king nodded. "I'm sorry. I didn't mean to bring up a difficult subject." They sat in silence for a moment. Darcius' eyes jumped around as if he searched for a change of topic. "Whatever happened to that friend of yours? Did you ever hear from him?"

"Morgan?" Veron said, cocking his head. "He lives here in Felting with Jeanette. You were at their wedding, sir."

The king waved his hand. "Not Morgan. Yes, I've seen him. The other one. Brixton."

A conflicting mix of hurt and longing formed in Veron's stomach at the mention of his old friend. Emotions swirled in him from the memory of the multiple betrayals. In the end, Brixton did genuinely change. Chelci would have died, and they would not have defeated Bale if it weren't for him.

Chelci shook her head. "No news since he left."

"It was around ten years ago," Veron added. "No one has seen or heard from him since."

Darcius sighed. "It's a shame. I thought he was doing better."

"My guess is his guilt caught up with him," Veron said.

"From killing his father?"

"From that or killing the king, killing his fiancé, betraying me *twice*, or betraying his entire kingdom. Pick any from the list. He grew more affected by shame before he left. We used to get together, but he became aloof. He poured himself into his baking, but that wasn't enough."

"As much as we both despised him for a while . . ." Chelci said. "We miss him."

"That's too bad." After a beat, the king hit his hands on his knees and stood. "Well, if you're going to the library, you should be off. It's getting late, and I'm heading to bed."

"We'll leave you, then," Veron said, rising.

"Father?" Chelci's voice rose at the end. She cocked her head and motioned with a knuckle to wipe under her own nose.

Veron glanced at the king where a bead of red formed under his nose. "Sir, you're bleeding."

The king pulled a white cloth from a pocket and dabbed under his nose. "Nothing to worry about." Darcius' voice muffled with the rag pressed to his nose. "It happens all the time."

"That doesn't seem like nothing, sir," Veron said. "You may want to see a physician if it happens regularly."

"It's probably from all the stress," Chelci said. "You've been king for—what . . . sixteen years now?"

"Seventeen," Darcius confirmed.

"That's a long time to be in charge, and I'm sure it's difficult."

"Don't worry," Darcius said. "I have one who sees me regularly. They're on top of it. And with you and your knights around, the job is not nearly as stressful as it could be."

The king led Veron and Chelci to the door, where Veron picked up the lantern again.

"Good luck in the library," Darcius said. "I hope you find something useful."

"Thanks, Father," Chelci said, kissing his cheek. "And you get some rest."

12

HUSHED CONVERSATION

Lia shook the rain off and stamped her feet as she entered Fetzer's Tavern.

"Packed house tonight," Danik said at her back.

The low roof of the tavern glowed a warm russet color, illuminated by lanterns spread around the room. Men and women sat around tables packed with ale, dice, and cards. Barmaids weaved between the patrons, hefting mugs of frothy ale and collecting piles of coins. A pair of men took turns throwing knives at a target in the corner.

"There's one." Lia pointed with her chin before walking to a booth. Her legs groaned in thanks as she collapsed to the bench with a sigh.

"You and me both," Danik said. "I'm beat."

"I can't remember when they last worked us that hard."

"Climbing, stealth training, boulder carrying, bows, and staff work all in the same day. I'm sure Mason and Bridgette are already asleep."

She chuckled. "Mason and Bridgette."

"What?" Danik asked.

"Nothing. They're just so . . . good. Always wanting to do what's right. It's nauseating."

"Mason's probably lying in bed, thinking of you right this second."

Lia hit him hard on the shoulder.

"Ow!" Danik groaned.

"Cut it out!"

He grinned then held up his hands. "All right! No more."

"Mason is . . ." She snickered. "He probably *is* thinking of me, isn't he?"

Danik joined her in laughter.

"He's harmless enough, but I could never be with someone that . . . earnest."

A woman with two large foaming mugs arrived at the table. "Welcome, you two. Ales?"

"Yes, please, Clara," Lia said, leaning away from the table to give her room to set the drinks down.

"We've got roasted garront tonight. You interested in plates?"

Lia's mouth salivated at the idea, but her full stomach said no. She shook her head. "Thanks, but we've eaten."

The barmaid left, and they scooped up their drinks.

"Here's to your final day of Tribulation," Danik offered.

Lia tipped her mug, foam pasting itself around her mouth. The cool ale slid down her throat, and she sighed. "I didn't think it was ever going to end. I believe Dayna took it out on the rest of you today, too."

"*We* didn't have to carry the boulders yesterday, though. Or be on guard duty two nights in a row."

"Or scrub every weapon until Gavin could see his beard in the reflection."

"At least now, we can come back here again," Danik gestured to take in the tavern.

"You always could," Lia pointed out. "I was the one forbidden."

"But what's the fun without you?"

She blushed.

The men at the knife target left, and Lia perked up, then pointed. "You want to go a round?"

Danik looked toward the target. "Against you?" He scoffed. "That's hardly fair."

Lia took a long drink then set her mug down and slid out of the booth. "Of course it's fair. You have as much of a chance to practice as I do."

"Yeah, but—" He didn't seem to know how to finish his sentence, but he followed, leaving his drink behind. "I don't."

Four concentric circles were painted on the wooden target against the wall. Lia pulled out three knives with red handles from where they stuck into the board. "And you think that makes it unfair?"

Danik sighed then laughed. "I just don't like getting beat." He pulled the blue-handled knives out then followed Lia to the black line on the floor.

"I'll let you go first then," Lia said, gesturing for him to start.

He shook his head then toed the line, his body square to the target. "So . . . If not Mason, then what's your ideal person like?"

Lia shrugged. "I don't know. Someone who's real—who doesn't just spout idealistic jargon."

"Like—" he lowered his voice "—the Code of the Shadow Knights?" He flung his first knife toward the target. It flipped through the air and stuck into the wood, just inside the fourth ring.

Lia looked around the room before turning back to Danik. "Don't tell my parents, but . . . yeah. It's fine. I don't *disagree* with anything. It's just a lot. Putting others' needs first. Not using your powers to elevate yourself. It seems . . . limiting." She stepped to the line.

"What about, *Never allow your abilities to be known*?"

"Exactly," Lia said. She flung her first knife, which stuck inside the second ring.

"I'm not sure your parents had a choice, though," Danik said. "The entire kingdom celebrated them after they defeated Bale. It'd be tough to hide from that. And they try now—always wearing their hoods around the city and disguising the training center. No one recognizes the rest of us." He threw his second knife, which settled next to Lia's.

"Nice," she said.

He grinned.

"Hypocritical is what it is. It's like our training." She glanced over her shoulder to make sure no one was near. "They're teaching us to be Shadow Knights, but we have to wear those stupid bands all the time. If we're supposed to learn to use the origine, then let us use it. We can do these incredible things, but all we do is protect people and stop uprisings in far-off cities who have nothing to do with us. We could run this kingdom if we wanted to."

Danik's eyes narrowed as if he played her words over in his head.

"Not that I want to do that," she clarified as she stood at the line, "but we could."

He nodded. "Yeah, I'm sure we could. Wouldn't that be something? Shadow Knights on the throne with everyone knowing who they were."

Lia's knife thunked into the wood, barely off center, but well inside the first ring.

"All I want is to be able to use my full potential," Lia said.

"You're better than me, that's for sure—as much as I hate to admit it. You're better than all the knights . . . possibly even your father."

Lia's mouth turned up at the compliment. "It's almost like he wants to hold me back."

"Maybe he doesn't want you to show him up?" Danik threw his last knife. It stuck inside the black mark of the second line, and he frowned.

"I wouldn't put it past him," Lia muttered. "None of them respect me."

"The knights?"

"Yeah. I run circles around them. I can disarm any of them in a fight, but they treat me as if I'm a kid, like my skills aren't good enough."

Danik chuckled. "You and me, both. Well . . . the respect piece, at least. Did you know that Gavin has never once sat down to talk with me one-on-one?"

Lia raised an eyebrow.

"It's true. He just sucks up to Veron, Chelci, and the others. It's like I'm some distasteful person he lives near but doesn't want anything to do with."

"Sounds familiar. He worked with me on my poison research, but only because my father made him." Lia held up her knife and sighted the target. She paused to let her breath exhale smoothly before she threw. The blade tumbled end over end until it sank dead center inside the first ring.

"This is ridiculous," Danik said, throwing up his hands and marching back to their table. "That's enough for me."

"Aww, come on!" Lia said, smiling. "It's just for fun! You did well."

Danik frowned, picking his mug back up and taking a long drink. Lia followed his example.

The door to the tavern opened, drawing Lia's eye as the four members of the Merryweather family entered. She frowned. "I've never seen them in here before."

Danik followed her eyes. "Who's that?"

"The Merryweathers?"

He stared at them with a blank expression.

"They live across the road from us?"

Nothing.

"The boy was the one at the dock with the loaf of bread?"

Danik's head tilted. "Oh yeah. That *is* him."

The conversation with Nathan played again in her mind. "That's right, it's his birthday. He was excited about eating at a tavern."

The family sat at a table close to their booth. Nathan and Anna stared around the room, grinning. Lia focused her hearing, amplifying it with the origine.

"What's your meal tonight?" Johann asked as Clara arrived at their table.

The children stared up at the barmaid with wide eyes.

"Roast garront with greens and carrots." Nathan's eyes brightened as Clara continued, "Six pintid a plate. You want four plates and a couple of ales and waters?"

Johann's mouth tightened. "Um . . . can we get just one plate? We're going to share."

"Father," Nathan said in a high-pitched voice. "Can't I get my own?"

Johann chuckled. "Sorry, son. Not today." He turned to Clara. "Just one please. And four waters."

The barmaid nodded then left the table.

"What is it?" Danik asked.

Lia raised her eyebrows then blinked as she looked at him. "I'm sorry . . . What?"

"You're frowning. What's going on?"

"Oh—" Her eyes drifted back to the Merryweathers' table. "They, uh . . . They're a sweet family."

She patted against her pocket then raised her other hand to flag down Clara.

"Here," Lia said quietly, pressing three copper tid into the barmaid's hand. ". . . for that family over there. Can you give them each a plate? It's the boy's birthday today. Say it's on the house or something."

Clara smiled. "Sure. I'll bet they'll love that."

Danik's chuckle broke Lia from her thoughts as the barmaid left. "What?"

"You're an odd one, Julia Stormbridge."

Her smile faded. "You're odd." She punched his arm in the meaty part of his bicep. "It's his birthday. Other than getting drinks like this, I don't have much to spend money on."

"What about the future? You don't think you'll want money for something down the road?"

She shrugged. "I don't know."

"You ever wonder what it will be like—your future?" Danik asked.

Lia nodded. "All the time. I keep hoping I'll have a Dream that will show me. Wouldn't *that* be incredible?"

Danik's face fell.

Lia inhaled quickly and cringed. "I'm so sorry. I completely forgot."

Danik waved the apology away. "It's fine. It was years ago."

Lia stared at her drink, wondering how to clear the awkward air.

"My father didn't believe my mother when she first told him," he said after a moment. "He thought she was making it up to get him to pay attention to her. They fought a lot. He was always spending his time making these stupid gourd houses."

"What's that?"

"They were . . . houses—miniature ones—carved out of gourds. He spent all his free time making them and my mother hated it."

"Why'd he make them?"

Danik shrugged. "I don't know. He didn't even sell them. Just gave them away to kids. He said he loved the look on their faces when he handed it to them. My mother always commented about how he could spend his time doing something that made extra coin, instead, but he kept making the houses."

"Seeing how you're going to die . . . that must have been awful. But they didn't tell you, did they?"

He shook his head. "They lived with the knowledge for months. When they saw the signs, they even knew which night it was going to be. They sent me to sleep at a neighbor's house." Danik balled his fist. A shimmer grew at the corner of his eye. "The thief showed up just like she Dreamed. He killed them both, just as she saw. It's as if they didn't even care. My neighbor told me about the Dream afterward. I was *so* angry at them."

"Because they didn't tell you?"

"Because they didn't even try! They could have—" He paused, shaking his head as he looked at his drink. "I would have tried. It's one of the reasons I jumped at the chance to join the Knights. If I had the power I have now, maybe they would still be alive, and he'd still be making those gourd houses."

"I'm sorry, Danik."

"I lived on my own for three years. The neighbors helped some, but—" He shook his head. "No one really cared. I was invisible—an orphaned kid living in a rundown shack of the Red Quarter. My parents didn't even get their own graves. Did you know that?"

Lia shook her head.

"They just dumped them in a pit with all the others who died that week. Nameless, forgotten, unappreciated . . . just like me."

He wiped at his eyes. A shrug indicated he wanted to move on. "So, uh . . ." He leaned across the table. "Tell me about this devion thing. What is that?"

Lia raised an eyebrow as she set down her mug with a thump. "Speaking of the Knights holding things back." She leaned forward, matching him. Her mouth opened.

"You got room for us?"

Lia turned to see fellow knights Ruby and Bradley standing before their table.

"Looks like the rain has everyone inside tonight," Bradley said, moving to sit without waiting for an answer to his question.

"Uh, sure," Danik said as he scooted toward the wall. "We have room."

Ruby moved next to Lia. "What are you two talking about?"

"Two ales," Bradley called, waving a hand and catching Clara's attention. He turned his attention back to the table. "Yeah, I hope we didn't interrupt you."

Lia's eyes jumped to Danik. She swallowed, then shook her head. "Nothing. Just talking about today's training."

Ruby whistled. "It was a rough one today, huh? I think Dayna might have been trying to make you all crack or something." She laughed.

"That was a lot," Bradley said. "You all appeared to do great, though—especially you, Lia. That looked like a rough few days of Tribulation.

Lia shrugged. "I lived."

"Remember our training, Bradley?" Ruby said.

He chuckled. "All I remember is us two trying to keep up with Gavin and Dayna."

"It was tough," Ruby said. She turned to Lia. "Your father pushed us hard."

"Your mother was the easy one," Bradley added. "She was always encouraging and supporting us on the tough days. But .. . we needed Veron to demand what he did from us."

A woman arrived with two large mugs, adding them to the collection on the table.

"I think Dayna takes the training demands to a whole new level now, though," Ruby added. "Once we grew older, it was easier. We trained less and went on more missions. Seeing what the Shadow Knights did—stopping oppressors and saving good people—helped me with my motivation."

Bradley set down his mug after taking a drink. "Me, too. The code felt purposeful then."

"Well, we've been going on missions for a while now," Lia said.

Ruby nodded. "Soon you'll be doing even more. You'll see, then."

"How did you two feel about the bracelets?" Lia's question drew a pointed look from Danik. She kicked him under the table.

"All I wanted to do was take them off once we learned how to use the origine," Bradley said.

Ruby chuckled. "Me too. But if we didn't keep them on during training, we would have never developed the skills we needed."

"The origine doesn't make you a good fighter," Bradley said. "It takes a good fighter and makes them great."

"Hmph," Lia said. The table grew quiet. "Yeah, I agree. It's good to practice without it." The words strained as she pushed them out.

Danik raised an eyebrow.

Ruby and Bradley led the conversation while the four knights downed their drinks. They started with the warming weather, then moved on to the political climate of the various kingdoms. Lia longed to take her leave, but Ruby pinned her on the far side of the bench seat. Bradley made an optimistic comment about the future of Terrenor and the inherent goodness of its people. Lia rolled her eyes at Danik, who covered his mouth with a hand to keep from laughing.

When the mugs dried up, Ruby and Bradley pulled coins from their pockets and set them on the table. "Well, it's getting late," Ruby said, yawning. "You ready to head back?"

"I am," Bradley said.

Lia's eyes jumped to Danik's. His face held an intensity reflecting unresolved questions. "I think I may go for one more round," she said.

"Me too," Danik added.

"Suit yourselves," Ruby said. "You kids don't stay out too late."

The older knights took their leave, allowing Lia and Danik to spread out on the seats. Clara returned. "Another drink?"

Lia waved her away. "No thanks." The barmaid left, and Lia craned her neck to make sure no one lurked nearby.

Danik leaned in. "So . . . the devion."

"You know how the origine fuels our body with energy . . . ?"

Danik nodded. "It lets you use as much as you want, all at once."

"Right, but it's all done through the code of the Shadow Knights—helping others, being humble, always learning, and so forth. Your intentions need to align with the code before the origine will work." Lia inclined her head forward. "So . . . what if your intentions don't align?"

"The devion?"

"Exactly. If your goal is money, power, or any selfish desire, the energy can still be there if your goal matches your heart. When you're filled with corruption and evil, strength will still follow. The devion is an ability just like the origine. It gives you energy, but supposedly, it lasts longer."

Danik's eyes widened. "*Really*? Then why don't—" He stopped himself.

Lia's eyebrows raised. "Why don't . . . what?"

Danik pursed his lips and paused. "Why don't . . . others use it?"

"No one knows about it. Otherwise, I imagine we'd have an army of them out there clamoring for power. My father has a theory that Edmund Bale, who learned to use it in a matter of days, was unknowingly fueled by the devion rather than origine."

Danik leaned back and whistled. "So, what happened with Talon Shadow?"

"The lure of power tempted the founder of the Shadow Knights. After stopping King Vitrion, he wanted his band of knights to be in charge. There was a split in their ranks—those using origine against those who turned to the devion. The side with origine won. They wrote the code after Talon's fall—to keep others from following the same path."

"So, why don't they teach us about it?"

Lia shrugged. "Maybe they don't want us to know it's a possibility—so we're not tempted."

Danik tapped his empty mug. "It's frustrating that they don't trust us."

Lia chuckled, mulling the word until it came out as a whisper. "Trust." She bit the side of her cheek and was quiet for a long moment. "Do you think the knights will ever respect me?"

Danik pursed his lips but didn't reply.

"I'm not sure what else I need to do to prove myself." She held the handle of her mug, staring at it. "Then there's my family. They don't even accept me for who I am."

"I think they love you," Danik said. "They may not show it well, though."

Her eyes raised to his. "If I tell you something, do you promise not to tell anyone?"

"Of course. I won't say a thing."

"I've thought some about leaving," she whispered.

Danik's eyes grew. "What?"

"I have. Think what it would be like to make your own decisions and have no one tell you what to do?"

"Yeah, but what about the Knights? What about your parents?"

"They don't care about me. They're busy with the crisis of

the day. All they want me for is to have someone to yell at and to see what I can contribute as a shadow knight. Did you know they have *never* said they love me?"

Danik spun his mug.

"What are you thinking?" Lia asked.

"I . . . I bet your parents would miss you." He shrugged. "I know I would."

"I'm not planning to do it, you know."

He waved a hand dismissively and chuckled. "Oh, I know."

"I like to talk, but . . . I don't think I'd ever actually leave." Her voice dropped to a murmur. "I owe it to Morgan."

"Morgan?" Lines formed in Danik's brow. "Your father's friend?" The furrows disappeared as a wave of recognition washed over his face. "Oh, you're talking about . . ."

Lia nodded at the unfinished sentence, trying to push the painful memory away. She eyed her empty mug and longed for the hazy fog that would have come had she taken Clara up on another round of ale.

"If you *did* leave the knights, what would you do?"

Lia paused. A grin grew on her face as she stared at her hands. "Anything I wanted."

13

TAKING A CHANCE

A wind picked up as Veron ascended the steps to the academy wall, blowing the steam away that swirled off his mug. He pulled his cloak closer with his free hand to keep the cold tendrils from reaching inside his clothing. At the far end of the narrow path, the shadow of a hooded figure sat on the stone fortification, their head scanning.

"Quiet night?" Veron asked, his footsteps drawing the head of the figure to him.

The hood lowered, and Chelci's gentle smile gazed back. "As always."

Veron extended the steaming mug. "I thought you might like some tea."

"Thank you." She accepted the drink and lifted it to her lips, taking a sip. "Mmm."

"I didn't bring one for Gavin." He glanced across the academy complex, where another shadowy form scanned the city in the other direction. "I hope he doesn't mind."

"I'm sure he'll be fine." Chelci nodded toward Gavin across the way. "How long do you think we'll need to keep up a double watch? Back in your father's time, they only kept one each night."

Veron's face turned down, and his jaw tightened. "And we know how well that worked."

Chelci's eyes grew. She rested her free hand on his arm. "I'm so sorry. I didn't think about that."

He shook his head. "It's all right. It wouldn't have mattered how many people were on guard that night. The problem now is the recognition we get. After coming back from killing Bale, everyone knows who we are. They don't fully understand what we do, but it wouldn't be too hard for a determined person to find us."

"Yeah, but the people love us. Why would someone—"

"Not everyone loves us. Not the Black Lanterns in Lorranis or that gang in Bromhill last year."

Chelci nodded. "That's true."

"And if people want to find us, it's not too difficult."

"Do you think it's time for the Glade?"

Veron glanced out at the darkened city and sighed. "There are so many memories here. I love this place."

"I do, too."

"It's not quite ready though. For now, doubling up on guard duty is better than nothing."

Chelci sipped of her tea. "So, what brings you up here so late? Shouldn't you be preparing for bed?"

Veron took a deep breath. "I met with Thajk tonight."

She frowned. "The spy from Tarphan?"

Veron nodded. "He petitioned our assistance at the Advisors Council, then I met with him privately. There's a group there planning to kill Grint."

"What is it with these people? Someone's always wanting to kill someone else." Chelci sighed. "So, they want our help?"

"I'm thinking of seeing if Lia wants to lead."

A long moment of silence followed. "You think she's ready?"

"I don't know. She doesn't follow through on responsibilities. She abandons her team when they need it. She complains and questions my authority."

"You're not painting a convincing picture."

"I know," Veron said, "but, she is finished with her punishment, and giving her the chance to make some decisions could be good for her. Maybe the leadership will bring out a new level of responsibility."

"Maybe it will help her see the purpose of what we do."

"More than anything, I'm worried about what will happen if we don't." Veron sighed. "We probably should treat all the trainees as full knights now. They've put in the time."

"Who else should go?"

"Maybe four in total. I'm considering letting her choose."

Chelci nodded. "I'll be one of them. Let her choose the other two."

"Are you sure you want to do that? It could be easier to not watch."

"We need to watch. Plus, it could be nice for us to have some time together."

Veron grasped her hand and gave it a squeeze. Her answering smile caught the light of the moon. "I worry that we're messing her up."

"How so?"

"Why is she the way she is?" Veron asked. "I feel like we did something wrong."

"Yeah, I know what you mean. But we've done the best we could."

"Only having one child makes me worry—like this is our only shot at getting it right. If we had more children, I don't think I'd feel the same sort of pressure, you know?"

Checi's jaw clenched. She glanced out to the city, moisture glistening at the corners of her eyes.

Veron's eyes widened as his own words hit him. "I'm so

sorry. I didn't mean it like that. We tried, and it's—it's no one's fault."

She nodded and whispered, "No one's fault."

The echoed words hit him hard. Memories of sorrow flooded through his mind. He pushed them away, the pain still too raw. "Well . . . you know what I mean." He swallowed hard. "I'm sorry."

"It's fine." She sniffed and wiped her eyes, then turned back to him and changed the subject. "Did Thajk have any other news? Wasn't he the one who thought he ran into Brixton?"

Veron shook his head. "He was wrong. Turns out it was *a* Brixton, but not *our* Brixton."

Chelci sighed. "I'm sorry. I know you had hoped it was him."

"It's fine. In other news . . ." He paused and exhaled a long breath. "I hear Norshewa is building their army."

She groaned. "Not them again."

Veron nodded. "Ambassador Dane spoke at the council meeting. They don't seem to be mobilizing yet, but who knows what ideas they have for the future."

"Any other news from Dane?"

"Apparently, a village in Rynor was destroyed."

"By Norshewa?"

He shook his head. "Unrelated. Some small village up in the Straith Mountains named Piryd."

"I've never heard of it."

"Me neither."

"What happened? Raiders?"

"No one knows. There are no other villages nearby. What's strange is that someone killed all the women and children and burned the buildings, but the men were missing."

"Missing?"

"Vanished, without a trace. They're looking into it."

"That is odd."

Movement along Rampart Way caught their attention. Their daughter's pulled-back hair shone in the moonlight. She walked with a young man, difficult to make out, but likely Danik as they always seemed to be together. Her steps crossed with a slight stagger. Veron's shoulders drooped.

"She's been out drinking," Chelci said.

Veron sighed and hung his head. "We do allow them the freedom."

"She needs to display more restraint, though. They both do. Are you sure we want to do this? That our 'Little Sunshine' can handle it?"

Veron puffed a laugh through his nose at the nickname he hadn't used in years. "I think we need to try. I'll gather the knights."

"This late?"

Veron nodded. "You'll need to leave for Searis at first light."

"Sounds good. That will give her the night to prepare . . . and to sober up."

"Make sure she's not drinking on the mission, all right?"

Chelci smiled. "Of course."

Veron walked the halls of the academy and knocked on doors, summoning the knights to the courtyard. Chelci and Gavin descended the steps down the wall once everyone had gathered. A lantern hung on a hook, lighting up the gathering of twelve elite warriors. Lia leaned against the wall in the back of the crowd with a frown on her face and Danik next to her.

"I know it's late, but I have a couple things to discuss," Veron said, raising his voice to quiet the others down. "First, we have a mission to Searis. Knights need to leave first thing in the morning."

Heads nodded around the courtyard. Leaving at a moment's notice was a familiar practice to them all.

"The mission is to stop a group of assassins, and," his voice wavered as he gestured to the back wall, "I'd like Lia to lead the four-person team."

Muttering filled the space as the knights spun around. Lia straightened, bringing her back off the wall, her arms hanging at her sides. Her eyes made round circles with whites showing on all sides. She glanced at Danik, who appeared to chuckle.

"If you're interested," Veron added.

Lia paused, looking unsure until, finally, she nodded.

"Chelci will be one of the team," Veron continued, "but Lia will choose the other two knights and she will be in charge." He kept his hand extended, inviting his daughter to step forward. A moment of silence followed while he waited for her to say or do something. With a bemused look on her face, she approached the front of the group. A mixture of pride and fear surged through Veron as Lia stood next to him. *I'm not sure if this will be a victory or a disaster.*

"Who would you like for the other team members, Lia?" Chelci asked.

Lia's eyes remained wide as she scanned the crowd. Gradually, the side of her mouth turned up into a grin. "I choose Danik and . . ." her shoulders fell, "and Mason."

Mason's chest puffed and his shoulders raised. A proud smile reflected toward Lia. Danik shuffled forward, frowning toward the other knight.

"Very well," Veron said. "You four will leave first thing in the morning." He turned to Lia. "Plan your food and supplies. It's a full seven days to get to Searis, even with horses. You'll need—"

"I know, Father," Lia said, her eyes twinkling. "I can do this."

Maybe this will be just what she needs, Veron thought. He nodded, a proud smile forming. "Run your supply list by your mother before you leave."

"I will," she replied with a tight nod.

"Very good." Veron turned back to the crowd. The knights began to talk amongst themselves.

"Is that it, Veron?" Gavin asked, his dark skin even more shadowed by the flickering torchlight behind him.

"There is one more thing I wanted to discuss." He glanced at Chelci, whose mouth formed a tight line. "Not that I *want* to discuss it, but I think it's necessary . . . before the knights leave." He took a deep breath and exhaled. "Some of you already know about this, but many of you do not. I need to tell you about the greatest threat to the existence of the Shadow Knights. This has the potential to wipe all of us out and send our kingdom into an age of darkness, all in one fell swoop."

The crowd of knights leaned in.

"I need to tell you about the devion."

14

THE WAVY MAIDEN

Lia led her horse by the reins, the clop of hooves on stone drowned out by the bustle of the city docks. Ahead, workers laden with goods walked up and down gangplanks, loading vessels. The material being loaded would head for Karondir, Karad, Lorranis, or Tarving, the cities reachable along the Benevorre and Felavorre Rivers. Trade by river was a bustling industry, and Felting sat at its center.

A dank smell of fish and dirt filled the air, wrinkling Lia's nose. She scanned the docks, looking for the *Wavy Maiden*. The masts of the lined-up boats rose high in the air, swaying with the roll of the water.

"Last one on the right," her mother said at her back. Chelci walked behind, followed by Danik and Mason, each leading their own horse.

"I know. I see it," she lied. Even though they were on the same team and her mother was only trying to help, Lia chafed at being told which boat it was. She headed in its direction.

The dock extended into the river with a gangplank angling up to the deck of a double-masted schooner. The masts and hull were a dark wood, aged and conditioned from years in the elements. Furled sails hung at each mast while the boat crew hurried about, securing crates and barrels of cargo.

"There y'are!" A grizzled man shouted down from the main deck with a hand on the rail. "Come along. We need to secure those animals before we can be off."

"Come on, Ginger," Lia said, patting her horse on its neck. Ginger snorted, then followed Lia up, ascending the ridged plank with ease.

"That's a fine mount," the man said when Lia arrived on deck. He nodded to a crewman who moved to take the horse's reins.

"Her name's Ginger," Lia said.

"Secure them in the hold," he ordered. The crewman nodded and clicked his tongue to lead the animal away.

Lia rubbed her back as Ginger walked off. Hollow thumps sounded on the wooden planks after each step.

Chelci arrived next, and another worker took the reins for her horse. "Thank you for making room for us despite this late notice," Chelci said to the man who greeted them, her head set deeply in a hood.

Lia's mother had come to the docks early to secure their transportation. On past trips, Lia would have been the one rising before it was light to set up the arrangements. She took great delight in having her mother do it instead. Lia expected her mother to resent being ordered around, but Chelci hadn't batted an eye.

"This is my daughter, Lia," Chelci said, motioning her way. "And these two are Danik and Mason."

"I'm Captain Vardan," the man said, flashing a grin. A missing tooth gaped back at Lia while she shook his callused hand. He winked before turning to welcome the other knights who had just arrived up the plank.

Cracked lines in leathery skin formed the captain's face. Around forty years old, he looked younger than most of the crew by five to ten years. He wore a dark blue coat covering a cream vest and shirt that puffed out from underneath. His breeches tucked into high black boots. A well-worn three-sided black hat sat on his head, which he tipped in greeting to them all.

"Welcome to the *Wavy Maiden*," Vardan said once they had all arrived. "Our boat's the fastest on the river. Our sails have a knack for finding even the slightest hint of wind. So, about the —um—fee?"

The captain looked at Chelci, who turned to Lia, raising her eyebrows.

Lia's hand jumped to her pocket where she kept the coin purse. "How much—" She cleared a catch in her throat. "How much was it again?"

"With horses, it's six tid per person," Chelci replied.

"That includes meals," Vardan added.

Lia's stomach turned. "Right." She counted out two argen four tid and handed it to the man.

The captain smiled as he accepted the coins. "The winds are favorable now. With a little luck, we should arrive in Tarving before supper tomorrow."

"And if we're not lucky?" Chelci asked.

The captain's mouth formed a line. "Then we'd have to wait on the wind at the mouth of the Taravorre. But don't worry, I've never had the trip take over six days."

"Yet we could make it on foot in four," Chelci said with a hint of an edge, "without having to pay anything." She turned to Lia. "Are you *sure* this is wiser than walking?"

Lia's teeth clenched at her mother's second-guessing and judgment.

A silence fell, the captain's eyes darting between the group.

"Yes," Lia said, her stubborn streak fueling her response. "I'm sure."

"Well," Mason said, stepping toward the hold, "I'm going to

unload the horses so they can rest—if anyone wants to join me."

Danik shuffled after him, looking less enthusiastic.

Vardan turned toward the center of the boat and took a deep breath. "Raise the gangplank! Cast off the bow lines! It's time to be off!"

The crew on the boat jumped into action—a few of them having to tear their gaze from Chelci and Lia. Ropes flew, hoisting heavy bolts of fabric. Knots appeared along the railing as weathered hands tied ropes, repeating tasks they'd done for years.

"Raise the mainsail! Ready the jib!" The captain navigated the deck, barking orders. The sails pulled taut, and the wind pushed the freed vessel into the current of the Felavorre River.

Lia grasped the railing and leaned forward, closing her eyes. The air brushed against her face. Her hair picked up the breeze, fluttering behind her as the boat moved forward.

Her mother's voice interrupted the moment. "You know, finishing the mission quickly doesn't prove you are a good leader."

Lia's eyes opened and her face turned down. Chelci stood at the railing in front of her. The insight in her mother's pointed comment left her shaken. "I want to rest the horses, so they'll be able to travel better." Her mind whirred to think of more excuses. "Plus, they said the king's life is in danger. The longer we take to get there, the greater a risk he's in."

"That's true, but if the winds aren't in our favor, it could take even longer."

"Mother!"

Chelci startled.

"Father asked me to lead, which I'm trying to do. My decisions may not be what you would do, but please . . . let me lead my way."

Chelci took a deep breath before exhaling. "A wise leader

will seek the advice of others, especially when they have little experience."

"A wise mother will question her daughter *in private* if she disagrees with her decisions—rather than doing so in front of the team she's supposed to lead."

Chelci stared for a long moment. Her hard eyes softened and she nodded. "I'm sorry. You're right. I shouldn't have questioned you in front of them."

Lia's shoulders relaxed. "Thank you. Now, let me do things my way."

Heavy footsteps approached. Lia turned as the captain and his broad grin arrived with Mason and Danik. "As I said," he gestured over the water, "we're the fastest on the river."

She looked past the railing. The boat cut through the water, sending ripples toward the shore, which zipped by some distance away.

"Come this way," he said. "I'll show you to your quarters."

The four knights followed the faded black hat. They passed men still working on the sails. A snigger pulled Lia's attention to where two men leered at her mother, whispering between themselves. Her eyebrows creased, and then her stomach dropped. *I know them.*

"Lia," Danik whispered.

She turned toward him, but her eyes stopped. Tying a knot against the ship's rail, a familiar bald man with a gray beard stared back. *Xander.* The corner of his mouth curled in a sneer. Next to him, a man with a scar across his cheek fingered the hilt of a dagger at his hip.

"It's those men from the dock!" Lia whispered to Danik. "What do we do?" The ship's movement and the land passing by confirmed the answer she already knew—*We sail.*

"How are the horses?" Chelci asked Mason, oblivious to the threatening crew.

"They're all set," the young knight confirmed. "We took off

their gear and made sure they were secure. Not a lot of space, but they can lie down if they like, and they have plenty of hay."

"Good."

The captain led through a door into the miniscule forecastle. A low ceiling and dim light greeted them. Danik had to hunch. The must of damp wood and mildew filled Lia's nose. They passed a primitive galley with bins of dried food. Hammocks lined the room, tied between the walls. Storerooms filled any open space, packed floor to ceiling with crates.

"Back here," Vardan said, pointing to a double stack of hammocks separated from the others. Stains covered the drooping fabric. "You can use these two."

Lia flinched when a rat skittered along the wall.

"Don't worry," the captain said, waving a hand at the animal. "They won't bother you."

Mason pressed down on a hammock and nodded. "I'll take the top," he said, climbing up. Close to the ceiling, he rolled over the lip and disappeared into the hammock's curved shape.

Vardan waved toward a door next to the hammocks and opened it with a creak. A cramped cabin with a set of bunked beds rested inside. "The other two can stay here."

The beds contained flat pillows and stained sheets. Lia's eyes twinkled at the thought of privacy. She glanced around the forecastle, noting the proximity of the crew's hammocks, then walked through the door. She pressed down on the bed before turning back to her team. "It's only fitting that Mother and I take the beds."

"Very good," the captain said. "Supper will be late in the afternoon, and we'll sail until nightfall—or until the wind leaves us. For now, find a relaxing place on the deck or wherever you like. And come to me if you have questions."

The weather remained pleasant for the remainder of the day. The boat made the downstream trip in no time and headed upstream mid-afternoon when they reached the mouth of the

Taravorre River. Progress slowed, but the winds remained favorable.

Lia and Danik found a place on the quarter deck where they could sit. They passed the time by playing cards and talking. Mason joined them some but spent much of his time wandering the boat. Chelci spent most of her time reading. She had brought books, which she pored through, leaning her back against the mast with the main sail providing shade. When night fell, the crew let down the anchor to keep them from drifting downstream. Having little to do on the boat, the four knights retired early.

A ROUND of laughter caused Lia to open her eyes. She had laid in the bottom bunk for over an hour, but the lumpy bed and sound of water running along the hull kept her mind from turning off and falling asleep. While the privacy was nice, the stuffiness of the cramped room left her wishing she had chosen a hammock instead. Deciding she needed some fresh air, she rose and opened the door to the cabin.

The creak of her door didn't appear to waken her mother, who breathed deeply in the top bunk. Outside the door, Mason's shape confirmed he lay on top, but the bottom hammock was empty.

Across the room, a gathering of men sat around a table. A lantern dangled from the ceiling, swinging just above their heads. Of the other hammocks scattered around the room, half were empty while snoring emanated from the rest.

"There it is," Danik's voice came from the group. Another man groaned while the others laughed.

"What are you doing?" Lia asked, touching Danik's shoulder. She froze when she recognized the men—the same ones from the incident on the dock. Xander smirked at her, his gray beard lifting to the side.

"Lia!" Danik shouted, his alcohol-induced voice much louder than hers. "Join us!"

The men mumbled in assent and flashed crooked smiles. The sailor with the scar across his cheek slid a stool over and patted for Lia to sit next to him.

She ignored the seat and leaned next to Danik's ear. "These are the men from the dock," she whispered.

Danik waved his hand and sputtered his lips. "We're all good. They apologized about that."

"It was an unfortunate incident, and we were out of line. We should have left both you and that boy alone," Xander said from across the small table. His smile grew with a sharp edge. "Now, we're just friends on a ship looking for ways to pass the time. Please, join us."

She pulled lightly at Danik's shirt. "Come on. Let's get some sleep."

"No way!" He gestured to the table. "I'm not leaving now. You'd love this, too!"

Lia eyed the free chair and reluctantly sank into it, her body tense and ready to jump. "Fine. I'm having trouble sleeping, anyway."

A cup appeared in front of her, slapping on the table and sloshing clear liquid over the side.

"You've got to try this," Danik said, lifting his own identical cup.

Her body tensed. She leaned close to whisper. "We're on a mission. You can't be . . . drinking."

A sheepish look washed over his face. "I know," he whispered back. "At the beginning, I forgot. Then, once we were playing, I didn't want to insult them. It's only a couple drinks, and it's nighttime anyway." He tossed a thumb behind his back. "And they're both asleep."

The responsibility of leading warred with her desire to have fun. She should be reprimanding Danik, but instead, she picked up the cup, barely touching the sticky sides with her fingertips. She sniffed. A fruity, medicinal odor reached her.

"It's good. Trust me," Danik added, bringing his drink to his mouth and tossing the contents back.

What's the perk in being a leader if you can't do what you want? she thought. *And he's right . . . We don't want to insult them.* She set the cup to her lips and tipped it. The drink had a buttery flavor with a sharp kick at the end. She swallowed but couldn't avoid a small cough, which prompted a laugh from the crew.

"What are you playing?" she asked, her eyes jumping around the table.

"Scorpion-eyes," Xander said.

She furrowed her brows.

"You take turns rolling the dice," Danik explained while picking up the objects. "Roll as many times as you like and you get points for however many dots you rolled, but if you ever show a one, you get zero for that round."

"And everyone adds a tid to the pot," Xander added.

Lia noted the pile of coins in the middle of the table.

"If you roll scorpion-eyes—two ones—you lose all your points," the scarred man next to her said.

"First person to one hundred wins the pot," Danik said as he rolled. The dice bounced off the weathered table and piles of coins to display a five and a four. He picked them up and rolled again. Two sixes displayed after a moment of bouncing numbers. "Nice!"

"That makes twenty-one," Xander said.

Danik picked up the dice and paused, pursing his lips. He took a deep breath before he shook his hands and spilled the dice. "Whew!" he shouted as two twos stared up. "I'm done. That's too close."

"That gives you eighty-five in total," a crewman said.

Danik passed the dice to his left, then turned to Lia. He

flashed his eyebrows, then exhaled with a grin. "That scared me."

"How long have you been playing?" Lia asked.

"Eh," he fingered his cup and spoke with a slur, "about four of these worth."

"You know," the bald man with the beard said, eyeing her across the table, "we rarely get cargo like you four. What's your business?" A hiccup jostled his beard.

Lia glanced at Danik. His goofy grin didn't help her answer the question. "We're traveling to Tarving," she replied.

"Well, clearly. But who are you? What are you doing there? Looking for more docks to swim off?"

Her stomach churned. "Our business is our own."

The man laughed until his face twisted in a wince and his hand moved to the side of his chest.

"What's wrong?" Lia asked. "Ribs still tender?"

His eyes narrowed. "I'm Xander, in case you don't remember. I'm quartermaster here. And you are . . . ?"

She paused before replying. "Lia."

The group cheered as a four and a one appeared on the table. The man who had rolled them waved his hands in disgust.

"That's one more for everyone," the man with the scar said.

Danik reached into his pocket, but his eyes wavered. "It's my last one," he whispered to Lia, placing a coin on the table.

Xander took his turn. He rolled two times and added nineteen to his total, bringing him up to sixty-eight before he passed the dice.

"So, Lia . . ." Xander said. "You seem young to be traveling between kingdoms like this."

Her head cocked while another crewman took his turn rolling. "Is that a question?" she asked.

Xander grinned. "You're the leader of the group, aren't you?"

Lia straightened. "Yes."

"I heard that other woman giving you grief. Is she always that irritating?"

Danik chuckled, followed by a hiccup. Lia looked back toward the closed door of the cabin. "She often is."

"Pretty though," the man with the scar added.

Xander nodded as he picked up a bottle and leaned across the table to refill Lia's and Danik's cups. A dash of the clear liquid spilled onto the table.

"Twenty," a man said as the dice passed around the table again.

A twinge of unease tugged at Lia from the wicked look on the quartermaster's face. Lia lifted her cup and took a smaller swallow. The kick of the drink gave her a slight haze, but she pushed it away.

"Is she . . . attached?" Xander asked.

Lia blinked before she connected the question. "Chelci? Yes, she's married."

Xander nodded but didn't reply. Rather, he looked at the man with the scar with a devilish smile. Chills ran up Lia's spine.

She turned to Danik and pulled on his shoulder. "Come on. We should try to get some sleep."

He sloughed off her hand. "Are you crazy? I'm about to win!"

Lia bit her lip and remained in her seat.

The man with the scar next to her picked up the dice. After a quick shake, he tossed them across the wooden surface, revealing a six and a one.

"Again!" the man shouted, hitting the table.

The rest of the crowd reached to add coins to the pot.

"Uh, Lia?" Danik whispered, prompting her to lean in. "Can you spot me?"

The coin purse in her pocket was already too light from the

fare of their river passage. "It's the money for our mission," she whispered with a tight voice.

"I'm close to winning. I need one tid, then you can have it right back." Danik's eyes pleaded.

Silence fell around the table as the men watched and waited.

Lia rummaged in her pocket and pulled out a copper tid. "I get a cut of your winnings."

Danik grinned. He took it, dropped it on the table, and scooped up the dice. A vigorous shake threw double fives.

"Ninety-five," he said, picking them back up. "Only five more."

A nervous energy surrounded the table. The men leaned in with bated breath.

Danik shook the dice. The hard cubes rattled in his hand over the silence. After a long shake, he released the spotted objects. They rattled over the wood surface and bounced off the scattered pile of coins. The first die settled to a one while the second one spun on its side. They waited and watched. The spinning number emerged when the die settled. Another one.

Danik clenched his fists and closed his eyes while the rest of the table laughed and cheered.

"Back to zero!" the man with the scar taunted.

Lia's jaw dropped. She stared at Danik, but he didn't take his eyes off the money.

A few rolls later, the man on his other side celebrated with a roll of an eleven, resulting in him raking in the table of coins. Lia watched as the tid she was in charge of fell into the man's open palm and ended up in his pocket.

A muttered word from across the table led to a lascivious laugh from the other men. Xander stood, running his hand through his thick beard as he moved around the table with his eyes on the cabin in the corner.

Lia's brows pinched together. "What are you doing?"

Xander glanced her way. "I'm going to say hello to your friend, Chelci. I expect she may enjoy sitting with me while we play another round."

Lia jerked her head to Danik, who continued to stare dumbly. She looked back at the quartermaster. "She's sleeping. You should leave her alone."

"She won't be sleeping once I wake her." The other men laughed. "Come on. You wouldn't deny us a little fun, would ya?"

"Danik." Her insistent voice shook. He finally turned her way. "He's waking Chelci."

Danik's brow furrowed, his eyes gaining focus. "Why?" He looked at Xander. "Let her be."

Xander's eyes hardened. "Don't come on our ship and tell us what we can't do. If I wanna wake her, I will."

Lia stood. She took a quick step and grabbed the quartermaster by the arm. "We said leave her alone."

Her commanding voice filled the cramped room. The men around the table hushed, watching with bated breath.

Xander grasped her hand and removed it from his arm.

"Do you plan to stop me?" Xander looked at his men. Chairs scraped as they stood, quiet, with their chins extended. "Do you plan to stop all of us? You got the jump on us last time, but you won't be so lucky today."

"If needed, yes, I will." Lia's jaw clenched tight. Her eyes bore into him. Her muscles quivered, tingling with the origine, ready to act.

"Lia?" a bleary voice called. Chelci was awake and poking her head out from the cabin. "What's going on?"

"Leave her alone," Lia repeated in slow, deliberate words to Xander.

The quartermaster chuckled. He looked between Lia and Danik, then back to Chelci. Finally, he shrugged and returned to the table. "Fine. There's no need to get in a fuss about it."

Lia motioned to Danik. "Come on, let's get some sleep."

Danik joined her in leaving the gang at the table.

Lia arrived at the door to the cabin. "It's nothing, Mother. Go back to sleep." Chelci's scowling form disappeared into darkness as Lia closed the cabin door behind them. "I'm tired. We can talk about it tomorrow."

Lia lay on her bed, and her mother climbed back up to hers. For a while, Lia stared at the dark underside of the bed above as adrenaline pumped through her. She listened for any sign of the crew coming their direction, but nothing else happened. Eventually, she drifted off to sleep.

15

TROUBLE IN TARVING

Lia slept until well past sunrise after the poor night of sleep and late-night conflict. When she exited her cabin, the hammocks were empty. A lone crewman bustled about in the galley, preparing food.

The wind tugged at her hair when she stepped out onto the deck. She gathered the wild strands and tucked them behind her ears, then frowned as she looked up. The sails remained furled. She looked over the ship's railing. They stayed motionless.

She walked to where Chelci, Mason, and Danik stood at the railing.

"It's about time," Danik teased.

"Did you sleep well?" Mason asked.

"It, uh . . . wasn't the best night," she replied. "Mother, are you all right?"

Chelci returned a smile. "I'm good. I hear you stood up for me last night. Thank you for that."

A flush creeped up Lia's neck. "The men were rude. It was nothing." She looked up at the tied sails. "Why aren't we moving yet?"

Mason pointed a finger up. "The wind is bad—blowing in the wrong direction. Captain Vardan says we could be stuck here awhile if it doesn't change. Danik suggested hiring local pack animals and hitching up a towline, but the captain scoffed and muttered something about the cost. He'd prefer to wait it out rather than eat into his profits."

Lia's stomach dropped. She looked around the deck. Xander curled a rope at the foremast, glaring at her. "Maybe it will change," she said.

The wind didn't change, and by early afternoon, it blew even harder in the wrong direction. Lia did her best to avoid Xander and any of the crew while waiting.

While she leaned on the rail, looking at the ripples of water lapping at the hull below, her mother arrived next to her. "Don't say you warned me," Lia said, her back straightening.

Chelci's head tilted. She extended a hand with an apple. "I was going to offer you a snack."

Lia sighed. She accepted the piece of fruit and turned her back to the rail. "Sorry. I guess I feel a little defensive. I thought going by water would be quicker. You were right. I wanted to impress—do the job quickly so others would see how good a leader I was, but unless something changes soon, it may have been better to walk after all."

"Leading is difficult," Chelci said. "You go with your gut and trust others will follow you—right or wrong."

"What if my gut's wrong?"

"Sometimes it is," she shrugged, "but that's all right. Learn from poor decisions and make better ones the next time."

Lia chuckled. "Sounds simple."

A wrinkle formed on Chelci's brow. "While we wait . . . I am curious about last night."

Lia's throat turned dry.

"Were you drinking and gambling?"

"No, I—I wasn't. Well . . . I woke up and found Danik. He was gambling with the men and had a few drinks."

"You realize it's against our rules to drink alcohol during a mission, right?"

"I know. He was out of line."

"And what about you?" Her mother's eyebrow lifted.

Lia tried to swallow the lump in her throat. "They served me a glass—only one. I know we can't drink, but I didn't want to insult them. Don't worry. It won't happen again."

Chelci rested her hand on Lia's shoulder. "Part of leading is not just telling others what to do, it's demonstrating what you expect out of them. *You* must set an example for people like Danik."

She hung her head. "I know."

"And you need to take action when rules are broken."

Lia took in a deep breath then blew it out. "I'll speak with him today."

Chelci nodded. "Good."

The furled sail whipping forced Lia to look up. "Ugh. Still in the wrong direction. What should we do now?"

"What does your gut tell you?"

Lia leaned against the rail, peering at the water. "Land is close. With the gangplank, I'm sure we could get the horses ashore. Maybe we should walk from here. What do you think?"

The corners of Chelci's mouth turned up. "I think that's a great idea, leader."

THE STEADY LOPE of her horse and the warm breeze brought a smile to Lia's face. Having left the stationary *Wavy Maiden* behind, she looked forward to making up some time. With their horses rested, and only a few hours till dusk, she set a brisk pace. It would be at least another two nights until they would make it to Tarving.

After a while, she pulled her horse back to an easier walk. The breeze slowed, settling thick and warm in the air.

"Tarphan sure is hot!" Mason said, clopping along behind her.

"Is this your first time here?" Lia asked.

"I thought you were on the mission to Portris last season," Danik said. "Was that not you?"

"That was Shawn," Chelci answered. "Shawn, you two, and Veron."

"Yes, this is my first time," Mason confirmed.

Behind a stone wall, a herd of rydanor grazed in the field. One moved in stride with them, its massive legs rippling as it looked in their direction.

"And I've never seen a herd of rydanor like that."

"Why don't we raise them in Feldor?" Danik asked. "They'd be useful for pulling carts and plowing fields, wouldn't they?"

"It's the temperature," Chelci said. "They need a warmer climate to thrive."

As if responding to the comment, the closest beast grunted, prompting the four knights to laugh.

While the group settled into an easy walk, Mason's horse trotted up next to Lia's. "I think that was a wise call, Lia," he said quiet enough to where the other knights wouldn't hear.

"What call?"

"Leaving the boat. We made good time to get to the intersection, and now we'll make steady progress on foot the rest of the way. Total time to Tarving should be around four days, so . . . nothing lost."

A smile tugged at her face. "Thanks, Mason." Her thoughts turned toward the coin purse, which was considerably lighter. *Something was lost.*

"I think you're going to be an outstanding leader with the Knights. I, uh . . ." He paused and fidgeted with the horn of his saddle.

Lia looked his way and waited on whatever he tried to say.

His voice dropped quieter. "I've been worried about you."

Her brows knit together. "What do you mean?"

"You left us in Lorranis. You've been drinking more and more. It seems like . . ." He paused as if deep in thought. "Like you've forgotten what we're doing as knights—to help others."

Her jaw dropped. *Who does he think he is to tell me how to act?* She rankled at the rebuke. "I haven't forgotten our purpose."

"I'm sorry. I know I'm not perfect, but I remember how you used to be kinder, years ago. I thought maybe I should say something. That's all."

"What you can do is mind your own business. If you—" The truth in his words tugged at her, cutting off her bitter retort.

Their horses continued to step along while they rode in silence.

Her mouth struggled to speak what her mind told it to say. "How do you think I can be a better leader?" she eventually muttered through strained lips.

Mason perked up. "Um . . . maybe you could look for input from others more?"

"Like, ask questions about what they would do?"

Mason thought for a moment. "Yeah, I think that could be helpful."

Lia nodded as the horse hooves clopped along. "Thank you," she said after a long moment.

"You're welcome. And I *do* think you're going to be a great leader."

LIA'S THIGHS and back ached as her horse walked into the city of Tarving. The sun fell behind the building's thatched roofs, shading the street and the people who bustled about. Muddy steps squished in all directions, proof of the rain that blanketed the region most of the day. A light, warm drizzle continued, resulting in a steady drip down her face. After two nights in the woods and a wet slog, she looked forward to a warm meal, a bed, and a chance to get dry.

At the central square, crowds grew dense despite the bad weather. People traded, bought, and bartered with the vendors while a clock tower rose from the street, standing taller than any of the surrounding buildings.

Along the Taravorre River, boats moored along the docks, their masts swaying with the river's movement. *The Water's Edge Inn* caught Lia's eye. "Let's try there," she said, eager to get out of the rain.

"Hey, Lia," Danik said, pointing toward the water.

She followed where he indicated with her eyes, and her stomach sank. *The Wavy Maiden* rested, tied up to a dock. She sighed. *I guess we should have stayed put.*

Lia dismounted, tying her horse to a post outside of the inn. The other three knights followed suit.

A wall of rowdiness greeted them as they entered. Tables filled with men and women lined the wall and spread through the room. Cards, dice, and ale covered every surface, and the sound of laughter and insults filled the air.

Lia flagged down a man with an apron behind a counter, her soggy feet squishing on the wood floor.

"*Qua re pouls voiss faytte?*" the man said.

Caught off guard by the Tarphic greeting, Lia's jaw dropped. She struggled in her response. "*Yoi . . . ce . . .*"

"Is Common Norshic better?" the man asked in a heavy accent.

"Yes, please," she breathed with a sigh.

"What can I do for you?"

"Do you have any rooms for the night?"

"We have a few. Two tid per double room, and that covers dinner."

"We have horses too—four of them."

"That's no trouble. Our stable is next door. Housing them will be an extra four pintid."

"We'd like two rooms then." Lia fished coins from her purse, wary about the diminishing weight of the pouch.

A harsh voice cut through the room as hollow steps approached. "Well, look who decided to arrive."

Lia's stomach twisted. She turned to find Xander, the bald quartermaster standing before her. The man with the scar and the other crew from the boat sat at a table behind him.

"Hello again, Xander," she said as professionally as she could.

"You ran away from our boat to get here faster, huh?" The men behind him laughed. "We've been here since this morning, so how'd that work for you?"

"Good for you for making it upriver quickly," Chelci said. "Captain Vardan must be pleased."

"It's a pity you all left. We could have used more of your money." Another round of laughter.

"Danik!" the man with the scar called out. Dice rattled in his fist as he shook it in the air. "Ya want a chance to earn back what ya lost?"

"Um," Danik hesitated, glancing at Lia. "Maybe later."

Lia opened her mouth to add to his comments, but Chelci spoke up first. "Thank you for the offer, but we won't be doing any gambling tonight."

"Mother," Lia muttered. "Let me handle this."

"Mother?" Xander said, his eyes wide. "I had no idea." A wicked grin pulled at his mouth while he looked between the two women. "Yeah, I can see the resemblance."

Lia took the two keys the innkeeper extended. "Come on," she said to her group. "Let's get our stuff."

She led the way outside to where they'd left their horses. Snickers echoed behind her, bringing a flush to her neck.

. . .

Lia lay in her narrow bed with her eyes closed. Her busy mind kept her up while Chelci's rhythmic breathing sounded from the other bed. The damp smell of drying clothes hung on lines through the room clung to her nose.

A rap at the door popped her eyelids open. *Who would knock?* She sat up and checked the other bed. Her mother remained asleep. Lia pulled back the sheets and stood. She padded across the room, ducking under a line of clothes, then opened the door. Xander stood in the hall with his arms crossed, wearing a scowl. The hair on the back of her neck bristled.

"Come with me," he whispered before turning down the hall.

Lia frowned, standing with her hand on the door. *What does he want?* She looked back at her mother, still asleep. The footsteps grew softer in the hall. While she had no interest in following Xander anywhere, her lack of metal to inhibit her abilities left her unconcerned about the danger. With a sigh, she threw on a riding cloak and slipped on her boots.

Xander waited at the bottom of the stairs when she descended to the common room. Darkness clung to the empty tables where chairs rested upside down on the flat surfaces.

"What's going on?" she asked.

The quartermaster led toward a side hall. "It's Danik."

Lia's heart jumped. "What's wrong? Where is he?"

"I'll show you."

Lia's pulse thumped as she walked down a narrow passage and through a sparse kitchen. Xander opened a door that led to a narrow alley.

Rain hit Lia in the face as she stepped outside. A covered lantern in the main street threw a faint light down the alley. She glanced into the dark backstreet and gasped. Crewmen from the boat stood around Danik. A gag covered his mouth while hands held his shoulders and arms. A bruise decorated the side of his face while a nasty looking cut dripped watered-down blood off his chin. At his waist, his hands strained against metal shackles.

"Danik!" She turned to Xander. "What is this? Let him go!"

"Danik wanted to win his money back," Xander said playfully. "He's been playing cards with us for the last several hours."

Danik's eyes, filled with fear and repentance, locked onto Lia's.

"What happened?" she asked, nearly yelling to be heard over the rain.

"He didn't win his money back, that's what happened."

"Why is he like this?"

"When we started, Danik petitioned us to play on credit—that his money was in his room. Once his losses grew, it became apparent he didn't have the money after all."

Lia's stomach dropped. Danik hung his head.

Xander's voice turned hard. "He insisted you were the one who carried the group's money. He said you would cover his losses."

The crewman with the scar on his face stepped forward. He held a length of metal pipe, tapping it against his hand.

Lia clenched her jaw. She stared at Danik until he raised his face and met her eyes. She shook her head, then reached in her pocket to pull out her coin purse. "How much does he owe?" Her fingers untied the leather drawstring.

"Four argen, three tid."

Her fingers stopped moving. Her mouth rested open, her breath escaping. "F—four argen?" Her voice wavered.

"He insisted you had plenty. Said it wouldn't be a problem."

Lia resumed untying the pouch, but her fingers shook. After tugging it open, she fingered inside, noting the contents. *That's nearly all we have.* She looked at Xander. "We still need this money for our—" She stopped herself. "We need it."

"I don't care what you need it for," Xander said. "You owe us. Pay us now unless you want us to beat more of it out of your friend."

Lia thought of her mother and Mason sleeping upstairs. *They're depending on me to lead this mission. I can't give away all our money! And using the origine would reveal who we are.* Blood running down Danik's face caught her attention. Her brows narrowed. *Why isn't he healing himself?* The sight of the shackles reminded her he wouldn't be able to.

She opened her mouth to speak, but before she did, the man with the pipe reared back and hit Danik in the stomach.

"Stop it!" she shouted.

Danik bent over, moaning through his gag.

"If you want us to stop, pay us what you owe!" Xander shouted.

The scarred man readied for another strike, but Lia didn't allow it. She pulled from the origine, the tingling power filling her body in a rush. She lunged at the man and took the pipe from his hand before he could move. Spinning between the sailors, she knocked them senseless, hitting them in the head or gut, one at a time. Pausing her flow of energy, she gave the men time to fall. Some passed out and others groaned as they hit the ground.

A click of keys drew her attention. She grabbed the metal object from a fallen man's pocket. It fit Danik's shackles. She twisted the key, unlocking the restraints from each of his hands.

Free, he pulled the gag down. "Thanks, Lia."

They both turned to the last man, Xander. With whites around his eyes, he stammered, "Are—are—are you . . . shadow knights?"

Danik took the metal weapon from Lia and approached the

quartermaster. A wicked grin covered his face. "We are. You messed with the wrong people."

"Let's get out of here," Lia whispered, moving toward the door.

Danik's arm whirled through the air as the older man raised his hands and cringed. A solid metal clunk filled the alley as the pipe collided with the side of his head. Xander's body fell limp against the wall of the building and slumped to the ground. Danik bent over him.

"Is he breathing?" Lia asked. *That was a hard hit.*

Danik straightened, the jangling of coins bouncing in his hand. "Uh, yeah, I think so. He'll be fine." He motioned with his hand to shake the coins before he dropped them into his pocket. "I had to get what should have been mine."

Lia pursed her lips.

"Let's go." Danik passed through the doorway.

"Hold on." Lia stepped out of the rain into the kitchen. She pulled his arm, spinning his body around. A hard shove knocked him against the wall with a *thunk*.

"Ow!" He winced and held his side.

"You idiot! What were you thinking?"

Danik dropped his head. "I'm sorry. I felt awful for losing all that money on the boat. I thought I could get it back."

"We're on a mission! You can't be gambling and drinking!"

"I wasn't drinking," he said quickly, holding up a finger.

"Danik . . ." She exhaled, frustrated. "I'm not always the best example, but I'm *trying* to do better."

"I'm trying, too."

"And this is my first chance to lead. You can't be doing this."

"Lia, I am *so* sorry. I won't do it again, I promise. If . . . If you need to give me some sort of punishment, I understand."

Lia paused for a moment then straightened his cloak. "I'm not going to punish you. I wish I could have been with you, to be honest. But I need to set a better example." She extended a loose sleeve and wiped at his face, cleaning the blood and water. "Don't do it again, or I *will* have to do something, all right?"

He nodded and smiled, resting his hand on hers and looking into her eyes. "Thank you for rescuing me."

"You'd do the same for me." She nodded toward his wounds. "Does it hurt?"

"Oh, yeah. Hold on." Danik closed his eyes and breathed. The cut on his face sealed before her eyes, making a tight scab that faded. The bruise faded to blend in with his skin. He exhaled, then reached an arm out to steady himself on the wall as his body wavered. "That's better."

"How'd they get the jump on you, by the way?"

Danik frowned. "They came from behind with the metal restraints before I realized what was happening. Without the origine, there were too many to fight off." He nodded toward the hall. "We should probably go before they come to."

"I'll help you," she said, wrapping her arm around his back and assisting him to walk.

"Thanks. I'll just need a minute."

They navigated back through the hall. Lia went second up the stairs to make sure he didn't lose his balance as he ascended. He stopped at the top of the stairs.

"I think I can walk all right." He nodded down the hall. "I'll wake Mason and pack our stuff. You wake your mother. We need to get out of here."

Lia nodded. "Agreed. Meet you at the stables in five minutes."

Lia rested her hand on the door to her room and paused while water dripped from her clothes. *She won't appreciate this.* She sighed and pushed.

16

FESTIVAL OF THE SEA

Two and a half days more of travel brought the four knights to the Tarphan capital of Searis. A festive energy filled the air as they walked their horses up the sandy, stone streets. Kids ran with handfuls of sweets. Colorful signs dangled from windows, and smiles covered the faces of everyone they passed.

Lia led Ginger by the reins with her mother following just behind. "What do you think's going on here?" she asked over her shoulder.

"It must be the Festival of the Sea," Chelci replied. "They celebrate it the sixth week of suether."

"I've heard of it," Mason called out. "They eat a lot of fish and dress up with seaweed and stuff."

A young girl ran across the street in front of Lia with green strands draped over her shoulders.

"The busiest harvesting of the year is about to start," Chelci said. "The festival is to wish the fishermen good luck."

Mason chuckled. "Poor fish."

"They host a big parade after dark, then on the last day,

they have public executions of prisoners to represent the killing of the fish."

"Sounds morbid." Lia hesitated at a fork in the street. "Which way was the castle again?"

"To the right," Chelci said. "Shouldn't be much farther."

The street grew wider and descended. When they turned a corner, the shoreline opened up and Lia's jaw dropped.

A tumult of crashing waves over rocks marked where the city met the sea. Frothing whitecaps gave the ocean an angry look while plumes of water shot into the sky after pounding against the craggy land. A narrow bridge spanned the water and connected the mainland to a rocky island where a castle soared into the sky with spires and towers reaching the clouds. Behind the castle, the sun rested low above the ocean, preparing to set over the horizon.

"Searis Castle," Mason breathed.

"Impressive," Danik said, leading his horse next to Lia.

"I'd hate to be an army trying to capture that," Lia said with a chuckle.

"Bale didn't even attempt it," Chelci said.

"What did he do?"

"After he conquered Feldor, he had King Jabari travel up to Felting to pledge fealty to him. They didn't even have to fight."

"Sounds like a wimp," Danik added.

"Jabari Grint was a good leader," Chelci said, "but he understood the realism of his situation."

"So, Constantine Grint," Mason said, "the king we're trying to save, is Jabari's son?"

"That's right. His father died ten years ago."

"Do you ever wish Feldor followed the same traditions as the other kingdoms?" Danik asked.

Chelci laughed. "You mean . . . do I wish I would get to rule after my father dies?"

"*I* do," Lia said. "That would make me a princess, or a

grandprincess, or something like that. Has grandfather ever thought about trying to change how they choose rulers?"

"I'm sure he hasn't." Chelci smiled, shaking her head. "I wouldn't want him to even if he could."

When they arrived at the bridge, Lia led the way across. A salty spray of water misted in the air, and waves kicked up around them. Her horse grew skittish. "Whoa, girl. It's all right." She patted Ginger on the side and pulled her forward.

A wooden gate built in a rock face forced them to halt at the far end of the bridge. A team of guards with spears stepped forward, blocking their path.

"*Atrad!*" the closest guard called. "*Qua re voiss tahvo?*"

Lia pulled a document from the pocket of her cloak. The folded parchment contained the symbol of the Shadow Knights printed on the top. "We're here to see King Constantine."

The guard's eyes narrowed as he accepted the paper. He passed his spear to another soldier and opened the sheet. His eyes widened as he progressed down the page. "Thank you for coming," he said in accented Common Norshic before turning around. "Open the gate, see them straight to the keep."

Lia's mouth turned up. *The power of being a shadow knight.*

"We're honored to have you here," the guard said, stepping out of the way. "The Shadow Knights are always welcome in Searis."

Metal twisted, and the gate in the rock trembled. The guards moved to allow it to open, revealing a maw of stony blackness behind it. The darkness stretched deep into the recesses of the island. Two guards held torches aloft and motioned for their group to follow.

Water dripped down the walls, glistening in the flickering light of the torch. A smooth path curved around a bend and angled upward. Lia strained her eyes, trying to peer through the void ahead. Ginger whinnied. Lia rested a hand on her neck, hoping the gesture would sooth the animal's nerves along with her own.

Cracks of light gave her a destination to focus on. A rumble preceded another gate opening, light spilling into the tunnel. She squinted as the group entered a walled courtyard of stone with towers and crags of rock shooting up in all directions. Relief from leaving the tunnel mixed with awe over the impressive sight.

"*Pertei meik*," a guard said, reaching to take the horses' reins. The animals followed, heading to a stable carved into the stone.

"This way," the remaining guard said, leading up a flight of steps to the main keep.

Smooth, carved stone blocks rose in a line, contrasting against a section of rough, dark-gray rock the keep seemed to grow out of. When they entered, the interior morphed into the familiar setting of rolled carpets, tapestries, and ornate decorations.

Passing through an arched doorway, a balcony stretched over the frothing waves, the salty taste of the sea permeating the air. In the distance, an orange sunset splashed across the low-hanging clouds. In the center of the balcony, a fountain spouted water into the air before it pooled in a shallow basin. A group of men stood by the railing of the balcony, speaking as they looked toward the ocean.

"Wait here," the guard instructed. Lia waited while the Tarphic soldier crossed the balcony and greeted the men at the edge.

A wisp of wind blew sand in Lia's face. She wiped it away and blinked repeatedly.

"Do they know?" Mason whispered.

Lia turned to him. "About the threat?" Her raised eyebrow angled toward her mother. "I imagine so, but you never know."

Chelci added, "Sometimes, even when they are aware, they may not believe it to be credible. Kings get a lot of threats."

"Why would we trust this spy of ours more than the king would?" Lia asked.

"Because Thajk has ears throughout the city, and he owes the Shadow Knights his life. He trusts us, and we trust him."

Footsteps turned Lia toward the approaching men.

"Chelci Stormbridge, it's good to see you," a man a few years older than her mother said. A faint Tarphic accent barely shone through. Prematurely gray hair fell past his chin. His beard matched the length and was more white than gray. Obscure stress lines showed on his face. He leaned on a shaking cane as he walked. A younger man paced next to him.

"Your Highness, King Constantine, thank you for seeing us."

"It has been some time since you've graced us with your presence, Chelci. How is your husband?"

"Veron is good. He asked me to send you his greetings."

"I remember when you and he came to help with the Bruxelian uprising." He chuckled, creases forming at the edges of his eyes until a racking cough sent shudders through his body. He cleared his throat and flagged an assistant with a wave of his hand. "My apologies. This dry throat's nagged me for weeks. I'm supposed to stay inside to help, but—" He gestured to the sea with a grin. "How can I avoid this view?"

The assistant arrived with a cup, which the king drank.

"I trust you remember my chief advisor, Victor Gannaway?" The king said after lowering his goblet. He motioned to the middle-aged, brown-haired man next to him, who bowed.

"Of course," Chelci nodded. "It's good to see you again, sir."

"Our kingdom owes you a great debt, Chelci," Constantine said. "What brings you back? A social call?"

Chelci answered with a grim laugh. "I'm afraid not. We're here to add to the debt."

The king's smile faded.

"We heard reliable word that an attack on your life is coming soon."

"Ha!" Constantine chortled. "We hear of threats every day from one source or another. They are generally nothing, and not worth troubling with."

"Yet you've come all the way here," Victor said, eyebrow raised. "Tell us more."

"Actually," she turned to Lia, "let me introduce you to our mission leader, Lia Stormbridge. She can go over the details."

Lia swallowed the lump in her throat and stepped closer. She bowed before the king. "Your Majesty, it's an honor to be here with you."

A twinkle shone in the king's eyes as he looked back and forth between Lia and Chelci. "Your daughter?"

Lia's upper lip twitched. "Yes, I am her daughter," she confirmed, standing straight with her jaw set. "But on this mission, she reports to me."

Chelci inhaled, but her smile didn't falter.

"Well then," the king said after a brief pause. He rested both his hands on his cane, his arms trembling. "Lia, please explain why the Shadow Knights felt it necessary to travel here to protect me."

Lia looked at her mother, then to Danik and Mason before turning back to the king. "We have a reliable source in Tarphan who keeps us apprised of notable activity. He informed us there is a plot to kill you and take over the throne."

The king coughed, covering his mouth. "And who is supposedly plotting this?"

"A group of medicinalists," Lia replied.

"The Searis Apothecary Guild?" the king asked, and Lia nodded. "We heard that rumor, but we didn't find it credible."

"They did petition for an audience with you a few days ago," Victor added.

The king nodded, his brow furrowed. "We declined them out of an abundance of caution but . . ."

"But maybe there's something to it?" Victor suggested.

Lia cleared her throat and stepped close. "Is it true that you raised taxes on medicines?"

The king's brows furrowed. "Yes, but it was only a small increase. We eliminated taxes on medicines years ago to lower the costs and hopefully boost health. I only raised back half of what it used to be. Surely, they can't be that upset about it."

"I've found people can get upset over just about anything," Chelci added.

"Hmm," Constantine pulled on his beard and looked out to sea.

Lia shifted her feet, unsure if she should say more or wait.

The king turned back and motioned. "Walk with me."

Two guards joined their group. Victor walked next to the king, and the four shadow knights followed behind as they passed through the arched doorway to re-enter the keep.

"I have no children," Constantine said with a wisp of regret. "My poor wife has miscarried four times, and we've just about given up hope. And now," he gestured toward his legs that struggled to move down the hall, "this illness leaves me weaker by the day."

"What's wrong?" Lia blurted. Chelci shot her a scathing look of rebuke, turning her stomach. "I-I'm sorry. It's not my business."

The king laughed and waved away the apology. "It's fine. I'm not shy. My physician is stumped. It's some sort of degenerative condition, but they can't identify it. It began mid-wiether but has progressed quickly once suether arrived. I've had other doctors give their opinions. They all declare it's something different, but none can give a definitive cure."

An ache twisted in Lia's heart. *Feeling worse each day until you die?* She shuddered.

Constantine's shaking walk halted, and he turned more fully. "They don't realize it, but . . . if this apothecary guild wants me dead, all they need to do is be patient, and they may get their wish. Then, if I die with no heir, the throne will be up for the taking."

"What are the Tarphic rules of succession in the case of—" Chelci paused and offered a hand of apology. "—if you were to pass away without an heir?"

"The executive council would meet and choose a successor," Victor said. "Billingsworth, Lavigne, Toussaint, Garnier, myself, and a few others—the chancellors and advisors."

Lia shook her head. "I don't buy it. They're mad about the taxes, so they somehow arrange to kill you. Then they *hope* someone sympathetic to their cause is chosen?"

"I agree," Chelci said. "It doesn't make sense."

A grand staircase loomed before the king in a room with a vaulted ceiling. Victor extended an arm, and Constantine grasped it before placing his foot on the first step. His body trembled as he ascended one step at a time. The grip on his advisor resulted in white knuckles and a shaking arm. The cane in his other hand pressed into the marble surface, pushing the man's body upward. Lia and the other knights followed behind.

Sweat dripped to the floor by the time the king made it to the top. He panted, looking around and taking a moment. The hallways split, and wide passages extended in either direction. "Sorry to hold you up, but stairs are a challenge for me."

"It's no worry, Your Majesty," Lia said. "With your permission, we'd like to speak with your guards and canvas the city."

"Of course," Victor said. "You will have anything you need."

"Thank you for coming," the king said, angling his body toward the left hall. "Now, if you'll excuse me. I must lie down for a bit before supper. Victor or any of my guards should be able to answer questions you have or provide anything you need." He turned to his advisor. "Please have some tea brought to me."

Victor nodded. "Of course, Your Majesty."

The shadow knights bowed as the king shuffled along, the guards in tow. Chelci's gaze caught Lia's eyes. Her mother nodded. *I guess I'm doing all right so far.*

Lia turned to the advisor. "What is the king's security like, especially at night?"

"This floor holds the royal apartments." Victor extended his arm where the king had disappeared. "His Majesty's quarters are just down this hallway—his bedroom, sitting room, private bathhouse, and breakfast room. He and the queen spend most of their time there."

"What are the access points?" Chelci asked.

Lia glared. She had been about to ask the same question.

"There is a royal balcony that views the city, but it is inaccessible from the ground." Lia opened her mouth to speak, but the advisor continued, "Still . . . We keep two royal guards there every night."

Her mouth clamped shut.

"Inside the keep"—he motioned behind them— "these stairs are the only entry point." He pointed down the hall to the left. "And this hall is the only way to reach the king."

"And you keep men there, I assume?" Lia said.

"Of course—two more midway along the hall."

She looked to the right. "What's down there?"

"My living quarters, along with those of the Chancellor of Justice, are in the east wing. There's also a library and a study for the king."

"And there's no way to enter the floor down there?"

Victor shook his head. "None."

Lia turned to the other knights. She opened her mouth to issue an order but hesitated at the earnest look on Mason's face.

"Do any of you have ideas about what we can try? I'd love to get your input."

The sides of Mason's mouth turned up, and Chelci's eyebrows lifted.

"I think we should stop them," Danik said, punching a fist into his other hand.

Chelci chuckled, shaking her head.

"Maybe we can scout the city for these medicinalists?" Chelci said. "Perhaps we'll get lucky and discover what they're up to."

"We don't want to leave the king unguarded, though," Mason said.

"He *will* be guarded," Lia said, motioning to the left.

"I mean with us."

Lia smiled. "I know what you mean, and I agree."

The other three stood, waiting for Lia to decide. She took a deep breath, then exhaled. "Mason and Danik, you wait here and guard the king's hallway, but stay out of sight. We want to capture these men when they come." She turned to her mother. "Chelci and I will check out the city and see what we can find about this group."

She looked between the knights. Mason stood tall with his chest puffed up, holding a confident smile. Danik rolled his eyes at the young man. Her mother nodded in confirmation.

"Okay then. Let's go."

17

NIGHTTIME ATTACK

The streets grew increasingly crowded the farther they pushed into the city. Lanterns and torches filled every street. People packed the roads, eating, singing, and toasting with mugs. Children ran together with a wild energy that matched the festive environment. It was well past midnight, but a parade of music, dancing, and laughter continued to wind through the stone paths of Searis.

Chelci snuck glances at her daughter as they moved, jostling between bodies. She struggled with the lack of control, but the focused look on Lia's face caused a surge of pride to grow. *I hope she makes good decisions, for both of our sakes.*

"I'm proud of you, Lia," Chelci said.

Lia turned her head. "For what?"

"For this—for leading."

"Even though I wasted money on that boat?"

Chelci paused. "It got us where we needed to go, and we made it here in time. Who's to say we wouldn't have been delayed another way had we only stuck to the road?"

"Yeah, I guess so." Lia laughed.

"You know, we don't get a lot of one-on-one time together these days. I'm glad to be here with you."

Lia's mouth opened, but she hesitated for a moment. "Being in charge is not easy."

"You're right. It's not."

Lia smiled and glanced at her. "I'm glad you're along, Mother."

"I am, too."

"I, uh . . . know I'm not always the easiest daughter, and I'm sorry that I push back against you and Father sometimes."

Chelci's smile grew. "Thanks. We just want what's best for you."

They stepped across a busy street, dodging people and entering the dark alley on the opposite side.

"You know, Lia, back when your grandfather William was in the Knights, relationships weren't permitted. Your father and I —well . . ." She chuckled. "We weren't a fan of that, so we don't enforce it anymore."

Lia nodded but didn't reply.

"Do you . . . have anyone you're interested in?"

A laugh bubbled up from her daughter. "I thought I was supposed to focus on being a knight and all of that."

"You're right. I'm just curious. I met your father when I was around your age, and I wondered if you had your eye on anyone." No response came back. "Mason seems like a nice young man."

"Ha!" Lia covered her mouth with her hand. She looked around to make sure no heads turned her way. "Sorry. Yes, Mason is nice."

Chelci's brows pinched together. "But . . . ?"

"I don't see him like that. Most of the knights are—I don't know . . . serious, I guess. They're not that fun to be around."

"The job isn't meant to be all fun and games."

"I know, but—Danik seems to have fun. He's friendly too."

"Danik?" Chelci scowled. "He seems to look out for himself a lot. It makes me worry."

"Just because he's not stuffy and serious doesn't mean he's not a good person, Mother."

"You remember our nighttime departure from Tarving, don't you?"

Lia squirmed.

"He has a problem with gambling and drinking," Chelci said.

"It's not a *problem*—"

"We're on a mission, Lia. If he can't control himself, he puts us all at risk. There needs to be consequences for actions like that."

"I told you, I gave him a *stern* warning."

Chelci bit her tongue, restraining from saying what she really felt about him. She replied when her calm had returned. "Do you think that warning will be enough to keep him in line?"

Lia hesitated a beat before speaking. "I do."

"I assume you will report on his actions to your father after we return."

Another pause. "Of course."

Chelci nodded. "Going back to the topic of the time you spend with young men . . . Be careful with Danik. That's all I'm saying."

Mother and daughter continued forward in strained silence.

"It should be just ahead," Lia said, snapping Chelci out of worried thoughts as she pointed at a tall building looming in shadow.

Before they had left the castle, Chelci dropped hints about inquiring on the location of the Searis Apothecary Guild. Lia's stubbornness had given in, and they got detailed directions before they left. They slowed as they approached.

"How do you think we should enter?" Chelci asked, eyeing a cracked window on the second floor.

Lia paused for a moment. "What would you do?"

Chelci smiled at the question, then waved her forward. "I'll show you."

Taking the lead, Chelci kept to the shadows along the wall of the alley. She raised the hood of her Shadow Knights cloak, and Lia followed suit. A sheen of sand covered the dark-gray stone of the building. Chelci rested her hand against the wall. Tiny ledges jutted out where the stones and mortar joined.

"The window," she whispered, indicating above them. Lia seemed to understand and felt along the wall as well.

Chelci used enough of the origine to give her the strength she needed to gain purchase. She pulled her body up, gripping the sandy ledges with the tips of her fingers and the edge of her boots. Moving hand over hand, a few stones at a time, she scaled the side of the building until the cracked windowsill was before her.

She peered inside, her eyes scanning the black room and finding nothing. She looked down at her daughter and nodded. Lia ascended.

Holding on to the sill with one hand and keeping her feet clinging to whatever semblance of a hold they could find, Chelci pushed the window higher. It slid in its pane, leaving a space just wide enough. She pulled, bringing her chest up to the sill and wriggling her body inside.

Rolling into the room, she crouched on the wooden floorboards and listened. The space she entered appeared to be for storage. Wooden crates filled shelves on one side of the room while jars of strange objects suspended in liquid covered the other.

Lia dropped into the room. "What's all this?" she whispered.

Chelci moved for a closer look. She lifted the lid of a crate and peered inside. Tall glass flasks stacked inside. The next crate held more of the same.

"Turnfoil Root. Spurnibus Bark." Lia whispered names of labels on the opposite side of the room. She leaned closer to a jar, squinting. "Ground *Valdor* Bones?"

Chelci looked over her shoulder. "*Valcor* bones. That must be rare."

"What are these?" Three small vials filled a shelf at head height. Lia picked up one and held it to the light. "Essence of Xolopyr Root."

"What's that? I've not heard of it," Chelci whispered. "I wonder if it's like the molopyr tree."

"Maybe you should read some of those herbology books you and Father are making me study," Lia smirked. "Yes, the two trees are similar. The molopyr has poisonous leaves, but it's only a mild irritant. The xolopyr is ten times as strong."

"What do they use it for?"

"I've read it's used as a setting agent in dyeing fabric. A drop or two in a solution prepares material to receive color, but"— she shook the vial— "it's also used as a poison."

Chelci looked at the shelf. "Let's hope they're going to dye fabric with it."

"There's more, though. Look." Lia pointed to the labels on additional colored bottles. "Philbius Powder, Ethydriline, and Kotoric Acid. If you mix those three chemicals, it makes a deadly gas that kills in seconds. These medicinalists have plenty of ways to kill someone."

Lia set the container of xolopyr root back on the shelf. She moved to the door and turned the knob. The door opened. Mother and daughter walked through to the dark hallway beyond. Moonlight splashed onto the floor through a window at the far end. Closed doors lined the hall.

"Let's check the others," Lia whispered.

They passed a flight of stairs that led down into a silent

darkness below. The next door opened to a similar room for storage, but the shelves were empty. They continued on. The knob to the next door didn't spin when Lia turned it.

"Here we go." Chelci pulled a metal device out of her pocket, and Lia moved to the side. She inserted the skinny metal rod and the skeleton key it paired with. Her fingers jiggled the device, feeling for the telltale catch she sought. The key slipped, again and again.

"You want me to try?" Lia whispered.

"I've got this," Chelci replied. Beads of sweat formed on her brow.

"Mother, let me give it a—"

A click filled the hall, and Chelci grinned. The knob turned, and the door swung open. An office lay beyond the door. A wooden desk waited in the center with smooth gouges cut into the top. Stacks of files lay on the desk with cabinets against the wall. Old leather chairs, ripped and faded, sat before the desk. A clock ticked where it hung on the wall, a pendulum swinging beneath it.

Lia went to the desk, inspecting the stack of papers, so Chelci examined the cabinets. Drawers opened, the smell of old paper wafting out. She grabbed a stack and held them to the light. *Toadgrass Elixir - For warts, boils, and skin rash.* The page contained ingredients and instructions for preparing the concoction. She flipped the page. *Tincture of Spotted Salamander - for headaches, infection, and mild dimothermia.* She continued to flip and found nothing but more recipes.

"This looks like invoices," Lia said, shuffling through her stack. "Inventory, supplies, dues."

"Anything interesting?" Chelci asked as she looked in another drawer. Dusty magnifying glasses stared back.

"I can't tell. Names of members . . . I don't recognize anyone here."

Chelci extended her hand. "Let me see."

Lia passed her a pair of sheets. Scanning through the pages revealed nothing of note.

"These invoices break down everyone they've worked with," Lia said, leafing through another pile. "But I'm not sure what we could—"

She paused, drawing Chelci's attention. "What is it?"

Lia moved the papers closer to the light and cocked her head. "It's odd. I can't think of why—"

A bang in the hall brought silence to the office. Chelci inhaled and spun toward the open door. Lia scurried, angling behind the door while stuffing the papers in the inside pocket of her cloak. Chelci leaned against the door frame and waited. Footsteps walking up the stairs grew louder. Her heart beat faster. She peeked around the opening and spied a figure entering the hall and turning in her direction.

She scurried away from the door and scanned the room. *The desk!* She ducked behind it and crawled into the kneehole, pressing her body against the wooden sides. Her breath felt like an alarm in the confined space.

Boots vibrated the floor. *They're in the room!* A drawer slid open, and another pair of feet arrived. Chelci held her breath.

"Did you leave the door open?" an unfamiliar male voice asked. The words were in Tarphic, but Chelci translated them.

"Not me," another man said. "Peirro was here last."

The first man sighed. "He'd lose his head if it weren't attached to his neck. Just grab it so we can go. The others are waiting."

"Just a moment. I need my dagger. And you're sure you trust this guard? It could be easy for him to turn us in."

"Yes, he should be waiting for us now. And he's on our side. He wants the man dead as much as we do."

"Not as much. Otherwise, he'd be the one killing him." A dagger slid into a sheath. "Are you sure about this?"

"Yes, I'm sure. Assuming it goes according to plan, we'll be heroes."

"Or if it doesn't go to plan . . . we'll be hanged."

"Come on. The others are waiting." After a moment, the boots left the room and faded down the hall.

Chelci poked her head out from under the desk and found Lia coming out from behind the door.

"What'd they say?" Lia whispered. "I made out something about people waiting, a guard, and heroes, but they spoke too fast."

"A guard is supposed to let them in somewhere. They're going to meet some others now, and they were here for a dagger."

"Did they say what they were going to do?"

"They're going to kill someone . . . right now."

"I think we're on the right track coming here, then," Lia said. "Follow them?"

Chelci nodded. "Let's go."

Lia and Chelci traveled the hall and returned to the room where they first entered. Chelci looked through the window. Two bodies shrouded in darkness walked down the alley away from them.

"That's them," Lia said.

The forms stopped at the end of the street before merging into the crowd.

"Let's not lose them." Lia extended a leg out the window. She slid through, then dropped, landing on the street below.

Chelci followed. She lowered her body through the window while holding onto the sill. After stretching to a full extension, she let go, strengthening her legs with origine. A quick bend of the knees absorbed the impact of the fall.

"Come on," Lia urged. They wasted no time in running up the alley, moving toward the sound of music and the glow of lanterns.

Both ladies stopped at the intersection ahead. The parade remained in full force, moving through the street before them. Two women with flutes weaved around a bare-chested man pounding on a drum. The crowd shouted and sang, foreign words jumbling together. Children held thin poles with colorful paper fish attached to the ends that poked above the adults' heads. As the children ran through the crowd, the fish seemed to swim through the current of bodies. Blue and green decorative costumes filled every direction. Hats with wide brims and bright tassels topped many of the revelers' heads, blocking Chelci and Lia's view.

"Where'd they go?" Chelci asked.

Lia pointed through the crowd, past a gap of people. "There they are."

Chelci's eyes scanned where the finger pointed. At first she saw nothing until two men pushed their way past a woman in a bright red outfit. "Don't lose them," she urged.

Lia led the way, pressing through the crowd. Chelci followed in her wake. The street seemed to flow in the opposite direction they traveled, making progress difficult. Some of the drunken partiers only laughed when they bumped into them, but others frowned and shouted Tarphic insults. A cacophony echoed in every direction. Lia moved forward, and Chelci stayed on her heels.

Monitoring the men became easier when the crowd thinned. Their casual walk appeared as that of an evening stroll.

"They're going in the wrong direction," Lia whispered. "Are you sure they said they were going to the castle?"

"I'm pretty sure—" Chelci paused, then cocked her head. "Well . . . they mentioned guards, but they didn't say anything about the castle."

"Where else would they go then? The king wasn't going somewhere else tonight, was he?"

"No, he said he was staying put."

The men ahead turned down a side street. Chelci and Lia hurried to reach the corner where they peered around. The men continued ahead, sauntering down the smaller alley.

"Should we intercept them?" Lia asked in a whisper.

Chelci shook her head. "We need to be sure before we act. We need to see the others they meet up with, too."

They followed for another ten minutes, making two more turns. A nervous feeling tickled at Chelci's brain. "I don't get it," she whispered. "They seemed set on acting now, but these guys—"

One man stopped at a door ahead and fiddled with the lock. The other man waved and wished him a "good night" while he continued forward.

The light voice carried up the stone street and brought chills along Chelci's spine. *That wasn't the voice we heard in the office.*

"We followed the wrong men," Lia said, echoing Chelci's thoughts. "The other men must be . . ." As one, they turned and ran.

The buildings blurred as they passed, their legs fueled with the origine.

"Mother, pace yourself," Lia shouted.

Chelci slowed a hair, not realizing the distance she'd put running ahead of her daughter.

"We need to be ready to fight when we arrive. Don't wear yourself out now."

Smooth stones pounded under their feet. Their cloaks billowed behind. Chelci rested her hand on the sword hilt at her hip to keep it from flailing about. *If these men slip by . . .*

"It's going to be fine, Mother," Lia said, as if knowing her thoughts. "We'll get to them."

The castle guards at the end of the bridge raised their

hands and bared their weapons until they realized who the blurred forms in black cloaks were. They hurried to the side.

"Has anyone come through here in the last twenty minutes?" Chelci asked breathlessly, slowing for only a moment.

The lead guard furrowed his brow. "Uh, yes, maybe fifteen minutes ago. There were some men—five of them—to do some masonry work on the new tower."

"At night?" Chelci asked.

The guard shrugged. "It's hot during the day."

Chelci groaned. "I can't believe you let them in!"

"They were cleared . . . on the list." The guard stepped in her direction as their distance grew farther. "Is something wrong?"

Chelci turned. She and Lia sped up, crossing through the dark tunnel then across the courtyard to the keep in only a moment.

"Danik and Mason will have stopped them, I'm sure," Chelci said as they sprinted down the hall.

"I don't think we need to worry about that," Lia said.

The nonchalant statement caught Chelci off guard. "Are you taking this seriously, Lia? The king's life is at stake!"

"Of course I am."

They entered the vaulted room with the grand staircase. Skipping several stairs at a time, Chelci was up it in seconds. Lia was just behind her when Chelci turned left at the top.

"Mother."

The word stopped Chelci in her tracks. She turned to see Lia pointing to the right of the stairs.

"This way."

Chelci's brows pinched together. "What are you talking about? The king is this way!"

"No, mother, *we* need to go *this* way."

Chelci's jaw hung loose. *What has gotten into her?*

"You put me in charge, right?"

"Yes, but—"

"Then follow my lead! Come on, we have little time!" Lia moved to the right.

Chelci looked behind her at the hallway toward the royal apartments. Her feet felt heavy, and her heart pounded. She forced them forward, her steps speeding into a run as she raced after her daughter.

A short way down the hall, a door loomed. Lia didn't even hesitate as she barreled into it, slamming the door open. It hit the wall behind it with a bang.

"What are you doing, Lia?" Chelci said, two steps behind. "This is the—"

Chelci froze. Two lanterns showed Danik and Mason standing with swords extended toward her, frozen with their Shadow Knights cloaks draped behind them. Victor, the advisor, held his hand over his heart with wide eyes, standing with a tall, dark man she didn't know. King Constantine, in a velvet robe that draped to the floor, stood with his head cocked and a curious look on his face.

"You found us," Danik said, dropping his guard and sheathing his sword.

Chelci's mouth hung open, and Lia looked just as surprised.

"What are you doing here?" Lia asked.

"There was an attack . . ." Mason motioned to the advisor, "on Victor."

"On Victor?" Chelci blurted. "But how did—" She looked at Lia and paused. Her daughter stared back with intensity. Her eyes quivered, and her head shook the slightest bit.

"How did . . . what?" Mason asked.

"How did you know?" Lia said after a moment, ". . . to come here? Weren't you guarding the king?"

"I patrolled the hall," Danik said, lifting his chin. "Mason wanted to stay back, but I thought it was wise to check the area.

I spotted five men sneaking into this room. They had daggers and were up to trouble, so I acted."

"And I'm so thankful he did," the advisor said. "He saved my life."

"Possibly mine, too," the other man said, reaching to shake the hands of the newcomers. "Chancellor Edgar Billingsworth, at your service, ladies." Not a strand was out of place on his short, black hair or his trimmed beard.

"It was the Apothecary Guild men we were after," Danik said.

"They weren't here for me," the king said, chuckling. "It seems your intelligence was wrong about this one. Still, I appreciate you coming all this way."

Chelci scanned the room. A four-poster bed rested against the far end of the room while chairs made up a sitting area near the door. A row of shelves with books, flagons, and trinkets filled the left wall.

Lia strolled toward the bookshelves. "Where are the men now?" she asked. "Did you kill them?"

"I didn't have to," Danik said. "As soon as I brought out my sword, they dropped their daggers."

Lia nodded, tapping her finger on the shelf while she walked along it.

"What'd they say?" Chelci asked.

Mason shook his head. "Nothing. They asked to see the king, but that wasn't going to happen. The palace guards hauled them off to the dungeon."

"That's right. We'll hang them in the morning," the chancellor said.

Lia turned. "So soon?"

"Not soon enough," Victor added.

"We caught them red-handed in the attempted assassination of a high-ranking royal official," the king said. "The penalty is death. There's no need for deliberation."

"We have the Festival of the Sea speech from the king tomorrow morning," Billingsworth said. "We always have a sacrifice to wrap up the festival. We'll just add them to the list."

Lia turned back to the shelf, leaning in to inspect something.

What is she doing? Chelci thought. She turned to look at the advisor. "Do you know why they were after you?"

The man shrugged. "Maybe they thought I was behind the medicine tax. Who can know with people like that?"

"Can I speak with them?" Lia asked.

"I'm afraid that's impossible," Victor said. "The men await execution after committing a crime against the crown. They do not deserve the privilege of visitors."

"I'm not a visitor," Lia said, turning to the king. "We came here to protect you, Your Majesty. While we may have been mistaken about the target, we saved the life of your advisor. Would you grant me this request?"

The people of the room turned to the king. He pulled on his white beard and nodded. "I don't see the harm."

Lia smiled. "Thank you."

Chelci's head tilted, her mind spinning. *What is she up to?*

18

CLARIFIED MOTIVES

Raiyn tapped his head against the damp stone wall. His closed eyes were an attempt to block out his grim reality. Without seeing, it was possible to picture himself back at his flat, sitting around the table, eating soup and laughing with his mother.

Mother.

He exhaled, letting the air tickle the two-week old facial hair. He adjusted a leg. The gritty feel of the sand on the rocky floor brought him back to reality. He opened his eyes.

The faint dripping he had tuned out became impossible to ignore when he saw the source again. In the corner of his cell, water pooled on the ceiling and fell in a steady drip every two to three seconds. The only thing he appreciated about his confined space was the fact that the floor sloped away, sending the water that collected in a narrow stream past the other cells and out of sight around the corner.

In the cell next to him, a spice addict leaned against the bars. He pawed at his face and muttered nonsense that turned into a faint laugh. Scratch marks raked the man's arms, some with thick scabs. He had been there a week after murdering a family in an attempt to get money to feed his addiction. The spice withdrawal grew more serious every day, but his pain would soon be over. He was to be the festival sacrifice the next day.

Raiyn groaned as he grabbed the bars and rose to his feet. A metal anklet pulled against his leg, a chain running taut to an eyelet on the wall. He pressed himself against the front and looked at the dungeon guard, who leaned back in his chair with the front two legs off the ground. A lantern in the hall lit the man along with the row of cells in the room. "Hey, Pedric."

The guard lowered his chair. "What?"

Raiyn beckoned with his hand. "Come here."

A grumbling noise preceded Pedric rising to his feet and coming to his cell. "What do ya want?"

Raiyn nodded to his right, whispering. "Have they talked yet?"

Pedric scoffed. "Other than asking to see the king? No."

Raiyn looked at the cell three spaces down from his. Five men in dark clothing filled the enclosure, some sitting, the others leaning against the wall. Dried blood covered most of their faces. "Did I hear they tried to kill the king's advisor?"

"Why do ya care?"

Raiyn shrugged. "Let me speak with them. I can get them to talk."

Pedric's eyes narrowed. "What are ya gonna do? Ya can't beat 'em much harder than the guards already did, and they didn't spill a word."

"Let me out of here, so I can get near their cell. It would only take me a moment, and I guarantee you, I'll get them to speak." Raiyn's stomach quivered. *All I need is a moment out of this cell without shackles.* When he had first arrived, as soon as they took off his arm restraints, the mysterious power returned. He was too shocked to have taken advantage of the opportunity, and it disappeared as soon as they attached his anklet.

"I don't care what they have ta say. If ya wanted to be an inquisitor, ya should have thought of that before ya turned to thievin'." Pedric rapped on the metal bars with a club, making Raiyn jump back. The guard walked back to his chair. "Ya got twelve more weeks in your sentence, Raiyn. Make yourself comfortable and get some sleep. These five are hanging in the mornin' along with this one."

He hit the bars of the next cell over, but the addict didn't flinch. Pedric paused and moved closer. "Hello?" He prodded the prisoner with his club—no response. "Stop playing dead. You—" He shoved with his foot, and the man fell to the side, unmoving. His head knocked against the stone floor with a sickening thud. His lifeless eyes remained open but his body was still.

Pedric sighed then muttered in the direction of the five men. "I guess you'll be hanging alone, tomorrow."

Raiyn leaned back against the wall and sighed. *Twelve more weeks—assuming I don't die in the meantime. What am I going to do after that?* His fingers found the metal shard that had been buried in the debris of the cell when he arrived. Keeping it behind his back, he scraped the hard splinter against his palm, letting it tickle his skin. He had considered using it to try and pick his anklet, which could be possible, but there was no way it would be effective against the massive door. So he kept it secreted away in case he ever found a use.

A clank sounded down the hall, bringing him to alert. He rested his hands on the bars of the cell and leaned against them, peering out. Footsteps approached. Pedric gathered himself and stood at attention.

Two guards rounded the corner, carrying torches. Their pressed and clean uniforms contained royal emblems on their lapels. *Royal guards. What brings them here?* Two women followed, wearing black cloaks. The one in front looked a few years younger than him, but he could barely tell from the confident way she held herself. The other woman was older, but both were similar heights with brown hair pulled back in loose braids. They approached the cell that held the men, but the prisoners didn't stir.

"You tried to kill the king's advisor," the young woman said, her voice bouncing through the austere space. "Why?"

The men stared back but didn't reply.

The older woman spoke up. "Tahvo attem voiss ol rei advisir. Percaoi?"

No response.

"You are to be killed in the morning. If there's more to the story, this is your only chance to tell it."

The older woman translated again, but the men said nothing.

The younger one stepped closer, grabbing the bars. "I believe there's more to the story. I need to hear what you know."

The older woman translated until one of the men stepped forward. "How do we know we can trust you?" he asked in accented Common Norshic.

"We're here to protect the king."

"And his advisor?" the man in the cell asked.

The young woman stood straighter. "Our mission is the king."

The two stared at each other for a long moment. The man beckoned her forward with a finger. Both of the women approached the bars, but the man backed up. "No!" he shouted. "Only her." The two women exchanged quiet words before the older one took a step back.

The man in the cell and the young woman leaned close with the bars between them. They whispered, only muffled sounds reaching Raiyn. After a few minutes, the young woman nodded and stepped back. She motioned to the older woman, and they left without a word.

.   .   .

LIA HURRIED up the winding stairs leading from the dungeons. The air freshened the higher they climbed, the stale smell of mold being replaced by the salty air of the sea. The two guards escorting them walked ahead with torches.

"Can we move faster, please?" Lia said. "I need to get back as quickly as possible."

The guards nodded and picked up the pace.

"What was that about?" her mother whispered from behind.

Lia continued a brisk walk, only turning her head to answer. "I needed to hear their side of the story."

"What'd they say?"

"What I expected they would."

Chelci laughed. "What? That they're innocent? That they weren't trying to kill the advisor?"

"No, they confirmed they *were* trying to kill Victor, and that they *weren't* here to kill the king."

"Why would they say that?

Lia paused and turned. "Because Victor is trying to kill the king."

Chelci's eyes widened and her jaw dropped.

Lia turned and hurried to catch up to the guards.

"What?" Chelci called, scurrying after her. "Is that what they said? You can't—"

"There's no time, Mother. We've got to get back."

The passages turned and stairs climbed. In a few minutes, Lia and Chelci arrived again at the grand staircase. Lia moved around the guards and ran past them, Chelci on her heels. After a sprint down the hallway to the right, Lia slammed against the door to the advisor's room for a second time.

An identical scene to the one before played out again. The shadow knights drew swords, their muscles ready to respond, while the other men stared back with looks of confusion. The only difference from before was that each man held a cup they'd been about to drink.

"Don't drink that!" Lia shouted, her breaths heaving.

The advisor's brows narrowed. "What do you mean?

Lia glanced around at the shocked faces, her chest rising and dropping. "Where did that drink come from?"

"Victor just poured the glasses," Constantine said.

"Don't drink it," she reiterated. "It could be poisoned."

The advisor laughed. "It's not poisoned. It's an aged brandy from my private collection."

"Lia," Danik said, his taut muscles relaxing. "The guildsmen were about to stab him when we got here. They didn't have time to poison his spirits."

Lia exchanged a look with her mother, who shook her head. Lia's palms sweat. She took a deep breath. *Here goes nothing.* "I don't mean the apothecaries poisoned it." She nodded to the advisor. "It was Victor."

Gasps bounced through the room.

Chelci grasped her on the arm. "Lia, you can't just—"

"What?" The advisor laughed, his mouth hanging slack as he looked around the room. "That's preposterous!"

"Your Majesty, your advisor has been trying to kill you," Lia said, her tongue feeling looser. "He planted the rumor about the guildsmen trying to kill you, in order to have someone to blame. They snuck into the castle to kill Victor in order to save your life."

The king's eyebrows lifted. "Why would you suggest that? What proof do you have?"

"I believe the proof is in those cups you hold."

Each of the five men looked at their cups. Mason held his to his nose and sniffed, while the chancellor held his at arm's length.

"Victor wanted you dead, and I believe he's using the attack tonight as a convenient excuse to serve you poison."

"These cups aren't poisoned," Victor said. "How dare you accuse me of—"

"Drink it." Lia said. Silence filled the room. "If you say they're safe, then drink yours. You poured them from the same bottle, yes?"

"He did," Danik confirmed, pulling his sword in sync with Mason and pointing them toward the advisor.

"If nothing's wrong with it, then you won't mind drinking your cup, will you?" Lia said.

Victor sneered at her. He looked around the room. With his chin stuck out and eyes locked on Lia, the advisor moved the cup to his lips.

The cup paused for a moment. Lia's heart thudded. With a flick of his wrist, the king's advisor tossed the contents of the cup into his mouth and swallowed in one gulp. Maintaining fierce eye contact, he slammed his cup down with alacrity.

"You've gone too far, Shadow Knight." The king's face grew red. "This is an absurd claim, and I will not have you sullying the name of my trusted men. Unless this is a joke of exceptionally poor taste, I want you all out of my city immediately!"

Lia turned to her mother.

Chelci's eyes pleaded with her. "Take it back," she whispered. "There's no proof of this."

Lia clenched her teeth together. Her breath grew ragged. *Could I be wrong?*

"What do you have to say for yourself?" the king barked.

The room leaned in toward her, waiting with bated breath. Her lips parted, trembling. "H-He must have built up immunity or something."

The room exploded into sound as the king, advisor, and chancellor of justice began speaking at once. Danik and Mason held their heads sheepishly while their sword points drooped.

"Chancellor," Constantine said. "Summon the royal guards. Have them escort these fools from my presence."

"I'm serious!" Lia shouted over the uproar. She crossed the room to the shelf next to the bed. She inspected books and bottles at a furious pace while she talked. "I believe he put essence of xolopyr root in the drink in order to kill you all."

"Lia," Mason protested. "He drank from the cup."

The chancellor exited the door and shouted down the hall outside.

Lia continued, "Yes, which means he probably consumed powdered pembrake to counteract it."

"Powdered pembrake?" Victor said, holding his hands up in exasperation. "You're making this up."

Lia lifted a container and peeked under its lid before setting it back. "Pembrake is a fungus found at high altitudes or deep forests."

"High altitudes? Deep forests?" Victor said, his lip curled. "Like the sandy shore of the ocean?"

"No, like the Parthe Mountains, a mere day's travel from here," she replied. "The powder works against the poison found in xolopyr root. They're usually found growing together, keeping a balance in nature."

"I have no idea what these things are," Victor objected, "much less where to find them."

"In addition to his last-ditch attempt tonight, Your Majesty, your advisor has been poisoning you for weeks."

"Lies, Your Majesty!" Victor shouted. "She's made this up."

"Chancellor!" Constantine shouted toward the hall. "Where are you? Get her out of here!"

Lia left the shelf and stepped toward the king. "You've been sick for weeks, right? Dryness in your throat, weakness, cough, needing to rest? These are signs of regular exposure to molopyr leaves."

"Molopyr leaves!" Victor laughed, bordering on hysteria. "Now there's another poison I'm supposed to know about?"

"Is he always the one who arranges your tea?" Lia asked, returning to the shelf and moving even quicker.

The king's brows knit together. He looked at his advisor.

"No!" Victor said. "I'm *not* the only one who gets his tea."

"But he does it frequently," the king said, his voice taking on a pensive tone.

"You're not listening to this slander, are you?"

Lia lifted books and checked in containers. She sniffed bottles and looked behind them. A commotion came from the door. She glanced over. Chancellor Billinsgworth arrived with four royal guards. Her heart raced. *No! Not yet! It must be here somewhere!*

"Take her away," the advisor shouted. "Toss her in the dungeons if she refuses to cooperate."

"Your Majesty, I'm telling you, your advisor is the danger here."

The guards grabbed her by the arms and pulled her toward the door.

"Your advisor has been trying to kill you, and I have proof!"

"Proof?" the king said. "What is your proof?"

The rough grip on her grew slack. Lia wrestled an arm free and drew papers from her cloak. She walked to the king and handed them over. "This is a receipt from the Searis Apothecary Guild for a purchase from your advisor, Victor Gannaway."

Victor's jaw dropped, his face growing pale.

"Your Majesty, would you read the items purchased by Gannaway five weeks ago?"

The papers crinkled as the king adjusted them. "Molopyr leaves, essence of xolopyr root, and . . ." The paper crinkled again before the king looked up. "Powdered pembrake."

"When the guildsmen heard of your weakening condition,

they put it together," Lia said. "They knew what Victor had purchased and determined he was making a play for the crown. They tried to set up a meeting to warn you, but they couldn't get through."

Lia turned back to the shelves, pressing her fingers along the grain while chaos erupted behind her. The advisor blubbered about it not meaning anything. The Chancellor of Justice asked for clarification, and the shadow knights moved closer to the king's advisor with their swords up.

A crack of wood under her fingers gave Lia a surge of hope. She pulled on the crack, sliding a panel of wood aside. The clamor in the room hushed as all eyes turned to her. She reached her hand into the cavity that had opened and pulled out three objects. Lia held her breath as she lifted the lid off two containers. The first one was half-filled with shriveled green leaves. The second container—a small one—contained a white powder with flakes of red. The final item was a small vial, identical to the ones she saw in the guild shop. She held it up, *XOLOPYR* visible in bold letters across the label.

"Victor!" the king boomed in as strong a voice as his feeble body seemed to manage. "I trusted you. I gave you a seat at the table. How could you do this to me?" He bored a hole through his advisor with his eyes, his chest heaving.

"But—" Victor's head jerked from side to side as the knights grew closer. "She's lying, obviously." He laughed, nervously while sweat dotted his forehead. "You don't believe *her*, do you?"

No one answered his pitiful pleas.

His face hardened. Grabbing a knife from his sleeve, he lunged toward the king with a yell.

Swords from Mason and Danik pierced him in the side. The advisor cried out, dropping the dagger. He fell to the floor, his face wincing as he clutched his side. Blood creeped down his tunic, pooling onto the floor.

"Victor, how could you do this?" Billingsworth asked, his furious brows at a sharp angle.

Gannaway pointed a shaking finger at the chancellor. "You said you supported me for the throne. You and Lavigne, both."

The king inhaled, his chest puffing.

"This is *not* what we said we supported!" Billingsworth turned to the king. "Your Majesty, Lavigne, Victor, Garnier, and I were considering what we would do in the terrible situation of your sickness growing worse. We did indicate that Victor was a leading candidate if we had to replace you, but we never had any intention for *this* to happen."

"You may not have," Gannaway said, wincing and holding his side. His ragged breath wheezed. "But I did."

The king shuffled across the room, hand clutching his cane as he moved. His advisor looked up, his face shifting between pain and anger. Constantine raised his foot, braced himself with a hand on the post of the bed, and kicked. The dull thud of boot against face reverberated through the room along with a sharp crack of bone. Victor's head went limp. His chest sank as a final breath exhaled.

After a few deep breaths, the king turned to Lia. "I owe you an apology."

Lia fought to keep a smile from showing.

"You stuck with your gut, and you saved my life. I'm sorry for doubting you."

"That's all right. We're just doing our job."

"Do you have any ideas of how to flush this . . . whatever it is in my system?"

She chuckled. "Molopyr is mild. It would have killed you had you continued drinking it much longer, but now you'll recover since you've stopped. Drink a lot of water."

"I will," the king said.

She scanned the room. Danik and Mason beamed, but the look on her mother's face held her attention. Chelci's head bobbed in approval while a faint smile tweaked her mouth.

"What do we do about the guildsmen then?" Billingsworth asked.

"Free them at once!" Constantine said. "They risked their own lives to save mine. They are heroes. Bring them for an audience with me in the reception hall tomorrow after the ceremony. I want to thank them personally and apologize for any rough treatment they've experienced."

"Nice work, Lia," Danik said, joining her by the shelf. He peered into the containers of poisonous items while keeping his distance. "I'm sure I would have figured it all out too . . . had I not been on guard duty."

Lia frowned and punched him in the arm. "You jerk."

He laughed. "I'm just teasing. That was impressive." Danik's attention focused on the hole in the shelf. He leaned forward and pulled a stack of bright coins from the darkened space.

"Whoa," Lia breathed. *Maybe that can pay the men back for the suffering they endur—*

Danik slipped the coins into his pocket. "I'll give you half later," he whispered. "*He* doesn't need it anymore."

Lia glanced at the rest of the room. Billingsworth had already left. Her mother and Mason spoke with the king while the guards dealt with the dead body of the advisor. No one noticed.

"Yeah . . . sure," she replied, her stomach twisting in a knot. A smile formed again. *This was my first mission . . . and it was a success.*

Raiyn had barely fallen asleep when footsteps woke him. He blinked his eyes open and turned to the faint lantern by the guard. Pedric stood as a tall and dark man entered the dungeon and spoke with the guard for an extended period. He nodded several times until the tall man turned to the cell at the end.

"You five are free to go," the visitor said as Pedric brought a ring of keys to unlock their cell door.

The men cheered, filling the damp dungeon with laughter and joy. Raiyn managed a weak smile, jealous of their luck.

After the men left, quiet settled in the dungeon like a blanket. Although the five men hadn't spoken, their presence helped him feel like he wasn't alone. With the dead addict's body removed as well, the quiet grew unnerving. Around the corner, moans and cackles of more prisoners reached him from time to time, but he'd never seen who was there or how many other prisoners lived in his temporary home.

Pedric approached his cell.

"What happened to them, Pedric? Are they really going free?"

The guard's head didn't lift. His face drooped as he rested his hands against the bars and leaned against it. "Yeah . . . apparently, it was a misunderstandin'."

"Good for them."

"Yeah . . . well . . . they were supposed to hang for the festival tomorrow." Pedric looked to the side. "We always have one. The people expect it."

Raiyn's brows pinched together. A queasy feeling grew in his gut. *Why won't he look at me?*

"Since the other men are gone, the chancellor wants someone else ta take their place."

Raiyn's breath stopped. The drip of water muddled in his brain as the bars spun.

Pedric looked at him, a soft pity hidden in his eyes. "I'm sorry Raiyn. Ya seem like a decent guy, but . . . you're taking their place on the gallows."

19

THE GALLOWS

Raiyn paced his cell, the thought of sleep far from his mind despite staying up all night. He repeatedly checked the seams of the metal cage and door surrounding him for weakness, but none were to be found. Pedric had rotated off guard duty, replaced by the sour-faced Bostich who rarely spoke.

"Come on, Bostich," Raiyn pleaded. "I'm dying today. At least give me a chance to breathe fresh air one more time. All I'm asking is for a moment to be outside . . . without shackles. You can guard me with as many men as you like." *Then I can use my power to knock you over and run out of here.*

The guard said nothing.

"I stole some medicine! My mother was dying! I know it was wrong, but is that cause to execute me?" Raiyn hung his head, tears trying to force their way out.

"It's not my call," Bostich muttered. "I just do my job."

"Ask someone, please! I'll behave. I just want to breathe air that's not filled with mold again."

"If you don't stop whining, I'm going to shove a spear through those bars and execute you myself."

Raiyn quieted. *Is this it? Mother is dead. My life is at a dead end.* He slumped to the ground, leaning his head against the wall. Greasy hair fell in front of his eyes. He focused on his breaths, counting them in and out. Hours must have passed, but he had no way to track the time.

A harsh rap jolted him awake. He blinked his eyes open to find Bostich at the door with four guards behind him.

"Arms through the cage," Bostich growled, holding a limp set of manacles.

Raiyn sighed and stood. He held his arms back and nodded at the metal rings. "I won't put up a fight. You don't need those."

Bostich chuckled. "Sure you won't. Arms through!"

Raiyn hesitated, hoping the guard would give up, but the man's face only grew angrier. Raiyn extended his arms through a space in the bars. A click sounded as one ring clamped around his wrist, the other soon following. He sighed as he stepped back, his shoulders and head drooping.

The door creaked as it opened. Two men entered his cell with spears and moved behind him.

"This way!" a guard barked after removing the anklet around his leg. Sharp tips pressed against his back, moving him forward.

"Sorry, Raiyn," Bostich whispered, his eyes holding a sorrow Raiyn had never seen in the man before. "I hope it's quick and painless."

Raiyn nodded in thanks. Pressed again by the spear tips, he followed the two guards who led the way out of the dungeon.

The sun blinded him when he stepped into the courtyard. His eyes had adjusted to the dim light of the underground cell, and the sharp contrast to the world jarred him. He squinted to see where the men led.

While walking, he tested the shackles that held his arms together. A pin held the ring tight around his wrist. He wriggled his hands to reach, but it was too small and tight. A ring dangled from the waist of the guard ahead of him with over a dozen keys strung on it. He stared as his feet marched, trying to envision which key would work on his shackles.

A sharp tip poked him in the back. "Don't even think about it, thief," the guard warned.

Raiyn sighed. *There's no way I could get the keys and unlock myself quickly enough.* With his hands hanging lazily before him, he reached to the waist of his pants and pulled out his hidden metal shard. *This might be my only hope.*

With one hand covering the other, he wriggled the metal pick into the hole of one of the restraints. It floundered as he dug blindly. After a moment, the metal clicked against something that pushed back. He tensed and forced himself to walk, keeping his eyes up. The sliver pressed harder, moving something inside the lock. It seemed the tension was about to give when a raised cobblestone caught the edge of his foot. The stumble was slight, but the pick slipped and fell against the back of the lock housing. The guards around him continued forward, oblivious to his attempt.

Keeping his face forward, Raiyn inhaled and tried again. He resumed digging in the lock, but nothing happened. The longer he tried, the more frustrated he grew.

He crossed a bridge and wound through the streets. The closer they grew to their destination, the more distracted he became. His mind soon became a foggy mess, trying to block out what was to come. His legs propelled him forward, each step jostling his body while he fiddled with the lock. A crowd grew around him. The guards pressed forward but moved tighter on all sides. Someone's voice projected ahead. The guards stopped, and Raiyn looked around.

They stood at the edge of the city square next to a raised stage. His four escorts surrounded him on all sides while a crowd of people filled the square. He wasn't the focus, though.

Raiyn turned his head to see the King of Tarphan speaking on the stage from behind a lectern. One arm gestured, punctuating his words while the other held onto the podium for support. The crowd cheered, but Raiyn's muddled brain couldn't discern what was said.

The king's tone grew serious. His face fixed in a hard look until his words crescendoed, then his hands rose to a thunderous applause. A young woman on the stage in a black cloak stood when the king gestured to her, the applause from the crowd growing. His mind sharpened when he looked at her. *That's the girl from the dungeon. I wonder what she did.*

The applause continued, and the king hobbled back to a seat, sitting at the same time as the girl in black. The clapping and cheering faded, and another man approached the lectern —the one who freed the guildsmen. A sinking feeling grew in Raiyn's stomach. For a moment, he'd forgotten why he was there.

In front of the stage, a gallows caught his eye, and his pulse sped. The man droned on about justice and peace, but Raiyn could only think of the noose dangling in the air.

". . . and as a demonstration of the justice this city stands for, today we execute one who spit in the face of our peace." Jeers came from the crowd as the speaker continued. "This vile criminal destroyed the property of hardworking businesses. He stole, vandalized, and attempted to murder innocent people of our fine city."

I didn't try to kill anyone!

"As we conclude this year's Festival of the Sea, I can think of no better way to celebrate than to demonstrate the justice our city clings to. This gives all of us hope, and it's what makes us great." The crowd cheered. The man held up his hand, accepting the applause, but as it settled down, the man turned to him.

Raiyn's stomach dropped. The entire city of Tarphan looked in his direction. Looks of anger and disgust covered their faces. A lone "boo" rang through the crowd, unleashing a torrent of scorn and abuse from every direction.

The spears prodded him forward. Raiyn walked, his feet feeling weighted with stone while his fingers labored frantically at the lock. A rotten piece of fruit hit him in the head. He winced and ducked his face. Several more items hit him, splattering rancid juice and chunks of spoiled food. Too soon, the gallows loomed before him.

Two guards ascended the steps first, then the ones with spears prodded him next. A grizzled man with yellow teeth grabbed him by the wrists when he arrived on the elevated platform. He jerked him forward and pulled him to a stop where the noose hung, swaying in the breeze. Raiyn blanched at the trapdoor under his feet.

The hangman didn't waste any time in grabbing the noose. Raiyn strained his head, trying to keep it away from the man and his circle of rope, but firm hands put a stop to his writhing. The rope dropped past his eyes and touched his neck. The knot slid tight.

Tears welled up, blurring his vision. He pulled at the shackles. The metal rings dug into his wrists, but the chains between held them taut. He scanned the crowd, and his breath caught. The familiar face of Kip Chilton stared back with a slack jaw. *There's nothing he can do for me.*

He felt a click reverberate through his arm, then he inhaled sharply. His breath caught in his chest. The unlocked hinge of the left shackle pivoted slightly, lessening the tension on his wrist. He kept it covered with his hands, and after a quick glance down, he shifted the pick to the other shackle. *One isn't enough. I need both free!* He furiously dug into the other lock.

The man with the yellow teeth stepped to the side of the platform, where a lever stuck up from the floor.

Raiyn's pulse raced. *I need more time!*

"Please," he said, quick and desperate. He turned his head to the guards who had brought him. "Allow me to say a few words."

The guards glanced at each other, hesitating. They turned to the hangman whose hand rested on the lever. Raiyn's fingers worked while he waited, the outline of the trapdoor waiting to engulf him.

The closest guard sniffed then raised his chin and spoke in a firm voice. "No. You have no rights here." He turned back to the hangman. "Drop him."

Raiyn's heart plummeted. He opened his mouth to protest when another faint click reached his ears, and the metal on his second wrist loosened. *That's it!*

The hangman's arm tensed. His fingers wrapped around the lever as he positioned his body to pull.

Raiyn shook both arms. The shackles opened—the left one followed shortly by the right. They dropped from his hands, falling to the wooden platform with a clunk.

A gasp sounded from the guards.

Raiyn flexed his stomach and sensed the tingling presence of the power he needed. *Now I just need to—*

A clunk sounded from the lever, freezing his thoughts. His stomach dropped as the door beneath his feet jerked open.

Raiyn pulled the power inside him at the same moment his body fell. The world froze, his weightless body stopped in time. His freed hands worked the slip knot of the noose in an instant. He managed it wide enough before his lowering chin brushed the side of the rope. The noose pulled upward, but his head was free.

His body sped its fall as he loosened his hold on the power. The stones of the city square rushed to meet him. His feet hit hard, and his body collapsed.

Shouts erupted around him. Through the wooden legs and

braces of the gallows, spectators scurried backward with wide eyes and gaping mouths.

"Get him!" a guard from the platform shouted. Feet thundered down the steps.

I've got to get out of here!

Raiyn dodged the wooden crossbeams and stood free of the structure. The guard who had unlocked him finished his descent from the stage and barreled toward him with a fierce intensity in his eyes.

The clearest path to get away was over the main stage. Raiyn pulled again at the waiting power and ran as fast as his body could move. The guard with the keys appeared to freeze mid-stride. The shouting crowd remained in whatever pose they held.

He flew onto the stage. The king sat in his seat, but his appalled gaze remained fixed on where Raiyn had been moments ago. Before he leaped off the back of the stage, the young woman in the black cloak caught his eye. While the rest of the crowd looked frozen in place, she turned as he moved. Her eyes narrowed and her head cocked in a curious inspection. He pushed the moment from his mind and jumped.

When he hit the ground, he slowed his speed but continued running. Slurred, slow-motion shouts reached his ears, but Raiyn didn't stop to pay attention. He raced around a corner, leaving the gallows, the crowd, the king, and the curious young woman in black behind.

A SIGN over the locked door to his flat indicated the Department of City Affairs had seized the space. Raiyn wasn't about to let that stop a fugitive prisoner escaping from execution. He rammed his body into the door, aiming just beside the knob. The door shuddered but didn't budge. He tried again with more force. The windows rattled, but the door remained. He backed up. His limbs felt exhausted from his run from the gallows. His chest heaved, his mouth gulping in breaths. He steeled his body and tapped into whatever strength he had left. When his shoulder hit the door, the casing splintered. His momentum carried him forward until he splayed across the floor.

Taking great effort, Raiyn pushed his body off the ground, then closed what remained of the ruined door. *I just need a moment, then I'll be gone.*

He passed through the opening to the next room, bracing himself for whatever he might find. The bed remained as it always had but was empty. His breath hitched. Where her body had lain, dark stains marred the sheets. *Where did they take her?*

He pictured a pleasant grave in the cemetery at the edge of Searis—a headstone marking her plot of ground, announcing the year she died with notes about her impact on the world. His hope fouled when he considered her reality—burned at the city crematorium with piles of other unnamed bodies, her ashes scattered to the wind.

I'm sorry, Mother. I wish I could have given you better than that.

Raiyn wiped his eyes and moved to the shelves in their sparse kitchen. No food was to be found, but he threw a water flask with a strap over his shoulder.

He crouched before the chest in the room's corner. The rusty hinge resisted as it opened, a moldy smell wafting out. A handful of clothes stared back. Raiyn rustled through the container, working as quickly as he could to flee the city before anyone recognized him.

He changed his tunic, tossing the damp, grimy shirt he'd worn for weeks to the floor and putting on a clean garment of faded blue. Next, he pulled out a threadbare brown cloak and wrapped it around himself. The hood was thin but should keep the average observer from recognizing his face. He found a blanket at the bottom. Holes riddled the fabric, but it would be better than nothing for sleep. He grabbed a sheathed dagger and attached it to his hip. The blade was dull and rusted but could still skin a rabbit in a pinch.

He closed the chest and stood. Before he turned to go, his eyes fixed on the leather pouch collecting dust on the shelf. His breath caught, and his body froze. He picked it up, his jaw clenching. His heart told him to toss it down and forget the reminder of his past, but his mind told him he might need it. With a shaking hand, he tucked the pouch into an inner pocket of his cloak.

"What's in the pouch?" a voice asked in Common Norshic.

Raiyn gasped and spun, his eyes wide. The young woman from the stage stood in his flat, leaning against the wall with a casual air. Her black cloak draped to the floor, and tendrils of loose, brown hair obscured her face.

"How'd you find me?" He replied, voice shaking. "Who are you?"

Her eyes narrowed. She nodded toward his cloak pocket. "I asked what was in the pouch."

Raiyn held his hand over his heart, pressing the item against his chest. "Nothing." His hand drifted to his hip, then slid the dagger free of its sheath in a quick flick.

The girl raised her eyebrows. "That's pretty fast. How did you learn to move like that?"

Raiyn extended the knife toward her. "Let me go, or you're going to find out just how fast I can wield this."

Her mouth curled at the edge. She leaned in. "Show me." She moved off the wall and bent her knees. Her hands raised as if she prepared to grapple. She appeared three to four years younger than him, but her toned arms and relaxed approach to fighting suggested years of experience.

Raiyn took a step back. *I can't stab a girl, but—* He looked past her and imagined freedom calling. He bent his knees and extended the blade again. With no intent to hurt her, he readied his legs to sprint past.

Power bubbled up in him, and Raiyn took off. He moved as fast as he could, angling to her side. He glanced at her in the split moment he came alongside, and again, her eyes tracked him.

Raiyn's chest slammed into an invisible force. His blurred body stopped its forward momentum as the young woman's arm stretched across his path. His feet continued, rising into the air while his body flipped horizontally. When he hit the wooden floor, his breath left him. He winced but forced his body not to move. The young woman stood over him, holding his knife and the pouch that had been in his pocket.

He gasped for breath.

"Nice try," she said, wiggling the pouch. "I guess I'll have to check for myself."

"Please!" Raiyn begged, the word laced with emotion. "Please, don't. It's personal. I beg you."

The girl stopped twirling the pouch and stared back. She extended the item back to him. "As you wish."

"How did you do what you did?" Raiyn asked.

"I was going to ask you the same question." She chuckled, then stepped back, offering him a hand, "but I already know the answer."

Raiyn grasped her hand and allowed her to help him up. "You have the power, too?"

"You know nothing about it, do you?"

Raiyn shook his head. "Very little."

"What's your name?"

He hesitated before answering. "Raiyn . . . Raiyn Crabtree."

She pointed her head in the opposite direction. "What was

all that about in the square, Raiyn? Why does the city want you dead?"

He scoffed. "Because the king wanted to put on a show."

Her eyebrow raised. "You're saying you're not a criminal?"

"Well . . . I stole medicine. Barkleaf elixir."

"Barkleaf? Was someone sick?"

"My mother." Raiyn nodded to the empty bed. "She died right there—before I could give her the medicine."

"I'm sorry," she breathed. "What about the 'attempted murder' charge?"

He sighed. "That was a lie—for the crowd. They wanted to give them someone to hate."

The young woman looked around the room, nodding. Unsure of her intentions, he studied her face. Her hair fell casually across her shoulders. Curiosity filled her eyes. The skin on her cheeks and around her nose were free from wrinkles but contained a rough edge, as if they'd seen plenty of action in their time.

"What's your plan now?" she asked.

"I, uh . . . need to flee the city. I thought I'd head east or maybe north."

She stared at him, tapping her chin as if evaluating a puzzle. He fidgeted, unsure if he was in trouble or not.

"If you're heading north," she said, finally, "maybe you can travel with us."

"Us?"

"I'm with three others. We leave today."

A flood of hope rushed through Raiyn. *A chance to learn more about this power and meet people like me.* His brows pinched together. "What's your name?"

The young woman extended her hand. "Lia." Her firm grip rattled his body. "I live in Felting and train with a group."

"Is this group . . . like you?"

"Yes, and like you, too. We're known as—" She paused, her mouth frozen.

Raiyn leaned forward and raised his eyebrows.

Lia pursed her lips for a long moment until the tense look on her face relaxed. "You'd be welcome to come with us."

Raiyn took several even breaths. After a moment, he managed a nod. "Yes. I'd love to travel with you."

20

THE ROAD HOME

Lia sat on Ginger, her body rising and falling with the horse's steps. The sandy city of Searis had faded behind them hours before, and the grasslands of Tarphan stretched ahead.

Danik rode next to her, his gaze holding a hard frown.

"What's troubling you?" Lia asked, getting Danik to turn to her.

He pursed his lips, his eyes jumping ahead.

Lia looked forward. Riding at the lead, Mason and Raiyn engaged in a friendly discussion. She caught snippets of their conversation about lumber, Searis, and road travel. Safe from the dangerous eyes of the city, Raiyn had lowered his hood, showing off his thick, black tussle of hair.

"You don't like Raiyn?" she whispered.

Danik paused for a moment. "Honestly . . . no, I don't."

"Is it his rugged beard or broad shoulders you dislike?"

"Wha—?" He turned to her, and she burst into laughter.

"I'm teasing," she said after her laughter subsided. "But . . . I bet he *could* wield a sword with arms like those."

"Sword fighting isn't just about strength." Danik snapped back.

"Whoa, I'm sorry." She chuckled again. "I didn't mean to hit a nerve."

"I agree with Danik on this," Chelci said, bringing her horse alongside Lia's. "We know nothing about him."

"That's not true," Lia said. "We know he's learned a bit of the origine and has potential to learn more."

"We know they sentenced him to death for attempted murder," Chelci added.

Lia frowned.

"We can't just take anyone who has ability and teach them the secrets of what we do. We are cautious for a reason, Lia."

Lia held up her hands. "He's only riding with us. I'm not suggesting we reveal all of our secrets, but . . . what's the harm in him coming along? We keep a watch at night already. This gives us a chance to know more about him. When we get home, we could give him a more thorough test to see if he's worthy of continuing."

"Why do you like him so much?" Danik asked.

"I don't—ugh." Lia reached to punch him, but he steered his horse just out of reach. She looked toward Raiyn and thought. "I've got a feeling about him. He's lost and alone. He needs to find something, and I think there's a good chance the Shadow Knights could be what he needs. I believe what he said about the charges being made up. He doesn't strike me as a killer."

"Even then," Chelci said, "he admits he stole."

"To save his mother," Lia noted. "I recall another young thief who was trained to be a shadow knight around twenty years ago."

"Veron? That was different?"

"Was it, though?"

Her mother didn't reply but only stared ahead to where Raiyn talked with Mason.

A stream trickled across the road ahead. Lia's mouth felt dry, and her back ached. "Let's take a break," she said. No one complained.

The riders dismounted at the stream, letting their horses dip their heads to drink. Chelci pulled some hard bread out of her bag and passed it around.

"Thank you, but I'm all right," Raiyn said when she extended a torn section to him.

"Are you not starving?" Lia asked, crouching by the stream to fill her water skin. "You came from the dungeons, didn't you?"

"Um, yes, I did but . . . You're kind enough to let me travel with you. I can't take your food. It's too much."

"It's all right," Chelci said. "Please take some. We have enough."

With twinkling eyes, Raiyn accepted the bread. He thanked Chelci and took measured bites.

"It's like he's never eaten bread before," Danik muttered low enough so only Lia could hear.

"Take it easy on him," she whispered, standing and capping her water skin. "His mother just died."

"So, Raiyn," Danik said, speaking at full volume. "Where'd you learn to use your . . . ability?"

Raiyn paused with wide eyes, the bread half in his mouth. "Um . . ." he glanced between the four people. "I just, um . . . kind of figured it out."

"On your own?" Mason asked. "With no one to help?"

Raiyn shrugged. "Yeah. I don't know that I've figured much out—just enough to be dangerous, I guess." He laughed. "What about you all? How'd you learn?"

Lia froze and glanced at her mother. No one answered, and a nervous energy filled the air.

"Sorry," Raiyn added. "I didn't mean to—"

"Where are you from?" Danik asked.

"Um . . ." Raiyn's eyebrows pinched in as he glanced around the group. "From Searis."

"But you don't have a Tarphic accent."

Raiyn's lip twitched.

Danik leaned in. "Did you move there?"

"I lived there most of my life. My mother educated me, so I never developed much of an accent."

"What about before that?"

"Before? I, uh . . . I'm not sure. I was young then. My mother had us move around a lot."

"You don't remember where you moved from?" Danik pressed. "Your mother never mentioned it?"

"Give him a break," Lia said, laughing to break the tension. "Do you remember everything you did when you were young?"

Danik's hard look morphed into a smile. "Sorry, I was just curious. How about swords?"

Raiyn raised his eyebrows. "Swords?"

"Yeah," Danik said. "Sword fighting. With 'the power' you experimented with, did you ever develop sword fighting skills?"

"I did a bit," Raiyn said, his eyes lighting up. "My mother showed me some things."

Danik muffled a snicker, and Lia shot him a scathing look.

"She said I was a natural, one of the best she'd ever seen."

"Oh?" Danik said, a hint of a laugh creeping onto his face. "Let's see it."

"I'd love to, but I don't have a sword."

"What'd you learn with?"

"My mother and I used sticks and brooms—whatever we could find. It's been a while, though."

"Well, you are in luck," Danik said with a flourish. He walked to Mason's horse and pulled a sword from the scabbard tucked into the blanket roll. "You can use Mason's." He tossed the sword.

Raiyn's eyes grew. He bent his knees to catch the hilt, but the grip bounced off his hand and fell to the dirt. "I'm sorry," he said to Mason, picking it up. "I didn't mean to drop it in the dirt."

"It's fine," Mason said, wincing.

Danik pulled his sword from where it rested in his pack. "And now we can see your skills."

"Danik, I'm not sure this is wise." Chelci said.

"I'll be careful. I want to see what 'the Natural' can do." Danik moved onto the grass beside the road. "Join me, Raiyn of Searis. Let's see what you've got."

Raiyn's face held a smile as he joined him in the grass. "Look, I don't claim to be greater than any of you. That my mother said I was great probably meant about as much as a stump telling a rock he was a great warrior."

Lia chuckled.

"But I'm proud of what I've learned, and I'm honored to be here with a chance to spar against you."

Danik wore a crooked smile.

"When you spar, do you use . . . whatever that power is?"

"Sometimes we do, sometimes we don't," Danik said. "Would you like to?"

Raiyn shrugged. "Sure. I'd love to see what you can do with it."

"All right then." Danik raised his sword, dipping into dragon stance with his sword over his head, pointed out.

Raiyn held his weapon, bouncing its weight in the air. The tip swayed while Danik circled with a smirk. Raiyn stepped first, his face focused. The blow was fast and heavy, powered by sturdy arms. Danik deflected the swing with a light parry and moved away. Not waiting, Raiyn swung again. The two swords clashed, scraping as the young men pushed apart, making space.

He's fast, Lia thought. *And strong.*

Raiyn's focus shifted. He paused for a moment, his body clenching before he moved again. A blurred form moved through the air, the sword whistling as it arced. Danik sped up at the same time. A frenzied crash of swords in rapid movement rang out.

Lia watched the indistinct bodies shuffle back and forth. Occasionally, a head or a back would take shape as someone paused for a moment, but then it melded again into the skirmish.

Come on boys, give this up.

Raiyn crashed to the ground, his body returning to normal speed. He paused on all fours, his chest heaving as he watched his opponent. Danik remained upright, holding his sword out. His breath seemed labored, but it was barely noticeable.

"Don't forget," Danik said, "you can use the power if you like."

Mason scoffed next to Lia's. "Danik, he *was* using—"

Lia elbowed him in the side. "He knows, Mason," she said, her mouth turned down. "He's taunting him."

Danik stepped forward, holding his sword out. "Sorry, that was mean. I was only teasing."

Through much effort, Raiyn got to his feet and held his weapon up. The sword barely lifted, the shaft shaking. "You sure are fast."

Danik lunged in a blur. Raiyn shouted, jerking his hand back. Lia blinked to find Danik holding both swords, the edges set on either side of Raiyn's neck. Raiyn held his chin up despite his panting breaths.

Danik's fierce look morphed into a smug grin. He lowered the swords.

The tight concern on Raiyn's face relaxed, and a smile

formed. "That was impressive, Danik. You must have been training your whole life to get that good." He shook his head.

Danik gave a quick laugh, his mouth trapped in a smile. "Thanks. You've got . . . potential. Maybe one day you'll get there."

Danik returned the swords to the scabbards where they came from, and Raiyn shuffled back. His body struggling to remain upright, and his hands pressed against his knees.

"Do you not get"—he took a deep breath—"tired after you use it?"

"We practice using it," Lia said, "resting any chance we can. Over time, it gets easier."

"Lia," Chelci said in a sharp tone. She shook her head in a tight path. "That's enough."

Lia's cheeks heated as the eyes from the group turned to her. She clenched her teeth and turned back to her horse. "All right, that's long enough of a break," she said. "Let's get moving."

Danik walked by, chuckling under his breath. "How was that?" he whispered with a grin.

She glared at him. "Don't be rude to him."

His smug look vanished.

Mason, Raiyn, and Danik mounted up. Their horses splashed through the stream as they resumed the journey. Lia tightened the roll on the back of her saddle.

"Teaching him is dangerous, Lia," Chelci said, throwing her leg over her horse. "We need to determine more about who he is first, and that's not your job."

Lia nodded, mounting her saddle. The rebuke stung, but her mother was right. "What do you think about him?"

Chelci looked ahead to where the three young men on horseback moved ahead. "I'm not sure yet. He seems kind, but —" She tilted her head. "There's something about him I can't put my finger on."

"Do you think we should tell him who we are? Invite him to join us?"

"We need to get Veron's input. For now . . . hold off teaching him any more. Understood?"

Lia nodded, her mother's wisdom both comforting and chafing. "Deal."

21

THE CAVERNS

Talioth's steps echoed in the narrow stone passage. The caves, formed thousands of years before, snaked through the mountain with sharp drops, grand openings, and twisting halls. Over time, the Marked Ones had carved out a city of their own. Cozy rooms and grand halls connected with dark passages. Bored shafts brought light and air, but the caverns kept a mildewy tang that never left the senses. His breath fogged as he walked.

Rounding a corner, the low ceiling sloped up, and the light intensified as he emerged into the Hub. The central meeting place of the caverns was where people gathered. A hole high in the ceiling allowed a large shaft of light to spread through the room. Twelve columns surrounded the expanse, and a mostly smooth stone floor spread flat across it. Halls disappeared down darker passages in several directions.

Children played by the fountain, where water streamed out of a hole in the wall and collected in a carved-out stone basin. A group of men sat around a small fire, holding mugs and laughing. Two women sat at a loom, threading wool through it and creating a colorful display of what would soon be a rug.

Talioth craned his neck and looked up. Wooden scaffolding stretched to the ceiling. Workers labored high on the platforms, pounding away at stone with hammers and chisels. A statue built of blocks took shape against the wall.

From a nearby passage, two men stepped into the light, pulling a two-wheeled cart filled with rectangular stones. Their shoulders slumped and backs bowed. Sweat ran down their brows, blackened with grime while the chains connecting their legs jingled.

"Too slow!" the foreman, Centol, yelled, cracking a whip over the men's heads. "Move faster!"

Startled, they moved quicker, their emaciated arms stretching taut while pulling on the handle. At the base of the scaffolding, they set down the front of the cart and took a deep breath. When Centol cocked his arm with the whip, they jumped into action, reaching for the cart to unload the cargo.

Talioth chuckled. "Such a motivator."

Centol turned to him and offered a slight nod. "Welcome, Talioth. The statue is coming along. Slower than I'd like, but—" He nodded to the workers. "They're doing better than the last bunch. Soon, you will see the likeness."

Talioth glanced up again, imagining the upper half bearing his own face. "I look forward to seeing it."

A deep thunk sounded from the workers. The older of the men by the cart had set a stone on the ground as he bent over and rested. His thinning hair was gray, and a scraggly beard grew down his neck.

"Get up!" Centol yelled, raising his hand with the whip.

Talioth placed his hand out, stopping him. "I've got this." He stood forward, his chin lifted, staring down his nose at the filthy worker. "You enjoy taking rests, do you?"

The aging man looked up as Talioth stood over him. His jaw hardened. "No . . . I don't enjoy it," he said with clenched teeth.

"Centol here is good at motivating people to work through

pain, but if it's not motivating enough, we can get more creative."

"I'll trade with him," a fresh voice said from above.

Talioth stepped back and looked up. A younger man leaned over the edge of the scaffolding, staring down.

"Who are you?" Centol asked.

"My name is Rippon," the man said, holding a hammer and chisel, his eyes earnest. "I'd be happy to switch jobs."

Talioth squinted at the young man's familiar face, then glanced between him and the older man on the ground. "He's your father."

Rippon's lips formed a tight line.

"I think we found some motivation," Talioth said, a smirk growing. He pointed up at the young man. "Bring him here."

"No!" the older man on the ground yelled. "Leave him alone."

Centol leaped from the ground, flying into the air to land on the third-level scaffold. He grasped the young man's hair and dragged him down the ramp.

The older man scrambled next to the cart. "I can work!" He strained to lift the stone from the ground, but it slipped from his fingers. He turned to Talioth, begging. "I can do it. Please, leave him alone."

Centol arrived with the young man bent over and held by the hair. The chains around the worker's feet clinked as he moved.

Talioth pulled a dagger and placed it against Rippon's throat. "Maybe I should carve my initials into his skin to remind you both who owns you."

The older man picked up the stone again and lumbered up the ramp, the struggle visible on his face. "There's no need. See?" he said.

Talioth laughed as the man disappeared up the ramp. With

a sneer, Centol flung his handful of the worker's hair toward the ramp. Rippon stumbled but caught himself.

"Get to work," Centol ordered.

When the older man descended the ramp again, he glanced at Talioth. "Sir, I will work hard. It's just . . ."

Talioth's face screwed up. "It's just, what?"

The man wouldn't make eye contact. "The stones are heavy. I try, but they're difficult for one person to lift."

"They're too heavy, are they?" Talioth said, his jaw clenching. He took a deep breath and let it out before stepping close to the cart. The power inside him hummed. His muscles ached to be used. He selected a stack of two stones and lifted them both free of the cart. Sliding a hand underneath them, he lifted the burden above his head with one hand.

The old man's eyes grew as the large stones balanced high in the air.

"Difficult for one person to lift, you say?" Talioth taunted.

Centol chuckled.

The effort felt simple. Not even a drop of sweat beaded on his brow.

"I'm sorry, sir," the worker babbled. "I'll try harder. If you're able to do that, then surely—"

An icy wave brushed through Talioth. His forehead wrinkled as his arm faltered. The effort to keep the stones raised felt immense and unbearable.

"Are you all right, sir?" Centol asked.

"Of course I'm all right," he snapped. The stones lowered as the strength in his arm faded. He tried to lower them with control, but the weight was too much. They fumbled, his arms unable to bear the burden.

Making a show of trying to set them back on the cart, the heavy stones tumbled out of control. One split in half as it hit the ground, and the other lost a chunk out of its corner.

Talioth gasped for breath. He glanced at the crystal around

his neck, its glow barely visible. His teeth ground together as he bent over, panting.

"Sir?"

Talioth turned to Centol, rage simmering inside. "It's time."

Gasps sounded from around the Hub where other marked ones watched. The tense room was silent for a long moment.

Centol nodded, glancing at his own dim crystal. "Who should we use? Someone from the mines, or one of these men?"

"I don't care as long as it's one of the strong ones." Talioth looked up the scaffolding. Rippon caught his eye. "Bring the son."

"No!" the older man yelled, stepping close. "Leave him be, please!" He reached out and grabbed Talioth's sleeve.

Talioth jerked his arm away. "How dare you touch me!" He smacked the man with the back of his hand across the face, sending him reeling. The man fell, scraping his legs on the rocky ground.

Talioth grabbed the whip that lay on the cave floor and snapped it at the man. Two cracks filled the air in quick succession while stripes formed along with tears on the man's shirt.

The worker yelled, writhing on the ground while Rippon clumped down the stairs, pulled again by Centol. Ropes bound his hands behind his back, and tears rolled down his face as he watched his father.

"Meliand!" Talioth shouted across the Hub.

An older woman stood amid a group of onlookers. Her flowing red dress hung on her wrinkled body. Long gray hair fell in wavy lines on all sides of her head. The stain on her neck stood in stark contrast to the bright-red fabric.

"Prepare the chamber. Gather everyone."

The woman nodded.

Talioth searched the room. All eyes looked at him already,

and it only took a moment to find who he sought. Valdok approached even before he called.

One of the largest of the marked ones, the man's broad shoulders and massive arms parted anyone in his way. He nodded when he arrived. "What do you need, sir?"

"Take this man to the chamber and get him ready."

Valdok nodded and grabbed Rippon's arm.

"What are you doing with me?" the worker asked, pulling away.

Valdok sent a balled fist into his side. A deep thud echoed, followed by a groan from Rippon.

"He'll be ready," Valdok said as he dragged the man away.

"I'll lock up the workers," Centol said, already signaling for guards to bring them down from the platforms.

TALIOTH ROUNDED THE CORNER, pressing his hand against the stone wall. The low lantern inside the room evened out the glowing red light. The chamber contained nothing more than a chair and a bed, where Balakolt lay under a covering of skins.

The attendant, Kolfian, noticed his arrival. She stood from the chair and nodded as she slunk against the wall.

"Hey," he breathed, gazing at his wife.

Balakolt turned her head then flashed a pained smile. "Hey." Her response was raspy and thin.

Talioth sat in the chair next to the bed. He took her hand in his. The wrinkly skin and bony structure grew more pronounced by the day. It was difficult to remember the vibrant woman she was not long before. "How are you feeling?"

She took a labored breath before replying. "I—" Violent coughs interrupted her. The air expelling from her lungs rattled and shook. She grimaced as her body contorted. When the fit ended, she groaned, pressing her hand against her chest.

"I'm sorry," Talioth said. "I shouldn't bother you."

"No." She squeezed his hand. "If I don't have these moments, what's left?" A faint smile returned.

"The coughs are getting worse," Kolfian said. "They're stronger and more frequent."

He nodded, keeping his eyes on his wife. "Are you eating?"

"Some," Balakolt replied, her voice barely audible. "But I've not been very hungry."

A cleared throat turned his head toward the attendant. "She hasn't eaten in three days," Kolfian said. "She tries, but it won't stay down."

Talioth breathed in through his nose then turned back. He caressed her hand, remembering the many years they'd shared. *How has it come to this?*

Her frail hand applied a faint amount of pressure. "Don't let me die like this." Her eyes pleaded with him. "I-I'm scared."

He swallowed the choked feeling in his throat as a tear pooled at the corner of his eye. "Don't worry. The people we gathered are ready. We're taking one to the chamber now."

Her eyes brightened. "Really?"

He managed a weak smile then nodded. "That should make a big difference. You'll be up and around in no time, you'll see."

She sighed, closing her eyes and letting her body relax. "Do you think we—" She paused to take a steady breath. "—made the right choice?"

"Choice about what?"

Her finger raised and formed a small circle. "All of this—being here."

He tightened his hold on her. "Of course. There was no choice to make."

Talioth and Centol were the last to arrive. They passed through a narrow opening into a wide, circular room. Red crystals were set into the walls on all sides. In the center of the room, a hole plummeted into darkness below. Suspended from the ceiling, an enormous red crystal hovered over the hole, emitting a faint hum. The object held a faded glow, throbbing in time with the humming.

Meliand, Valdok, and their entire group were already gathered. Standing shoulder-to-shoulder, people filled the room. Children clung to parents' legs, and those who were shorter stood on rock ledges near the walls to see.

Rosalik, one of the younger marked ones, looked on with a clenched jaw and furrowed brow. Her brown hair was pulled back in tight rows, her arms folded across her chest.

Centol gasped, staring at the central crystal. "I've never seen it this low."

Talioth grimaced, nodding. He turned to the older woman across the hole. "Meliand, are you ready?"

She nodded.

Valdok stood behind Rippon and pushed the young man to his knees. Positioned next to the hole, he faced the large crystal.

"What is that? What are you doing with me?" Rippon's questions came quickly, his breath heavy.

Valdok moved to the side while Meliand approached. She positioned her hands around the worker's head. He thrashed, but her fingers tightened. Her long nails dug into his scalp, lines of blood seeping through his mat of hair and dripping down his neck. He screamed.

"Hold still!" she ordered. "If you do, this will hurt less."

"Wh-what are you doing?"

"We need your help," Talioth said, his voice tired. "The crystal is fading."

"Help? I-I know nothing about it! I can't fix your crystal!"

"Yes, you can," Talioth breathed, nodding to Meliand.

"Wait! I have a daughter back in Piryd. Her name is Annabelle, and she's only four. She has blonde hair and a beautiful singing voice. Please, think of her. Don't take away her father."

"If your daughter was in Piryd, then she's a pile of ash right now."

The man stopped struggling. His wide eyes locked on Talioth while his jaw dropped.

"Likely, the wind has taken her charred remains and blown them across the land. If you prefer, I will think about her blowing ashes while we proceed." He nodded more forcefully.

Rippon's body went rigid, his mouth locked with his jaw tight. His head jerked forward and his wide eyes fixed on the crystal. The red glow pulsed, growing brighter. The humming grew louder as the light intensified.

His shaking head was held in place by Meliand's firm grip. Tremors began in his arms. His skin rippled, white light emanating from the pores in a collective glow. Talioth shaded his eyes. The walls of the room brightened, pulsing in time with the central crystal and the ones around their necks.

The man groaned. It began as a low rumble but intensified until it felt as if the room shook. With a last shriek, the sound died. The light coming from him faded, and he slumped.

Talioth released his breath. All the glowing crystals in the room, along with the one in the center of the room, faded. The men and women watched, waiting. He leaned forward. *Come on, stop.* The light continued to dim. He swallowed hard as it settled—barely brighter than what it was when they started.

"Argh!" Rosalik yelled, clenching her hands above her head. "It's hopeless!"

"It's not hopeless," Talioth muttered.

"No, it's not," Meliand said, releasing the worker's head.

His body crumpled. The once young skin was now ashen-gray and covered with wrinkles. His eyes looked sunken in their sockets. A moan escaped his lips. His body swayed as if he attempted to move but was unable.

"Talioth," Rosalik said, "what do we do?"

The men and women turned to him. Stains on their necks and barely glowing crystals around their necks waited for his wisdom.

"The power is spread too thin," Talioth said. He pointed to the crumpled heap, moving to stand behind the man. "These *ordinary* men cannot replenish it anymore. We can continue to sacrifice them, but it won't last long." He pressed his foot against the shriveled man's back and kicked. The pile of skin and bones fell forward into the pit, disappearing into the void. No cry came from his mouth. No sound of him hitting anything echoed back.

"Is it time?" Rosalik asked.

Talioth locked eyes with her and nodded. "It's time we find the Shadow Knights."

Gasps filled the room.

"You mean, go past the mountains? Centol asked. "No one has done that for, what . . . twenty years?"

Talioth nodded, clenching his fist.

"Will this be enough?" Centol pointed toward the central crystal.

"It will have to be. We won't be able to go far, though."

"Do you know where they are?" Rosalik asked. "You know more than any of us."

Talioth shook his head, wishing for knowledge their secluded lives couldn't produce. "Twenty years is a long time. We'll scour the nearby cities, seeking information."

"What if they're not there?" a man in the back asked. "What if we don't find anything?"

"We will find them eventually."

"What if our power doesn't last that long?"

He took a deep breath, wondering the same question. "It will."

Shuffling drew his attention to the entrance, where Kolfian

entered. He frowned. *Why would she leave her?*

The attendant's face carried a fearful sorrow he'd not seen in some time. She stared at him, shaking.

"What is it?" he asked, his voice nearly failing him.

With a tight jaw, she shook her head.

"Kolfian, what's wrong?"

Her head lowered to look at the ground while her arms clasped before her. She breathed in as if to speak, but nothing came out.

"Speak!"

She startled, then opened her mouth.

Silence filled the room as every marked one stared, waiting to hear.

"She's dead."

22

———

EVALUATION

Veron leaned against the side of the building with his arms crossed. He and the others gathered in the square down the street from their training center. His eyes fixedly watched the others. A group of knights surrounded Raiyn, shaking hands, talking, and laughing. Lia stood next to him, hanging on his every word.

"What do you think about him, sir?" Danik asked, shuffling his feet as he approached.

Veron turned toward the young man. "I'm not sure yet. He seems friendly enough."

"Suspiciously so, if you ask me."

Veron chuckled. "What makes you say that?"

Danik propped his back to the wall, looking at the crowd. "I don't know. It seems convenient, don't you think? We stumble across this guy who can use the origine, and suddenly he's in Felting with hopes to join us."

"We have to *invite* him to join us," Veron said.

"Are you going to?"

"I don't know yet." Veron paused. "You traveled with him for a week. What was he like?"

"Cocky. Trying to impress everyone. He bragged how he learned to use the ability on his own, and that he was one of the best sword fighters ever." Danik scoffed. "Trust me . . . he's not that great. Also, he seems like he's got a secret."

Veron's brows narrowed. "What do you mean?"

"I asked about his past, and he avoided the question. He grew up in Searis but doesn't have a hint of a Tarphic accent, and he conveniently can't remember anything before he moved there. It sounds fishy if you ask me. He may have the potential to develop the origine, but I don't trust him."

"Interesting," Veron lingered on each syllable while nodding. "How about the mission overall? How did Lia do?"

Danik's face brightened. "She was brilliant—a natural leader. Her decisions were confident and good. King Constantine would have been dead if it weren't for her."

"I'm glad to hear it." After a beat, Veron pushed himself off the wall, his mouth settling into a hard line. "Also, Danik . . ."

The young knight stiffened.

"I heard about your drinking and gambling on the mission."

"It was only a couple of—"

Veron silenced him with a raised hand. "I don't want to hear it. You know the rules."

Danik's eyes dropped to the street.

"I put Lia in charge, so I'll abide by her handling of it, but know this"—he met Veron's eyes—"if you flaunt the rules again, you will answer to me. And I promise you, it won't end with just a warning."

Danik swallowed and nodded. "Yes, sir."

Veron pinned him to the wall with his hard gaze. After a moment of watching Danik squirm, Veron turned back to the crowd. "Now . . . I think it's time I meet with our new friend."

Picking up a sack from the ground, he slung it over his shoulder. The lumpy objects inside pressed against his back as he crossed the square. The crowd of people talking with Raiyn looked his way, one by one, their conversations halting.

"Raiyn, come with me. I'd like to talk."

Lia's eyes widened, but Raiyn seemed unaffected. "Yes, sir," he said, running a hand through his shaggy black hair. "I'd love to speak with you."

Raiyn and Veron left the square, walking down Rampart Way toward the river. The afternoon sun threw shadows on the street.

"I appreciate your daughter sticking up for me," Raiyn said, interrupting the silence.

"Hmm," Veron mumbled. "I hear you were in some trouble with Tarphan law. Tell me more about that."

"Did you speak with Lia yet?"

"I did," Veron said, "but I'd like to hear it from you."

"I, uh . . . I made a mistake." He looked at the ground. "I wanted my mother to live. She was sick, and I couldn't think of any other way."

"So you stole?"

Raiyn nodded. "It wasn't my place to take the medicine. There are other things I could have done instead."

"Like what?"

Raiyn turned his head. "I'm sorry?"

"What other things could you have done?"

"I, uh . . . guess I could have asked people for help. Maybe the apothecary would have taken pity on me and given me some."

"Do you think so?"

"Eh . . . probably not."

"I imagine they hear many heart-wrenching stories." Veron turned down a tighter alley. Buildings bordered each side, and the city wall rose ahead.

"People in Searis don't seem very keen to help others," Raiyn said. "I doubt that would have worked, but I know stealing was wrong. Maybe the right thing was to have let nature take its course. Maybe she was meant to die."

"Let her die?" Veron asked. "Even if you knew medicine could cure her?"

"I don't know," Raiyn's voice wavered. "I stole and almost ended up dead for it."

"Which would you say is more right," Veron asked, "letting your mother die when you know of a medicine that can save her, or stealing from someone to get the cure?"

"Uh . . ." Raiyn fell silent, the crunch of boots on dusty stone bouncing off the walls.

"Not a simple question, is it?" Veron asked.

Raiyn chuckled. "No, it's not. What would you say?"

"What's your mother's name?"

"Catina."

Veron stopped at the end of an alley where a ladder continued upward. He rested his hand on a rung. "Letting Catina die when you can stop it is wrong. But at the same time, stealing from someone else is wrong. Whichever you choose, you're going to live with the guilt and have to face the consequences."

"Do you think they should have executed me?" Raiyn asked. "They were only going to because they needed someone for the festival sacrifice."

"Different kingdoms have different legal responses. It's not my place to dictate what Tarphan does." Raiyn opened his mouth, but Veron continued before he could speak. "I agree they should have punished you. As soon as you legitimize stealing in questionable situations, the slope becomes slippery. But . . . I don't believe execution was the right consequence."

A memory of his childhood flashed through his mind—working the streets of Karad and stealing from anyone he could. He laughed, earning a curious look from Raiyn. "I know something of stealing to survive. It's a tough life."

Veron set his foot on the bottom rung and pulled himself, hand-over-hand, up the ladder. At the top, he set down the sack he carried and scanned the view.

To the left, the castle of Felting towered into the sky with spires and turrets dominating the air. Ahead, the Felavorre River rolled by, pushing a cargo vessel along at a casual pace. Two men sat in a small boat anchored by the shore. Their fishing lines dangled in the water as they waited. Veron turned around. The wall ended a short way downriver, beyond which Felting sprawled in all its glory. Streets, buildings, and squares meshed together in a web.

Raiyn grabbed the top of the ladder and pulled himself up. He turned to take in the view. "Wow, this is impressive."

"Yes, Felting is quite the city."

"These walls surround the entire thing?"

"Most of it, except along the river. They are formidable. I've helped defend them as well as breached them."

Raiyn turned, looking at the late-day glow cast upon the mountains.

"How did you learn the . . . power?" Veron asked, his hands braced on the top of the wall. "One generally doesn't just 'figure it out.'"

Raiyn was quiet until Veron turned to the young man. "My mother, she—she taught me some."

"How did she—"

"I don't know." Raiyn shook his head. "She never said."

"Was she able to use it?"

"No," he breathed after a pause. "She knew of it, though. I don't know how."

"Tell me about her."

"My mother?" Raiyn smiled. "She was pure love—made me feel like the most special boy in the kingdom. It was just us, but every day was a joy. She taught me herself—insisted I know about the world. We had little, and we needed little.

She did laundry to earn money until—" His words stopped short.

"Until she got sick," Veron prompted.

Raiyn nodded. "I did what I could, but . . . she didn't recover."

"I'm sorry. What about your father?"

Raiyn inhaled sharply. His eyes narrowed. "I have no father."

"Everyone *has* a father, but not everyone knows them."

"He's dead," he said, voice wavering.

"I'm sorry to hear that," Veron said. "You know, I grew up most of my life without a father, too. He left me when I was young. I thought he was dead until I found him again later in life. We had a short period to reconnect before he passed. Tell me about yours."

Raiyn's jaw tightened. "He was a thief, and a liar, and—" His words choked. "And he beat my mother." A glint of moisture formed at the corner of his eyes. "He was a lord . . . in Rynor." He sniffed. "I'm glad he's dead."

Veron nodded, glancing at the mountains. "My daughter thinks we should train you."

Raiyn jerked his head in Veron's direction and wiped his eyes.

"Others are more hesitant. What do you say? Is that something you would want?"

"Sir, I appreciate anyone who would look out for me. But . . . I don't even know who you are. No one will say anything. I gather you're a group who understands this hidden ability, and I understand you sneak around, fighting others and—"

Raiyn froze mid-sentence. His eyes grew, and his bottom lip quivered. "You're the—Are you the . . . Shadow Knights?"

A smile spread across Veron's face. After a moment, he nodded slowly.

Raiyn exhaled a nervous laugh. "I—Yes! Of course I want to join you! I'm ready to learn—to do anything you say."

"The life of a shadow knight is not glorious. We don't live lives of luxury. We don't live in opulent palaces. We're servants."

Raiyn's eyebrow raised.

"That's right, servants of Terrenor. We defend peace and help those who need it."

"I love that," Raiyn said. "I want to make a difference and defend others. I don't need luxury."

"It's dangerous too."

Raiyn paused, then spoke with a slight tremble. "I'm not afraid of danger."

"We put ourselves in harm's way when others can't or won't, and we don't always come back. My father died on a mission, fighting next to me. I will always miss him, but his death had purpose. That was the day we saved the people of Terrenor from Edmund Bale."

Raiyn's eyes grew.

Veron turned and cocked his head.

Raiyn's lip quivered. "My-my father. He—" His words stopped.

"Did Bale . . . kill your father, too?"

Tears formed at the corner of the young man's eyes. He nodded. "I'd rather not talk about it."

"I'm sorry. There's no need for me to press." Veron crouched and opened his sack, pulling out objects, a wooden rod, a ball, a heavy rock, and a metal training bracelet.

Raiyn sniffed and wiped his face again. "What is that?"

"I'd like to run through a few tests with you, if that's all right."

"What tests?"

"Balance, focus, reactions—things like that. We do it with all future knights."

A grin grew on Raiyn's face. "Future knights?" he said, clearing his throat. "Sure, I'm up for anything."

Veron opened the door to his room and entered. The sun had set, but a glow filtered through an open window along the far side. His and Chelci's bed filled the room. An arched opening led to another small space where he found his wife seated at a desk, facing away.

"Welcome back," Chelci said. She looked over her shoulder and smiled. A book lay open before her. "How did it go?"

Veron pursed his lips and exhaled through his nose. "Well . . . I think. He has a lot of natural ability. His instinct to use the origine kept creeping in, skewing his results, but . . . still, he was good."

"What about as a person?"

"Despite his sentence to be hanged, I like him. I see a lot of myself in him."

"I do too," Chelci said. "He seems genuine."

"I worry about bringing him in this late, though. Who knows how he learned and how he uses the origine now. It could take a lot of work to reform bad habits."

"But that can be done, right?"

Veron nodded. "What worries me most is . . . I feel like he's holding something back."

Chelci's eyes narrowed. "What do you mean?"

"There's something he's not sharing about his past—his mother, his father, how he's learned what he has."

"I sense that too, but . . . could we let him go with all that he knows?"

Veron sighed. "He'd decide on his own what's right and how to use the power."

"It would be risky to kick him away."

"It feels risky either way." Veron sighed. "I'd rather keep a close eye on him than let him go with all this knowledge."

He crossed the room to peer out the window. Although the sun had disappeared, red-and-orange clouds filled the horizon, holding on to the vestiges of light from the day. "William once mentioned something about a training program they used to put candidates through."

"Really?"

"They didn't tell them about the origine until they proved their character—sometimes years later."

"What did they do with them?"

Veron shook his head and turned back to her. "There was some sort of test—the Criterion, he called it. He never said what they did, but it was supposed to make sure the knights would follow the code. I wish we had something like that now."

"You're worried about Raiyn?"

"Well . . . yes, him too. But I was even thinking about our current knights. Sometimes I wonder if they're all the right sort. We should give it some thought as to what that might look like. In the meantime . . . I say we give Raiyn a chance. Do you agree?"

Chelci closed the book and stood. "I agree."

"Good, because, uh . . ." He pointed over his shoulder. "He's already downstairs with the others."

A picture on the table beside the bed caught his eye. Veron smiled as he picked it up. The simple wooden frame held a crude sketch of a man and woman holding swords in front of a castle. A simple smile turned up on both of the figures' faces. The words 'Father' and 'Mother' scrawled across the bottom with a small heart at the corner.

"Can you believe that was ten years ago?" Chelci rested her hands on his shoulders.

Veron smiled, remembering the early days when things seemed simpler. He set the picture back down and turned to his wife. "You saw Lia in action on the mission. You think the responsibility helped her? Do you think she's ready for more?"

Chelci's mouth curled in a playful smile. She pulled him closer. "I do. I also think . . . I missed you while I was gone."

Veron smiled in return, the beat of his heart growing stronger. He leaned forward and pressed his lips to hers. The sweet and soft kiss filled with a tender love that had waited in anxious anticipation. His hands wrapped around her back and drew her body to his. When their lips parted, he looked into her eyes. "Not as much as I missed you." They hugged each other tight, her head tucking into the crook of his neck. He breathed deeply, savoring the embrace, not wanting to let go.

When they pulled away, he held onto her hand and squeezed. "Give me a moment to speak with her. I'll be back."

"You had better be," she said with a sparkle in her eye.

Veron winked and left the room.

The courtyard was quiet as Veron descended the steps from the living quarters. One lone lantern hung on the wall, casting flickering light across the dirt space. He turned down the hallway, following the sound of conversation, and found the young knights in the common room. The crowd sat around a table, laughing at Danik, who stood, trying to balance a ball on his head. Lia sat next to Raiyn with Bridgette, Mason, and Shawn opposite them.

"Sir," Danik said, grabbing the ball, his laugh settling.

"Please, don't stop on my account," Veron said.

Danik slid into the seat next to Lia. "It's all right, sir. What can we do for you?"

"I'm sorry. I didn't mean to break up your fun." Veron turned to Raiyn. "We've decided."

The young man's chest lifted as he inhaled. He adjusted his arms on the table, seeming to search for a natural way to hold them.

"You may stay with us," Veron said.

Raiyn's shoulders relaxed. His mouth, along with Lia's, turned up into a grin.

"We will teach you to use and control your power and train you in the ways of the Shadow Knights."

Chatter filled the table as Bridgette, Mason, and Shawn offered congratulations.

"And Lia . . ." His daughter's face jerked to his, "will be your trainer."

Lia's eyes widened. "Me?"

"Yes," Veron confirmed. "You conducted yourself well in Searis, and we would like you to take charge of Raiyn's training. Do you feel up to the task?"

Lia glanced at Raiyn, her mouth hanging open. The young man smiled back at her. A grin formed on her face as she looked back at her father. "Yes, I can do this."

Veron masked the pride he felt. "Good. I will take my leave, then. Don't stay up too late."

On the other side of Lia, Danik's scowl stood in contrast to the festive mood of the room.

Veron rested his hand on the frame of the door. "And Lia?"

Her eyebrows raised.

"Training starts tomorrow."

23

TRAINING RESPONSIBILITY

Thump, thump. Lia pounded on Raiyn's door and waited. After a moment, she pounded again. Sounds of shuffling came through the door until it opened. A bleary-eyed young man stood before her with black hair sticking in all directions. Shirtless, his loose trousers hung to the floor.

Prepared to bark orders, Lia found her words stuck as she stared at his chest. His shoulders, arms, and upper body rippled with muscles. He ran a hand through his hair, squinting.

"Hey, Lia," he croaked. "What's wrong?"

"Get dressed." She cleared her throat. "Training begins now. Meet me in the courtyard." She turned and left, the image of his chest sticking with her.

The chill morning air hit her as she stepped outside. She yawned as she descended the stairs, remembering her early years of training. Danya or another knight would wake her early every day with a new torture planned. Eventually, the pre-dawn wake-up became easier to bear, but she never fully adjusted to it. *Now, I am the one planning the torture.* She chuckled to herself, nervous at the responsibility weighing on her.

After a few minutes, Raiyn shuffled down the steps. He dressed in a light gray tunic and plain brown training pants, both provided by the knights. "It's not even light yet," he said.

"You don't need light to train," Lia responded. "Come on. We start with a run."

Lia led the way out of the training center. Light from the moon splashed off wet stones, damp from rain the night before. She broke into a jog, not even glancing behind to make sure Raiyn stayed with her. A moment later, he came alongside, matching her, stride for stride.

"So, I get you for my trainer, huh?" Raiyn said.

"What? You disappointed?" Lia asked.

He laughed. "You seem . . . younger than the rest."

The hairs on her neck prickled. "You think I don't know what I'm doing because I'm young?"

"No! I'm sorry, that's not what I meant. I intended to say . . . it's impressive."

Her hairs settled. "Thanks." Lia turned left, down a dead-end alley toward a ladder.

"This is where your father brought me yesterday."

"Yeah, he likes it here. I do, too. But we're not testing with rocks and balancing balls today." Lia arrived at the ladder and scurried up first.

Raiyn arrived at the top moments later. "Are we running along the wall?"

Lia nodded.

"How far?"

She chuckled, nodding ahead to where the dark shadow of the city wall extended in an arc from the Felavorre River to the Benevorre far ahead. To her right, a faint light grew, peeking over the Straith Mountains.

She took off.

The battlements along the wall of Felting were wide enough for two people, but without a railing on the inside edge, it was too dangerous to run side-by-side. Raiyn's heavy footsteps sounded behind her. His breathing soon grew labored.

"So, what all sorts of training will we do?" Raiyn asked.

"*You* will do anything I tell you to do," Lia said, speaking over her shoulder. "Shadow knights are warriors—the best of the best. We're not that way because we have special abilities. We're the best because we train for it. You will run, climb, swim, carry heavy objects. You'll drill with swords, knives, bows, staffs, axes, any weapon you can get your hands on."

"Sounds fun."

"You say that now, but wait until your entire body is sore and you're exhausted. You get used to it though. The rest of the knights still train every day, but it's less grueling than at the beginning. Us young knights have had to do twice what everyone else has on any given day, and now . . . it's your turn."

"So how does that energy power thing . . . factor into all this training?" he said around breaths. "What exactly is it?"

The wall widened. Lia slowed to come alongside Raiyn. "We call it the origine. It's your source of energy, like a pool inside you. Every time you walk, jump, think, heal, breathe, or move, you use some of it. When a shadow knight taps into it, they can use as much of it as they choose."

"That's where my speed and strength have come from," Raiyn said, puffing. "I've been using the pool quickly, but when I stop, I'm exhausted."

"It takes a bit to recover after using it—especially if you use a lot at once."

"Can you . . . use it all?"

"Yeah. If you use it all, you'll find yourself weak and exhausted, unable to do the simplest things until you recover."

"So when you fight . . . you make sure you don't use it all."

Lia nodded. "If you're in a battle and use it up, you're as good as dead. That's one of the greatest dangers we face."

"Is that the only way you can die? You can . . . heal from injuries, right?"

"No, we can die. We're still mortal. Running out of origine is the greatest danger. As long as we have energy left, our bodies can do amazing things—heal from stabbings, arrows, poison, nasty wounds. My grandfather healed from five arrow wounds and a slit throat, and they say my mother came back from the dead. I'm not sure I believe that one, though."

"That's incredible."

"But if a wound is severe enough, or if our origine is depleted, we can't heal. We worry about head wounds, neck wounds, and any wounds where someone stabs and twists their blade."

Raiyn cringed.

"Damage in those cases is often more than our bodies can handle, even using a full supply of origine."

The Feldan Arena approached, below the wall on their left, and Raiyn's head turned. "Whoa! What's that for?"

The overgrown arena lay nestled in the dark. An oval shaped spectator area encircled a grassy open floor.

"Now? It's mostly for growing weeds. They used to host combat spectacles there to entertain the people, but it's been hundreds of years since it was used."

"What sort of spectacles?"

"Men fought animals. Men fought each other—usually slaves or prisoners."

"And people came to just watch?"

"Yeah. Feldor used to have a more barbaric side. I think the Shadow Knights helped reduce that."

The path ahead connected to the castle. Walls grew taller, spires rising into the sky. A short set of steps left Raiyn groaning as they ran up.

Above the steps, a pair of guards stood and collected their spears as the runners approached. Lia didn't slow, and the uniformed men tensed. She waved a friendly hand and nodded as they passed, leaving the guards staring after them.

Raiyn gaped at the castle, slowing while they skirted around it. "So how does the . . . metal thing work?" Raiyn asked.

Lia chuckled. "I'm not sure, to be honest. It's something about how our bodies conduct energy. I don't understand it. Avoid armor, bracelets, chains, shackles, or anything metal wrapping around you. If it happens, your connection to the origine will be gone."

"Do other people know about that?"

Lia sighed. "Back in the day, no one knew *anything* about the Shadow Knights: abilities, weaknesses, or even the fact that they existed. After my father killed Bale and saved Terrenor, everyone learned about us. We keep our training center a secret, and we don't advertise who we are. People don't understand our abilities, but there are rumors about our weaknesses. We train to avoid metal lassos."

"What's that?"

"In a fight, one person could sling metal chains or some object, trying to wrap it around us. If they're successful, a partner could be ready to move in for the kill."

The wall narrowed after they passed the far side of the castle. Lia resumed her place in the lead while Raiyn struggled along behind her, his breath growing more labored by the minute.

"With all this . . . running and stuff, do you . . . ever use origine?"

Lia thought back to her own training and how she used it to beat the others. "No," she said while wearing a half-grin. "We train to be skilled without using it as a crutch. The origine only accents our abilities, but we must refine them first."

"I feel like . . . I need it to . . . keep up with you." A breathy laugh punctuated his words.

While Lia jogged, a presence moved past her, taking the lead on the wall. Raiyn's blurred form darted ahead a short distance before he stopped and waited. A grin plastered on his face while Lia caught back up.

"Sorry," he said as she approached. "I was curious how it would—Whoa!"

Lia slowed to a halt and shook her head.

Raiyn steadied his hand against a merlon while bending over. His other hand waved in the air as if trying to maintain his balance.

Lia pressed a hand against his back. "Don't fall over the edge on me. You'd make me the first trainer to have her trainee die on day one."

"I'm sorry," he panted. "I . . . Hold on."

"Sit," she instructed, "back to the wall. Take deep breaths and close your eyes."

Raiyn sucked breaths in and blew them out. He leaned his head back against the stone and grimaced. "Ugh, this is worse than normal."

"It's because you were fatigued. You used from your pool of energy, which was already low from the running, depleting you more than you're used to."

Raiyn took several deep breaths, then blew out. "So don't use origine when you're tired then, huh?"

"You can, but you must control it. Listen to your body. It will tell you when you're getting low and require rest. How do you feel now?"

He laughed. "Tired. I'm not sure I can run."

Lia nodded. "Come on," she waved her hand. "We'll walk back."

.   .   .

"Wow," Raiyn said, running his hand along the wall of weapons. "You train with all of these?"

"I have," Lia replied. "Which ones do you know?"

"I've only used a sword before." He lifted a battle-axe off the wall and bounced it in his hands. "This one's heavy."

Lia chuckled. "Yeah, that's not my favorite." Bending over, she picked up two wooden swords that leaned in the corner. "We'll work on the other weapons soon, but let's start with these for now."

Raiyn accepted one by the hilt and swung it through the air. His frown gave away his displeasure.

"Don't worry. We'll get back to steel soon, but we always begin with wood." She handed him a metal bracelet, wrapping one of her own around her wrist. "And put this on."

"To keep us from accidentally using the origine?"

Lia fought to keep from blushing at her own training habits. "Accidentally . . . or on purpose. I should have given it to you before the run." She led the way out of the weapons room into the sunny courtyard. "Do you know your stances?"

"Um . . . how to stand with a sword?" Raiyn kept his hands by his hips with the sword tip pointed up. "Like this?"

"That's horn stance."

He raised his sword above his head, angling it behind him. "And this?"

"That's owl."

"That's all I know."

"Move your arms like this," she ordered, waiting for him to follow. "Elbows in. Knees bent. Good. That's snake. Now raise your chest and angle your sword down. Farther. That's shovel. And finally—" She raised her blade above her head, pointing the tip at him while bending her knees. "Arms farther back. Nice. That's dragon stance."

"I like it. Variety."

"Now, we practice the forms with the positura."

He cocked his head. "Positura? What does that mean?"

She laughed. "I have no idea, but it's what we do."

As if materializing out of invisible rooms, other knights showed up in the courtyard with their own swords.

"You mind if we join you?" Gavin said, stretching out his legs. Dayna, Ruby, and Bradley joined in a line.

"Not at all." Lia turned to Raiyn. "The positura is all combinations of the stances, flowing between the forms one at a time."

"All right." Raiyn's eyes shifted.

"Don't worry, I'll call them out each round," Lia added.

She stood next to Raiyn and brought her sword above her head. "Dragon-horn-shovel-owl-snake."

Lia led, moving one-by-one between the stances, her arms and legs flowing smoothly while her weapon danced. The knights behind her followed step-by-step. Raiyn fumbled each round. His sword jerked. He tripped over his feet as they shuffled to find the right place. He watched Lia the entire time, struggling to match his movement to hers. The minutes passed steadily, her body in tune to the endless moves she'd rehearsed for years. By the time she called out, "Snake-owl-shovel-horn-dragon," to complete the exercise, Raiyn's arms struggled to hold his weapon, and sweat dripped off his brow.

"Good," Lia said, relaxing her tense muscles after finishing the last combination.

Raiyn panted. His wooden sword drooped to the dirt while a weary smile played across his face.

"Nice work," Gavin said to Raiyn as the other knights walked away. He patted him on the back. "It gets easier."

Chelci approached while the others left. She extended a water skin. "Either of you like a drink?"

Lia grabbed the container and took a long drink. The air was already hot despite the sun having barely climbed across the sky. She smacked her lips and passed the skin to Raiyn.

"How did the morning run go?" Chelci asked.

Lia glanced at Raiyn, whose eyes grew as he tipped the water back. "Um . . . it was good," she said. "A nice starting point to build from."

"It was early," Raiyn said, chuckling as he lowered the water.

"Get used to that," Chelci said. "Training days are long and hard." She turned to Lia. "What do you have planned today?"

"We're about to spar so I can see where his skills start. Then I thought we'd try out a few other weapons—maybe the staff and axe. I thought we'd do some swimming and climbing later in the day."

Raiyn's eyes grew wider the longer she spoke.

"What about the boulders?" Chelci asked, one side of her lip curling.

Lia grinned. "Definitely the boulders. Then, I thought we'd do some stealth training after dark."

Chelci nodded. "Sounds like a full day." She looked at Raiyn. "Good luck."

"Uh, thanks." Raiyn leaned to Lia after Chelci left. "What's this about boulders?"

"You'll see. For now, let's see those sword skills."

Raiyn shook out his arms. He took in a deep breath and exhaled. Lia stepped back, giving space for movement.

"What should I do?" Raiyn asked. "I weigh twice as much as you, and I don't want to hurt you."

Lia held back a laugh. "We'll get to more specific drills later, but for now, see if you can hit me. Don't worry about the fact that you're older, taller, heavier, and stronger."

Raiyn gave a tight nod, his jaw fixed. He approached in horn stance, stepping toward her. His eyes flared the moment before he swung. Even with the bracelet on, Lia saw it coming before he moved.

He grunted, slinging his weapon, but she deftly moved,

leaving him hitting nothing but air. He tried again, going for the other side. Her sword deflected the blow as she stepped forward and knocked the strike out of the way. Her elbow rammed into his gut while his weapon flailed.

"Oof," he uttered, stumbling backward. He regained his footing, but his confidence had waned.

"Again!" she called.

He toed his way forward, his sword held vertically, accomplishing nothing but blocking his body.

What kind of stance is that? Raiyn didn't strike or move. "Are you just going to stand there or attack?" she taunted.

She blocked his half-hearted swing to her shoulder and another to her head. A few jabs fell short, but his confidence seemed to return.

That's better.

He circled, coming closer. When he reared back for an overhead strike, Lia stepped in. She deflected his blow before it could generate momentum, sending his arms to the side. With no sword or arms to defend himself, Lia hooked a foot around the back of his legs and pushed his chest. His arms flailed, his feet having nowhere to move. His sword dropped as his body tumbled to the ground. Lia extended the wooden tip of her weapon toward his neck, pinning him to the ground.

"I guess I've got farther to go than I thought," Raiyn said, his voice shaking.

Lia lowered her sword and replaced it with a hand to pull him up. "Don't be hard on yourself. Your forms are . . . all right. A few tweaks and they'll get there. Your reactions are decent. We need to work on your strategy and timing."

"I always figured whoever was the strongest was the one to win a sword fight."

"As my father says, 'A sword fight shouldn't be a long battle where you trade blows back and forth. It should be two or three moves intended to disarm your opponent.'" She held back an ironic laugh at the idea of her quoting her father. "Strength is good, but more important is quick thinking and anticipating your enemy."

Raiyn nodded.

Lia picked up the fallen sword and dusted it off. "For now, let's put these away and try a new weapon. Did you have any in particular you wanted to use?"

Raiyn's eyes twinkled. "How about a battle-axe?"

Lia nodded. "Sure, we can work with that."

24

———

PLANNED RETIREMENT

Veron ascended the last flight of stairs, his pulse rising despite his peak physical condition. A dark-red rug led down the hall. He padded along, nodding to the guards posted outside the king's chambers. His black Shadow Knights cloak left no room for doubt about who he was. Before he arrived at the door, it opened, the sound of a muffled cough preceding the king's exit.

"Your Majesty," Veron said, bowing his head as his father-in-law entered the hallway.

Darcius Marlow wiped the look of the anguished cough away and smiled. "Veron? A tad early, aren't you?"

"Yes, sir." Veron halted. "I had hoped to catch you before the meeting began."

"You have caught me, indeed." Darcius waved for him to follow. "Let's head down."

The Advisors Council chamber looked the same as it did when Veron first entered it seventeen years before. The oval table contained the same leather-backed chairs. No one gathered yet, and the king continued across the room. He passed through the center of three archways and strolled onto the balcony.

A light breeze stirred the air. With the sun blocked by the surrounding castle, the temperature felt pleasant. No clouds filled the sky, and the view was stunning. The Straith Mountains dominated the eastern horizon, and forest and rivers meandered to the north.

Veron found his gaze drifting to the far side of the balcony. He would never forget the night he confronted his friend, Brixton, as well as Edmund Bale there. Veron could have ended the tyrant's reign, but he went after Chelci instead. It took him a long time to live down the selfishness of that choice, but after he could see the big picture, he was thankful he had done it.

"What's on your mind, Veron?" Darcius asked.

Veron turned to the king. The man's shoulders looked heavy, his eyes kind. He leaned on a cane, his arm shaking.

"Would you like to sit?" Veron asked.

Darcius waved the comment away. "I sit all day." He motioned to the land out over the balcony. "The fresh air does me good."

"I'm worried about you, sir."

The king didn't reply.

"The job is stressful, and you seem to be . . ." Veron searched for the right word, "struggling."

Darcius nodded, quiet for a long moment. "I am," he said. "My doctor says the sickness has infected my bones—whatever that means. He gives me two, at most three, seasons to live."

Veron gasped.

"I told Chelci earlier today, but made her promise not to say anything. I plan to inform the Advisors Council in a moment."

"But . . . surely, there's something to be done."

"There is . . . rest and reduced stress. I intend to retire from the throne the finweek of suether—assuming I make it that long. That will give the council time to prepare a peaceful transition."

Veron's jaw hung loose. After a pause, he shook his head. "I'm so sorry. Is there anything I can do to help?"

Darcius smiled. "Keep taking care of my daughter and granddaughter. How is Lia, by the way?"

"She . . . uh . . ." Hundreds of distracting thoughts rushed through his head. "She's doing well. The mission to Searis, training the new recruit . . . she's risen to the challenge. She seems happier and has done well."

Voices chattered through the archway as people arrived.

"That's a relief," the king said.

"It is. And the new recruit . . ." Veron exhaled. "He's doing well. He trains hard and listens. I think he'll be a good knight."

Darcius nodded, then motioned toward the room. "Shall we?"

Veron followed. Four people had arrived and the rest approached through the open double doors. Veron selected a chair and sat, ignoring the others. His mind spun with the thought of Chelci losing her father, of himself losing his friend, and of Feldor losing its king.

What will this mean for the Shadow Knights?

"Welcome!" Darcius' voice jolted Veron back to the room. The king suppressed a cough and sat at the top of the oval table, a servant helping him push the chair forward. "Let's begin with departmental reports." He nodded to a man just older than Veron with blond hair and a tight vest. "Magnus?"

Magnus Hampton, the High Lord of Treasury, stood. "The treasury remains strong. We completed wiether's tax report and the rate reduction has not had the negative impact some feared." He looked pointedly at Quentin Cotterell, one of the king's advisors, who sniffed and glared. "Less tax rate resulted in more spending, which puts the treasury balance the highest we've seen since my father retired. We have a surplus."

"That's great," the king said.

"With those extra funds, perhaps, now we can supplant Feldor's defenses, as we've discussed," Geoffrey Bilton said. "Our border defenses are less than adequate, and the needed extra funds are long overdue."

"Let's not get too hasty, Geoffrey," Darcius said. "Defense is important, but the lighter forces have served us well. We haven't needed them since, well . . ." The king glanced at Veron. "Since seventeen years ago, when you, Veron, and I sat in this very room debating whether or not Bale would attack."

"You can't wait until you need an army to decide to outfit one," the High Lord of Defense grumbled. "You must plan ahead."

"A point well made," the king said. "Still, I'm sure everyone has an opinion about how to use a surplus of funds."

A throat clearing turned the heads of the room to where Marie Windridge sat with a stern face, her erect posture reaching for every bit of height she could manage.

"As High Lord of City Affairs, I insist a portion of these extra funds go toward city infrastructure," she said.

Mutters surrounded the table.

Suzanne Quigley, the other advisor besides Cotterell, nodded.

"Carriages break their wheels in potholes, the privies in the warehouse district need a new drainage system, and the trade merchants still push for a new bridge to span the Benevorre north of the city."

"No bridge!" Kennith Stokes yelled. The High Lord of Commerce pounded his fist on the table for emphasis. "We *need* travelers to come through the city. If we add a bridge outside the walls, we'll miss out on the commerce that comes from them passing through."

"What about the Felting Orphanage?" the advisor, Quentin said.

Windridge frowned. "What about it?"

"Last meeting, you mentioned how much it cost per week to run. If we were to close it, that would free up money for both defense *and* infrastructure."

The king raised a hand. "We're not defunding the orphanage. Yes, it costs, but taking care of the next generation is worth the investment."

Windridge nodded in thanks.

Veron's mind drifted as the high lords and advisors continued to argue. Darcius' health troubled him. *I wonder how Chelci took the news.* Darcius had been a great king, ruling with fairness and wisdom. He thought through various candidates and who would be able to fill the role, but none compared.

Eventually, the council's arguments segued into more departmental reports until everyone got a chance to share.

"I have one more topic to discuss," the king said, "but before I do, we have two representatives who have petitioned for an audience." He raised his hand to the guards at the door. "The first will be Ambassador Dane from Rynor."

Bilton frowned. "Good. Perhaps we can find out more about their incident."

"What was this?" the High Lord of Justice, Herman Miligan, asked.

"Maybe, if you'd showed up to the meetings, you'd know," the advisor, Quentin, muttered.

Miligan's face soured. "I was on my death bed, sick! I'm sorry I wasn't able to be here and infect you all!"

"Blue fever, right?" High Lord Stokes said sarcastically. "Isn't that the sixth time you've gotten it?"

Sniggers echoed around the table.

Miligan wiped spittle from his reddened face. "It's a wonder I'm still alive, much less able to walk around."

"We're very pleased that you're feeling better, Herman,"

Darcius said, his face genuine, "and we're glad to have you back. The justice system would be lost without you."

The guard returned and Athrian Dane stepped through the door. He stopped just beyond the doors and bowed low. The short and plump man wore clean, elaborately designed clothing, richly adorned with gold and vibrant threads that stood out against his pale skin. His thinning hair was combed neatly and set off by his short, gray beard, which was trimmed into precise lines, accenting his round face. His piercing eyes conveyed a sense of wisdom and experience.

"Ambassador, welcome!"

"Thank you, Your Majesty, high lords, and others. It is my honor to return before you."

"What news do you bring from Rynor? Anything further on the attack?"

His round face fell. "Some, but I'm afraid not much. As best as we can tell, it seems to have been an isolated incident."

Miligan interrupted, "I'm sorry but can someone fill me in on what this is about?"

"Rynor had an attack," the ambassador said, his strong words silencing muffled laughter. "Piryd . . . a remote village high in the mountains. No males from late teens through their fifties were anywhere to be found in the aftermath. Whoever led the attack burned and slashed the women, children, and elderly, along with the rest of the village. No one living remained."

Miligan leaned against the back of his seat, his features hardened and drawn.

Dane looked to the rest of the room. "King Tomas' troops scoured the area and found nothing."

"Was there anyone of note who lived there? Or any treasure to be found?" Magnus Hampton asked.

Dane shook his head. "It was mostly baltham miners that

made up the village, but the mine's production had grown sparse. Shouldn't have been anything worth attacking for."

"So, the attackers just wanted the people?"

The ambassador shrugged. "We don't know for sure, but that may be the case."

"What can Feldor do to help?" Darcius asked, his face kind and hands folded on the table before him.

"Are you here to petition for assistance from the Shadow Knights?" Veron asked.

Dane turned to him and shook his head. "Not at this time. The king thanks you for your help in Bromhill last season, but he doesn't feel it is necessary to request your presence with this."

Veron nodded as the ambassador looked to the others.

"I don't imagine it would be the case, but I wanted to check if anyone has heard any news that could be related." Dane scanned the room, but no one appeared to hold any helpful information.

"I don't believe we have heard anything here in Feldor," Darcius said.

"It's as I expected, but I still wanted to check. We do ask that you all keep your ears open, and if you hear anything, please relay the information to me. Our hope is that no other villages befall the same fate."

"We hope for the same," the king added. "Any news from your neighbors to the north?"

The ambassador frowned. "King Darian's army grows. Our expectation that they would have learned from Bale's overzealous aggression seems misguided. Norshewa wasted no time in replacing its leaders and growing its army again. There are rumors of—"

Veron's ears perked at the hesitation.

"Of what?" the king prompted.

Dane forcefully swallowed. "Rumors that they have discovered Bravian Fire."

Silence filled the room. Eyes flitted nervously around the table, and Veron's stomach dropped.

"Please tell me you're joking," Bilton said.

The ambassador shrugged. "Like I said, they're only rumors. Easy to spread to instill fear in an opponent. I've heard no first-hand accounts."

"But with a weapon like that . . ." Bilton faded out.

"We'd need thicker walls," Hampton said.

Bilton frowned. "We'd need a lot more than that."

"Any signs of advancement on your borders?" Darcius asked.

"Nothing yet, thankfully, but our army is mobilized and ready, camped outside of Molvaigh, just in case."

"Do you need assistance?"

A faint smile formed on Dane's lips. "Thank you, Your Majesty, for the offer. So far, our ranks are sufficient, but we may call on you if the situation changes."

King Darcius nodded. "Thank you for reporting to us, and please keep us informed about Norshewa and any further news about this Fire." He gestured toward the door.

The Rynorian ambassador left the room, escorted out by the guard, and in a moment, another man entered.

"Richard!" Kennith Stokes called out as he stood. "I didn't realize you were here."

Richard Gillbanks served as the Lord of Commerce for Karondir. In his mid-forties, the man wore a crimson doublet and black tights. His brown goatee came to a sharp point below his rounded chin. He smiled and shook hands with his High Lord in the commerce industry. "I just arrived, sir. Baron Devenish asked me to come personally to the council." Gillbanks' eyes flitted toward Veron. "We need some help."

"Welcome to the Advisors Council, Lord Gillbanks," King Darcius said, extending his hands. "How can we be of service?"

Gillbanks bowed. "Your Majesty, there is trouble in Karondir."

"Of what sort?" High Lord Bilton asked.

"A group of trade leaders threatens the merchant guild. They claim the merchants are holding back sales to punish them for raising their rates."

Stokes cocked his head. "Sounds like a task that would be right up your alley, Richard. You can't handle it within the department?"

"We have a problem—Isidro Cusk."

"Who's that?"

"Cusk leads the trade guild. It's rumored he killed the previous leader and threatened the families of some merchants. Everyone knows it's him, but we've never been able to catch him. We fear worse things are coming. Our local law enforcement has been ineffective. We're worried that, uh—" Gillbanks stopped, touching the hem of his doublet.

"Worried about what?" Bilton asked.

He sighed. "The Lord of Defense is afraid Cusk's influence has permeated the department."

Bilton rubbed his chin. "So . . . you need help. Do you want us to bring Feldor troops to Karondir?"

Gillbanks shook his head, his eyes flicking back to Veron. "We feel this may require a more delicate touch involving stealth as well as action."

"You want the Shadow Knights," Veron said.

Gillbanks swallowed and nodded. "Yes, sir. I know you serve throughout all four kingdoms and you can't appear to show favorites in where you spend your time. But . . . we could really use your help."

"A need is a need," Veron said. "The Shadow Knights would be honored to assist. Of course we will come."

The visitor's worried look melted into one of relief. "Thank you!"

"I will meet with the others. We'll send a pair of knights tomorrow."

Gillbanks' shoulders relaxed. "Very good. I will depart this afternoon and inform the baron. He will be most pleased. Thank you, Veron."

Veron nodded, and the visitor from Karondir departed through the door.

The king nodded to himself. "Very good. Very good." A moment of silence lingered. The advisors watched him, waiting. The king's mouth turned down. "I have one more topic to discuss."

Veron sighed. His heart going out to his father-in-law. Darcius pushed his chair back and stood, gripping the table in front of him.

"I would like you all to consider who is the right person to replace me."

A tense silence filled the room. The men and women glanced between each other, looking as if they couldn't determine if it were a joke or not.

"You're not about to die," Bilton said.

"Oh, but I am, Geoffrey," Darcius said. "I hope it will not happen too soon, but I intend to step down the finweek of suether."

Voices exploded around the room. Veron couldn't discern who spoke or what they said. The king raised his arms and brought them back under control. "Please, don't fight me on this. According to my doctor, I have a few seasons left to live, and I'd like to spend them in peace. I can leave the decisions about bridges and taxes to someone younger and healthier." He managed a half-smile.

"Your Majesty," High Lord Bilton said, "no one can replace you. The wisdom you've shown—your strength as a leader—"

The king chuckled, which devolved into a fit of coughing. "You don't need to ingratiate yourself to *me*, Geoffrey." He motioned around the table. "The high lords will choose the next king."

The shock on Bilton's face only lasted a moment. "Of course," he blustered. "I'm not trying to—I didn't mean—" He looked around the table. "I *do* think I would make an excellent king. I'm sure you all are aware of my record over the last—"

"Of course, everyone knows your record," Magnus Hampton said, cutting him off. "But don't we want someone who is younger and will live longer? I've been on this council for almost five years, and in that time—"

"Live longer?" Bilton said, his jaw agape. "What? Do you think I'm about to keel over?" He pointed at Magnus. "I could still take you in a duel!"

The shouting grew until Darcius raised both hands. "Please . . . this isn't how I want to spend today. You'll have plenty of time to make your cases, but I hope you *also* consider candidates from outside the Advisors Council."

Bilton grumbled.

"Your Majesty," Veron said. "High Lord Bilton *is* right, though. Finding someone as wise and fair as you will be difficult. I'm thankful for your time of service. I know I, as well as all of Feldor, are better for it."

The king smiled as a chorus of assenting voices echoed around the table.

25

MEASURED PROGRESS

Raiyn woke early of his own volition. After two weeks of early mornings and constant training, his body had adjusted to the schedule. A light breeze blew in from the open window, the cool suether morning a welcome respite from the hot days. The window in his room faced east, and the sky past the distant mountains lightened.

He sat up and tossed his legs over the edge of his bed. Stretching his arms above his head, he yawned and craned his neck to either side. His gaze drifted to his pillow, and his heart sped. The leather pouch he kept hidden behind the thin casing of fabric around his pillow poked out.

He stared for a long moment, then stood. Walking to the door, he slid the bolt in place, the nearly silent creak making him cringe. With the bolt ensuring no one would burst in, he returned to his bed and pulled the leather out from the compressed straw.

He jerked his head toward footsteps outside his door. Holding his breath, he listened as they passed his room and continued down the hall. He exhaled and turned back to the pouch.

Flicking the clasp open, he folded back the flap. The smell of worn leather replaced the scent of straw. A cold rush washed through his veins. *If they knew about this . . .* He peeked inside. *If they knew everything, they would never have let me in here.*

A knock rapped on the door, causing him to jump. "Just a second," he muttered, folding the flap in a hurry and stuffing it back in the straw.

"Time for training," Lia replied through the door. "Meet me downstairs."

He sighed, allowing his shoulders to relax. "Will do." His heart pounded as he dressed.

RAIYN PUFFED as he jogged up the street. The boulder balanced on his shoulder weighed him down, but his legs felt strong. Two weeks of constant training left him tired and sore, but he had seen the progress.

Rampart Way seemed to stretch forever as he lugged the final rock back to the training center. The walls lingered in the distance, but his heavy steps didn't get him there as quickly as he liked. *At least I'm not having to take breaks in the middle anymore*, he thought.

He pictured the hourglass waiting for him, taunting his effort, demanding he move faster. Raiyn pushed his exhausted legs as fast as they would carry him.

After the never-ending slog, he turned through the open door to the training center. His labored breath bounced off the tight hallway until he emerged into the courtyard.

Lia stood in the shade, chatting with Danik. She turned her head at his arrival. "All the way!" she shouted.

Raiyn trudged across the dirt and dropped the stone from his shoulder to the dirt. A dull thump sounded as the rock fell. He dropped to the ground, his legs finished, his body exhausted.

"Closer," Lia said, holding up a spent hourglass. "But not close enough. It needs to be faster next time."

"*Much* faster," Danik called from behind her.

Raiyn cried out, his chest rolling as he sucked in breaths. "I don't . . . think . . . I can . . . faster."

"Sure you can." Lia crouched next to him. "You've dropped your time a great deal already. Your sword work is much better. Your skill with the axe is impressive. You're making significant progress, Raiyn. You should be proud of yourself."

Raiyn allowed himself to smile. The compliments felt good, despite his exhaustion.

"We'll take a break from physical work for a bit—let you rest. You want to learn about the Shadow Knights' history?"

He groaned as he sat up, but then nodded. "Absolutely."

Lia extended a hand, pulling him to his feet.

Raiyn paused and rested his hands on his knees. "Whoa!" His vision spun, the ground tilting. He blinked several times, and the world settled again. "All right. I'm good."

She laughed. "Rest for a moment. I need to get something."

Raiyn didn't argue. Lia disappeared down the main hallway, leaving him alone with Danik.

"Lia told me about how you cheated during training," Danik said. "Your first day, on the run."

Raiyn's eyebrows lifted, his heart speeding. "I didn't mean to cheat! I was trying things out. I didn't know—"

Danik's laughter stopped him. "Don't worry about it. No one cares. It's tempting—when you're new, with plenty to learn."

"Do you all still train?" Raiyn asked, sitting on a bench against the wall.

"We do, but not as often," Danik said. "It's just to keep us on our toes now. By this point, we know everything we need to." He turned to Raiyn. "I can see the improvement you're making. I think you're going to make a fine shadow knight one day."

Raiyn smiled.

"I don't care what Lia says."

His smile faltered. "What do you mean?" Raiyn asked. "What did she say?"

Danik frowned. "I shouldn't have said anything. I'm sorry. Just . . . just forget it."

A sinking feeling grew in his stomach. "Did Lia say I wouldn't cut it?"

Danik sighed and chewed on his lip. After a pause, he turned to Raiyn. "You can't say anything to her about it. You promise?"

"Of course."

"She told her father you wouldn't be good enough—that we should let you go."

Raiyn's eyes widened. "What? When?"

"The other day. She said your training wasn't moving as quickly as it should, and she thought it was a waste."

"She just said I was making great progress—that I should be proud of myself."

"I think she's afraid to be honest." Danik shrugged. "Like I said though—I think you're going to do great. It will just take time."

Raiyn's forehead scrunched, and he stared at the dirt, debating the veracity of the information. "Well . . . thanks for telling me."

Lia reappeared in the courtyard and walked to a door containing a faded emblem of the Shadow Knights in the corner.

"You won't say anything, will you?" Danik asked.

Raiyn shook his head, his stomach twisting.

Danik nodded. "I'll leave you to your training. Good luck." The other knight shuffled away.

At the door, Lia fiddled with the lock for a moment before it opened, revealing storage shelves beyond. She closed it after grabbing a large book.

"What's that?" Raiyn asked when she returned.

Lia handed him the thick book and sat on the bench next to him.

Chronology of the Shadow Knights stared back with a dark cover and gilded edges.

"The book of the Shadow Knights?"

Lia nodded.

He opened it. "Code of the Shadow Knights," he read aloud. "Serve the kingdom above self and others. Consider the needs of anyone less fortunate than you. Never use your position as a knight to elevate your status in life." He skimmed down the page.

"It's the code we live by," Lia said.

"I like it." Raiyn frowned and read the last line aloud. "Never allow your abilities to be known?"

Lia scoffed. "Yeah, well . . . we keep some closer than others. You don't get kicked out for not being perfect. Trust me."

Raiyn flipped through the book. Pages and pages of history discussed the events of the early knights. He flipped a page at the end of the section and cocked his head. Torn edges of paper stared back. He ran his finger down the jagged line. "What's this?" he breathed.

"That used to discuss the origine," Lia said. "What it is, how it's used. Supposedly, it was pretty cryptic though, and not too helpful. Some of it's still there, but the early pages are gone."

"How long has it been like that?"

She shrugged. "As long as I've been alive."

"How do you learn, then?"

"Oral tradition—from my parents. They've written some notes on it." Lia flipped a few pages farther and showed where untidy handwriting had added lines to a blank section of pages.

She flipped a few pages more. "The last part is an archive of knights."

A set of boots crunching the dirt called his attention from the book. The older knight, Dayna, approached, wiping her hands on a rag. "I need help in the kitchen," she said. "Can you two peel potatoes?"

Lia frowned. "We're training."

"That's great," she said without emotion. "Come train him how to peel potatoes."

Lia sighed. "Fine." She took the book back from Raiyn and closed it up. "Come on, we can talk in there."

Raiyn followed as the women led across the courtyard and down the hall. His mouth turned down as he thought of Lia telling her father he wasn't doing well. *Does she really think that about me, or is Danik trying to get to me?*

A small fire burned in the hearth of the common room, making the room even hotter than standing in the baking sun. The small open windows set high on the walls didn't seem to bring much relief. Shawn, the only shadow knight he hadn't heard speak yet, bent over a pot hanging above the fire, stirring.

"Over there," Dayna said, returning to what appeared to be her work station at the counter while she pointed out a sack leaning against the wall.

Lia gathered a large bowl and two knives. "Grab those, will you?"

Raiyn picked up the sack of potatoes and lugged it to a table where he sat with Lia. He took a knife and followed Lia's example of cutting the peel off.

"Wow, it's hot in here!" Lia said, wiping her forehead with the back of her arm.

"Try working in here for a couple of hours," Dayna muttered. "You're lucky your training gives you an excuse to skip out on your regular rotations."

Raiyn finished his first potato, dropped it into the bowl, and grabbed another. A bead of sweat trickled down his nose. "So, you do plenty of running and fighting for training. What sorts of things do you do to work on the origine?"

"The priority is improving your physical ability," Lia said, sending a long peel of potato flying from a clean stroke with her knife. "Shadow Knights must be great warriors without the origine. All it does is focus your ability. Typically, we don't even teach its existence until someone is well into their physical training. You seem to be quite far along on both, though."

Raiyn frowned, remembering what Danik said about what she really thought.

"We'll get into more directed origine training soon, though."

"Like what?" he asked.

"Ha! I can't give away our training secrets."

"Why not? If I know ahead of time, does it defeat the purpose?"

Lia paused, appearing to think before resuming her work. "I guess not. We'll run through tasks like lugging heavy objects around the courtyard and running the city at night—when no one sees. You'll have checkpoints to do certain things in certain amounts of time, forcing you to practice using the origine."

"Sounds fun."

"We'll also practice a variety of origine-powered abilities like holding your breath, thinking quickly, healing. And—of course—you'll train to fight with it."

"Do the older knights still practice the origine? Like your parents?"

Lia paused, her knife dug halfway through a potato while she turned her head. "Some. My father practices—" She stopped.

"What?"

Lia sighed. "He says there's this thing called a 'pure connection.' He's been working on it for years."

"What is it?"

"It's supposed to give you unlimited power or something like that."

Raiyn raised an eyebrow. "Wow! That sounds awesome."

"No one knows if it's a real thing or not, though."

"It's real," Dayna interrupted from her place at the counter.

"And you know this because . . . ?"

"Have you never talked with your parents about it?"

"I've heard the story." Lia leaned closer to Raiyn and whispered, "Danik and I don't think it's real."

"Why do your parents think it is?" Raiyn asked.

Lia dropped a potato in the bowl and turned to Dayna. "You want to tell the story?"

Dayna set down a knife from where she'd been chopping an onion. "It happened the day Bale was killed. Veron had used all his energy. He was spent. Useless. Suddenly, however, he was filled with origine. When Chelci died, he—"

"*Supposedly.*"

"She died," Dayna insisted.

"You don't know," Lia muttered. "You weren't there."

"I believe what the Shadow Master says, and he *was* there."

Lia turned to Raiyn and bounced her eyebrows.

Dayna continued, "Filled with the pure connection, Veron poured healing into Chelci's body and brought her back to life."

"You can do that?" Raiyn asked. "Pass healing into others?"

"Not that I've ever seen," Lia said.

"No one has found the pure connection since that day," Dayna said, "but Veron continues to search."

"That sounds . . . incredible," Raiyn said.

"It sounds made up," Lia added. "Anyway . . . he works on that, and my mother works on the metal issue."

His forehead furrowed. "Metal issue?"

"You know how having a circle of metal around you takes away the ability to use the origine?"

"Oh yeah, that."

"My father doesn't have the same problem."

He paused, waiting for clarification.

"Metal dampens his abilities, but they're not gone."

"He can still use the origine?"

"It takes more effort to do anything, so he wears out quickly, but he *can* use it."

"And he's the only one?" Raiyn asked.

"As far as I'm aware." Lia dropped the last potato into the bowl, then wiped her forehead again. Her hair stuck in clumps against her face, her cheeks rosy. "Ugh, I can't take this heat!"

She took the bowl to Dayna and set it on the counter with the knives. "We're going to go out into the city to continue training." She turned to Raiyn and winked.

His brows pinched together. *What is she up to?*

"Come on," Lia urged. "Enough rest. It's time to work again."

26

COOLING OFF

Raiyn followed Lia down the hall and outside into the street. The harsh sun heated his skin, but the faint breeze brought a hint of relief. He looked down at his shirt, drenched from sweat. A whiff of his own odor turned his nose. He held his arms tight by his side and kept a decent length between him and Lia. *I hope she doesn't notice.*

Lia walked through the city, turning down various streets. Older men and women sat under awnings in front of shops, fanning themselves. Children played in the shadows of leafy trees.

"What are we going to work on now?" Raiyn asked.

Lia grinned. "One of the most important parts of being a shadow knight—being invisible."

"You mean stealth training? Like what we've been doing at night—sneaking in the dark, hiding on roofs and stuff?"

Lia turned off the street, where crumbling grassy steps sloped down. Lapping water sounded ahead, hidden behind overgrown dangling tree limbs. Raiyn pushed branches out of his way and ducked as he followed down the steps.

"If we're to sneak around successfully, no one can notice us."

"I doubt anyone is going to notice us hidden in these branches," Raiyn said with a laugh.

They arrived at the bottom of the steps. Moss covered stones formed a small square. Trees above blocked out the sun, providing a private area hidden from the surrounding city. Beyond the low-hanging branches, the Felavorre river flowed past, gurgling against the stones at the edge.

"If you're on a mission, hiding from someone, they may notice you by sight, sound, or . . ." she paused, turning to him, "smell."

Raiyn's shoulders fell, his cheeks flushing. "Sorry. I was hoping you wouldn't notice. I know I smell. It's the—"

Lia burst into laughter, stopping him. "I'm not talking about you! It's me. I reek!"

"What?" Raiyn's mouth fell. "I hadn't noticed."

A disbelieving grin grew on her face. "I don't believe you, but . . . thanks."

"I thought you use the city bathhouses?"

"We do, when we're here. A shadow knight needs to ensure their smell doesn't give them away—not always a simple task, given the time we spend traveling and hiding. I figure with the oppressive heat today, a rinse in the river is the perfect 'training' opportunity to prepare you for when it's needed."

She leaned in closer and mocked a whisper. "But really, I just wanted an excuse to cool off."

She bent down and unlaced her boots, removing them one by one. Raiyn did the same, his curiosity growing about what 'a rinse in the river' looked like.

When Lia tossed her second boot onto the ground, she walked to the water's edge, barefooted. She leaned over, dangling a foot into the water. "Oh! It feels great!"

Is she getting in with her clothes on? Raiyn watched out of the corner of his eye. *Is she getting in without her clothes on?*

She pulled at the hem of her shirt, ruffling it and pulling an arm through a sleeve. Raiyn's eyes widened, locked on her while he tossed his boot down.

Lia paused, glancing his way. She lifted her eyebrows and motioned her finger in a circle. "Turn around!"

His eyes grew even wider. "I'm so sorry!" He spun, covering his face despite looking in the opposite direction. Rustling of clothes made his ears strain and neck redden. After a moment, a splash preceded drops of water hitting his feet.

A giggle sounded from the river. "All right, your turn."

He turned, blushing. Her clothes lay haphazard on the ground. A body length into the river, her head bobbed above the water.

"I'll face away while you get in," she said, her head turning.

Raiyn stood, frozen. He glanced around one more time, confirming no one was around. His damp shirt stuck to him as he pulled it off. It took a moment to extricate himself from the tangle of fabric before he tossed it to the ground. He paused at his trousers. *Did she even take off . . . ?* He used his toe to brush through her pile of discarded clothes. *No sign of underclothes.* He sighed with relief. His trousers took only a moment to remove. He dropped them on the ground and moved to the edge of the river, eager to get under the water.

The cool river sent chills up his bare leg as he stepped in. "Oooh, it's cold."

Lia's laugh bounced away from him. "Don't be a baby. Get in."

Raiyn brought his second leg in and took a step deeper. The water was up to his mid-thigh. He tiptoed deeper.

"Are you in?" Lia asked.

"Almost. I'm working on it." He stepped farther and gasped.

The water reached the hem of his underclothes. "I didn't expect it to be so cold."

"Dunk yourself. It's easier that way."

"I'm getting there."

Lia sighed. "Well . . . I'm turning around either way. So, if you're—"

Raiyn submerged himself under the water. The river covered his upper body and soaked his hair. With a split-second delay, a rush of cold washed over him. He flung his head out, pressing his hair back and gasping for breath. "Whew! That's—" He breathed. "Ah! That feels good!" He opened his eyes, a grin plastered on his face. He took a step back, keeping plenty of space between them. The depth left the upper half of his chest out of the water.

Lia held a mocking smile. "Cold? You . . . are weak."

His jaw fell before she burst into laughter. While Raiyn stared back, she dunked her head underwater. She stayed under for several seconds, her hands tossing her hair around. When she emerged, her soaked hair fell across her face in long strands. He glimpsed her eyes peering from behind the brown tendrils.

They both giggled. "That's a good look on you," Raiyn said with a smile.

Lia dunked her head again and smoothed her hair behind her before she came up. "That's better," she said, blinking her eyes.

Raiyn leaned his head back, allowing himself to feel the gentle pull of the river running over his body. The chill of the water didn't feel as shocking anymore. The heat he'd battled all day faded in his memory. "This feels wonderful."

Keeping only her head and graceful neck above the water, Lia lifted an arm across the surface and scrubbed it with her other hand. Mesmerized by her bare skin, Raiyn followed suit.

He scrubbed his arm, feeling the thick grit of sweat and dirt slough off.

"What's that?" Lia asked.

"What's what?" Raiyn traced her pointing finger and glanced at the side of his chest where a dark patch of skin stood out. "Oh, my birthmark. I've had it since I was born. With the five sides, it looks kind of like a star."

"That's pretty cool."

"I guess so. My mother always said, 'You're marked, Raiyn, destined for greatness.'"

"Destined for greatness." Lia smiled. "I like that."

"So, uh . . ." He cleared his throat, thinking of how to change the subject. "Do you do this often?"

Lia shook her head. "Like you said, we typically use the bathhouse."

Raiyn raised his legs under the water and scrubbed them with both hands. "On a hot day like this, I'm surprised this place isn't filled with people."

"Kids like to play down at the docks. They run and jump off the end, splash around a moment, then climb up the ladder and do it all over again."

"Is that what you did, growing up?"

Lia nodded. "Sometimes it was nice to have some privacy though, so I'd come here." She smiled. "It's been a few years, but my brother and I used to come—"

"You have a brother?" Raiyn asked, halting his scrubbing and leaning forward. "I didn't realize. Where is he?"

Her eyes widened, and she stopped speaking. "I—uh . . ." Her face fell, silence settling heavily over the water. "I'd rather not talk about him."

Raiyn's curiosity scrambled unsuccessfully to fill in the blanks. "I had a sister," he said after a pause.

Her head tilted.

"Amelia was her name—or was going to be. The midwife

kicked me out of the room when she was born. I was four. My mother told me she died minutes after birth—that her lungs gave out."

Lia's eyes were soft and caring. "I'm sorry. I've heard of that happening to many people. I can only imagine—"

Raiyn silenced her with a shake of his head. "I listened at the window. I remember Amelia's cries. I heard the midwife's gasp and my mother's cries of joy turn to horror. They whispered—something about her face. It wasn't right. The midwife was going to take the baby and run, to hide her . . ."

Lia leaned forward, hanging on the moment of silence. "What happened?"

"My father showed up. They shouted, argued." Raiyn inhaled, his bare chest expanding. He pursed his lips and dropped his gaze to the flowing water. "My mother screamed and I ran. She lied to me about what happened. She didn't want me to know that—" His words choked up.

Lia's hand touched his arm under the water, soothing him.

"I didn't want to remind her of the horror, so I never asked about it again." Raiyn pulled his arm free and scooped water to wash over his face.

"What was your father like?" Lia asked.

Raiyn paused for a moment, scrambling through his memories. "I'd rather not talk about him."

They exchanged wistful smiles, then turned their attention toward the center of the river.

"Do you think I can do this?" Raiyn asked, his heart thumping.

"Do what?"

"Become a shadow knight. Serving others, putting their needs first, and all of that. I'm not sure if I'm cut out for it."

The water rippled as she turned to him, her forehead furrowed in lines. "Why do you say that?"

Danik's words played through his mind. "I'm not sure I'm

getting any better. You all are these elite warriors, and I can barely keep up. I wonder if I ever will."

Lia chuckled. "I'm sorry," she covered her mouth.

Raiyn frowned, folding his arms across his chest.

"I'm not laughing at you," she added. "You've only been here two weeks, Raiyn. I've been doing this all my life. Danik and Mason have been here for four years. Be patient with yourself."

"I don't want to let you down."

"You won't let me down. At two weeks, your skills are *far* past anyone I've seen or heard of before. You're going to be great. Give it time."

Raiyn nodded. "All right. Will you let me know if I'm not cutting it, though?"

The side of her mouth curled up. "Sure. I'll let you know."

Lia ducked her head under the water again. When she emerged, her arms and bare shoulders peeked above the water while she positioned her hair. Raiyn averted his eyes, the image of her bare collarbones fixed in his mind.

"We should get out and head back. I asked Bradley to go through a session on archery with you this afternoon. He's the best."

Raiyn groaned.

"What is it? You don't like archery?"

"No, it's not that," Raiyn said. "I just realized we have to put those sweaty clothes back on."

Lia laughed. "Yeah. Had I planned better, we could have brought something to change into."

Raiyn turned away, facing outward. "You can go first. Let me know when you're dressed."

His ears burned as he listened to her exiting the water and collecting her clothes. A warm feeling crept up his neck. He shook away the thought of her standing behind him and trained his eyes across the river. A bird swooped into the water and emerged a moment later with a fish in its mouth. He smiled. *Four weeks ago, who would have thought I'd end up here?*

XANDER SLUNK BACKWARD, deep under the building's awning. It was hot and bright in the middle of the day, but the shade left him obscured. A young man and woman walked up the street, laughing. Both had wet hair and water dripping down their clothes. The young man with the black hair didn't look famil- iar. The girl, however— He grinned. *I'd recognize her anywhere.*

RAIYN CLOSED the door to his room and placed a lit candle on the table next to his bed. His legs groaned as he lowered his body to the mattress. *That must be from carrying the boulders . . . or running the castle steps over and over.* He swiveled his torso from side to side, stretching his back and his arms. He felt stronger, though. The runs grew easier. His speed with the sword grew faster, but the axe had become his weapon of choice.

He thought back through Lia's words. *Does she really think I'm doing well? She sounds encouraging, but maybe she's just trying to be nice.*

A light knock drew his attention. "Come in," he said.

Danik poked his head into the room.

"Oh, Danik . . . hello."

"Hey. Just wanted to see how you're doing."

A smile pulled at Raiyn's face. "Thanks, I'm . . ." He consid- ered the state of his body. "Tired and sore, but feeling stronger."

"Good. For me, it was around that two-week point that I felt a difference. It will keep getting better."

"I'm enjoying the chance to focus on it without other distractions . . . like chopping lumber."

Danik was quiet for a moment, his mouth forming a tight line.

"Is something the matter?" Raiyn asked, an unsettled feeling building in his stomach.

Danik paused again, the tension growing. "I found your leather pouch."

Raiyn's heart stopped. His head turned toward his pillow until he caught himself.

"That's right. In your pillow."

He fought to keep from panicking and returned Danik's gaze. "You looked through my stuff?"

"*Your* stuff? It doesn't really belong to you, does it?"

"Did you, uh . . . open it?"

Danik nodded. "And I know enough to understand what it means."

Raiyn filled his lungs with air as his pulse pounded in his head.

"Don't worry," Danik said, his face softening. "Your secret's safe with me." He flashed a smile.

The tension in Raiyn's body faded. "I was, uh, planning to, um—"

"Everyone's got something they're hiding," Danik interrupted, "a secret . . . an unknown desire. I'll have your back."

"Thank you, Danik." Raiyn breathed aloud. "You don't know how much that means."

"It's nothing."

"I'll probably tell Lia. I think she'd understand."

Danik's face twisted. "I don't know. I suggest keeping this one close."

Raiyn sighed. "You may be right."

Danik grabbed the door handle. "I'll let you rest. More intense training coming tomorrow, I'm sure."

"Hey, Danik," Raiyn said, causing the other young man to

stop closing the door. His pulse sped again. "What do you think about Lia?"

"Lia? She's, um . . . she's good. Why?"

Raiyn allowed himself a grin. "I notice most Shadow Knights don't have . . . attachments, but I hear it's allowed. Do you, uh, know how she feels about that?"

Danik's eyes narrowed, and Raiyn squirmed. "Why do you care?" Danik asked, his voice carrying a surprising edge.

"I was just curious."

"You think she'd be interested in you? You've barely been here for two weeks. You can't just saunter on in here and lay claim to anyone you want."

Raiyn held up his hands. "Danik, I'm sorry. I didn't mean any offense. I'm not . . . claiming anyone. I simply wondered about her. It's stupid though. Sorry . . . Forget all about it."

A forced smile returned to Danik's face. "I'm sorry for snapping. I guess I can be protective of our knights. When attachments form, it distracts from our purpose—'for the good of the kingdom.' You know?"

"Of course," Raiyn said. "I won't bring it up again."

Danik nodded. The grim line returned to his lips as he closed the door.

27

KNIGHTS AT WORK

The walls of Karondir grew as Veron's horse trotted closer. Grass and clusters of grazing cattle filled the fields outside the city. Veron's mind turned to the siege engines, tents, and rows of soldiers he encountered there years before, but the ripe smell of manure brought his mind back.

"Sir," Shawn said, riding beside him, "Thank you for choosing me for the mission. I know some others are older, and I appreciate the vote of confidence."

Veron turned back to the city walls. "Your skill with the sword is exceptional, and your control over the origine is impressive. I'm lucky to have you here, and I think us two should manage just fine."

"Do you think we'll have to fight?"

"That depends on Isidro Cusk," Veron said. "We'll learn what we can then go from there."

Guards stationed at the gate eyed them as they trotted through but didn't ask questions. The rough brown traveling clothes gave the impression of country farmers and helped them keep a low profile.

Veron chuckled. "That was easier getting in than the first time I came here."

Shawn raised his eyebrows. "What was different?"

Veron pictured the dark watery tunnel under the walls, where he had almost drowned in a desperate attempt to stop Bale. "Well, it was wetter for one thing."

Veron led the way through the city, dismounting in front of the central keep and tying his horse to a post. The guards stationed at the tall, metal doors stopped them that time.

A young man leaned a spear in their path and spoke with a voice that seemed falsely deep. "State your business!" His helmet rested askew, too large for his head.

"We're here to see Baron Devenish," Veron said in a friendly manner. "Tell him Veron Stormbridge wishes to speak with him."

The young guard's eyes grew. He nodded to another by the door before turning back to Veron. "Yes sir, Mr. Stormbridge. We'll get him right away. Do you mind waiting here for just a—"

"Veron Stormbridge?" a distant voice called from behind the cracked door.

The guard who had just slipped through the opening to locate the baron mumbled a reply and backed through the opening, pulling the door wider.

The wrinkled form of Baron Devenish shuffled out, a broad grin growing on his face. He flung his arms open and greeted Veron with a friendly embrace, saving a more professional handshake for Shawn.

The baron hunched as he stood, his back containing a significant curve that seemed to be held in place by the velour suit hugging his form. His thin hair was white, and his skin sagged. "It's been too long. Please, come in." He waved his hand toward the door and led the way.

The tall ceiling of the room inside stretched to the far end of the keep. The baron led them to where a group of people gathered. A familiar man in uniform sporting a sword at his hip grinned in their direction.

"Captain Boyd?" Veron extended a hand to the man. Images of rescuing the soldier from the dungeon after Bale's men took over the city popped into his head.

"*Lord* Boyd now," Devenish said.

"That's right." Boyd smiled. "Lord of Defense for Karondir."

"Congratulations," Veron said. "It's good to see you again."

"And this is Lord Gillbanks of Commerce," the baron added.

Veron turned to the man as he approached. "Of course. It's good to see you again, Lord Gillbanks."

Veron shook hands, then introduced Shawn to the group. "We've come about the trade issue."

The baron's face turned down. "I appreciate you coming so soon."

"Tell us what you know about Cusk."

Devenish looked between the other men, then replied in a lowered voice. "Isidro Cusk has led a group of traders for years. He skims from the top, taking from anyone he can."

"No one can pinpoint an actual law he's broken," Gillbanks said. "People are too afraid to turn on him lest he make good on his threats, so he skirts by. He's . . ." He looked at Boyd. "He's not someone you want to mess with."

"You'll understand when you see him," Boyd added.

"It's strange because we've never had issues until recently," Gillbanks said. "It's like his ambition came out of nowhere."

"And you think your men may be bought off?" Veron asked.

Boyd sighed. "I feel it's likely."

The Baron continued, "Cusk made up accusations about the merchant guild, saying they're cheating him out of money. A week ago, a guild leader, Lohen, wound up dead, slit from navel to neck, hanging from a hook on the city wall. Everyone knows it's Cusk, but . . . there's no proof. We could use your help."

Veron nodded. "Of course. Can you show us where he lives?"

Veron crouched in a shadow where a wall blocked the light from the street lantern. Across the street, a gray stone structure rose from the surrounding buildings, its towers peeking over the high city wall. Archways connected stately columns in front of a large door where two guards posted. Another man paced along the far side of the house, disappearing in a moment around the corner.

Above the door, a covered balcony extended away from the building. The faint light of a lantern glowing through a window proved someone was home and awake, despite the late hour.

"What do you think?" Shawn asked. "The balcony?"

Veron nodded. "I think so."

"We could climb up the side of the building." Shawn pointed.

Veron lowered the young knight's hand. "Don't be so obvious. The balcony's not that high. We can jump for it."

Pulling the hood of his Shadow Knights cloak, he stole across the street. He crouched behind an empty carriage, Shawn stopping beside him. Through a wheel spoke, he watched the door. The guard at the house hadn't moved. Veron crept along the ground, keeping the vehicle between them until he made it to the alley.

"So, we run across the alley, then leap to the balcony, right?" Shawn whispered, leaning into Veron.

"That's the idea," he whispered back. "Once we're—"

Veron held his breath. One of the door guards walked past the edge of the portico and peered down the alley, mere strides from where they hid. Veron's arm, motionless, resting on a carriage wheel, tensed. After a moment, the man turned and left in the other direction.

"What do you think that was about?" Shawn whispered.

Veron's eyes narrowed. He nodded forward. "He's checking the streets." Veron leaned back to glance down the main road. *Empty.*

A click sounded ahead. The door to the house opened and a man exited. He nodded to the guards before tossing a covering over his head, but the momentary glimpse from the lantern illuminated a dark scar running along his chin. The guards made to follow until the man held up a hand, indicating they should stay put.

"That's him," Veron whispered.

Cusk was a monster. A full head above his guards, his shoulders bulged underneath a black tunic. Daggers tucked into sheaths at each hip, and his legs powered his massive frame forward as if he were a battering ram.

Veron leaned back as the man rounded the corner and proceeded down the dark alley. With his face covered, a sneer was the only visible feature.

"Let's follow," Veron said, rising as Cusk faded into the darkness.

"Are you sure that's a good idea?" Shawn's voice contained a slight wobble. "Did you see him?"

"Don't forget who we are," Veron said, already moving. "Where is he going in the middle of the night? This is what we're looking for. Besides, what's he going to do to us?"

Their soundless feet traveled the alley, dodging pebbles and slivers of light. They turned several corners, keeping to the shadows and maintaining a distance. The buildings showed higher levels of disrepair the farther they traveled from Cusk's place, and before long, the entire neighborhood looked deserted.

A faint light ahead grew more pronounced. Soon, Cusk

stopped where a man held a lantern, standing in the center of the ruins of an old structure. Some walls and most of the roof had collapsed—likely remnants from Bale's attack years before.

The mouths ahead moved, but Veron couldn't make them out. He pressed against the remaining wall of the building, straining his ears.

"I wish I could hear anything," Shawn whispered.

Veron held his finger to his lips. He strained his ears, but the origine's effect on listening didn't amplify as much as he needed. He glanced up and scouted the roof as an idea formed. "Wait here," he whispered.

He jumped, fueling his legs with origine and using his hand to guide his body as he flew into the air. The slate roof held, and he padded his way to a hole. Veron leaned over the space, finding Cusk and the other man below him.

"Are you sure?" Cusk asked. "Even after Lohen's death?"

The other man shook his head. "They're afraid, but . . . not enough, I guess."

Cusk growled and paced. "What do you think, Ganz?"

"I think they'll cave, but it may take a few more examples."

Cusk appeared to think while he walked.

The man called Ganz continued, "The rates are fair, sir. You need to stick with it."

"I don't care if they *are* fair," Cusk said, his voice rising. "They shouldn't be holding back from me, and Lord Gillbanks should support me."

"What do you want to do next?"

Cusk tapped his chin. "Maybe we need to put some pressure on Gillbanks."

"Gill-banks," a raspy voice echoed in the darkness, slowly pronouncing each syllable.

Veron jerked his head toward the gloom where the sound came from as the men below did the same.

"Who's there?" Cusk asked, his question sounding like an order.

Gravel crunched. Veron heard his own breathing. Ganz extended his arm, raising the lantern to no effect. A small red glow materialized in the darkness ahead. Cusk took a step in that direction as a robed figure melted out of the shadows, passing the crumbled walls of the building.

Cusk exhaled with a heavy breath. "I told you not to contact me. I'm doing my part, but causing chaos takes time and careful planning." His words held an edge. "Not to mention that I lose business, the worse things get."

The man wore loose clothing, draping from his head to his feet. The fabric matched the long strands of gray hair that fell to his chin. A swath of linen wrapped his neck, tucked behind a short, thick beard. A thin necklace draped against his chest with a faintly glowing red crystal.

"I paid you handsomely, which should *more* than compensate for any temporary dip in business," the man hissed.

"Uh . . . who is this?" Ganz's voice betrayed him by shaking. "What's going on?"

"Who I am is unimportant," the man replied. "But I'm losing patience."

Cusk raised his hands. "What is it that you want? More bodies? More fear? Why do you want this city in chaos?"

The man in gray laughed, a crooked grin forming. "I don't care about what happens in this city."

Cusk tilted his head.

"What I want is for the *Shadow Knights* to show."

Veron fought a gasp and nearly lost his grip on the edge of the roof.

"Shadow Knights?" Cusk scoffed. "That's what this is about? I'm not—" He glanced at Ganz. "We're not *summoning* them. And I don't want their kind here. This deal is over."

The man in gray's face turned hard. "You don't have the luxury of backing out."

"We're done. Get out of this city. If I ever see you again after today, you'll regret it."

The man in gray pulled a curved blade from a sheath. Something between a knife and a sword—it extended the length of his arm. The weapon angled in a concave shape with jagged spines along the back. He stepped forward, his body remaining casual as he held the blade up. "I offer you a chance to keep your lives. You will keep doing this until the Shadow Knights show."

Cusk chuckled. "Keep our lives, huh?" He stepped aside from Ganz and rose to his full height. His shoulders squared, and his chin lifted. He pulled two daggers from their sheaths and glared at the man with his arms bulging. "That's a bold statement. Do you know who I am? Do you know what I do when people cross me?"

Ganz pulled a bludgeon off his belt, a smirk plastered across his face.

Cusk stepped closer to the other man. "Your knife doesn't scare me. I could still cut you up with a broken leg and a missing arm. Don't you dare come here and—"

A hideous crack filled the air, and the flame of the lantern sputtered. A blood-curdling shriek bounced off the walls of the buildings. Veron blinked, trying to determine what happened. When the light returned, a ghastly scene unveiled before him. Cusk lay prone, screaming. His left arm rested on the ground, severed from his body but still holding a dagger. Blood ran down his side where his upper arm ended in a stump. He clutched his leg with his remaining arm. The appendage bent unnaturally just below the knee, a hard bulge trying to break through the surface of the skin.

Cusk's scream rang through the night, echoing off the stone walls along the deserted street.

Veron's pulse raced. The injury was gruesome, but what bothered him was the ability of the mysterious man. *No one could do that, unless . . .*

"Let's see it, shall we?" the man taunted, holding his arms out in mock invitation. His curved knife dripped red from the long blade. "I'd like to see you cut me up with a broken leg and a missing arm."

Ganz backed away, mumbling and shaking. He dropped his bludgeon and lantern, then turned and ran.

The man in gray rushed ahead of him in the blink of an eye. "Where do you think you're running off to?"

Ganz skidded to a halt. "I-I-I don't—" His voice sputtered. He turned and tried a different direction, but the man appeared in front of him again.

The man in gray held his knife out. "What will it take for the Shadow Knights to come?"

"P-p-please, I-I don't—"

A fresh wail from Cusk drowned out his words. The man in gray moved closer, but Ganz's feet looked stuck.

With his pulse pounding, Veron sprang off the edge of the roof. His heart jumped in his throat as he fell. The origine strengthened his legs as he hit the old stone floor. A loud crack shattered the air from the broken tiles under his feet. The men in the room spun, staring. Veron lowered his hood and pulled Farrathan from its sheath over his shoulder. "Leave him alone," he growled, enunciating each word. "You seek the Shadow Knights? Then you seek me."

The man in gray's eyes grew wide. He approached Veron with a malicious grin growing on his face. The crystal around his neck grew brighter, filling the ruins with a red glow.

No longer with any attention on him, Ganz ran. He fled into the darkness and didn't look back. The mystery man didn't seem to care.

Cusk remained on the ground, groaning and whimpering.

As the man in gray moved past him, he ran his curved knife across the man's giant neck. A moment of gurgling led to silence as Cusk's body fell back, limp.

"Shadow Knights," the man hissed. "Where are the rest of you?"

"Here," Shawn said, stepping from behind the wall and entering the red glow.

"Stay back, Shawn," Veron warned, bending his knees and moving into dragon stance.

"How many of you are there?" the man asked.

"Don't answer," Veron ordered without averting his eyes from the man. "Who are you?"

"My name is Talioth. And you?"

Veron hesitated before answering. "Veron Stormbridge."

Talioth stiffened. His eyes twitched as if searching the recesses of his memory.

"It's good to meet you, Veron Stormbridge."

"I lead the Shadow Knights. What interest do you have in us?"

"You have something I want."

Veron gave a short laugh. "We have nothing. If it's money you seek," He nodded to Cusk's body, "you should have talked more to *him*. The Knights keep nothing of value."

Talioth's mouth curled at the corners. "Oh, you *do* have something of value, *Veron*. And unless you want to end up like this man, you'll tell me where the rest of the knights are."

Veron paused, his brows pinching together. "How did you . . . do what you did?"

Talioth's grin broadened. "Be more specific."

Veron swallowed, his heart pounding. "How do you know about—" He shut his mouth.

Talioth's head tilted the opposite direction. "The origine?"

Veron gasped. "Is that what you used? How did you learn?"

Talioth laughed, a rumbling, throaty chuckle that bounced in the night. "There's so much you don't know."

Veron's mind raced. *What is going on? Who is this man?* He glanced at Shawn. The younger knight posed with his sword ready. "Shawn . . . Now!"

Veron flexed his muscles, pulling from deep inside. He moved as fast as possible, intending to circle around the man, pinning him from behind with his sword. Instead of the warm, tingling feeling of energy, a sinking sensation rushed through his body. He stumbled. His body tried to move faster than his legs could manage, and he tumbled to the ground, Farrathan clanking at his side.

He raised his head. His vision spun, mind muddled. Shawn had remained on his feet, but the other knight stood rooted in place, staring at his arms. "What's wrong?" Shawn asked.

An evil laugh turned Veron back to Talioth, the red crystal around his neck glowing stronger than ever. "What's wrong?" he asked in a mocking voice. "Are your powers not working?" His boots scraped on stone as he walked forward.

Veron scrambled to his feet and grabbed his sword, his breath shaking. He moved backward, keeping distance between him and the man. Desperate attempts to use the origine only succeeded in sweat beading on his forehead and his breath growing ragged.

With a flurry of movement, Talioth blurred. He spun around Shawn, then disappeared.

Veron's arms jerked behind him. His sword hit the ground. He struggled against an invisible force, but resistance was futile. A kick sent him sprawling forward again, his face skidding on the stone. With his cheek pressed to the ground and his arms locked behind him, he spat to clear the grit out of his mouth. He made it to his knees, then froze as Talioth's curved knife appeared in front of his eyes.

"Let's try this again from the top, shall we?" Talioth said.

Veron glanced to the side. Shawn was on his knees, just like him. His arms pulled behind his back, locked in a set of metal shackles. *Metal!* He pulled his own wrists—held fast.

Talioth took a few steps back and stood between the two knights. The red crystal dimmed to a muted glow as when he had first arrived. "How many knights are in your organization?"

Veron clenched his jaw and stared back. He didn't reply.

"Where do the Shadow Knights live?" Talioth's voice grew in intensity. "Tell me where they are, or you will die."

Veron's stomach turned. He made eye contact with Shawn, a mixture of fear and sadness filling the young knight's face. *I'm sorry, Shawn,* he thought, shaking his head. *We can't tell him.* Veron turned to Talioth and spoke in a clear voice, "No. We will die instead."

Talioth's playful look was gone, replaced with a grim expression. He strode to Shawn and rested the curved knife against the younger knight's bare skin at the base of his neck. "Are you sure about that?"

Veron gritted his teeth. Talioth's arm slowly moved sideways. Shawn kept his jaw clamped tight, wincing and groaning as a trickle of red dripped down his chest.

"He's going to die unless you talk!" Talioth shouted.

Veron locked eyes with Shawn, who shook his head. A twisting pain radiated through his gut. Nausea bubbled in his throat. He lowered his gaze. "I can't," he uttered, the faint words barely reaching his own ears.

The groaning stopped. Veron looked up to find Talioth staring at him with narrowed eyes. The man inhaled, his chest filling up before he blew it out. "In that case, you're both going to go on a trip. You may not talk *here*, but . . ." He paused for effect. "You will when we get to the others."

"What others? Where?" Veron asked.

Half of Talioth's face curled into a wicked grin. The man

scooped the discarded bludgeon off the ground and turned to Shawn.

The younger knight's eyes danced. "What are you gonna do with—" *Thunk!* The hollow sound of the club hitting the side of his head turned Veron's stomach. Shawn's head slumped, and he fell to his side. After a beat, his chest moved with a slow, steady rhythm.

Veron sighed, but his relief fled as Talioth turned to him and crossed the space. Instinctively, he reached for the origine and shocked himself to discover the faint tingle of its presence. His breath caught. *Is it back?* He pulled deep from within. The metal shackles around his wrist deadened the power, but it was there. He strained, a dull roar growing from his gut. His arms bulged, pulling apart and using the origine at a frightening pace.

Talioth's confident demeanor fell and he checked his stride.

Veron's power crescendoed. The faint tingle grew into a muted rush of power. Metal snapped, chains clinking as his arms pulled apart.

The man in grey stared, frozen, with wide eyes. "How did you . . . ?" His unfinished question hung in the air, matching his loose jaw.

With shackles still around his wrists, but free to move his arms, Veron battled through the damper holding him back. He flew to his sword and brandished it with a fierce cry, his source of power rapidly depleting.

The red crystal's glow surged again while Talioth stumbled backward.

Veron's power waned, the tingle dissipated. He felt as if something sucked the energy out of his body. He stood motionless, holding his sword out, unable to move.

"That's impossible," Talioth muttered. "You can't—" His eyes darted around. In a flash, he grabbed Shawn's unconscious body and hefted him over his shoulder. He turned back to

Veron, eyes wide and filled with fear. The flurry of action loosened the swatch of fabric around his neck.

Veron's eyes narrowed. *What is that?* The flickering light of the lantern illuminated a dark stain covering the man's throat.

After a brief pause, Talioth turned and fled, carrying Shawn. In an instant, he was gone, disappeared into the dark city.

Veron gasped and collapsed. His body had nothing left to sustain the energy he needed. He rolled on the ground, panting for breath and trying to look where the man disappeared. He tried to rise to his feet, but his body wouldn't cooperate. He longed to run after Shawn, but he couldn't. Talioth and the shadow knight were gone.

28

BROUGHT TO THE LIGHT

"Thank you!" Danik shouted as the knights gathered around the tables in the common room. "If we had to eat *hot* soup one more day . . ."

"Maybe you should take a turn cooking, Danik," Bridgette said, setting plates of chopped vegetables, bread, and smoked meats on the two tables, "since you seem to care so much about it."

"Please, no," Bradley said. "I can still taste that *sludge* he made last wiether."

"All I'm saying," Danik clarified, "is that when it's as hot as the surface of the *sun* outside, I'd rather not put boiling soup inside my body."

Raiyn laughed, settling into a seat beside Lia. The smoked meat smelled good, his stomach rumbling. "How do you rotate duties?" he asked. "Not everyone cooks?"

"We divide the chores," Lia said. "Cooking, cleaning, laundry, watch duty, weapon care. Speaking of which, it's time you took on some duties." She leaned down the table. "Mason, are you on watch tonight?"

"With Bridgette," he said, nodding and chewing on a piece

of bread. The blonde young woman serving food looked over at the sound of her name.

"Which of you wants a break tonight?" Lia asked.

Bridgette raised her hand so fast a piece of bread nearly fell off her plate. "Me!"

Lia turned back to Raiyn. "All right then. Raiyn, you're on night watch with Mason tonight."

A flutter of nerves flowed through him, but he smiled. "Sounds good."

A rush of footsteps echoed up the hall. Raiyn jumped when Veron flung himself through the doorway. The Shadow Master leaned his arms against the frame as he panted, his face laden with worry.

"Father?" Lia said. "You're back already? What's wrong?"

Silence filled the room. All eyes were on Veron as he stood, catching his breath. Finally, he straightened. "We have a problem."

"So, you have no idea where he took Shawn?" Dayna asked, leaning over the table while Veron sat, drinking water.

Veron shook his head. "There was no sign of them by the time I regained my strength. I checked with the guards at the gate, but they saw nothing."

"Maybe they're still in Karondir?" Gavin suggested.

"It sounded like his intention was to take us somewhere— that we'd 'go on a trip.' I searched for hours, scouring for fresh hoof marks outside the gate or anything that could be a clue, but I found nothing."

Raiyn sat in the corner of the room, nibbling on forgotten vegetables while the other knights gathered around Veron, peppering him with questions.

"Are you sure the origine was gone?" Chelci asked. "You didn't have some sort of metal on you?"

"Both Shawn and I? At the same time?" Veron raised his eyebrows. "It was gone—inaccessible."

"But only while the crystal glowed?"

"It seemed so."

"Could that be what gave him his powers?" she suggested. "The crystal sucked the ability to use the origine from you and somehow passed it to him?"

Veron pursed his lip for a moment. "I don't think that was it. He used it before I even showed." As if suddenly remembering, he pointed to his throat. "And he had this . . . stain—a black mark on his throat. It was odd."

Danik edged forward. "So, what was that bit again about him trying to find *all* of us?"

The crowd of knights muttered at the question.

"That was all he wanted to know," Veron replied. "How many knights we have, and where we are."

"And now they're going to torture Shawn to get the answer from him?" Lia asked, bringing quiet to the room.

Veron looked up and glanced between the faces. He nodded. "It sounded that way."

"Do we need to move . . . in case they break him?"

Veron sighed and ran his eyes around the room. "Possibly. Shawn's tough. I doubt he'd give us up, but . . . it may be wise."

"Talioth," Chelci said, tasting the word on her tongue. "The name doesn't ring a bell."

Veron set his drink down, thumping the table. "We need to gather supplies and take a team to find him, right away."

"And go where?" Chelci asked.

Veron raised an eyebrow.

"The guards saw nothing. You found no tracks. Where will you begin?"

Veron inhaled. "I don't know. But we need to do something."

Raiyn raised a hand. "I'll volunteer, sir. If you need people."

Chelci bit her lip as her husband stood.

"What is it?" Veron asked.

"Yes, we need to find Shawn," Chelci said. "But without somewhere to look . . ."

"He's a shadow knight. We can't abandon him!"

She nodded. "I agree, but . . . Do you plan to scour all the forests? Maybe the mountains?"

Veron blinked.

"What if you visited the King's Library? Perhaps we can find references to powerful crystals or some sort of black stains."

Veron's sigh filled the room. He bobbed his head. "You're right. We should see what we can find here, first."

Raiyn paced the wall of the Shadow Knights facility, his head on a swivel and eyes scanning. Every shadow moving in the street set his hair on edge.

"Raiyn."

He jumped, turning toward the voice. Mason approached along the wall.

"Take it easy," Mason said.

"I'm sorry," Raiyn said, laughing nervously. "I guess I'm on edge. It's my first time on watch, plus all this talk about crystals and losing powers."

"You'll be fine. The night has only just begun. You need to pace yourself or you'll wear out from stress before we even reach midnight. And it sounds like this Talioth person doesn't know where we are."

"At least, not yet." Raiyn took a deep breath to settle himself. "I feel like I need to prove myself or something."

"Just keep an eye out. If you see anything suspicious, call me over." Mason nodded back in the direction he had come. "I'll be over there."

Raiyn turned back to his section of the wall and resumed pacing. *Report anything suspicious. Prevent intruders. Protect the other knights.* Four figures walking his direction in the street drew his attention. Raiyn held his breath and crept closer, as if another stride length would tell him everything he needed to know.

The figure in the front was a man—shaggy hair peeking out of a deep hood, broad shoulders, dark cloak. He angled toward the door to the Shadow Knights facility. Raiyn's pulse pounded. *Should I call Mason? Should I cry out?*

The man looked up, stopping Raiyn's heart. *Who is—* He laughed, his shoulders relaxing as a slender, dark form below waved. Veron, Chelci, Gavin, and Lia had returned. He forced even breaths, holding his hand over his heart, trying to calm himself.

After a minute, steps sounded behind him, leading up to the wall. Veron's cloaked form arrived.

"First time on watch?" Veron asked, resting his hands against the edge.

"Yes, sir," Raiyn replied, fidgeting with the hilt of his sword. "Any luck at the library?"

Veron shook his head. "Not tonight, but we'll keep looking. Shawn's out there somewhere. I won't stop until we find him, but the trouble is . . . I'm not even sure where to look." He cocked his head, peering at Raiyn. "Are you all right? Nervous?"

"Mason just asked me that. I'm trying to do the best I can. Do you have any advice, sir? For keeping watch?"

Veron stroked his beard and paused for a moment. He chuckled. "Show up . . . and don't fall asleep."

Raiyn smiled. "Thank you. I'll stay awake."

"How has your time with Lia been?"

His thoughts ran through sword fighting and running but turned to their time bathing in the river. "It's been, uh . . . Training's been great," he said, thankful the darkness hid his blush. "She's an excellent teacher."

"I'm glad to hear it."

Raiyn's face grew solemn. "Sir, Lia mentioned she has a brother. Is he not trained as a shadow knight, too?"

Veron sucked in a breath and stood still for a long moment. *Maybe I shouldn't have asked.*

"Morgan was born three years after Lia." A faint smile grew on his face. "He looked like me and acted like his mother—caring, sweet, but didn't like to be told what to do. He was a natural at all of this." He motioned around to the training center, then turned back to Raiyn. "Did she tell you what happened to him?"

Raiyn shook his head. "What happened?"

Veron pursed his lips and stared out into the city. "He, uh . . ." His voice wavered. He wiped away a shimmer from the corner of his eye. "He passed away around four years ago—drowned in the river. Lia's now our only child, and the doctor says we won't be having any others."

"I'm so sorry," Raiyn said, looking out to the city as well.

The wind picked up, the warm breeze chasing away the thick heat of the night as the two men stood a moment in silence.

"Sir, do you have any advice for me?" Raiyn asked. "About becoming a better shadow knight?"

Veron's forehead creased. Raiyn imagined his mind churning through various words of wisdom. "First off . . . train hard," Veron said. "It may be painful now, but it will pay off later. Second, believe and live the code of the Knights. There's no room for compromised priorities with what we do. And third . . . be honest about everything—your abilities, your desires, even who you are."

The Shadow Master's eyes bored into him. *Why's he looking at me like that?* Raiyn felt himself shrinking, terrified he'd been found out.

Veron's head cocked, his eyes squinting. "Is there something you need to share?"

Raiyn's breath left him. He clenched the wall to keep from shaking. His heart pounded. After as long of a pause as he dared, he shook his head. "No, sir, there's nothing."

Veron nodded as another set of footsteps climbed to join them.

Raiyn felt sweat beading on his brow as he turned. "Lia," he said, a smile growing as his pulse settled.

"Hey," she looked between him and her father. "What are you two up to?"

"Raiyn's on his first watch. I was checking in," Veron said, a strained smile showing on his face. He turned to leave, speaking over his shoulder. "Raiyn, you're our first line of defense. Tonight, nothing is more important than protecting the rest of the knights." His steps faded as he disappeared into the darkness of the courtyard below.

"Everything all right?" Lia asked.

Raiyn laughed. "Yeah, I guess. I've felt on edge since I started though, so . . . What do I know?"

"How's the watch going?" Lia nodded toward the darkened city.

Raiyn glanced out, scanning the street but finding nothing of note. "It's fine. More conversation than I expected."

"I'm sorry," Lia said, turning away. "I didn't mean to bother you."

"No, no!" Raiyn touched her shoulder, stopping her from leaving. "It's great. It makes the time better. So . . . nothing at the library, huh?"

"Nothing helpful." After a moment, she leaned against the wall. "I always hated watch nights."

"You'd rather be sleeping?"

"Sleeping, ha! More like, out at a tavern."

Raiyn frowned. "Really? I wouldn't have guessed that."

Her eyebrows pinched together. "Well, not as much, recently, I guess. I haven't been out in a while."

A cat yowled in the street, an awkward silence following.

"Your father told me about Morgan," Raiyn said.

Lia's head jerked to him.

". . . that he drowned. I'm really sorry. I know you don't want to talk about it, which is fine. I just thought you should know."

Her eyelids remained wide. Her breath grew rapid. "Did he say how it happened?"

Raiyn shook his head.

Lia looked back toward the city. Her chest rose and fell several times. "There used to be some kids my age who lived nearby. When I was little, we would play together. It was a hot suether day—much like today—and I wanted to go with my friends to cool off in the river. My mother made me take Morgan. He was nine."

Her gaze dropped to her hands, resting on the stone wall. "So, there we were . . . at the docks, jumping off and swimming around. Morgan kept saying annoying things and embarrassing me. I wanted to ditch him. It was my idea to swim across the river. We jumped in the water, waving for Morgan to follow. I knew he wouldn't. He could swim, to a degree, but he was terrified of jumping off the docks. We teased him to come after us the whole length of the river. When I clambered to shore on the far side, I turned around, but he was gone. I thought he'd gone home—we all did."

She sighed. "My parents found his body later that day, caught in the current, wedged under a cross beam at the docks. They've never forgiven me for it. They hate me."

"I'm sure they don't—"

"They hate me," she repeated. "Right before we left for the river, my father and mother were playing with him in the courtyard. I remember it as clear as ever. My father tickled him, sending him running in circles around my mother. They were all laughing and panting with huge smiles on their faces. 'Take your brother with you,' Mother yelled at me. I had to wait while they both wrapped him up in huge hugs and told him how much they loved him and were proud of him. They both wish it had been him who lived instead of me."

Raiyn debated how to respond. He couldn't decide between empathy, shock, or sorrow, so he said nothing. Heavy silence followed until a sniff preceded Lia wiping at her eyes.

"Morgan was so eager to become a knight one day. He wasn't old enough to train yet, but he watched as the others did, waving a stick in the air, mimicking sword movements and learning all he could." She huffed a mirthless laugh. "It was the thing he cared about most. I've never had the same passion he did, but I feel I owe it to him. You know? Be the best knight I can since he never had the chance."

She turned to him with puffy eyes. "Most of the knights here don't know what happened. I'd appreciate it if you wouldn't say anything."

"Of course," Raiyn said. "I would never."

Her vulnerability drew him in. His heart pounded, his own secret eating him alive from inside. If he couldn't share it, he felt he would burst.

"I have something I want to tell you, too," Raiyn said, his hand gripping the wall. Her soft eyes beckoned him to share everything. "I, uh haven't been entirely truthful since we first met."

Her head cocked. "What do you mean?"

"I didn't share everything about . . . how I knew the origine."

Lia's eyes grew, but rather than back away, she drew closer.

"It's about my father." Raiyn's words caught. His jaw hung open, but he struggled to form the words.

Multiple sets of rapid footsteps knocked him from his stupor. He looked over Lia's shoulder as Veron, Chelci, and Gavin arrived, all armed with their swords drawn. Danik lurked in the shadows over their shoulders.

"What's this?" Lia said, backing away, her eyes on her father.

Veron pressed closer, his sword tip up. "I need to talk with our friend Raiyn *Crabtree*."

Raiyn flinched.

"But that's not your real name, is it?"

Raiyn's eyes darted between the knights. Pressed against the wall, he looked over the edge to the street below. The tip of a blade pressed against his chest.

Mason arrived after jogging along the wall, and the other knights gathered in the courtyard below.

"You're Raiyn, son of Catina," Veron said. "You've lived in Tarphan for most of your life. You kept a low profile—didn't draw attention, and you never answered questions about your father . . . who was *not* a lord of Rynor."

Raiyn clenched his jaw.

"Your father . . . Edmund," Veron said in a low voice.

Raiyn gasped, his eyes wide. "How did you—"

Veron lifted a handful of papers with his free hand. "I found *this* hidden in your room."

Lia leaned forward to look at the pages, but Raiyn already knew what they were, the scent of leather wafting his way. He glanced at Danik, who smirked.

"The Origine?" Lia said, reading the pages, her brow furrowed. These pages are torn. Are they—" She turned to him. "This is from the Shadow Knights book! How do you . . . ?"

"His father tore them from the book," Veron said, "shortly before I killed him."

Raiyn's heart pounded, but he didn't react.

"I imagine your mother grabbed them in the chaos that followed, and that makes you Raiyn Bale, son of the late King of Norshewa."

"What?" Lia yelled, turning to him.

Raiyn stared back, his chest heaving and head swiveling between the knights.

Veron pressed the sword harder. "Most of Terrenor would kill you in a heartbeat—the son of Bale, alive and with a claim to the Norshewan throne. Why are you here?"

Swallowing hard, Raiyn stood as straight as he could. "I want—" His voice broke. "I want to be a shadow knight."

"He's here to learn our secrets!" Danik yelled. "He probably wants to build his own army of men to pick up where his father left off!"

"No!" Raiyn shouted. "I don't want any of that. I only want to live a normal life."

"You lied to us, Raiyn," Veron said. "We took you in and taught you, but you broke our trust."

"Lia," Raiyn pleaded. "You must believe me. I didn't want to deceive anyone. I've lived with this my whole life, plagued by the truth behind my family name."

"He *was* going to tell me, Father," Lia said. "Just as you walked up, he was telling me about it."

"That's right, sir," Raiyn stammered, "only a moment ago. I want to be honest with you all. At first, I was afraid of what you'd do if you knew, but now I need you to know."

Lia's face softened, lines of concern forming around her eyes.

Raiyn looked at the surrounding knights. "Give me a chance, please!"

Chelci spoke softly. "It would be a risk to keep him here, Veron."

The Shadow Master's jaw clenched. He stared back into Raiyn's eyes, holding a sad kindness deep inside. "I'm sorry, Raiyn," Veron said, shaking his head. "You may be telling the truth, but we can't take that risk. You must go."

Raiyn felt like someone had punched him in the gut. His breath struggled.

"Give him some food and coin," Veron said to the darkness below before turning back to Raiyn. He motioned with his free hand toward the steps while keeping his sword ready with his other. "Leave your sword and gather your things."

Raiyn hung his head and shuffled his feet. His legs felt heavy as he descended the steps toward the courtyard. His neck burned with all eyes watching him. Reaching the dirt, he unbuckled his sword belt and handed the weapon to Dayna, who accepted it without reaction. He headed toward the stairs that led to his room but paused halfway. *I have nothing there to collect.*

Partway down the main hallway, Bradley met him with a sack. "Some food, and—" A small pouch jingled when the other knight set it in his hand, "a few coins." Bradley's mouth turned down. "Good luck."

Raiyn nodded, continuing forward on numb legs. The front door took effort to push. His body seemed weaker than normal. In the street, he looked up. Several of the knights stared down from the wall. His eyes fixed on Lia. A glistening trail ran down her cheek. She lifted a hand and offered a wave. He smiled back before turning toward the city.

Now where do I go?

29

MISSING WATCH

Chelci polished a sword, sitting on a bench in the shade, but it was her daughter, across the courtyard, who held her attention. Lia's feet shuffled forward, forcing Danik to retreat. Her quarterstaff pivoted through the air, hard and fast, side-to-side. Danik blocked with his own staff, the wooden clacking filling the courtyard. He slipped to the side, keeping his weapon up and ready. Lia advanced again.

The smell of sweat and dirt wafted to where Chelci sat. Lia's heavy breath reached her ears as drops of perspiration flung from her daughter's arms and forehead. Danik glanced her strike away, but the other end of her staff caught him in the side. He groaned, weakly lifting his staff again. She blasted it free of his hands with a punishing blow.

Lia braced her leg and made to strike until he raised his hands.

"Whoa, whoa! You got me!" His eyes were wide, his body cringing against a wall.

Lia exhaled in a huff, then flung her staff to the dirt.

"Are you sure you had that bracelet on?" Danik asked with a nervous laugh. "I've never seen you move that fast."

Lia yanked the metal object off her wrist and threw it across the courtyard, storming toward the wall.

"Lia!" Chelci called out. "Pick those up!"

Lia ignored her, taking the steps, two-at-a-time.

Chelci stood and pursued. "Lia!" she repeated.

A quick run up the steps brought her to her daughter as she stared toward the city, her hands clenching the stones of the wall.

"Lia," Chelci said, softer, but not quite gentle. Lia didn't turn. "Don't take out your feelings on everyone else. Talk to me."

Lia spun, her lip in a snarl. "You want me to talk? Let's talk about you and Father—telling me I have potential to be a leader—challenging me to train Raiyn." She stepped closer. "I did it. I poured everything I had into him, and he was great!"

Chelci felt eyes on them from below in the courtyard.

"He's kind," Lia continued. "He wants to please. Everything he does is from respect and humility. Who cares if his *father* did some bad stuff?"

"Lia, please," Chelci said. "He seemed kind, but—his background . . . There's a chance he was putting on a front for us. He's already dangerous after only a few weeks, but what if he stayed here for years, learning all of our secrets and honing his abilities? What if he returned to Norshewa, claimed the throne, and trained others to use the origine? We can't afford to risk teaching him anymore. He could wind up on the same path as his father."

"But he's *not* his father!"

Chelci nodded. "But that's always a risk. People are free to make their own choices, but we all have some of our parents in us. No one can escape the blood running through their veins."

"I wish they could," Lia snarled, "because I don't want to be anything like you. I hate you!"

The words stung. Chelci clenched her teeth together and

fought to keep from snapping back. She pressed her eyes together for a long moment to push out the hurt, and when she opened them, Lia descended the steps. "Lia, wait!"

The young knight stormed through the courtyard, sloughing off Danik's hand when he tried to rest it on her shoulder.

Chelci slumped to the rough stone, leaning against the wall. An ache in her chest grew. The lowered height blocked her line of sight to anyone below, and the control over her emotions shattered. Tears sprung from both eyes. She lowered her head and sobbed, taking jerky breaths.

"Hey," Veron's soft voice said.

She opened her eyes. Veron crouched next to her.

"How are you doing?"

Her lips trembled. "Lia, she, um . . ."

"I heard. She doesn't mean it, you know."

"I—I know . . . I think."

"She's young and frustrated. Give her time. She'll understand and come around."

"I wish she'd let me talk to her."

"Let her cool down, or . . . maybe write her a letter."

Chelci nodded and sniffed.

Veron dropped to his knees and leaned in with his arms out. Chelci blocked his hug, then sniffed and wiped at her face. "You don't want to hug me. I'm a mess."

He shook his head with a gentle smile. "You're not a mess. You look beautiful just as you are." He held his arms out, palms up.

His tender smile and kind words melted her heart. Chelci leaned forward and welcomed the embrace. Strong arms held her fast. His light breath tickled the back of her neck. Her eyes dried as she leaned into him, her worry fading.

"Do you think I did the right thing?" Veron asked.

Chelci pulled back. "About Raiyn?"

He nodded. "I'm worried I made a mistake."

She breathed out in a long breath. "I don't know. He could have—" She stopped, frowning. "I just don't know."

CHELCI TOUCHED the hilt of the sword at her hip, bouncing the blade against her leg. She paced the courtyard and looked at the sky—nearly dark. *Where is she?* Lia had been absent since their blow-up earlier in the day, but they were both scheduled for guard duty that night.

She walked down the hallway again, losing count of how many times it had been. Chelci poked her head in the common room where knights talked and played games. Veron popped his head up, raising his eyebrows. Chelci understood the silent question and shook her head in response.

Veron joined her at the door. "Should we get someone else?"

Chelci inhaled. "I guess, but I worry about—"

The front door to the center clicked, and footsteps approached down the hall. Chelci pulled her head out of the doorway as Lia and her sour face rounded the corner.

"We're on watch tonight, right?" Lia said, passing Chelci with little sign of emotion.

A hand grabbed Chelci's. She turned back to Veron. He offered a faint smile and squeezed her hand. "Good luck," he whispered.

Chelci followed her daughter, who was already on the steps by the time she made it outside. She hurried, hoping to have a moment before they split up.

"Stay on your side," Lia muttered, walking along the wall to the right and stopping Chelci in her tracks.

Chelci watched as Lia followed the wall and disappeared around a corner at the far end. She sighed and turned left. *I guess we're not talking then.* Finding her favorite spot to watch from, she leaned against the stone rail with a clear view down the street. She glanced down the wall, gazing at the barrier separating her from her daughter. *I wish I knew what went through her head.*

Lia stared ahead at the dark street, her eyes focused on nothing—her mind mired in frustration. She kept the barrier behind her, wanting to keep her mother's eyes from boring into the back of her head.

"Psst," a faint voice called.

Lia's hand went to her sword grip. She leaned forward.

"Lia, hey." Danik stood below, calling up to her.

"Danik, what are you doing?"

"I'm going out—grab some drinks—maybe throw a few dice." He grinned. "You wanna come?"

Her body ached at the invitation. "I can't. I'm on watch."

"How many times have there been attacks, huh?"

Lia chuckled, unable to argue his point.

"That's right . . . zero. Plus, your mother's on guard, too, isn't she?"

Lia glanced behind. The wall blocked her view, and tendrils of rebellion tickled her mind.

"We'll grab a few drinks and be back soon."

She shook her head. "I'd get in so much trouble."

He shrugged. "She won't even know you've gone."

Her anger toward her parents made her want to do anything *but* what they expected, and their recent dismissal of Raiyn only fueled the desire. The edge of her mouth raised. "All right." She lifted a foot on the edge of the wall and glanced behind her again. *No one.* She dropped. Her hair blew above her as she fell, using the origine to catch her fall in her powerful legs.

They hurried away through the shadows.

· · ·

"Ahh." Lia smacked her lips after a long draught of ale. She set it on the table with a loud *thump*.

"Tell me this isn't better than standing on watch," Danik said.

"This is *way* better than standing on watch." Lia laughed, glancing around Fetzer's Tavern. Most of the tables were empty at the late hour.

Danik watched her, his face a curious mix of raised eyebrows and a quirked mouth.

"What?" she asked.

"It's good to have you back."

"I haven't gone anywhere."

"I know, but—" He spoke slowly as if choosing his words carefully. "I've missed you."

Her face softened. "I'm sorry. I spent most of my time with Raiyn. But I *was* in charge of his training."

"I'm sure it's disappointing for him to leave—for all your training to seem . . . wasted. But, for what it's worth, I'm thankful to have you back . . . as a friend."

Lia nodded, offering a wistful smile. "Yeah, I've missed you too." They both drank. "I can't stand my parents right now," she said after swallowing. "They push me, yell at me, and when I finally do something they like, they take it away. They never *ask* me if I want these things! I keep wondering if I should just leave." She took another drink.

Danik paused, his mug halfway to his lips. "How serious are you?"

Lia shrugged. "I don't know."

"Where would you go?"

"Tienn. The mountains are beautiful there. I could find work—do whatever I wanted."

"Sounds like you've thought this through. So, you could leave the Knights? Your family?"

"Ha!" she scoffed. "I don't have a family. I have people who order me around. It could be good to get away."

Her brother's memory sent a wave of guilt shuddering through her. "I'm not sure if that's what I want, though." She drank again, a haze from the ale washing over her. She welcomed the dulling sensation, wishing it would block more of her memories.

Danik clasped his hands together on the table and looked into her eyes. "If you decide you've had enough . . . If you can't take your parents anymore and need to forge out on your own . . . I'll go with you."

Lia's eyebrows lifted, her body lightening. "You'd leave all of this, too . . . for me?"

He nodded with a soft chuckle. "You're the only one here I really care about. If you left . . ." He didn't finish his thought.

"Thanks," she breathed.

A chorus of groans came from a table where a grinning bald man raked in a scattering of coins, pushing a pair of dice out of the way.

Danik looked at her with a mischievous grin. "You wanna join them?"

Lia glanced at the table, her mind battling between a sense of duty and the pull of fun. She picked up her mug, downed the rest in a large gulp, and slammed it on the table. "Let's do it."

CHELCI WRUNG HER HANDS, pacing the wall, rehearsing what she'd say. The feeling of Lia being angry with her didn't sit well, and she'd been distracted since the watch began. She looked up, peering at the part of the wall where her daughter posted. *Still no sign of her.* The lights in the Shadow Knights training center were out. Everyone would be asleep—everyone except them two. She checked the street one last time—*no one*—then turned to walk along the long end of the wall to meet up with Lia.

When she turned the corner at the end, her eyes squinted, trying to see better through the darkness. *Where is she?* Chelci stood where Lia would have been on watch and spun. *I would have seen her descend the steps.* She sighed. *She left her station.* Chelci hung her head and shook it. *Lia, why do you have to—*

The hair on the back of her neck prickled. *Something's wrong.* She spun again, her eyes peering into the shadows. A whipping sound filled the air. She pivoted a moment too late, and a metal bolo wrapped around her waist. Chelci looked down, her mind slow. She tried to snap into action—pull her weapon and spin out of danger—but her body wouldn't move as fast as she asked it to. A click sounded as pressure surrounded her ankle—a metal cuff. She gasped. A man splayed across the ground rolled out of the way before scrambling to his feet.

"Who are you?" Chelci asked, pulling her sword.

Two men materialized from the shadows as more clambered over the wall. Chelci spun, her mouth gaping. More approached along the wall from the other direction. She tried to cry for help, but her voice caught.

"Hello again," a voice said, chilling her blood. A bald head caught the light of the moon, and the man's gray beard came into view. "Remember me? Xander? From the boat?"

Chelci's eyes grew. She held the sword firm and counted. Eight men surrounded her. She inhaled and opened her mouth to sound an alarm.

"Don't do that!" Xander hissed, seven swords raising at once, pointing at her chest.

She paused.

"If you call them, you're dead," Xander said, nodding to her ankle. "I've heard about how the metal works."

"What do you want?" she breathed, her arms tense and ready to strike.

Xander's mouth curled. "You disrespected us in Tarving and stole what was ours. Now, you will pay. Where are Lia and Danik?"

Chelci's stomach lurched. Her hand gripped tighter on the hilt. "Lia's not here. I don't know about Danik."

"Don't lie to me. We can kill you now and *then* find them, or you can live and help us."

"She—" She looked at the spot where Lia was supposed to guard. "Honestly, she's gone. She was supposed to be on watch, but she must be out in the city."

The men paused. A flutter of hope moved through her as the men shuffled their feet.

Xander turned to the man next to him with a scarred cheek. "They're here somewhere. Find them, and—"

"Knights! Alert!" Chelci shouted. A metal clash rang as she knocked the blades away. She ducked a man's sword that stabbed the stone wall where her body had been. She jabbed short and fast into his stomach and sprinted toward the open section of the wall, ringing the alarm bell mounted there. "Wake! We're under attack!"

Another man materialized from the darkness, halting her run. She glanced over the side of the wall, tempted by the open courtyard below. *I'd break my leg without the origine.* She attempted to pull the power from inside, but the metal anklet rendered the effort useless.

A swing of a weapon brought her attention forward. The man wielded a short sword, fast and deadly. She pivoted her light blade, stroke-for-stroke. Footsteps behind her forced her to glance back. She almost missed the arcing blade from behind but parried it away. Facing sideways, Chelci alternated her sword on either side of her body, knocking two steel attacks away. The men pressed close. After a quick dodge, one man's lunge found the chest of his partner. Chelci finished off the other. Both men tumbled off the wall, but more took their places.

She looked across the courtyard toward the stairs that led to the sleeping quarters. *Where are they?*

Facing a line of attackers, Chelci charged. Their eyes widened as she flew through them with measured desperation and a desire to protect. She spun and flashed her sword. Metal rang out, but she didn't stop moving. Her body felt one with her weapon, the wall, and the night. Men fell on either side of her as she pushed forward. Their swords couldn't keep up with the speed of hers. The motions were natural, honed through years of practice.

Commotion sounded from the sleeping quarters. Chelci glanced across the courtyard to see Gavin and Veron appear at the top of the stairs. Their curious expressions hardened. "We're under attack!" Veron shouted back into the hall. "To arms!"

Veron turned back to her, and their eyes met. Chelci smiled. Veron's face held a fierce determination. He rushed down the steps until his body froze. His body arced, neck strained. A silent scream bellowed from his lungs while a searing pain in Chelci's chest blocked out the rest of the world.

Chelci faced forward. Xander, the bald quartermaster, stood before her with a seething expression. She followed his arm with her eyes. It extended toward her, motionless, grasping the hilt of a sword. The long steel blade continued forward, disappearing into her chest.

She gasped and shuddered. The pain turned dull, as if her nerve endings blocked it out. Her body lurched. She tried to lift her own sword, but her arm didn't work.

Xander leaned forward, his face in a snarl. "If you speak with your daughter again, tell her . . . This was for her."

Her head lowered in time to see the sword yank free. She

screamed, the horrid sound of her own cry sounding foreign and distant. Blood ran down her tunic, pumping in spurts, dripping to the stone walkway. Her legs gave out. She slumped to the ground, leaning against the wall.

The knights arrived with shouts and swords. With origine surging through them, they dispatched any remaining men in a blink of an eye. Xander, the farthest from the stairs, was the only one to disappear over the wall unscathed.

Chelci tried to shout and point in his direction, but her words wouldn't form. In a moment, Veron was there, kneeling before her. His hand pressed against the wound. She braced herself for agony, but her body was numb.

"It's all right, Chelci," Veron said, his words fast. "You're going to be okay. This wound is—" His speech faltered, his face fixed on the bloody mess. Tears ran down his cheeks.

Chelci's eyelids felt heavy. She allowed herself a long blink, then struggled to keep them open.

Veron's eye caught the anklet, and he gasped. "We've got to get this off!" He pulled at the metal cuff, but it didn't budge. He glanced in all directions. "Help! Help me get this off!"

The other knights gathered. Their faces were long, but there was nothing for them to do.

Veron stood. He stretched her leg straight and held out his sword.

"Veron, leave it," Chelci whispered.

"I can do this," Veron said. "I can cut it off."

"Veron!" Chelci yelled, the effort taking all her strength.

Veron paused and looked at her. His desperate face dripped with tears.

"I don't know I could heal from this . . . even with the origine."

Veron's body shuddered. He dropped his sword and kneeled next to her, turning back to the wound. "I've healed you before —the pure connection. I can do it again."

Chelci was too weak to argue. Veron closed his eyes. His tense arms pressed against her. A rumble grew in his throat as his neck strained, but Chelci felt nothing. Finally, his arms went slack. Veron's chin sank to his chest, and he took in heaving breaths. "It's not working! It's—I can't—" He wiped at his face, his fingers trembling. "Chelci, I—" His words failed.

Chelci grabbed his hand. She didn't know if he'd be able to feel the squeeze she offered, but it was all she could do. "I love you, Veron."

Tears sprang anew from Veron's face. He pressed a tender hand against her face. "I love you, too."

"Tell Lia I love her, and—" She took a gasping breath, fighting to keep her eyes open. "Tell her . . . it's not her fault."

"Here!" Dayna's muddled voice shouted. "I found them!" A rattle of keys sounded distant.

Chelci's vision blurred. The crowd around her seemed to sway. A vague tug at her ankle resulted in a metal clank and renewed attention from Veron and the others.

"Try it!" She heard Veron's voice as if through water. "Heal!"

A tingle grew in her gut. *The origine is back.* Chelci closed her eyes. She pulled as hard as she could with her weakened body, and a prickling sensation grew inside her chest. She looked, but her bloody shirt showed nothing. Depleted to utter exhaustion, the look on Veron's face kept her going. She pulled harder, a groan escaping her lips. More tingling spread, moving from inside her body to the surface.

With a sudden gasp, it was gone. No more energy. No more origine. And no amount of pulling would change it. Her eyes shut, blackness covering her.

Danik hit his head on the door before he and Lia stumbled into the street. Both of them erupted in laughter.

"Looks like you need to practice sparring against doors," Lia said, her words slurred. She laughed again.

Danik turned toward the door, his body swaying. "I could take him."

"Come on," Lia said, tugging at his shirt. "I need to get back. I'm gonna be in so much trouble as it is."

"At least it wasn't wasted." Danik jingled a pouch, the clanking of coins sounding.

"Yeah," Lia said, grinning. "What's my half?"

Danik opened the pouch and fingered through the contents, pulling out some into his palm. A coin fell to the ground, and he awkwardly bent to pick it up. "Here you go . . . one argen, three."

Lia grinned as he dropped the coins into her hand. "I think I like dice games," she said.

Running feet turned her head. A blurry form rushed past, leaving her dizzy. She narrowed her eyes. "Was that the guy from the boat?" She turned to Danik, hovering her hand over her head. "You know, the one who was, uh . . . What's the word?"

"A hat?"

"No, not that. You know when . . ." Her foggy brain fought against coherent thoughts. She shook her head, then waved forward. "Never mind. Let's go."

They stumbled down the street. The facility was a short walk from Fetzer's, but their unsteady steps lengthened it.

"You think you can get back up the wall?" Danik asked, their destination approaching.

Lia waved her hand. "I think I'll take the steps."

"What about Chelci?"

"I'll tell her nature called."

Danik fumbled with his key to the door, and it swung open with a faint creak. The hallway was dark when Lia closed it behind them.

"How much longer do you think until daylight?" Lia whispered.

"A few hours, maybe. I'll tell you what . . . I'm sleeping in tomorrow."

"Hopefully, I can stay awake on watch. This ale has me—"

Lia stopped as they entered the courtyard, her heart jumping. She expected the facility to be silent with everyone in bed. Instead, everyone was awake. Torches hung on the walls. A few crumpled bodies lay in the dirt, and some dangled over the edge of the wall. A few knights stood in the courtyard, but several clustered on the ramparts above. Every set of eyes looked at her.

Pulling from the origine, she flushed the alcohol from her bloodstream. She sobered immediately, but the rush of consciousness and the use of energy left her weak. She pressed a hand against the wall for support. Danik's arm followed suit a moment later.

"What happened?" she asked.

Sorrow filled the faces staring back, but no one answered.

Lia walked slowly, trying to maintain her balance. Her stomach churned. "Mason, what's going on?"

The younger knight's face was pale. His lips trembled. "I-it was the man from the boat—Xander."

Lia remembered the man running a moment before, outside the tavern. She leaned forward. "What? Who are all these bodies?"

Mason glanced toward the stairs but said no more.

Lia felt herself pulled up the stairs. Knights parted to allow her to pass. She dodged splatters of blood to make her way. Dayna held a torch, the flickering light illuminating the grisly scene before her.

Lia gasped. She struggled to make her lungs work. She blinked and her hand shook. Leaning against the wall, her mother's eyes were closed, a peaceful look resting on her face.

A nasty black-and-red wound peered from beneath a gash in the fabric. Blood stained the lower half of her body. Nothing moved. *Wait.* A faint breath stirred her chest.

Movement tore her gaze away to where Veron crouched in front of Chelci. Blood stained his hands and shirt. His eyes were red and puffy. His mouth formed a tight line while his chin quivered.

"Mother?" Lia whimpered, too shocked for tears to fall.

"She's alive," Veron spat, his eyes hardening, "barely." He stood, facing Lia.

She shook her head, her eyes wide.

"Where were you tonight?"

The question took a moment to register. She turned to her father. "I, uh . . . I—" She hung her head, her answer barely over a whisper. "I was at the tavern."

"You were on watch!" Veron shouted, causing Lia to jump. He stepped closer. "You and Chelci were to protect us, but *you* went out drinking! You left her alone!"

"Sir," Danik said, stepping between them. "It was my fault. I persuaded her to leave her post."

"Danik!" Veron roared, turning to him. "I'm sick of you corrupting my daughter. I want you out of here, *now!* You're not worthy of being a shadow knight."

"Father!" Lia shouted. "I-I—" She wanted to argue with him, but the sight of her mother turned her mind blank.

"Sir," Danik protested. "I've been with the Knights for four years."

"I don't care how long you've been here," Veron said. "I should never have allowed you in to begin with." He pointed toward the city. "Out! Now! And don't come crawling back."

Danik stumbled, stunned.

"Father, I'm so sorry," Lia said, the tears arriving. She stepped toward her mother but Veron barred her way.

"You don't deserve to be comforted," Veron said, angry tears falling through the venomous words. "This is your fault."

Lia's mouth hung open. She struggled to breathe, gasping in spurts. An invisible searing pain stuck her somewhere inside. After a pause, she turned to Danik, who had backed up toward the stairs. "Danik. No, you don't have to—" She stopped, his sunken face confirming he needed to leave. She turned to her father then back to Danik.

"Did you mean what you said earlier?" Danik asked, his voice quiet but hopeful. "About going?"

Lia inhaled. She looked around the crowd. The knights' faces didn't plead for her to stay. Veron—her own father—directed a look of fury toward her. Finally, she looked at her mother, her body slumped and pale—barely alive.

She undid the clasp on the Shadow Knights cloak and held it in her hand. It felt heavier than normal. With a held breath, she tossed it down, the cloak crumpling in a heap. She raised her shoulders and stared into her father's face, lifting her chin. "There is nothing for me here."

She took an extended hand that Danik offered and followed him down the steps. Her neck turned red. Looks of shock and sorrow bore down on her from all directions. Tears fell, but she didn't let herself wipe them away.

They each took a moment to stuff a few possessions from their rooms into sacks, then met on the steps to head toward the exit.

"Fine! Go!" Veron shouted from the wall. "We're better off without you! First, it was my son. Now—" His words cut off.

Lia disappeared into the hallway. "Go, faster," she urged Danik, eager to be gone. They slammed open the front door and entered the street. Lia took off, trying to outrun the tears. Behind her, five words echoed through the night and stuck in her brain.

"We're better off without you!"

PART II

FREEDOM

30

MOUNTAIN DAY

Lia's feet ached, shuffling along the road. The sack over her back grew more uncomfortable the longer they walked. The sun beat down on her. Sweat made her shirt cling to her skin. The serene pastures by the side of the road had long lost their allure. Cows chewed their cud, staring back over the rail fence as if judging her for being tired.

"How much longer do you think?" Danik asked.

"I thought it would have been by now," she replied. "Hopefully soon. Although I'm still not sure what we'll do when we get there."

"We'll figure something out."

"Any thoughts about what sort of jobs we can do?" she asked, pulling out her flask of water to drink. "The money we made gambling won't last long."

"The only thing that comes to mind for me is some sort of guard. With the origine, it would be easy. I don't know anyone would hire you as a guard unless they knew who you were. You still think we shouldn't tell anyone?"

She nodded. "It would draw too much attention. I don't

want anyone knowing who we are . . . or *where* we are. You'd be a great guard. I can do something else."

She extended the water, but he shook his head. After returning it to her sack, they continued walking.

"Any ideas?" he asked.

"I'd like it to be something where I could use my abilities. Maybe something like a stonemason, a blacksmith . . . something along those lines."

Danik laughed.

She turned to him with a glare. "What?"

"Sorry . . . I'm picturing you stoking a forge and pounding molten iron with a hammer. It's a funny image."

"You don't think I can do it?"

"It's not that," he said. "There's probably only a handful of young women in Terrenor your age who could do it . . . but I know you could."

"Thanks." She looked at him with a reserved smile. Ahead, buildings rose from the landscape, catching her eye. "Finally!" The proximity of Tienn gave her legs the life they needed.

When they entered the city, the shade from the buildings offered immediate relief from the heat. Carts filled the streets with goods to sell. Shops with display windows and opened doors tempted anyone passing by. Above the shops, drying clothes hung out of windows while flowers and herbs filled planter boxes. After a short distance, the street opened to Tienn Square.

"What's going on here?" Danik asked.

A festive mood filled the square. Tables set up in rows. Colorful decorations strung from posts.

"It's like we stumbled into a party," Lia said.

"Again? Is the rest of Terrenor in a nonstop party all the time? Felting needs to get its act together."

Lia flagged down a woman passing with an armful of bread in a basket. "Is there a celebration going on?"

The lady's face screwed up. "Of course. It's Mountain Day."

"Oh, of course!" Danik chuckled after she left.

"Nice timing, I guess." Lia turned to the east. The Straith Mountains towered above the city. Jagged peaks and remote passes provided a beautiful backdrop. "So . . . we need to find a place to stay, food, and money. Any thoughts on how we begin?"

"I don't think food will be a problem. At least not tonight."

Lia followed his eyes. Several of the tables filled with food, and vendors passed samples out from their carts. "That's a good start. We'll need to find jobs before we can get money, so where can we stay in the meantime?"

Danik pointed at the far end of the square. "Let's try over there."

The buildings at the far east side of the square lay in ruin. Roofs had fallen in, walls crumbled, and doors hung on hinges. Scorch marks marred several of the walls that remained. They crossed the space to get a closer look.

"What happened here?" Danik asked, peering through a threshold.

"I bet this was from Bale's visit."

"*Edmund* Bale or Bale Junior?" Danik grinned at his joke, but Lia glared back. "Sorry. Poor taste."

"I wonder how Raiyn is," Lia asked. "You think he went back to Tarphan?"

Danik shrugged. "Probably."

Lia rested her hand against the crumbling doorpost. "Likely living someplace like this."

"He's back to doing whatever he was doing before we found him."

Lia frowned. *Grieving his mother's death. Preparing to be hanged.* She sighed. "My father chased Edmund Bale to Daratill, and when Bale's army passed through Tienn, they tore up the city . . . or so I've heard." Lia looked back toward the square, noting the tower watching over the area. "Looks like they rebuilt the clock tower since then, but I guess they didn't get around to fixing up this area."

"This one's not bad," Danik said, having wandered into the next building.

The two-story structure still had most of its roof. Windows were knocked out and several chunks of stone lay fallen on the ground, but overall it was mostly intact. One wall leaned precariously inward. A staircase wound up from the ground floor, and Lia followed Danik, the wooden steps bowing and creaking as they climbed.

"It's even got a bed!" Danik shouted as he entered the room on the second floor.

An old frame with a rotten mattress sat in the corner while the rest of the room remained empty.

Lia turned up her nose. "You can have it if you want it. I'm not touching that thing." She tossed her pack onto the floor and leaned up against the wall with a sigh. "The floor works for me."

"Suit yourself," Danik said, testing the mattress by sitting on it. A crackling noise filled the air, along with a waft of decay. "Ugh, never mind. The floor sounds good to me, too."

Danik set his pack on the floor and leaned against the wall next to Lia.

"We made it," Lia said, looking over at him.

Danik smiled. "Yes, we did. We're in this together, and no matter what, I'm always going to have your back." He held an arm out next to her, palm up.

Lia clasped his hand. They both squeezed, firm at first, then the touch becoming lighter. A tingle ran through her at the physical connection. She leaned her head back against the wall and sighed.

· · ·

THE CALL of music filled the square with people after night fell. Content with their lodging, Lia and Danik left their meager possessions to explore the festival.

Lanterns hung on posts, bathing the entire area with light. A six-person band set up in the center of the square, thumping out a tune that had the crowd clapping and dancing.

"Come on," Danik said, shouting over the music.

Lia followed, swerving through the throng to keep up. They stopped in front of a series of long tables. Several men and women sat talking. Others lay passed out, sprawled across the tabletop. The sight between the groups of people had Lia's mouth watering. Platters of half-eaten food lay in wait for whoever came along. Jugs of ale waiting to be poured sat with stoppers already removed.

"Now this is a party," Lia said.

Danik passed a group of drunken, mumbling men and sat on a bench. A platter of roasted chicken stared back.

"Are you sure we won't get in trouble for taking some?"

Danik grinned, then reached forward to yank a drumstick off the cooked bird. "Nope."

Lia glanced around. No one seemed to monitor the food or the people. She tore off a portion for herself. The meat was delicious: juicy, warm, and full of flavor. She moaned as she chewed.

"Careful," Danik said, his mouth full of chicken. "Someone might think we haven't eaten in two days." They both laughed.

After a moment to gorge on the meat, Lia leaned across the table to where two empty mugs sat unused. "I guess no one minds if we use these."

"Here, let me help." Danik grabbed the nearest jug and filled the mugs with ale.

They clinked them together and took long swigs. Lia looked over the top of her mug and noticed Danik still drinking. His eyes jumped to her, and she tipped her drink farther, gulping the frothy liquid. *He won't beat me.* His cup moved higher. She chuckled, bubbles forming in her mug. Danik laughed in response, and Lia lost it. Ale went up her nose. She jerked her mug down and spewed liquid across the table, coughing and sputtering.

Danik's mug set down with an empty clink. "Good drink?" he asked with a grin.

Lia shook her head, laughing and wiping tears from her eyes.

A basket of bread and a platter of cheese followed. They both gorged themselves, making their way down the tables, partaking in whatever suited them.

Leaning back in her seat, Lia held her stomach while a burp escaped her mouth. "Excuse me!"

Danik waved it off and sank his teeth into the remains of an apple. "Don't worry about it. We're here to enjoy ourselves, not worry about our manners."

"I don't think I can eat much more."

"Me neither." Danik set the core down.

Lia stared forward, her eyes glazing over. "Danik?"

He turned to her.

"Thanks for doing this with me."

A warm smile covered his face, reaching his eyes. "You sound like I was the one making the sacrifice."

Her brow furrowed.

"*I* was kicked out. Remember? Thank *you* for coming with me."

"We've always been a team, ever since you joined the Knights. I couldn't let you go on your own." She smiled back, her stomach full and a glimmer of hope trickling through her.

Her eyes turned to the crowd. The people looked cheerful, matching how she felt. *We can do this. We can build a new life here.* The steady beat of the music lulled her into a blissful trance.

As she watched the crowd, a woman twirled, her brown hair flying behind her. She gasped. *Mother?* Her heart pounded for a brief second then settled. *No, only someone who looks like her.*

"Are you all right?" Danik asked.

Lia blinked, her mind playing over the night they left. She pictured her mother lying against the wall, blood covering everything. Her stomach twisted in a knot. *I was supposed to be on guard duty. Father was so furious.*

She flashed a weak smile. "Just thinking about my mother and everything that happened that night."

"Hey, stop that. No good will come from reliving the past."

"Yeah, I guess so, but . . . I wonder if she's all right."

Danik's hand grasped hers, causing her heart to jump. "Lia," he said looking in her eyes, "she's gonna be fine. Her wound was healed. She was breathing—just passed out from using her energy. She'll recover in no time."

Lia nodded. "I know. You're right. She'll be fine." Saying it out loud helped it sink in.

"And now, *you're* free. You can do whatever you want—be whoever you want. It's the ultimate adventure."

"Is that how you see it?"

Danik cocked his head. "See what?"

"Leaving. Being here, you seem . . . alive. What about it is exciting?"

A slight smile crossed his face. "I think I've been wanting this for a while, actually. Growing up in the Red Quarter, I was a nobody. No one gave me a second glance. People kicked dirt on me, laughed in my face, even spit on me when passing in the street."

Lia's heart ached. "I had no idea."

"When my parents died, it grew worse. No one knew who I was and no one cared. I was a dirty face in a sea of bodies.

When your father found me, I was excited to make a name for myself."

"Fighting right?" Lia asked. "He found you beating up someone?"

Danik chuckled. "Yeah, some older kid who tried to take bread from me. When I joined the Knights, I couldn't wait to stand out. I wanted people to know the name Danik Bannister." He grew quiet.

"But that didn't happen."

"It was great, all the skills, and the power, but . . ." He shook his head. "I was still a nameless face, hidden under a hooded cloak instead of behind a mask of dirt. So . . . I guess that's what I'm excited about."

"Making a name for yourself?"

Danik grinned. "Yes. Doing whatever I want. Being great at something, and people knowing who I am."

"Yeah," Lia nodded. "That does sound pretty good."

A smile grew on Danik's face as he nodded toward the music. "Come dance with me."

A nervous spike of adrenaline rushed through her. "What?"

"Dance!" He pulled on her hand, bringing her to her feet. "Come on!"

Thoughts of her future faded. The memory of her mother's injured body disappeared. The ale-induced haze in Lia's mind convinced her to go with it. Danik led her away from the food, around the tables, and past other bodies. Close to the band, the music surrounded her, filling her soul. They turned to each other. He rested his other hand on her hip, and she draped hers on his shoulder. His touch was tender but strong.

What do I do again? Do I start? Does he? What do I do with my—

With a goofy grin, Danik moved. Lia held on, allowing him to lead. They bounced and twirled, spinning between the other dancers, lost in the music. A mountain breeze swept through the square, lifting the thick blanket of warm air generated by the mass of bodies. Her hair fluttered behind her, the wind cooling her neck.

Her mind jumped between various thoughts: Danik's presence, the bounty of food, the joy of the party. But one thought dominated her mind. One idea covered the rest, helping her to feel good about her choices.

I'm free.

31

JOB SEARCH

Lia gradually emerged from her slumber, the ale and late night making the process more difficult. Despite being the middle of suether, the high elevation of Tienn left the nights cooler than she was used to. She appreciated the thin blanket she'd grabbed before leaving Felting.

The ruffled blanket a short distance away lay flat. Danik was already up. *Where did he go?*

Lia made it to her feet, stretching her neck, trying to work out a crick in it. She glanced around, frowning at the state of their lodging. The abandoned building seemed great the day before, but the thought of living there long term gave her pause. Footsteps ascended the stairs. She turned as Danik's disheveled hair rounded the landing.

"Want to start your day off right?" He extended a hand holding two pastries. A trace of steam emanated from them, and the warm, buttery smell filled her nose.

"Where'd you get those?" Lia asked, taking one while salivating. "They look fresh."

"Just . . . around." A wry smile grew on his face.

"Did you buy them?"

He raised his shoulders. "They were . . . free."

She put a hand on her hip. "Did you steal them?"

His smile grew. "I . . . selected them from a sheet, and . . . the baker didn't ask me to pay."

"Did he see you?" After a moment of silence, her eyebrows lifted. "Were you using the origine?"

He chuckled. "Maybe."

"Danik!" She hit him playfully with her free hand while misgiving rumbled in her gut. She sighed as she looked at the pastry. The sweet aroma hit her again. She took a bite. Warm, sugary goodness filled her mouth. "Oh, that's good," she mumbled with her mouth full.

They made quick work of the pastries and washed them down with water from their flasks.

"What should our plan of attack be?" Lia asked.

"You want to attack someone?" Danik replied.

She hit him again. "Finding jobs, you idiot."

He laughed, shielding his body.

"Should we stick together or divide up the city?"

"We're interested in different things so . . . How about we split up—come back here midday to check in?"

Lia nodded. "Sounds good."

The morning air felt crisp when Lia left the shelter. She took a deep breath, filling her lungs. *We can do this,* she thought. She wandered back to the square, noting the results of the long night. Garbage littered the cobblestones. Some decorations remained hanging. Several partiers lingered, passed out on the tables or the ground.

Lia turned along the main street. The road was quieter than the day before, but dedicated vendors were already up and out. They hawked scarves, hats, food, meat, and clothing. She nodded, acutely aware of her light pockets.

We need to make some money . . . and fast.

Two hulking men caught her eye. Medium height with

broad shoulders and enormous arms, the men turned up a side street, heading east. *I wonder what they do?* Confident the origine could make up for her lack of physical size and strength at whatever they did, she followed.

The city proper ended after a ways, but the men continued. A dirt path wandered through stones and around bushes. The slope continued up, and Lia remained at a distance.

After a short walk, a wooden building materialized around a bend, and the path seemed to vanish into the mountain. Workers gathered, milling in groups. They looked strong. Some carried lanterns. Some held pickaxes slung over their shoulders. Behind them, a dark opening just over a man's height cut into the sheer face of the mountain. Wooden supports framed the black hole. *It's a mine.* She checked the building again and noticed *Benjamin's Baltham* posted over the door.

A whistle blew from the building, making her jump. The men stood ready as a middle-aged bearded man dressed in a button-up shirt stepped outside. "Time to go!" he shouted. "Bowcott, take your men to the Granger Line. Richter, keep working on the Serpent Strain. Don't forget the grand bonus . . ." The men nodded and mumbled. "A baltham line larger than my thumb earns a gold sol for the man who finds it! Now get at it!"

The miners dispersed. Ones with lanterns not yet lit sparked them to life. Each miner lifted a hand cart of supplies with lanterns hanging on the ends. The men followed each other, one-by-one, pushing the wooden vehicles into the mouth of the mountain.

The miners dwindled to nothing, and the man in charge disappeared back into the building. Lia's curiosity led her to the unlocked door.

Inside, the man stood at a table where a map rolled out, covered by a maze of lines. He traced lines, frowning. When he glanced up, his demeanor changed. A smile formed, and he stood up straight. "Why, hello! Who are you, and what can I help you with?"

"Is this your mine?" she asked. "Are you Benjamin?"

"Benjamin Edkins, at your service. You can call me Ben." He crossed the room and extended an arm.

She shook his callused hand. "I'm Lia."

"How can I help you?"

"I'm curious if you're looking for any new miners. Also, how much do you pay?"

"I'm always looking for good workers. Outdoor laborers make three tid per week. Those in the mines make five plus a bonus if they discover baltham." He smiled and returned to the map. Starting at one side, he rolled up the parchment. "Our workers do well. You have a father or an older brother looking for work?"

"Um . . ." She fiddled with the tips of her fingers. "Me, actually."

Ben's head jerked toward her, his eyebrows lifting as the corner of his mouth raised. "You?"

Lia stood straighter. "That's right."

He shook his head and chuckled. "Thanks for coming to visit, but I'm sorry—not interested." Taking the rolled-up map, he crossed the room to a shelf with squared holes then tucked it into one of the open spots.

"You *just* said you're always looking for workers."

"I said I'm looking for *good* workers."

"I'll be good!"

A placating smile crossed his face, and he exhaled through his nose. "My wife, Mary, is an exceptional woman. She works tirelessly to take care of our family. When I get home, she always has dinner ready. Our home is clean, my daughter is cared for, and we all have the clothes we need. Lily, my daughter, is probably just younger than you. She enjoys playing with her friends, making herself up, and painting—she's a great artist. When I first started this mine, my wife offered to come work with me. Money was tight. I was in the mines every day, and she offered to labor next to me. Do you know what I told her?"

Lia didn't reply.

"I told her I wouldn't let her work here if she were the last person in Terrenor. Not because I didn't think she could do it, but because it was too dangerous." A warm smile formed. "Mary and Lily are my life. Everything I do is for them. We don't make a lot of money here at the mine. Sure, there's always the chance of landing a big one, but for now, we get by selling the baltham dust we can process. I don't need to be rich, but with my girls, I consider myself the richest man in Tienn."

"What does that have to do with me?" Lia asked.

"We find baltham at the intersection of borlium and sandzite. Do you know what you find when you mine at the intersection of borlium and sandzite?"

She shook her head.

"Shifting rock. Collapse. Death."

Lia swallowed.

"You seem like a nice girl, and you remind me a bit of my Lily. It's true that I *don't* want to put you in danger, but even more . . . you can't do it."

Lia raised her chin. "I can. Give me a chance. Let me decide if I'm up for the danger."

After glancing out a window, Ben motioned for her to follow as he led out a back door. Behind the building, a work area spread out, tucked between the cliffs. A sluice of water ran underneath wooden roofs for shade. A mountain of slurry lay in a heap down the hill. Various equipment lay strewn everywhere: broken tools, carts, and sacks. Men dressed like the ones who entered the mine were hard at work, breaking up large rocks into smaller chunks, rinsing piles in pans, and carting loads of discarded rocks away.

"You see him?" Ben asked, pointing at a massive man in his late thirties wheeling a cart.

Lia nodded.

"That's Bones Hopking. He collects discarded rocks and gravel in that cart, then wheels it to the pile over there. He's been doing it for fifteen years and is one of the strongest men in Tienn. You want to do what he's doing?"

She shook her head. "No. I want to be in the mines. I want to find the baltham."

He covered his mouth, but a laugh trickled out.

Lia frowned.

"The work in the mines is even tougher than what Bones does, and there's no way you could do that. Everyone starts as a laborer—no exceptions."

Lia pursed her lips. She looked out and stared at the worker as he returned from a trip with an empty cart. "So, are you giving me a shot?"

Ben's head tilted, his face lit in a humorous glow. He looked toward the worker. "Bones! This girl thinks she can do your job better than you."

"I didn't say—"

"Are you backing down now?"

Lia paused, then shook her head.

"Tell you what . . . if you can load one of those carts and deliver it to that pile over there before Bones, I'll give you a job."

Her heart thumped louder. "Deal."

She crossed the dirt to join the worker by a collection of rubble and empty carts. Bones watched every step, his face curious.

"I'm Lia."

Suspicion laced his smile. "Boneham Hopking. They call me Bones."

She looked at the empty carts and piles of rubble. "So, you, uh, fill these carts with that stuff and take them over there?"

He nodded. "Pretty much. You ready?"

She nodded.

"Go!" Ben called.

Surprised, Lia looked around to gain her bearings. Meanwhile, Bones squatted to lift a sizable boulder from the ground. He dumped it into his cart with a loud thud, shaking the wooden container.

Lia stepped to the closest empty cart and crouched next to a large rock beside it. Curious how it would feel, she tried to lift it. Halfway up, the stone slipped. She heaved to throw it over the lip of the cart, but the bulk caught the edge and fell back to the ground.

A laugh sounded behind her, and heat creeped up her neck. She clenched her jaw. *Enough of that!*

Lia crouched again and used a slight amount of origine to lift the rock. Her legs were sturdy. Her arms held on. In a moment, the burden fell into the cart with a satisfying thump. *I can do this!* She glanced at Bones. He just completed dropping in his third armload.

Maintaining a low simmer of extra power, Lia fell into a groove. She lifted the rocks and tossed them into the cart. Her back was strong, her arms and legs solid. Before long, her pile had passed that of the other laborer.

When the larger stones took up all the space, she grabbed a shovel from a nearby pile and scooped loose gravel to fill in the extra gaps in the cart. Bones did the same. After a final scoop, she grinned. There was no more room in the cart.

Lia glanced at Bones' progress. *He has several shovelfuls left to go!* With her heart pounding, she lifted the handles. The weight of the cart surprised her. She set it back down, the balance jostling and settling the load. Ben's laugh rankled her again.

She pulled stronger from her well of power. The energy

flooded her body, a warm tingle reaching the ends of her limbs. The cart lifted as easily as if it were empty. Lia moved forward, walking slowly at first, then increasing into a jog. The distance to the slag pile wasn't far, but her arms and legs quickly tired. Sweating and puffing, she dumped the contents of the cart against the pile and turned around with a smile. Bones continued to shovel gravel into his cart.

With a grin, Lia jogged back—no origine needed. When she set her empty cart down, Bones finished his final scoop of gravel. "Here, let me take that," she said. She ran the second cart across the yard, dumping it next to her pile.

A slow walk back gave her a moment to collect her breath and recover her energy. She sucked in lungfuls of air and worked to steady her pulse. Bones' jaw dropped when she set down the second cart. A laugh reached her ears. It wasn't a scornful laugh of judgment and doubt. It was one of awe, as if someone had seen something they couldn't believe.

She turned to Ben. The owner smiled at her, shaking his head.

"So, I have a job?" Lia asked.

He raised an eyebrow. "Are you *sure* you want to be a laborer?"

She lifted her chin, the side of her mouth tweaking up. "Like I said . . . I want to be a miner."

"Danik!" Lia called as she ascended the stairs of their crumbling building. The second-floor room was empty except for their sacks of stuff. She frowned.

"Lia? Is that you?" a voice called from outside.

She poked her head out a missing window to see Danik approaching. "I'm here," she called down.

He waved up with a smile. "Grab our stuff. I've got something to show you!"

Lia collected their things and jogged down the stairs. She exited the building and passed Danik's sack to him. "What is it?"

Lines formed at the corners of his eyes, his face glowing. "Come on."

Lia followed as he led down the street, turning a few corners. They left the rundown buildings behind, moving into a nicer area.

"I've been busy today," Danik said. "I met some people around town."

"Like who?"

"Some traders. Some guards . . . A variety of people. I love this city. The people are so friendly."

Lia nodded. "Yeah, I agree."

"A guy I met—a guy who trades jewelry and valuables—he had a connection and found this." Danik nodded ahead to a building where a set of double doors lay closed.

Lia touched the doors. "What is this?"

Danik pulled out a key and grinned. "A place to live."

Lia's eyes bugged. "What?"

He turned the key in the lock and swung the doors open. "It's ours, the entire building."

Lia gaped as she entered. An arched foyer with a marble floor welcomed them. A dining room, complete with a table for eight lay to the right, and signs of a kitchen peeked through the doorway beyond. Straight ahead, a sitting room with chairs and loungers was large enough to hold a dozen people. A staircase with a rich wooden railing curved around the outside of the foyer, leading to a second floor.

"And there are four bedrooms upstairs, all furnished," he said.

She continued to spin, at a loss for words.

His grin faltered. "What do you think?"

"What do I—?" She looked again up the stairs. "Why do we need four bedrooms?"

"Well, we don't *need* them, but . . . Isn't this great? There's even a private bathing room!"

"Yeah! Of course, it's great, but . . . we don't have this sort of money!"

A flush crept up his neck. "I was able to trade some stuff I found."

"You found?"

"Yeah, that trader . . . He pays for valuables and resells them elsewhere."

Her forehead pinched. "What did you *find*?"

"I, uh . . . got some necklaces."

She stared at him, but his eyes looked anywhere but back at her. An unsettled feeling worked through her gut. "You stole them, didn't you?"

His eyes danced some more. "It's hardly stealing when someone just leaves them out. It's like they wanted to give them away."

"Left them out? Where?"

"In the market."

"From a jewelry vendor?" His eyes confirmed her hunch. "Danik! That's stealing! We can't just *take* things from people to get whatever we want. Pastries is one thing but—"

"But we have these abilities, Lia." He blurted, his eyes alight. "It's *nothing* to swipe something from one of these vendors. No one will see us. No one will catch us. We can live like *kings* here!"

She pursed her lips, staring back.

"Look at this place! It's amazing! This is much nicer than those excuses for rooms we lived in at the training center."

"It is nice," she said grudgingly with a quick laugh. "If we *stay* here, moving forward, I want us to earn our living through honest work, though."

He rolled his eyes. "Fine. We can do that. I can find guard work, and you can—"

"I've already got a job," she said, smiling.

His head cocked. "Doing what?"

"Mining baltham." Lia glared at his subsequent explosion of laughter. "What's wrong with that?"

"You? You're going to mine baltham?"

"I am. I start tomorrow."

"Lia." He ran his hand down his face and looked around. "I think we should do something *bigger*. Mining is great for common people, but we're special. We can do things no one else can."

"Like swipe jewelry?"

"Yes—No!" He sighed. "We can do whatever we want!"

"And *I* want to mine."

He threw up his hands. "Fine. Mine. Have fun. I'm going to look for something better."

"Danik?" Lia said, waiting for his attention. She took his hand and squeezed. "Thank you."

His face softened.

She gestured around the room. "This place is great. Thanks for being here and working it out."

32

———

BENJAMIN'S BALTHAM

Lia arrived at the mine just before starting time. A thick heat hung in the air despite the early hour, and sweat already dotted her shirt. Butterflies filled her stomach. She held her chin high, confident in her ability to work. But most of the crowd gathered outside of the mine didn't seem to share the sentiment. The men gave her odd glances, and none spoke to her. *I guess I need to prove myself to them, too.*

The familiar face of Bones Hopking nodded in her direction. She crossed the yard. "Good morning, Bones."

"Morning," he replied. "I see you were serious, huh?"

"You didn't think I was?"

"Ben and I debated after you left. I told him I thought it was some sort of hoax . . . but here you are."

"I'm here to make money, just like everyone else."

"You surprised me." He chuckled. "Who would have thought? Be careful down there, all right?"

"I will."

Bones' face turned serious, his voice lowering. "I don't just mean the risk of cave-ins. Keep an eye on the other miners.

Baltham is a precious resource. Some men will do anything to get their hands on it."

Lia nodded, noting the crooked eyes looking in her direction.

Ben emerged from the mining office, and the gathering of men quieted. "It's time, men! Those of you on the Granger Line, nice work yesterday. You netted a half-vial of powder."

Half the crew nodded with celebratory smiles.

"Keep it up." He turned to the other half of the men and frowned. "Richter."

A red-haired man with leathery skin and broad shoulders stepped forward. "Yes, sir."

"I know the Serpent Strain is new, but we've got to see better production. That's three days straight with next to nothing."

The miner hung his head.

"I've got a new worker for your team." Ben pointed in Lia's direction.

A flush rolled across her face as all eyes turned to her.

"I'm adding Lia to your crew."

A chorus of shouts and protests filled the air.

"But, she's a girl!"

"As a miner? She can't do that!"

"She'll get us killed!"

Lia's eyes fell, aware of the burning stares in her direction.

"I realize who she is, but this is my call," Ben said. "Teach her what we do. She may surprise you. Understood?"

The man named Richter repeated, "Yes, sir," but lacked the conviction of the first time.

When Ben released everyone, Lia shuffled her way toward the red-haired man. No one made eye contact with her or acknowledged she was even there while they gathered their supplies. She cleared her throat. Still, no one turned. "Excuse me, are you Richter?"

The red-haired man turned to her, his lips forming a hard line. "I am."

"I think I'm on your crew."

The miner sniffed. He glanced around at the other surrounding men before looking back at her. "What was your name?"

"Lia, sir. Lia Stormbridge." She blurted her real name out of habit, cringing after it left her lips.

"Stormbridge. Ha! Like that hero knight." He turned to his men. "What was his name? Vernon? Vermin?"

His crew shrugged. Lia didn't correct him.

"All right, Lia, so this is how this works. I lead our crew of eight." He gestured toward the other seven men who huddled around. They nodded back, most with scowls but at least a couple with looks of pity. "If you get in our way, you'll be sorry. If you do something stupid and die, we *won't* be sorry. Got it?"

Lia nodded.

"Grab some gear and don't get lost."

The men grabbed carts, loaded up pickaxes, and headed toward the mine in a pack. Lia looked around and found extra gear. She hung an unlit lantern on the hook at the end of the cart and tossed in an axe. After wiping the sweat off her brow, she hurried to catch up with her crew, who had already disappeared into the dark.

The punishing temperature dropped as she entered the mountain, and the smell of rock dust filled her nose. The cart rolled down the well-worn path. She kept close to the man in front of her, the light from his lantern being the only source to see from. Lia kicked an unseen rock and winced.

The man ahead turned his head and stopped moving. He rustled in his pocket and tossed a shadowy object in the air. "Here, use this," he said.

Lia caught the object.

"It's a flint starter. You'll want to have your lantern lit."

She smiled. "Thanks." Scraping it by the wick, her lantern roared to life. The man's features came more into focus. In his mid-thirties, the man had short brown hair and a trimmed beard. She moved to toss the flint back, but the miner held up his hand.

"Keep it," he said. "It's an extra."

She put it in her pocket.

"I'm Dodd." The man's smile was refreshing after the gruff attitude of the rest of the team. He nodded his head forward. "We better catch up."

The man moved with long strides, and Lia pumped her legs to keep up. Soon, the string of lanterns returned ahead, and they settled back to a walk.

When the tunnel widened, Dodd slowed to allow Lia to come alongside. "Some guys don't take well to newbies—not to mention we've never had a girl in here," he said. "Give them time. They'll warm up."

"How long have you been here?" Lia asked.

"Five years, next week."

"What made you want to be a miner?"

"I used to be a farmer. My family has a large plot of land north of the city. We grew every kind of produce you could imagine. After I got married and my son was born, I got it in my head that I needed to do something bigger. I wasn't content to just be a farmer. I wanted to get rich."

"So you hoped to discover huge baltham deposits?"

He nodded with a wry grin. "Edkins pays well enough, but . . . I never hit that big lode I hoped for."

"Not yet," Lia added.

He chuckled. "Right . . . not yet."

The mine reached a junction where three narrower passages split in different directions. Lia frowned at the crossed beams blocking one. Dodd led the way down the passage at the far left.

"Where do the other tunnels go?" she asked.

"Bowcott's team works the Granger Line. They're down the center passage. It's been paying out for a season, so they'll keep working it until they capture every ounce of dust. The other tunnel's been closed for years."

"It ran dry?"

No answer returned.

Did he hear the question?

After a long moment of silence, Dodd spoke. "From what I hear, there was good powder down there. It paid out for over a year. Some of the older miners talk about it when they get drunk." He stopped moving and set his cart down. His voice lowered. "Word is that they found a line of baltham. Not just powder, the *actual* mineral."

Lia's eye widened.

"The men fought over it. Things got violent, and one of the tunnel supports failed. They say there was a massive cave-in, and four miners died that day."

"That's awful," Lia said. "So, what happened to the baltham?"

"They made another attempt. They dug it out and set more braces. From what I hear, just as they were getting to it, the mine collapsed again, and three more men died. People said the tunnel was cursed. Edkins paid restitutions to the men's families. It nearly ruined him. He blasted the tunnel shut so no one else would go after it."

Dodd picked up his cart and resumed moving. "That was years ago. Just recently, we opened a new line down this tunnel, so our team is working on it. It hasn't resulted in much payout so far, though."

The tunnel continued to wind along, passing other junctions. They sloped down and up and eventually caught up with the rest of the team. While not a large space, the room where they stopped had a higher ceiling and more space to move. The gathering of lanterns made the room appear bright as day.

"We wondered if you got lost, Dodd," a man said, "you and your girl." The miner cackled to himself.

"All right, men," Richter said, his booming voice filling the tunnel. "You heard Ben. We need to produce. This area has a lot of potential. Volume equals payout, so fill your carts with the highest quality you can and leave it to the guys outside to sift through. Then, come back and do it again."

The men mumbled in assent.

"Spread out! Get to work!"

The men rolled their carts in various directions, chattering and boasting about what they were going to find.

"Dodd," Richter said, turning the miner's and Lia's heads. "Show your girl what to do. And make sure she doesn't get any of us killed."

Dodd nodded, then turned to her. "I guess you're with me, Lia."

The miner led the way, pushing his cart past others who had stopped. Lia squeezed through the narrow passage, trying to steer clear of the other men. She stumbled, tripping on an outstretched foot. The handles of her cart were the only things keeping her from a face full of dirt and rock.

"Careful there, pretty," the miner she tripped over said. "It's a long way to the surface if you hurt yourself."

A muffled echo of laughter filled the narrow tunnel. Lia stared ahead, reminding herself to ignore them.

The hairy man next to him removed his shirt and tossed it on the edge of his cart. He spoke in a raspy voice, "You know, sugar, on hot days, us miners always work with our shirts off." Someone in the darkness snickered. The miner ran his hand through his shaggy brown hair. "Are you going to fit in and be like us?"

Lia's anger bubbled over as the laughter grew. When the

man grabbed at the edge of her shirt, she abandoned her attempt to ignore him.

Her cart skidded as she dropped the handles. Lia pushed against the man's bare chest, using the origine, and flung him into the rock wall. His back hit with a thud. In one motion, she grabbed the man's pickaxe from where it leaned against his cart and held the end under his chin. She pushed—not too hard, but enough to keep him in place.

"Don't you *ever* speak to me like that again." Her words rattled in the tunnel, low and menacing.

The tunnel was silent except for the gurgle of the miner pinned against the wall. He pulled against the axe head and shuffled his feet, but her force kept him in place.

"You got it?"

After a silent pause, the man nodded.

Lia released the man and tossed his axe down. He gasped, rubbing his neck and scowling at her. With a smug look, she picked up the handles of her cart and continued down the passage after Dodd.

"Watch out for Rankin," Dodd said when they stopped at the end of the line. "He doesn't take too well to being embarrassed."

"I guess you could say the same about me," Lia replied.

He nodded. "Just watch out. He's a nasty one."

Dodd hung his lantern on a wooden tunnel brace and motioned for Lia to do the same on the next one down.

"So, what is this Serpent Strain, exactly?" Lia asked.

Dodd pointed along the wall in the direction they had traveled. "You see that wavy line?"

Lia stepped to the side, giving the light a new angle. A silvery line undulated near the bottom of the passage.

"Below that line, the light shade of brown is sandzite. Above it, the black rock is borlium."

"And that's where baltham forms," Lia breathed.

He nodded.

"That silver line—Is that . . . baltham?"

Dodd chuckled. "I wish! No, those are sublimation crystals —worthless. The pressure between these two minerals forms a gas, leaving the crystals behind. The gas seeps up through the rock, accomplishing two things." He looked at her, holding up two fingers and raising his eyebrows.

"It passes through the borlium and transforms some of it into baltham?" she guessed.

He nodded and lowered one of his fingers. "And . . . ?"

She pursed her lips, then shrugged.

Dodd continued, "And it makes the rock very unstable. You see these beams?"

Lia glanced along the passage. Twice as many supports lined the area as what they passed through to get there.

"We need the extra support so it doesn't collapse."

The other men down the way had already begun working. They swung their axes into the wall, chipping off chunks of rock a small bit at a time.

"So, we dig into the rock, pile it in the carts, and take it above ground to be sifted for baltham powder?"

"Exactly." Dodd grabbed his pickaxe out of his cart. "You ready?"

Lia hefted her pickaxe, holding onto the worn wooden handle with both hands. *It's not too heavy.*

"Give it a shot," he said. "We mine the black rock above the line. Chip it off the wall and pile it into your cart. Most of the guys finish around three or four cartfuls in a day. Make sure you're getting at least two, otherwise you won't be around for long."

Lia squared her stance, moving her right hand near the head of the axe. She took a deep breath, then exhaled. Lifting the axe over her head, she slung it against the wall. The metal point bounced off the hard rock.

Laughter echoed down the tunnel. Lia turned to see every head turned in her direction. She clenched her jaw, hoping the red of her face wouldn't show in the tunnel.

"You need to put more power behind it," Dodd said. "Watch." He raised his axe and stepped forward, turning his shoulders to power the force of the tool. The pick chipped into the rock, knocking a small chunk loose. "Use your shoulders and your legs. If you only swing with your arms, you'll be wiped out after a few minutes. It's a long day, so you need to pace yourself." He bent over and tossed the tiny piece of stone into his cart.

Lia nodded, her jaw set. Turning back toward the wall, she repeated the motion Dodd demonstrated. As she turned her shoulders, she tapped into the origine, pulling the tool harder. A deep thunk reverberated through her arms. The pick sank into the rock halfway along its length, a web of cracks forming around it. She grimaced. *A little too much.*

The sound of picks stopped, and the tunnel grew quiet. The men who laughed moments before stared wide-eyed at the buried pick.

"Uh, yeah . . . that's *much* better," Dodd said. "A few more hits like that, and boulders will come loose. Keep at it."

Lia took a moment to wrench her axe free, requiring some extra strength from her hidden source of power. Her second swing used only the faintest trickle of origine as she pulled with her shoulders. The rock splintered, multiple large chunks falling off the wall.

Dodd chuckled, shaking his head. "I think you've got it." He turned to his section and began hacking away in slow, steady strokes.

She set down her axe and picked up the stones she'd knocked free—four of them, each requiring two hands to lift. When she picked her tool back up, the man to her left caught her eye. He nodded with a faint smile, then waved before returning to his work.

Lia worked steadily. Her section of rock crumbled under her punishing swings of the axe. Her cart filled before either of the surrounding men were even halfway done. She worked a little longer to help Dodd complete a load, so he could show her what to do with it.

Pushing the cart back up the mine shaft was difficult. She could barely even lift it without the origine. Using her stored energy, she kept up with Dodd, but the effort drained her.

After a steep section, Dodd set down his cart and leaned against the wall.

Yes! Thank you! Lia thought. "You all right?" she asked, stopping as well. She took deep breaths and bent over with her hands on her knees.

"Me? How about you? Most grown men can't lug a full cart this far without resting. I was pushing myself out of curiosity to see how you'd do."

She felt like grinning, but her aching forearms and rapid heartbeat prevented it. "Believe me, I'm tired. Just trying to prove myself, I guess."

"Well, I'm impressed. It must be those young legs, huh?"

"Yeah, something like that."

They drank water, shook out their arms, and gave their legs and lungs a chance to rest. Before long, the carts were up and rolling again.

The sun was high in the sky when they emerged from the mine. Lia squinted, her eyes having grown accustomed to the dim tunnels. The heat caused beads of perspiration to pop on her skin. Her sweaty shirt clung to her skin. *Rankin's idea to take it off wasn't too bad,* she thought, chuckling at the irony.

"Over here," Dodd said, leading the way. "We check in with Karlson."

Karlson, a bald man with a clipboard, stepped out from the

shade and inspected their carts. "A full cart each for Dodd and Lia." He glanced up at the sky. "Fast work today, huh?"

Dodd chuckled. "She's a natural."

"I've got an excellent teacher," Lia added.

Karlson pointed at two separate sluices. "Dodd, dump your cart in slot one. Lia, take yours to slot two."

Lia rolled her cart the short distance and upended it into a trough. Bones smiled at her and went to work, hacking through the chunks and shoveling the black rubble into the sluice box.

"We separate loads, so they can track production," Dodd called out, shaking his cart to empty the contents. "Plus, if you happen to land a chunk of baltham, they know who found it, and you get a nice bonus."

Lia wheeled the empty cart back to where Dodd finished up. Without a load, pushing it felt like a breath of fresh air.

When the other miner was ready, he turned to her and exhaled with a smile. "And now we do it again."

33

LOST OPPORTUNITY

After wiping the sweat from her forehead, Lia swung her axe into the wall. The solid thunk of the pick and the tumble of rocks had become a comforting sound. She gathered the stones and tossed them in her nearly full cart.

Her first day in the mine drew to a close. She'd already taken four loads up and worked on her fifth. The other miners stopped teasing her after the incident with Rankin first thing in the morning. As she lapped many of them with loads of stone, their respect seemed to grow. Two of the pleasant ones, Lightfoot and Govier, even took time to show her how to erect support beams as she excavated.

Having obliterated the section of wall she started on, she jumped around to other areas, looking for new sections with promising veins of the sublimation crystals.

A hard swing knocked another chunk of black rock loose. Behind it, a small pocket of gray stared back at her. *That's odd.* She looked around, but no one was near. Dodd was on a run to the surface. She ran her finger over the discolored section. The rough edges pulled at her fingertip. *Probably nothing . . . Still . . .*

Lia directed her axe around the gray section, taking several careful swings to knock a chunk loose with the gray rock. Once free, she tossed the chunk on top of the pile. *That should about do it.*

The trip to the surface was a challenge. After four other trips and a full day of hard labor, her supply of origine became more difficult to refill. She stopped several times, thankful to be alone with no one to judge her.

When she reached the steep portion of the route, a man ahead panted and struggled his way up. She gained ground on the miner, and her heart sank. *Rankin.* The man glanced behind him, his shoulders rising and falling with his breaths. At the sight of her, he redoubled his efforts.

The moment had the same effect on Lia. As much as she wanted to hold back and let him move ahead, she pulled from her reserves to speed up. Near the top of the incline, she wheeled her full cart past him as he panted, dripping sweat and grunting from the effort.

She couldn't continue when she reached the flat portion of the mine. She leaned against her cart, gasping. The wooden squeak of a wheel arrived next to her. *I want to get out of here!* She placed her hands on the cart handles, but the thought of lifting them made her dizzy. *I can't. Not yet.*

Rankin collapsed onto his cart. His face was red, and his hair matted against his face and neck. His hairy chest glistened in the lantern's light, heaving to recover. "How do you—do it?" He rasped between wheezing breaths. "That's, what, your fourth load?" He looked at her cart and froze, staring. His breath seemed to settle instantly.

"Fifth, actually."

Rankin nodded and walked forward. He ran his hands over the rubble in her cart. "Did you know that almost all of this is worthless?" he asked.

Lia didn't reply.

"It's true. With fifty carts filled like this, you'd be lucky to get enough powder to fill one small vial."

He pushed the rocks around, the stones clacking together. When he lifted his hand, a small, black rock the size of a cherry balanced between his fingers.

"But we do it because there's a chance we get lucky. If we found a deposit of baltham this large," he shook the small rock, "it would mean wealth, riches, never having to work again."

"For Ben, right?"

He sniffed out his nose, the corner of his mouth turning up. "That's right. *Ben* gets rich." He tossed the chunk of borlium back into her cart. "But we get a bonus."

Rankin returned to the handles of his cart. "Fair warning . . . If you were to get a bonus from a find like that, having just started, when most of us who have worked for over ten years have never seen one . . ." His mouth formed a hard line. "Let's just say, it wouldn't be received very well."

"Good luck to you then," Lia said, biting her tongue. "I hope you're successful."

He looked back at her with a sneer.

Lia lifted her cart, pulled from what origine she'd been able to recover, and marched forward, leaving the miner far behind.

The sun hung low in the sky when she exited the mine. Next to the mining building, a half-dozen men gathered around, their empty carts appearing finished for the day. She rolled to check in with Karlson and dumped her load of rock at the assigned place.

Dodd shuffled up, taking a swig from a flask. "No more loads for today," he said. "Day's about done. Is this five?" He pointed at her pile.

She grinned. "Yeah. How'd you end up?"

"Four—well . . . Three and a half when you consider that you finished half my first load. So . . . your first day. What did you think?"

"I liked it. It's hard work, but it feels good. Say . . . I wanted to ask you something." She turned to her pile of rubble and sifted through it. "I found something different and wanted to check with you. It was a pocket of gray."

"A gray deposit, surrounded by the borlium?"

Lia nodded.

Dodd's face grew rigid. "Are you sure?"

"Pretty sure."

He turned to the pile and assisted with her search. They tossed rocks out of the way and rolled stones over.

"The stone was about the size of a fist, and there was a small gray spot in the center."

Both of them continued to turn over rocks. "I don't see it here, Lia," Dodd said.

Lia sat on the backs of her legs and tossed her hair out of her face. "Where did it go?"

A shout rang out. Lia and Dodd turned toward the mine to see Rankin rolling his cart toward them. "I found one!" the miner shouted.

Lia's brows knit together. She thought back to their moment in the narrow mineshaft, and her stomach turned. "Oh, no," she whispered.

Rankin dropped his cart, the men gathering around.

Ben Edkins opened the door to the office. "What's this?" he called, hurrying down the steps to join the crowd.

Lia walked forward, her steps hesitant and tense.

Rankin raised his arm above his head in triumph. His arm flexed as he showed off a small chunk of stone.

Lia squinted, getting closer. The stone he held was black, similar to everything else she'd hauled all day. When he spun his hand, she gasped. *The gray pocket!* Her breath left her.

Rankin passed the object to Ben, who inspected it. "This is definitely baltham," the owner said, "and just over a thumb's width. Great job, Rankin, you'll be well rewarded."

"Thief!" Lia shouted before she could stop herself.

The excitement in the air vanished, and all heads turned to her. Rankin shot daggers at her with his eyes.

"You took it from my cart!" Lia said, waving a finger at the miner as she approached.

"I did no such thing!" the miner shot back.

She turned to the others. "I found it in the mine. I met Rankin in the shafts walking back, and he took it from me."

"You saw him take it?" Ben asked.

"Well . . . we were talking. I think he took it then."

"You *think*? Stealing baltham is a serious accusation."

"Well, I *know* he did . . . I'm pretty sure."

A mutter grew in the crowd at her lack of confidence.

"I found something that looked like that," Lia explained, pointing to the rock, "and it was in my cart, but now I can't find it."

"This is absurd." Rankin said. "I didn't take it from the little girl. She's delusional."

Ben's brows knit together. "You're saying you found a deposit of baltham, but you carelessly tossed it into your cart. You didn't tell anyone, and now when you rummage through your pile, you can't find it anymore. So, the only explanation is that someone else took it?"

"I didn't know what it was!" she shouted.

"How can you claim someone steals baltham from you when you don't even know what it looks like?" Rankin said.

The crowd laughed in response.

Ben raised his hand. "Lia, do you have any proof you found this?"

The crowd was quiet, waiting for her. She dropped her head. "No."

"In that case, the find is credited to Rankin."

The miner cheered.

Lia kicked the dirt and wandered back to her pile of stones, where Bones had already set to work. She kicked a few of the rocks over, but nothing with a gray spot appeared. "Bones, will you keep an eye out for a black rock with a gray spot in the center?"

Bones returned a weak smile. "Of course."

LIA'S SHOULDERS slumped when she opened the ornate double doors. Losing the baltham bonus was difficult to swallow. *At least I put in a full day's work, which I'll get paid for.* Everything was quiet. "Danik?" No one responded. She walked upstairs and peeked in each of the rooms. "Hello?" The house was empty. *I guess he's out.* Back downstairs, two gleaming swords caught her attention on a table. She picked the smaller of the two up. *This reminds me of my sword back in Felting.*

Leaving the house, she scanned up and down the street, looking for a sign of where he might have gone. Her eyes settled on a hanging wooden display noting *Barfield's Tavern*. She laughed to herself. "That's a sign, all right."

A bell rang when she opened the tavern door, but no one inside would have heard it. Men and women filled every chair in the packed room. A buxom lady in a brown-and-white uniform walked between tables, carting three pints of ale in each hand. A serious card game filled the table closest to her, but Danik wasn't there. The rattle of dice on a table drew her attention across the room. No Danik.

On a stage, a man played a lute, strumming so fast Lia thought the strings would break. A woman sang with him, and several in the room followed along in various musical keys. A lofted ceiling showed a second floor. Doors spaced along the wall with a railing looking on the room from above.

"Can I get you a seat, miss?" a lady asked. Her uniform matched the woman with the ales, but her chest was less endowed.

"No, I'm looking for a friend."

"What's their name? Maybe I can help."

There! Leaning against the bar, Danik stood with another man. "Thanks. I've found him."

Lia crossed the room, weaving between tables. Danik's attention turned when she arrived.

"There you are," Danik said, holding a drink, his words louder than necessary. "I wondered if you'd find me, but I figured you knew me well enough."

She laughed. "This was the first place I checked."

His eyes scanned up and down her body. "Your clothes are in quite the state." He grabbed his nose and moaned. "And you smell. Wow! Did you just sweat all day?"

"Hey!" She hit him on the shoulder. "At least one of us worked today."

He continued to waft his nose. "It reminds me of our early days of training with the—um . . ." As if he remembered to be careful of his words, his eyes jumped to the man he was with.

"Who's this?" Lia asked, changing the subject.

"Ah! Yes . . . this is Nicolar Gudrun. I told you about him yesterday. The trader."

"The man who resells stol—" She stopped herself. Danik raised an eyebrow.

"The man who sells things that need selling," Nicolar said in a heavy Norshewan accent. He extended his hand with an enigmatic smile. "You must be Lia."

Nicolar had shaggy black hair and a messy goatee. A scar on his bottom lip disappeared into his facial hair. His brown eyes narrowed as he spoke, but his smile insisted he was a friend.

"I am," she replied, shaking his hand.

"I was fortunate enough to run into Danik yesterday. It seems we share many of the same passions."

She raised her eyebrows and looked at her friend. "I'd love to know what those are."

"Ale for one," Danik said, lifting his mug and taking a drink. "And gambling for another."

"I met him here, playing cards," Nicolar said. "But the key similarity is neither of these." He leaned forward and whispered. "We aren't afraid to do what needs to be done to get what we want." He flashed a wicked grin before taking a long swig of his drink.

Lia's stomach felt queasy at the way he spoke. "Your accent . . . Where are you from? Norshewa?"

He nodded. "I was . . . until I was twenty-two. After Bale fell and they placed that figurehead, Darian, on the throne, the country went downhill fast. I got out of there as soon as I could. I was young and wanted to see the world, so it worked well. I spent some time in Rynor, in Kandis by the sea, then did a few years in Karondir. A while ago, I settled here in Tienn."

Danik stepped in and pressed his finger against the man's chest. "Nicolar knows everyone in Tienn."

The man raised a hand and chuckled. "Well, not everyone."

"Everyone!" Danik repeated, his speech slurring. "And he can do anything. You should meet his friends." He turned to Nicolar. "They're here, aren't they? You should bring them over."

Nicolar turned and waved across the room.

"It's all right," Lia said. "I'm sure you are busy. Plus, we need to get back soon."

"It's no trouble," he said. "They're coming now."

Lia turned and followed the group with her eyes. Four men and one woman approached.

"Hey guys!" Danik shouted, saluting them with his mug. "It's good to see you again." He leaned toward Lia. "This crew is the best."

"This is Cedric, Alton, Broderick, Donte, and the scary-looking one is Jade."

Jade lived up to the description. Her jet-black hair lay flat against the back of her head. Her eyes had a black shade painted on the upper lid, matching the color of her lips. The leather top she wore crossed over her chest, forming a deep V shape between her breasts. On her arms, one sleeve extended to her wrist while the other cut off just past her shoulder, showing off a full arm of dark-olive skin. She wore pants—like Lia, but unusual for the city. They weren't comfortable ones to be useful for running and climbing, though. They were tight and made of leather.

How would she get those on? Lia wondered.

"Scary-looking one, huh?" Jade said, her eyes narrowing. She used a dagger with a blue handle to pick at her teeth.

"Don't play with her daggers," Nicolar added. "She has a nasty habit of tipping them with poison."

Jade tapped at her hip, where another dagger with a green handle sat in a sheath. "Only this one."

Lia tried not to stare.

The other guys looked like run-of-the-mill thieves and spice users: shoddy clothes, dirty faces, and rotten teeth. Cedric leered at her with a crooked smile through his messy beard and a telltale ring of red around his nostrils.

"It's good to meet you all," Lia said. "And what is it you do?"

"Whatever Nico tells us to do," Cedric said with a laugh.

Nicolar turned up his palms and shrugged. "We work together—finding things, selling things . . . a little of everything." He tapped Danik on the shoulder. "Nothing quite as impressive as this guy."

Lia raised her eyebrows. "What did he tell you?"

"We heard he recently stopped an assassination attempt on the King of Tarphan. Quite impressive."

Lia cocked her head and rolled her eyes toward Danik. "Oh, really?"

Danik looked like he'd been caught in the act of taking the

last piece of cake. "Yes, well . . . Lia was with me, too. She had a big part to play in it."

"It was nothing," Lia said, pulling on Danik's arm. "Well, it was a pleasure meeting you all. We need to leave, though. We've got . . . things to do."

Danik downed his mug and slammed it on the bar. He fumbled in his pocket, took out some coins, and tossed them by his empty drink. "Yes. We. Do. Let's go!"

Lia waved politely to Nicolar's group and held onto Danik's arm as they made their way back through the room.

Lia took a deep breath when they stepped into the street. The fresh air was a welcome change from the stuffy tavern. Danik teetered as he stood, staring into the sky. "This way," she said, pulling on his arm.

"You're the boss," Danik replied, stumbling along.

What began as concern turned to frustration and full-blown anger by the time they finished their short walk up the street. She helped him stumble through the double doors of their house, then closed them behind her. She leaned against the doors, taking a moment to breathe, trying to work up the courage to say what she wanted. *You've got this,* she told herself.

She spun around, ready to speak, but her words failed her. Danik was there. Before she could speak, he wrapped an arm around her and pulled her body toward him. His head tilted forward, and he pressed his lips against hers.

As soon as the shock faded, Lia pushed him away. The shove—infused with a trace of origine—sent Danik reeling across the room and flipping over a chair. He hit the ground, his feet flailing in the air.

"Ow!" he yelled.

"What was that?" Lia yelled.

Danik struggled to get to his feet. "I thought you wanted me to kiss you."

Lia held her hands up in question. "Where in the world did you get that idea from?"

"I don't know. Maybe all of that 'We need to get back, wink wink, ha ha.'"

"No! None of that was about wanting to kiss you!" She screwed her face up in distaste at the idea.

He scratched his head, staring at the wall.

"It was about us trying to start a new life here and you, drunk at the bar with—" She shook her head, losing track of what she wanted to say. "What are you doing with people like that?"

Danik's eyes were opened wide. He grabbed the wall to steady himself. The shock of her reaction seemed to sober him up. "What do you mean?"

"A week ago, we were shadow knights, defending the good of the kingdom and protecting those who couldn't help themselves. Now, you're stealing jewelry and consorting with"—she motioned back toward the tavern—"whoever they are."

"Now, hold on. I've done nothing wrong."

"You didn't *steal* anything? You didn't pay for this house with property that wasn't yours?"

A sheepish look came over Danik.

Lia stomped across the room and picked up a sword from the table. "You didn't buy things with money that wasn't yours?"

"We need to live, Lia! I'm not stealing *everything*! I took a couple of things, but that's it. Let's enjoy it while we can. It will give us a chance to figure out jobs and make connections. Then we can be whoever we want to be!"

"We can do that without all of this!" she shouted, motioning to the surrounding room.

"So if I didn't do what I did, what would we be doing right now, huh? Sleeping in that crumbling room with growling stomachs? What did *you* do to help?"

Lia's jaw dropped. "I'm *working*! I worked hard all day. I even found a baltham deposit today."

Danik leaned in. "Really?"

"I did. Someone stole it from me, but I found it."

"Ha! See! People steal. It's going to be them or you."

Her forehead wrinkled. "It doesn't have to be that way. I *am* earning money. I'll get paid at the end of the week."

"And until then, it's a good thing I made the money I did."

Lia sighed, then shook her head. "I don't want to do this. I'm tired. It was a long day, and I just want to sleep."

"Lia, hold on."

She stormed up the stairs, not bothering to look back.

"Come on. Let's talk about this!" he shouted. No footsteps followed.

Lia slammed the door to her room and collapsed onto her bed.

I can't believe he kissed me!

At one point, a kiss from Danik would have been a welcome surprise, but the more time she spent with him, the more muddled her feelings for him became.

How do I feel about him?

She pressed into the softness of the bed. *The bed Danik got with the money he made.* She sighed. *I don't know how I feel.*

34

GRIEF

Veron leaned forward. He ran a hand across Chelci's pale forehead, brushing the strands of hair off her face. His finger felt the side of her neck. A pulse beat, faint but steady. The slow rise and fall of her chest gave only a faint relief from his gutted feeling.

Beneath the loose tunic, her wound had mostly healed. Whatever remains of origine she had mustered were enough to keep her alive, but it had been four days, and she had yet to wake.

Veron rolled his head, stretching his neck. His legs ached and back was sore. The hard chair in his room was not made for multi-day vigils. He stood with a sigh and paused at the door, glancing back. Her face looked peaceful, but its pallor troubled him. Exiting the room, he descended the steps, crossed the courtyard, and climbed to the wall around the facility.

The midday sun beat down on his head. Sweat trickled down his face, mixing with the dirt that had accumulated over the previous week. He hadn't bathed since the attack. His shaggy hair stuck out in several directions. His unshaved beard itched, but he didn't bother to scratch it. He stared over the city from the wall, his eyes unfocused. His stomach growled, but he didn't pay it any mind.

"Veron?"

The voice was Gavin's, but Veron didn't bother turning his head.

"Have you eaten? Could you use some water?"

Veron offered a faint smile and shook his head. The questions were kind, but he didn't want to be bothered.

Gavin came alongside him and sat on the edge of the wall, looking out in the same direction that Veron did. The younger knight's shaved head glistened. He ran a hand through his thick beard but said nothing else.

"What do you want, Gavin?" Veron asked.

The man's head turned, a weak smile forming. "You've been by her side for days. We're worried about you." He motioned down toward the courtyard. "Me, Dayna, Ruby . . . everyone."

"*Everyone.*" Veron scoffed. "Shawn's taken. Lia and Danik are gone. Chelci's—" He stopped as he choked up.

"Chelci's alive," Gavin said, "and she's going to recover."

Veron sniffed and wiped his eyes. "I know. I believe she will. All this has me thinking, though. Why do we do any of this?"

"Sir, we're Shadow Knights. We serve Terrenor. We stop injustice. We stand up for those who can't. We—"

"I know, but—" Veron stopped and covered his mouth with his balled fist. His jaw quivered as tears rolled down his cheeks. "What if she doesn't recover, Gavin?" His voice trembled. "What would I do without her?"

Gavin pursed his lips, remaining silent.

"Does what we do make a difference? Does it matter?"

Gavin's mouth gaped. "It does matter." His weak words fell flat.

Veron gripped the stone wall harder. "I've spent practically all my life serving Terrenor, and now everything is falling apart."

"Sir, I believe in what we're doing. I've seen the good we've accomplished." He motioned toward the courtyard. "Come train with us. It will do you good to move and sweat. The rest of us were about to drill a circuit of archery, staffs, and throwing knives.

Veron wiped his face and stared ahead. After a quiet moment, he pushed off the wall and turned away. "I'm leaving," he said as he walked to the steps.

"Leaving?" Gavin questioned. "As in . . . for a bit? Are you coming back?"

Where am I going? He didn't know, so he didn't bother answering. Taking nothing with him, he pulled up his hood and left the Shadow Knights training center, not even bothering to take the secret exit.

Veron wandered the streets for hours. He passed the warehouse district and the docks, the sharp tang of fish filling his nose. He ignored the line of stands where men hocked their daily catches.

When the docks ended, he turned right, following the slope into the backside of the Red Quarter. The people's faces were long, their backs bowed by hard labor and their skin sagging from malnutrition. Some congregated under trees and awnings, watching the street as if waiting for a gift of food or coins to fall from the sky.

Veron passed the center of the quarter, and a memory of rescuing Chelci when they were young picked at him. Seeing the ferociousness of how she fought a group of men was one of the things that had helped him fall in love with her when they were young. He picked up his feet, eager to leave the area and the memory behind.

After exiting the poor area of the city, he ventured through Turba Square. The sun hardly seemed a deterrent to the packed crowd in the market. Food, clothes, and supplies changed hands from carts while people shouted. Others entered and exited doors of permanent shops around the edge. The lively bustle perked him up for a moment until his eyes fell on his statue.

Deliverer of Freedom. Veron shook his head as he stared at the massive stone figure bearing his likeness. The sword and the cloak looked realistic, but the face never struck him as a true resemblance. He strolled closer, craning his neck. The statue used to be King Darrick, the leader when King Vitrion of Norshand was killed hundreds of years before, but when Edmund Bale took over, he had the affront to the history of Norshewa destroyed. *They should have left it blank instead of making this.*

With a tight jaw, he wandered out of the square. Making his way east, with no intended destination, a shop brought his feet to a halt. *Fenster Foods* stared back at him. It had been a season or more since he'd seen his old friend, Morgan Fenster. A pang of guilt tugged at him for letting time and distance grow between them, but he shook it off. *Today is not the day to reconnect.* He pulled his hood farther and turned to leave.

"Veron?" a woman called.

He stopped, trying to hide his grimace. He turned to see Jeanette, Morgan's wife, through the shop doorway. Her graying hair bounced next to her face while her rosy cheeks glowed at the sight of him.

"Jeannette." He forced a smile and stepped in her direction. "How are you?"

She beamed, walking outside and wiping her hands on a stained apron. "We're good." Her face dropped, and she leaned forward. "We heard what happened to Chelci. How is she?"

Veron frowned and shook his head. "We don't know yet. She hasn't woken."

"Morgan and I were planning to come by." She waved him toward the shop. "Come in. He'd love to see you."

"I can't," Veron replied. He glanced up the street and pointed. "I have to, um . . . I should get back."

Jeannette reached out and grabbed his arm. "Just for a moment?"

He took a deep breath and blew it out before he nodded. Lowering his hood, he followed the woman through the door.

The Fensters' shop, with its low ceiling and bins of food, reminded Veron of the old grocery he used to work at in Karad. Fruit and vegetables lined the rows. A counter sat at the side. He smiled at the memory of learning how to run a business with Morgan many years before. The major difference in the shop was the back row. Where the old shop ended, this one contained a small kitchen. A counter for chopping ingredients contained knives and bowls, and a small fire held two large pots hanging over it.

"Can I get you some soup?" Jeannette asked, moving to the pots and grabbing a ladle off the counter. "This potato soup is a new recipe and may be my best yet."

Veron held up a hand. "Thank you, but—" He stopped speaking as a man entered the shop from the back room.

Morgan's short hair remained brown, but his trimmed beard grayed. His slightly overweight body still held a youthful look, despite being in his mid-fifties. He carried a crate of leafy vegetables, but at the sight of Veron, he stopped. A broad smile formed, and he set down the produce.

"Veron! What an honor!" Morgan said, stepping forward. His mouth turned down, and his brows knit together. "Anything new on Chelci?"

Jeanette shook her head. "She's still asleep. They don't know yet."

Veron let his head drop toward the floor. Morgan stepped closer, holding his arms open. Veron allowed him in, and the older man wrapped him in a tight embrace. After a moment, Veron released his grip but Morgan held on. The tension in Veron's body faded. He tightened his arms around the man again. Moisture formed in the corners of his eyes. Morgan's grip grew tighter, and Veron sniffed. Memories of Chelci and the life they'd had together flashed before him. Tears streamed down his face, and before he realized, he sobbed. Morgan rubbed his back, not saying a word. When the tears subsided, Morgan loosened his hold, and the two men pulled away, wiping at their eyes.

"I'm sorry I haven't visited sooner," Morgan said.

Veron nodded. "It's all right."

"I heard about Lia, too."

Veron raised an eyebrow.

"Gavin came by yesterday and filled us in. Is there anything you need? Anything I can do to help?"

"Please take some soup," Jeannette said.

Veron smiled and shook his head. "Thanks, but I'm not hungry." He turned back to Morgan. "I don't need anything. These past few days, I've thought a lot." He turned his attention to the rows of food and strolled down them, allowing his hand to brush against the contents of the bins. "I've come a long way from when I was a thief on the streets in Karad."

Morgan laughed. "Yes, you have."

"But, I wonder what's been the point of it all."

"What do you mean?"

"I've given my life to learning the ways of the Shadow Knights. I've rebuilt the group and given all my time and energy to it, but . . . why? I don't feel like I'm any better now than when I lived on the streets."

Morgan's head cocked.

"I've lost my daughter, and who knows about Chelci? Our group of knights is dwindling. And now there is some group bent on hunting us down who can take away our powers. Part of me wishes I had never done any of it. I could have created another business like North Karad Market."

Morgan smiled at the reference to the business they'd worked at many years before.

"I could have lived a quiet life. Everything would have been simpler, and Chelci would be fine."

"Your life has mattered," Morgan said, his eyes piercing as they stared intently.

Veron took a deep breath and breathed it out as he bobbed his head. "I know. I know it has. I just—" The choking feeling returned. "I hope she's all right."

Morgan turned to his wife. "Do you mind watching the store for a bit?"

Jeannette smiled sweetly. "Of course not."

"Come with me." Morgan waved Veron toward the door.

Veron followed, and the two men entered the street. Morgan turned toward the square.

"When Bale killed Catherine and my kids, I thought my life was over," Morgan said. "Nothing I did seemed to mean anything. I went through the motions of my day, but I was a shell of a person. The others at the market tried to cheer me up and give me hope, but I wanted nothing to do with it. Do you know why, Veron?" Morgan stopped and looked him in the eyes.

Veron wiped his eyes and shook his head.

"I *wanted* to be miserable. My family was gone. I didn't deserve to have anything good because it wouldn't be fair to them. Do you know what pulled me out of it?"

Veron didn't respond.

"It was *you*." Morgan winked and resumed walking.

"What did I do?" Veron asked, shuffling to catch up.

"You showed up at the market. You had a task to complete. You had passion and urgency, and you welcomed me into it."

Veron's forehead pinched. "Of course I welcomed you. You were my friend."

Morgan shook his head. "You were off to battle the most dangerous man in Terrenor and the massive army at his command. You had special skills that few could even imagine. You had the ear of the king and the army, but I . . . was a mere grocer. What could I contribute? I didn't know, but I had a goal —to help you achieve yours."

They entered the edge of the square, and the volume of the crowd grew. Morgan raised his voice as they weaved between carts and people.

"It was on that journey that I met Jeannette. We got married, and now we have two children of our own. I could never have pictured it back in my darkest days, but I'm happy now."

"So, what are you saying?"

Morgan stopped and faced him. He set his hands on Veron's upper arms. "I thought my life was over, but *you* helped me find something that gave me meaning." A grin formed. He turned toward the center of the square and motioned toward the enormous statue. "What do you see here?"

Veron laughed. "A showy reminder that I did something seventeen years ago."

Morgan pursed his lips together. "Do you remember what this square looked like back then, when you, Chelci, your father, and I came through?"

Veron shuffled his feet but didn't reply.

"I remember an old statue right here that was toppled into rubble. I remember abandoned carts and shops. People lived in ruin and fear. Soldiers attacked Chelci and me in this very square. Look at it now."

Veron glanced around. The people appeared happy. Vendors sold products. The atmosphere was lively.

"What do you think changed?" Morgan asked.

Veron swallowed but didn't answer.

"*You* overthrew Bale. You saved Terrenor from his oppressive rule and gave everyone the freedom they craved. Now, the kingdom thrives! This statue is here because they owe it all to you, Veron."

Veron glanced up, moisture pooling in the corner of his eye. He wiped it away.

"You rebuilt the Shadow Knights. Didn't you save King Constantine's life recently in Searis? Didn't you stop the raiders in Palenting and that criminal alliance in Molvaigh? You're saving people's lives and making Terrenor a better place!" He motioned to the people in the square. "These people here wouldn't have the lives they do if it weren't for you. What you and the Shadow Knights do has a purpose."

Veron nodded. "I know you're right."

"Of course I'm right," Morgan said with a grin. "I'm the greatest grocer in all of Felting, and who could possibly be better to give advice like this?"

Veron managed a laugh. He stepped forward and wrapped his arms around his friend. "Thank you, Morgan," he said, pulling away. "I needed this."

"I bet I know something else you need?" Morgan said. "Dinner. Tonight. Let us bring a meal. It's been too long, and the kids would love to see you, too. I insist."

Veron smiled, nodding. "I would be honored."

35

CLUSTER DEPOSITS

Lia struggled to open her eyes. Her body felt stiff. It argued when she told it to move. The sun peeking through the window told her she had to get up, no matter how sore her body was. She tossed back the sheet and sat up on the side of the bed. Her yawn broke the silence. She pressed her fingers into her eyes and rubbed. *I did it yesterday. I can do it again today.*

Lia stood and dressed. She pulled her hair back then leaned to the side, stretching the individual muscles. Her shoulders, arms, and legs ached in ways she'd never experienced, even at the height of Shadow Knights training. But the more she moved, the better it felt.

A fresh breeze filled the room after she pushed open the shutters. The mountains in the east glowed, backlit by the rising sun. Between buildings, the Talon Tower rose majestically, displaying the time to the city. She took in a deep breath, filling her lungs with the crisp morning air.

When she entered the upstairs hall, Danik's steady snores emanated through the door across the way. *I wonder what he's going to do today?* She poked her head in the kitchen before she left. A pile of apples and a block of cheese made her pause as her stomach grumbled. *More stolen goods.* She sighed but grabbed an apple anyway.

A CIRCLE of men hunched together, talking when she approached the mine. A man she didn't know seemed to recognize her and snapped to get the others' attention. Conversation stopped, and the men glanced in her direction.

Rankin stood in the middle, glaring back with a smirk. "You gonna try to claim other people's stuff again today?" he asked.

Lia ignored him. She walked to where Dodd stood, but he didn't see her. "Hey, Dodd," she said.

His eyes shifted farther away.

"You realize I told the truth yesterday, don't you?"

The miner shrugged while keeping his eyes elsewhere.

Despite knowing the man for only a day, the snub hurt.

"Lia!" Her name turned her toward the office. Ben leaned out the door and beckoned her toward him.

With a last look toward Rankin, she followed the summons and entered the office.

"Eventful first day, huh?" Ben said, motioning for her to sit in a dusty chair while he took another one.

She nodded.

"I hear you brought out five loads. That's impressive."

"Thank you, sir."

"I don't know how you do what you do in that little body, but the other miners are feeling shown up."

Lia cocked her head.

Ben chuckled. "They're grown men and have been doing this for years. Now a girl comes in and shows them up on her first day? I think there's some embarrassment going on."

Her mouth curled.

"On top of all that, for another miner to find a load of baltham and you to claim it was yours . . . that won't sit well."

She sat up straight. "Sir, I promise. I found—"

He held up a hand. "We don't need to rehash it. I've worked with Rankin for ten years, so I know him well. That means . . . I know you're probably telling the truth."

Lia inhaled, her eyes growing.

"Don't get all excited, though. It's your word against his, and he was the one with the rock. There's nothing I can do about it."

Her shoulders slumped. "Yeah, I get it."

"Keep your head on straight and work like you did yesterday. Don't let the guys get to you."

Ben's smile comforted the lonely feeling she wrestled with. *Him believing me feels almost better than getting the credit.* "I will, sir. So, I'm curious. What do you do with the baltham?"

"I have a weekly appointment with the bank on Finday where I cash out. Stones go to jewelers and powder to druggists."

Lia raised an eyebrow.

"They mix it with some other stuff to make baltam powder —expensive, but something every apothecary needs."

"How much was yesterday's find worth?"

"I don't know yet, but . . . it should cover a full season of expenses."

Lia whistled. "And you just keep it lying around until then? Is that wise?"

He laughed. "Oh no." He nodded across the room at a black safe set into the wall. "It's secure. It's good timing, too. My loan with the bank was a few weeks behind in payments. Without some good days, we were going to be in trouble soon. This catches us up, and then some."

He pressed an object into her hand. Lia held it up, gasping. "A silver argen!"

Ben shrugged. "Like I said . . . It was Rankin's find, but that doesn't mean you can't get a little something."

She squeezed the coin in her hand. "Thank you, sir."

LIA HUNG to the back of the line again while the miners made their march through the tunnels. The other men kept their distance. Her lantern swung from its hook on the cart. The creak of the turning wheel filled the shaft. The route felt familiar.

Around a corner, a miner waited, his cart parked to the side. The short hair and trimmed beard revealed the one man she hoped to see. "Hey, Dodd," she said.

He resumed moving when she caught up, the passage just wide enough for two. "I want to apologize," he said. "In five years, I've never found any baltham deposits. Whether it was you, a girl getting lucky on her first day, or Rankin, a jerk who has no business being that fortunate, I felt put out a bit. What I'm trying to say is . . . Of course, I believe you, and I'm sorry I was rude about it."

She smiled. "Thanks, Dodd."

He opened his mouth again, but his words seemed to catch.

"What is it?"

He stopped moving and set his cart down. After glancing in each direction, he leaned in, his voice lower. "Baltham deposits are extremely rare. It takes very specific geologic conditions to create them."

Lia leaned in. "What are you getting at?"

"In those rare conditions, it's not unusual for *multiple* deposits to form."

Her eyes grew. "You're saying there's a chance there is more where I found the one?"

He nodded, a grin forming. "A pretty decent chance."

"Let's get down there, then!"

He placed his hand on her shoulder. "Rankin knows this. *All* the miners know this. They're going to follow him and work as closely as possible to wherever he was yesterday."

"But Rankin knows I was the one who found it . . . which means he's going to follow me."

He nodded. "Did he know where you were?"

She shook her head. "I don't think so. But he could follow me today, right?"

Dodd grinned. "A new miner wouldn't know to go back to the same place, though."

Lia pursed her lips, her mind whirring. "What do you say we work together? Split the bonus of anything we find?"

Dodd smiled. "Sounds great."

LIA SET DOWN her cart near Dodd's in the main hub. Richter and the rest of the men chatted while they waited. Dodd busied himself, fidgeting with a lantern out of earshot. Dirt crunched as one of Rankin's cronies, Cross, approached. His shaved head and black skin nearly disappeared in the dim light of the mine.

When he looked toward Lia, he jerked his head as if he were acting surprised to see her. "Hey . . . Lia. I forgot you were here. Nice job yesterday, by the way—all those loads." He shook his head and whistled. "It's impressive."

"Thanks," she replied, tense, ready for anything.

Cross fidgeted with the hem of his shirt. "Which shaft were you, uh, working yesterday?"

Lia tried to act casual, while inside, her heart pounded. She motioned across the room. "Down there—the far shaft, at the end of the line."

"Huh," he looked falsely disinterested. "You going back there again today?"

She shrugged. "I thought I might try somewhere new instead."

Cross nodded then glanced around. "Right. A change of scenery can be nice. Well … good luck today."

Lia laughed to herself as the miner walked away. She glanced across the room at Dodd, who had been watching. He winked.

"Rankin! Where you working today?" a miner called.

Rankin smiled, and several others laughed at the question. "I'm not telling you fools," he said, smiling.

"Come on," another man urged. "You've already got your payout. Give the rest of us a chance."

"I guess you'll just have to wait and see, won't you?"

Lia acted as if she wasn't looking, but out of the corner of her eye, she caught Cross standing next to Rankin. He whispered something that caused Rankin to smile. They both looked down the decoy shaft.

"Looks like that worked," Dodd whispered after returning to her side.

"All right, men—and lady," Richter said, raising his hands. "Yesterday was a big day. We had our first baltham deposit found since last suether."

The crowd cheered, stamping the ground with their boots.

"Edkins is happy. I'm happy." He motioned to Rankin. "This guy is definitely happy. Let's hope we can have more of that success today. Now, get to work!"

Lia and Dodd lingered a moment, giving the others a chance to disperse. Everyone followed Rankin down the far shaft. When they were alone, Dodd motioned with his arm. "You lead the way."

Lia rolled her cart down the shaft from the day before. The walls looked identical, and she panicked until a familiar section stood out, close to the end of the tunnel. A smile grew on her face and she set down her cart. "This is it." She rubbed her hand along the rough wall, her fingers finding the indentation she sought. "Right here."

Dodd held up his lantern, peering close at the surrounding area. He nodded. "All right then. If there are any clusters, they're going to be within an axe length around that spot. You start here," He pointed to the right of the indentation, "and I'll work over here. Work in small chunks, inspecting debris closely. If there's something here, we want to see it."

Her body fresh and filled with energy, Lia chipped away at the rocky wall. Nervous she would miss something, she restrained the origine, forcing herself to knock off smaller bits of rock than the day before. The morning progressed, but no signs of gray deposits appeared. Dodd made similar progress, and they both took a load of stone up to the surface at the same time.

When they returned to the hub, Cross came out of the far shaft with a full load. He eyed the two.

"Any luck?" Dodd asked in a friendly tone.

Cross squinted, stopping his cart. "Nothing yet. Where are you working today, Dodd?"

Dodd motioned vaguely toward their shaft. "Down over there."

Cross stared back as if waiting for a further explanation. The unasked question of why Dodd hadn't joined the others hung in the air.

"I figured you all crowded together down there," Dodd added. "I wanted more room to work."

Cross nodded, his lips pursed. After an awkward silence, he picked up his handles. "Well, good luck to you." He stared Lia down as he rolled past.

"You think they're suspicious?" she whispered when he was gone.

Dodd nodded. "I think *he* is. Nothing we can do about that, though. Come on."

．　．　．

THE AXE SANK IN, chipping off a small section of rock. Lia picked it up, then tossed it into the cart. Her arms grew tired. Sweat dripped off her forehead. *Time for some water.* She removed the stopper from her water flask and took a long drink. Dodd joined her in a break.

"Time for another support," he said, pointing to the ceiling over the section they'd been excavating.

Lia swallowed and cocked her head. "Another?" She glanced around, noting the other beams. "We already have three just in this area."

"If there are baltham deposits here, that means a higher concentration of gas, which means increased instability. We may not need it, but it's better to be safe."

Lia nodded, dragging a beam from a nearby pile of wood. Dodd helped her position it and held a crossbeam in place while they fastened the extra support to the existing structure. Finished, he tapped his palm along the wood. "Good. Now, we keep working."

Lia hefted her axe and sank it into the wall. It made a thunk, but nothing came loose. "Do you think we'll find something?"

Dodd heaved a stroke into the wall, knocking a sizable chunk loose. "Not likely."

Lia stopped and spun to him. "Really?"

He chuckled, tossing the chunk into his cart. "Sorry if I got your hopes up. Cluster deposits *can* happen, but they're not common."

"Why are all those men so caught up with following Rankin, then?"

"It's the hope. They've got to work somewhere. It might as well be a wall that has a higher chance of something great." He sank his axe into the wall again with no result. "You know that small chunk you found yesterday?"

Lia hit the rock, flecks coming off. "Yeah."

"The bonus alone will be almost as much as a miner makes in an entire season."

Her stomach sank. "Don't tell me that. Now I hate Rankin even more."

He laughed. "Sorry."

She readied her axe. "Well, bonus or not, I kind of enjoy the work."

She sank her axe into the wall, using only a bit of origine. For a moment, only a web of cracks formed, but as she wrenched the tool out of the wall, a large chunk fell.

Lia froze. Her jaw trembled, and her lungs struggled to take in a breath.

"You all right?" Dodd asked, preparing to swing.

Lia couldn't respond. She couldn't look in his direction. Her eyes locked on the gray lump in the wall, staring back at her.

"Lia," Dodd whispered, leaning in. His voice trembled. "You found more."

Her breath returned. She set down her axe and stepped in, touching the gray rock with her fingers. It was short but the length ran three fingers.

"That's larger than what Rankin turned in yesterday," Dodd said.

A nervous laugh bubbled from Lia's lips. "Let's get it."

They worked carefully, chiseling around the seam of gray, careful not to miss any. With a gentle levering of the pick, the rock came free. Dodd picked it up and extended it to Lia with a broad grin. "You did it."

"*We* did it," she corrected. She took the stone and turned it in her hand, gazing in awe. "I wouldn't have known to look here without you. Like I said, we'll split the bonus."

"Split what bonus?" The raspy voice sent a chill up her spine. She spun. Rankin and Cross blocked the passage, Cross with his pickaxe leaning against his shoulder and Rankin leveling a crossbow.

"Rankin! What are you doing?" Dodd asked. "Where'd you get a crossbow from?"

"It doesn't matter," Rankin said, raising his weapon. "Give it to me."

Cross readied his pickaxe, leaning in with his knees bent.

Lia's fist tightened on the rock, taking a step backward. "You stole mine yesterday. This one's ours."

Rankin's eyebrow raised, the corner of his mouth curling up. "Ours? You're a team now, are you?" He aimed to the side, pointing the crossbow at Dodd. "In that case, give me the stone, or your *teammate* dies."

Dodd gasped. Lia extended an arm in front of him. "Give it up, Rankin," she said, a warm tingle running through her body. "Trust me, you don't want to do this."

"What? Are you gonna push me against the wall with a pickaxe again? I'd like to see you try. Your friend will have a bolt in his skull by the time you can move."

"Try me," she said, her voice slow and even. She narrowed her eyes. "Shoot him. I dare you."

"Lia?" Dodd's voice trembled.

"Hand. It. Over." Rankin said, pronouncing each word.

Lia stared back, still as a statue.

Rankin's eyes bounced between them while a tense silence filled the tunnel.

Cross rocked forward and backward, bouncing the axe in his hands. "Are we gonna do this, or what?" he asked after a long moment.

Rankin's mouth formed into a sneer. "Yes. Yes, we are." His finger moved.

Lia didn't give the weapon time to respond. Dropping the rock, she dashed forward, grabbing the front of the crossbow and yanking it from Rankin's hand, the loosed bolt flying harmlessly sideways. Without pausing, she grabbed the pickaxe from Cross. She turned the tool around, clubbed him in the stomach with the handle, then slammed it into the side of Rankin's head. Time sped up as she released the origine.

The two miners dropped to the ground, yelling and clutching their injured areas. Lia held the axe out, ready to strike again. With wide eyes, the men scrambled to their feet. They stumbled backward several paces, then turned and sprinted through the tunnel.

Lia took a deep breath, then tossed the pickaxe to the ground, disgusted. "I warned them," she muttered.

"How did you do that?" Dodd asked.

Lia turned. Leaning backward with his back pressed against the wall, Dodd's jaw hung loose.

Lia shrugged. "Just something I picked up."

"You moved like—" His eyes grew. "Stormbridge!" He pointed his finger and shook it. "You're a shadow knight, aren't you?"

Her breath caught. Her eyes drifted, staring at the wall. "I was . . . once."

"That's amazing," he breathed.

"We should get to the surface," Lia said, picking the chuck of stone off the ground and shaking it in the air. "If Rankin gets there first, he'll tell everyone I stole this from him."

A rumbling sound filled the passage. Lia glanced in both directions. The sound seemed to come from everywhere at once, but the darkness hid its source.

"What is that?" she asked.

Dodd shrugged. "I don't know." His eyes grew large, and he pointed over her shoulder. "Look out!"

Lia turned, unprepared for what awaited her.

A mining cart exploding out of the darkness, barreling toward her. Rankin ran behind it, pushing the handles forward, his crazed eyes wide and vengeful.

Lia jumped. The cart ran underneath her as she extended her legs forward, catching Rankin in the chest. The man's momentum was more than her body could absorb, even strengthened by her extra power inside. She knocked into the wall, a dull thud shaking her head.

An enormous crash filled the air. Splinters of wood exploded, and the ground shook. Dodd was nowhere to be seen.

Lia's sight dimmed, pain searing her head. A low groan enveloped everything—a steady rumble intensifying from deep in the ground. Her eyes jerked open.

Rankin stumbled around, clutching his chest and scanning the ground. "Where is it?" he yelled, his voice high and manic.

The cart had demolished the wooden beam over them, and one of their two lanterns lay broken, shards of glass littering the ground. The wall shuddered. Lia pressed her hand against it, trying to stand. Her legs wobbled.

She spotted the prone body of Dodd, and alarms rang in her head. She stumbled forward.

"Where did it go?" Rankin yelled, his body flailing in the dim light. He waved his arms across the ground.

Lia knelt next to her friend. "Dodd, are you all right?" His chest moved, but his eyes remained closed. Scanning down his body, she cringed. A wooden brace crushed his legs, bloodied and broken by the impact of the cart.

Something grabbed her shirt and yanked her. "Where did you put it?" Rankin yelled, leaning toward her face.

"I don't know!" She pushed him away and turned back to Dodd.

The corridor rumbled. Dust fell from the ceiling. She pulled at the wood pinning him, but it wedged between the walls and wouldn't budge.

"Help me with this!" she yelled.

Ignoring her, Rankin bent and picked up an object. He held it up to inspect it in the light—a black stone with a gray streak.

"Please!" Lia shouted. "Help him!"

His cackle filled the shaft. He clutched the stone, then turned and ran.

Lia stared after him as small rocks hit her on the back. Rankin disappeared into darkness.

A squeeze on her arm caught her attention. "Run for it," Dodd whispered. His eyes filled with pain. "I can't move."

She clenched her jaw, took a deep breath, then set her hands on the wooden beam. With a loud grunt, she pulled harder, using her well of energy. A crack filled the air, the thick wooden beam splitting in two. Her heart leaped, but as she tossed the beam clear, the ceiling collapsed.

A mountain of dirt and rock fell as one. Unable to grab Dodd and move away in time, she flipped the nearest intact cart. The cart covered her, and she covered Dodd.

The light disappeared first, followed by a crushing weight like nothing she'd ever experienced. Her back shuddered, the upended cart pressing into her. She braced herself on her elbows and knees, yelling as the pummeling rock rained down.

When the tumult ended, she opened her eyes. Inky blackness surrounded her. Her arms and legs strained. Her limited supply of origine draining.

"Dodd, are you there?" She sensed him but heard nothing.

Summoning whatever strength she had in reserve, Lia pushed. Her arms and legs shook, like pushing against a wall. When she had almost abandoned hope, the weight on her back shifted. Rock tumbled against the wood of the cart. She redoubled her effort, and more of the burden sloughed off. Her arms straightened. She got a foot underneath her, then a second. She pushed with her legs. A roar escaped her throat as the wooden shell moved higher. With a final heave, the remainder of the rock and dirt against her cart fell.

Lia stumbled free, more shocked by being able to see again than in standing. A lone lantern, knocked a distance away, revealed a rounded pile of dirt and rock where she had just been. The tunnel collapse angled from the ceiling to the ground. Fortunately, she and Dodd had been near the edge, but unfortunately, they ended up on the wrong side.

"Dodd!" She lifted his body enough to wrap her arms around his chest. With her hands grasped together, she pulled. Rocks and debris covered his legs, but the rubble shifted, and he came free. Lia staggered backward, then fell to the ground, Dodd's unconscious form leaning against her legs.

She lay her head against the ground, breathing deeply. Her body was spent, wiped from the use of the origine. The corridor spun. She pressed her eyes together and focused on breathing. Her chest rose and fell as her wheezing breath labored. Drifting, drifting, her body sank until her mind went black.

36

RESCUE PLAN

The air shimmered, a haze blowing through the city. Fog curled around buildings, spilling over the cobblestone street. Walls appeared in the gloom as the clouds came and went.

Raiyn pivoted, checking in all directions. A force pulled at him, but he couldn't see or understand it. *Something is wrong*, he thought. His head jerked to the two-story structure next to him. *What was that? A voice? A cry?* His ears trembled, straining for confirmation.

Acting on instinct, he pushed open the nearest door and sprinted up the stairs. The doors on the second floor were closed, but somehow he knew where to go. He turned the knob and pushed. The door swung open.

It was a prison, like the one from Searis. A moldy stench filled the air. Water dripped from the ceiling and rolled down the mossy stone walls. Bars covered an open window where the haze blew through the city. A break in the cloud showed several buildings. A tower jumped out of the fog, standing twice as tall as anything around it.

Chains rattled, and a cough filled the room. Raiyn stepped

forward. A young woman sat against the wall. Her arms, covered in black-and-blue bruises, fixed in tight restraints. Her head slumped forward, brown hair falling in front of her face.

He ran to the woman and crouched. "Hey. Are you all right?" He brushed her hair back and she looked up. His gasp filled the room.

Dried blood mottled her face, and a nasty cut ran down her cheek. Her glassy eyes seemed to see through him, as if he weren't even there.

"Lia!" Raiyn yelled. He rested his hand on hers. "What happened?"

As he spoke, a ring of flames burst to life, encircling them. He shielded his face and turned back to Lia.

Her forehead creased, but her eyes still didn't focus. "Hello? Is someone there?" she asked.

Her voice sounded distant, as if spoken underwater, barely audible over the roar of the flames. Raiyn tried to speak louder, but the effort only made his vision blur. *What is going on?* "Lia . . . what's happening?"

RAIYN SAT UP, blinking his eyes open. His shirt clung to his chest, damp with sweat. *What was that?* He wiped his forehead and checked the room. The thatched roof dripped water onto the bare floor. The rickety door lay open as he'd left it. He scrambled to his feet and peered out the window. A light patter of rain fell on the river outside, and the sun had only just begun to rise.

I was asleep, but I could see . . . something. His eyes widened. *It was a Dream!* Raiyn's heart pounded. It had felt real, like he was there. *Is that happening to Lia now? Where was she?* He paced the hut, trying to remember the detail, the setting. *Should I go back and say something to her?* The Dream was fuzzy and grew more distant the longer he was awake. *It didn't look like Felting.* He frowned.

It had been six days since he left the Shadow Knights. He had found an abandoned hut by the river to sleep in while he looked for work. He tried to make the food the Knights had given him last, but it had run out the day before. His stomach growled. He had yet to delve into the lean pouch of coins they gave him, but the time had come. He needed food.

Before long, the rain stopped, and the clouds thinned. A hazy shine of daylight blanketed the city. Raiyn left his hut and stepped into the muddy streets. *Time to look for work, again.* He'd received a tip about a lumber company outside the south-west gate and intended to check it out.

After the rainy night, the city felt sluggish. Shoulders drooped, and people walked slower. Raiyn passed a shop grilling chicken. The smell turned his head and made his stomach ache. He hesitated a moment before continuing forward. *No, not yet. I need to wait until it's necessary.*

Lazy guards didn't even glance his way as he passed out of the city gate. The bridge over the Benevorre River arched. Raiyn peered over the edge, smiling at the beauty of the flowing water before he continued.

On the far side, the road continued south with trees lining the way, but what he sought was immediately on the right. A wooden sign leaned against a tree with *South Felting Lumber* scrawled on it. An area of cleared trees stretched west. Piles of logs and lumber stacked around the site, and a collection of men worked hard, hacking and sawing.

Raiyn entered the site. He flagged down someone taking a break from swinging his axe. "Excuse me. Can you tell me who's in charge here?"

"Meekins. Over there." The worker pointed to the side where an older man with broad shoulders and a thick beard spoke to a woman. The man's beard hung well below his chin, and he crossed his bulging arms over his chest. Raiyn approached and stood at a respectful distance to not interrupt.

Noticing his presence, the man stopped his conversation and turned to Raiyn. "Yes?" he barked.

His gruff, booming voice made Raiyn take a step back. "I'm so sorry. I didn't mean to interrupt, Mr. Meekins. I hope to speak with you about a job."

The woman chuckled, turning Raiyn's head. "You must be looking for Ms. Meekins," she said.

The woman was around forty years old. The upper portion of her dress was a faded yellow color, but the hem carried a brown stain from where it nearly touched the mud. The skin on her arms was dark and leathery, and her hair wrapped up in a messy bun on her head.

Raiyn's eyes grew. He glanced at the man then back to the woman. "I'm so sorry. I just assumed—"

"You assumed wrong," she said, then looked at the bearded man. "Just make it happen, Henry." She turned to leave and waved for Raiyn to follow. "What job?"

Raiyn stepped quickly to keep up. "I'd love to work for you." He motioned to the men working. "I can saw logs, cut boards . . . anything you need."

"I've got more workers than I need already. Sorry, kid."

Raiyn's heart sank. "I'm the best, though! I promise you'll be glad you hired me. I can produce more than any of these men!"

She stopped walking and faced him with a quirk in her mouth. "You have references?"

Raiyn hesitated. "I worked at the Goss Lumber Mill in Searis."

"You have a letter from Raymond? He and I go way back. If he's vouching for you—"

"No, I don't."

She pursed her lips and stared. "Can you get one? If he says you're great, and you bring me his reference, I'll consider you."

She pointed. "And don't even think about forging one. I know what his seal looks like."

"I, uh . . . I can't."

Her eyes narrowed. "What do you mean?"

He hung his head. "I can't go back there—to Searis."

She sighed and rested her hands on her hips. "If you're in trouble with the justice department, then I definitely can't hire you."

Raiyn kicked at the dirt, then nodded his head. "Thanks for your time." He turned and walked back to the road.

The walk back from the lumberyard felt longer than the trip there. His steps were slower, his posture slumped. *That was my last lead*, he thought. *Where can I go now?* The idea of trying to land a job with a bank crossed his mind. If it worked once, it could work again.

When he arrived at his hut, he jumped as someone exited the cramped room. The familiar face glanced around before settling his gaze on Raiyn and smiling.

"Hey, Mason," Raiyn said, smiling back.

"How are you?" Mason asked, lines forming on his brow.

"Getting low on ideas. I haven't dipped into my coins yet, but I'll have to before the day's up."

Mason pulled a cloth bundle from a bag and handed it over. "Maybe this will help."

Raiyn smelled the bread before he even opened the bundle. Two apples, some dried meat, and a chunk of bread wrapped up inside. His eyes grew. "Thank you!"

"Veron saw when I grabbed this. I think he knows."

"He didn't stop you?"

Mason shook his head. "He's a good man, even if he can be strict."

"How's Lia doing?"

Mason hesitated. "She's . . . good."

Raiyn narrowed his eyes at the forced response.

"Are you sleeping all right?" Mason asked, changing the subject and nodding toward the hut. "I can't imagine it's too comfortable in there.

Raiyn shrugged. "It's all right. Not much worse than my old bed in Searis." The memory of the previous night rushed to the tip of his tongue, but he held it back.

"What is it?"

Raiyn winced. He hadn't decided whether to share the Dream with anyone. "It's, um . . . nothing."

"Something's on your mind. You can tell me."

He pursed his lips. *Do I tell him even if it makes me sound crazy?* He took a deep breath and exhaled. "I had a Dream last night."

Mason's eyes grew.

"I've never had one before, so I'm not sure what it's supposed to mean."

"What was it?" Mason breathed.

"I guess it was a vision of the future, but—" He shook his head. "I don't know."

"What happened?"

"It was Lia."

Mason stared in rapt attention.

"She was trapped. It was a prison of some sort, but it was on the second floor of a regular building—almost like a large home, but it began to burn. Her arms were in chains, and blood and cuts covered her face. She looked like—" He shuddered at the memory.

"Like what?" Mason asked, leaning forward.

"Like she was about to die."

Mason blinked several times. His mouth hung open.

"I don't know if I should tell her or not. I guess so, but . . . What could she do about it if she knew? Would you want to know?"

Mason continued to stare but didn't reply.

Raiyn's brows pinched together. "What is it? You think we should tell her?"

Mason's chest heaved. He moved his mouth, but nothing came out.

"Mason! What is it?" Raiyn blurted.

The young shadow knight jumped. "Lia is . . . um . . . She's not here."

"What do you mean?"

"She left the night after you did . . . with Danik."

"She left? She left the Knights?"

Mason nodded. "Chelci's hurt—"

"What?"

"It's a long story," Mason said. "She was injured in an attack. Veron blamed Lia. He kicked Danik out, and Lia followed."

"Why didn't you tell me all of this when you came here the other day?"

Mason raised his shoulders. "Sorry. I wasn't sure how you'd take it."

Raiyn huffed. "So, Lia's with Danik. Where are they?"

"No one knows. They disappeared."

Raiyn's pulse thumped in his head. "Then, my Dream. It could be . . . soon."

"It could be *now*."

Raiyn's eyes grew. "We've got to find her. She needs to be warned! Can you help?"

Mason nodded. "Of course. Where was the Dream? Could you tell?"

"I—I don't think it was Felting. The buildings were stone, but—" He snapped, pointing at Mason. "There was a tower— four sides, pointed at the top with a clock on one side that rose above the city. Her window faced the clock."

"So, she's in a city with a clock tower where a second-floor window faces it."

"Tarving has a tower. I didn't see a river in the Dream, but it could have been there."

"Tienn does too. I'm pretty sure they're the only ones."

"Should we tell the other knights? Get them to help?"

Mason shrugged. "She's not a knight anymore."

"What about Veron? Surely he'd want to know."

Mason hesitated then frowned. "Maybe, but . . . If he knows the Dream comes from you—the son of his enemy?"

"Good point. Maybe not." Raiyn glanced around and patted his pockets. The coins rattled. "I've got all I need. I'm ready to go. I've never been to Tienn. Do you want to check there, and I'll go to Tarving?"

Mason nodded. "That sounds like a plan. I'll find us horses and more food. Meet me outside the stables in an hour, all right?"

"Can you find me a weapon, too?" Raiyn asked.

Mason flashed a grim smile.

"Just in case?"

"Of course. See you soon."

37

TRAPPED

"Lia! Lia!"

The voice sounded muddled and distant. Lia struggled to open her eyes and blink. *What happened?* She braced with an elbow and sat up. A dim light filled the corridor. Jagged black rocks lined the wall, and a sloped pile of debris stared at her. Her shoulders slumped.

"Lia, are you all right?" Dodd asked.

She jerked her head. Her friend leaned against the mine wall. A torn portion of his shirt wrapped his leg where blood stained the ground. "Dodd," she croaked, then cleared her throat. "I'm fine. That looks ugly." She nodded toward his leg.

"The bleeding has stopped, but I think they're both broken."

Lia winced. She struggled to her feet, bracing her arm against the wall. The pile of collapsed dirt and rock blocked their exit. She approached the pile and set her hand on the rubble. "Now, what do we do?"

"The lantern tipped over," Dodd said. "It's stable now, but we lost over half the oil. I turned the light as low as possible, but it will be out in . . . probably two hours."

Lia's heart raced. "Will they rescue us?"

Dodd pursed his lips. "It's unlikely. Who knows what Rankin will tell them? Either way, they'll assume we're dead. After a collapse like this, Edkins won't risk another cave-in. He'll close off this tunnel like they did the other."

She turned in the opposite direction, the dead end taunting her from only a few paces away. "So . . . we're trapped with about two hours of light, and no one will come to save us."

"Exactly."

Lia pressed her eyes together and sighed.

"Being a . . . shadow knight, what are you able to do?"

Lia perked up. She scanned the tunnel, taking inventory of what they had. *Two pickaxes, a shovel, a lantern, and some wooden beams.* "I can dig . . . quickly." She snatched the shovel.

Dodd adjusted his body, as if he wanted to rise, but a loud groan preceded him sinking back down.

Lia stood on the edge of the slope and used the shovel to chip into the pile of rubble at the far side of the ceiling collapse. The rocks were loose and easy to dig into. She flung the contents of the spade behind her. After a few shovelfuls, a depression formed, and her spirits rose. "I think this may work. If we can dig enough—"

Lia jumped back as a rumble of rocks filled the air. Debris rolled down the slope, filling in the depression and cascading to the ground.

"That's what I was afraid of," Dodd said. "Without support, it's loose and will continue to settle."

Lia pursed her lips and stared. Her mind whirred. "We need supports." She looked at the wooden beam laying askew on the ground and smiled.

"What are you going to do with that?" Dodd asked.

"You'll see." She managed the joist to her shoulder, spending only a small amount of stored power to get it balanced. The weight was incredible. Her legs felt like tree trunks, buckling under the weight. She used one hand to support the front while the other slid to the rear.

Lia took several deep breaths. She forced her body to calm, allowing the origine to simmer deep inside. Her arms tensed. Her core tightened. Closing the distance in a brief but spirited run, Lia flung the beam. It struck the mountain of rock and dirt near the ceiling, sinking into the pile several feet before it caught.

"Ugh," Lia groaned, pushing at the end of the wood. It wouldn't budge.

"Oh, I see." Dodd's face lightening. "You aim to punch a hole through. It shouldn't have to go far. That may be possible."

Lia wiggled the end of the beam, pulling it back until it popped free. She moved underneath it and lifted with her shoulder.

"I wish I could help," Dodd said.

Lia shuffled forward, ramming the joist into the same place. The distance it sank seemed farther, but it stopped again. "Come on!" Lia shouted, pulling it out again.

The lantern sputtered, spinning her around. The light appeared dimmer than before. "I thought we had two hours. It's not going out, is it?"

"Oh no." Dodd's jaw tightened. "The oxygen."

"What about it?"

"There's no ventilation. The flame is burning it up."

"So we're going to suffocate?"

"The flame will extinguish first. We'll be left in the dark . . . Then, yes, we'll suffocate."

Lia turned back to the mound of rock, her breath coming quicker. She readied for another attack. "How long do we have?"

Dodd hesitated, staring at the flickering light. "A minute? Maybe less."

She gripped the end of the brace. After three quick steps,

Lia flung the beam forward using all the origine she could manage. She yelled as it collided with the pile. Debris shot in all directions as the timber sank into the rubble. She strained, pushing with all her strength.

Resistance loosened, and her eyes flared. "It's through!" She spun, holding out her hands. "Quick! The shovel!"

Dodd tossed it. Lia stepped on the slope of rubble and dug furiously to the side of the beam. Rocks and dirt flung behind her. A hole formed, but the pile didn't resettle. Farther and farther she progressed until the spade broke through.

"I'm at the end!"

"Watch for it to move."

Lia eyed the beam. A creaking groaning filled the tunnel, but the joist stayed put, pressing against the ceiling. She continued digging. The dark hole grew. At first the size of a hand, it grew to the width of a body.

Lia tossed the shovel down and spun to Dodd. "That's as wide as I dare. You ready?"

The miner took a deep breath, then nodded. "Can you help me through?"

"I don't think there's an easy way to do this, but I'll do my best." Lia crouched next to him and lifted under his back and upper legs, drawing a yell from the man. "I'm sorry."

"It's all right," he puffed. "I can take the pain."

Holding the awkward weight, Lia climbed the slope. "Are you ready?"

Dodd nodded, his teeth clenched.

Lia positioned his head at the opening and rested his upper body in the tight passage. The height of the hole looked just enough. *He fits!* Lia pushed his torso while Dodd wriggled. *Halfway through.* Her options to push grew limited. She wrapped her arms around his upper-legs and heaved. He slid farther. *Nearly there!*

Dodd's body squirmed until it stopped. "I'm stuck!" a muffled voice called through the pile of debris.

Looking at the jammed passage, Lia's heart raced. The only visible parts she could push against were his bleeding and broken legs. "Can you use your arms?"

"They're pinned!" He yelled. "Push my legs!"

Lia blanched. Dark-red blood dripped from wounds. A black-and-blue bruise marred his skin.

"I'm almost there. Just push!"

Lia rested her hands against his boots. "Ready?" She paused until she heard a mumble. "Go!"

She pushed against his legs. A scream tore through the rubble, but enough resistance remained for the pressure she exerted to move his body. It slid farther until the legs went limp.

Lia gasped. "Dodd?" Nothing. "Dodd? Are you there?" She waited, but no response came. His legs rested limp against the rocks. Taking in a deep breath, Lia pushed again. His legs bent at the knees. She extended her arm, finding a hint of pressure. His body slid—slowly at first, then his legs disappeared, leaving a dark hole behind.

"Dodd?" she called through the hole. "Are you all right?" The mine was silent.

Lia skittered back down the debris pile and grabbed the lantern. The hole looked even smaller. She took a deep breath and exhaled. *If Dodd can fit through, I can too.*

She pushed the lantern ahead of her and clawed her way into the tight passage. Rocks pressed against her cheeks, her face tucked to her shoulder. The hand with the lantern stretched ahead while the other remained by her side, helping her wriggle forward. When her hips made it to the passage, her feet dangled in the air, no longer touching the rocky slope of debris. Lia gritted her teeth and pulled her body along. Sharp rocks pulled at her skin and clothes, but she continued. Her breath bounced back into her face. Shadows of arms and rocks played across her narrow field of vision. The space seemed to grow tighter the farther she moved. Her breath quickened.

A surge of hope filled her as her hand with the lantern found fresh air. The lantern dangled, extended somewhere ahead of her. *I'm almost there!* She pressed her elbow against the side and squirmed her hip forward. A rumbling sound took her breath away. The beam in front of her face shook and pressed in. She gasped. The narrow space she crawled through shrank.

Lia dropped the lantern. It clanked through the other side of the hole and, somehow, remained lit. She braced both arms against the wooden beam, stopping its movement. Pressure pushed against her. Her back slid to the opposite end of the hole. She groaned, her breath fast, her body pinned between the rocks and the beam. *I've got to get out of here!*

She glanced ahead. The opening lay just beyond her head. Using whatever reserves of origine lay inside, she pushed against the wood. She raised a knee as a brace. Using a freed arm, she pulled her body. It slid forward, propelled by her unnatural strength. Her head emerged through the other side of the hole, and she gulped a lungful of air. A distant rumble combined with pressure against her feet indicated the beam gave way on the far side. In a swift motion, she pulled both arms out and grasped the rock pile. An origine-fueled push propelled her body through the opening. She fell down the backside of the debris, bouncing off Dodd's limp body. The rumble continued a moment longer. Rocks settled, and dust puffed from the opening she passed through, but it ended as quickly as it began.

Lia lay on her back. She breathed in the new air and gave her body a few minutes to recover. *I can't believe I just did that!* She turned her head. Dodd continued to breathe, but his eyes were closed, and he didn't move. *I need to get both of us out of here.*

She sat up. A moment of dizziness washed over her but passed quickly. The pile of caved-in rocks looked the same as it had on the other side. About to turn away, something caught her attention. *What is that?* Her eyes narrowed, squinting in the dim light. She struggled to her feet and stumbled forward.

The weak light of the lantern splashed across the rubble. Her body threw a long shadow against the wall. She leaned over and paused before a broad grin curled her lips.

Lia's legs felt like lead as they stumbled forward. Her lantern creaked, the metal handle held away from her body. Dodd's unconscious body slumped over her shoulder. The weight of the grown man seemed to push her into the ground. In her gut, the warm simmer of the origine fueled her and was the only thing keeping her standing.

The other miners and their carts were gone by the time they'd escaped the collapsed passage. Shouting brought no one, so Lia trudged toward the surface, carrying Dodd.

The walk seemed interminable. Her body ached but she continued forward, one step at a time. When she thought she could go no more, sunlight shone at the end of the tunnel. *Only a few more steps, Lia.* A weight seemed to fall off her when she exited. She took a deep breath, her lungs giving thanks for the fresh air.

The other miners gathered around the side of the office, their sight obscured from her while heated debate rang through the air. Lia approached the office, continuing to carry Dodd.

"It was awful," Rankin's grating voice rumbled.

She peeked around the corner. Ben observed from the porch with his arms crossed, looking over the men. Rankin and Cross stood together while the rest of the miners listened.

"That girl went crazy," Rankin continued. "She stabbed Dodd in the chest with her pickaxe."

The crowd groaned.

"That's right." Rankin touched his sternum. "Right here. Dodd gurgled and shouted how he never should have trusted her before he collapsed."

"I was there, too," Cross added. "Her eyes were wild. She came after us."

"Clubbed me in the side of the head," Rankin said, pressing where matted blood and a large bruise showed. "Then she went for the support beams."

"Went for them?" Ben asked.

Rankin nodded. "Hacked at them with her axe while yelling. We begged her to stop, but she wouldn't listen. Even when the tunnel rumbled, she continued."

"And laughing about it," Cross added. "It was disturbing."

Ben lifted his chin. "And you think this is all because she wanted the baltham you found?"

"That's when she broke," Cross said, motioning to the rock with the gray streak Rankin held. "Everything was fine until Rankin found that. Two days in a row. I guess the girl couldn't take it."

"Yeah," Rankin added. "Now, she and Dodd are both dead." He chuckled. "I guess she's not as strong as everyone thought."

"How strong did you think I was?" Lia asked, stepping from around the corner, her boots echoing on the boards of the porch.

The crowd gasped. Rankin's and Cross's eyes widened, the whites forming a full circle.

Lia lowered Dodd from her shoulder and leaned him against the wall of the building. "He's still unconscious," she said. "Can someone clean his wounds and bandage his legs? I think they're broken."

After a tentative few steps, one miner rushed into the office to obey.

"You're alive!" Ben said.

Lia nodded, sitting on the edge of the porch. She took deep, steady breaths to aid her body's recovery. "We're *both* alive."

"Sh-sh-she's lying!" Rankin sputtered, shouting and pointing a finger at her. "We didn't take it from her. She tried to take it from me!"

Lia cocked her head and stared at the man.

"She didn't accuse you of that," Ben said, narrowing his eyes.

"Oh. Uh . . ." Rankin's head was on a swivel. He scanned the crowd and crept backward. "She said that . . . in the mine. Like she deserved to be the one to find it."

"Bones, would you shut him up?" Ben said, nodding to the massive laborer.

Bones approached Rankin, crossing his arms and standing next to him. Rankin's mouth remained shut.

"Lia, would you tell us what happened from your perspective?" Ben asked.

Lia nodded. "I will, but first—" She rummaged in her pocket. "I'm tired of this weighing me down." She pulled out a black stone the size of a fist and extended it toward Ben.

He stepped forward and accepted the rock. "What is this?" When he turned the stone, the crowd of miners gasped. The opposite side faded from black to a sharp gray. Over four fingers wide and tall, the entire rock was baltham.

Ben's voice caught. After a moment of silence, a nervous laugh bubbled out of his mouth. He glanced at Lia, his mouth curling into a broad grin.

"Now, do you want to hear what really happened?" she said.

38

CLEANING OFF

Although exhausted from the grueling ordeal, Lia's steps felt light on the walk home. Putting Rankin in his place, earning the respect of the miners, saving Dodd's life, and discovering baltham made for an eventful day. Her stomach grumbled as she made her way through the streets. *I hope Danik has some food.*

A raucous cheer sounded inside the house as Lia approached. *What is that? Sounds like a party.* Lia opened the door to a roomful of people, and her jaw stiffened. Mugs covered the table with stains of liquid across the surface. Picked-over bones and fruit rinds lay discarded on platters. Around the table sat the group of thieves from the tavern.

Standing beside the table, Danik held a rock in an open palm. The room had quieted, the crowd at the table leaning toward him.

Danik's eyes flitted to her, and a grin turned up the sides of his mouth. He held up a finger toward the others, then looked across the room where a sword leaned against the wall. "I'm ready," he said, continuing to watch the wall.

The man named Cedric stood with bits of foam in his

scruffy beard. He stepped next to Danik, extended his hand, and paused. His body wavered. He waved his arms to regain his balance. With a quick snap of his wrist, Cedric swatted Danik's hand away.

Danik turned into a blur. His speeding form crossed the room and returned. As fast as Lia could have blinked, he held the sword still with the rock balanced on the flat of the blade.

Lia's eyes opened wide, her chest tightening. *Don't show them that!*

The crew exploded into applause. Several stamped their mugs on the table, and Cedric clapped him on the back.

"That's 'mazing," Cedric slurred.

"Danik!" Lia yelled, drawing all eyes to her.

Danik's face cocked in a curious expression. The thieves' leader, Nicolar, held a reserved grin. Jade stared with narrowed eyes as she twirled a dagger, tip down, on the table.

"Ooh, Danik, show her the dagger one!" Cedric called. An enthusiastic round of approval followed.

"What are you doing?" Lia asked, her eyes boring into him.

Danik shrugged, a mischievous smirk on his face. "Just having a bit of fun."

"Come on!" Cedric encouraged, hiccuping. "Do it again!"

Danik nodded while the crew cheered. He pranced across the room and stood with his back against the far wall, raising his chin and taking in a deep breath. Jade stood and moved clear of the table. She raised a blue-handled dagger, holding it by the blade and sighting past it toward Danik.

Lia watched, her stomach churning. *You fool. What are you thinking?*

Jade pulled her arm back, then flicked her wrist. The knife flew, twirling end over end. The crew of men stared, their mouths hanging open and eyebrows lifted. When the dagger was about to reach Danik, his arm jerked. He caught the weapon by the hilt, the blade stopped just shy of his chest. The crew threw up their hands and shouted again, clapping and cheering.

Danik exaggerated a bow, then spun the dagger through his fingers. "Thank you, thank you."

"Danik," Lia said, her teeth clenched. "Can I talk with you, alone?"

"Oooh," Cedric teased. "She wants to *talk*." He returned to the bench seat and sloughed himself down, knocking his mug over and spilling ale on the table. He responded to the spill with a cackle of laughter.

Danik chuckled, then turned to Lia. He shrugged and followed her up the stairs.

The crew around the table watched as Lia climbed. Her neck grew hot. She turned into her bedroom and waited for Danik to enter before closing the door behind him.

"What are you doing?" she hissed, keeping her voice down and hitting him on the arm.

"Ow!" He said, shrinking back. "We're just having fun."

"You're showing off the origine."

"So what? Why do you care?"

Lia opened her mouth but paused. *Why do I care?*

"We're not shadow knights anymore. We don't have to 'follow the code.'"

"Yeah, I guess, but . . . why are those guys here?"

Danik's face brightened. "I ran into them again today and invited them over."

"Danik, they—" She lowered her voice. "They don't seem like . . . good people to hang around."

"And that's coming from you?" He scoffed. "What was that place you 'hung around' in Lorranis? The place with the viper pit?"

"That was different."

"Was it?" He held her hand and took a step back to sit on the bed.

She remained standing and wriggled free of his hand.

"Lia, I'm not trying to become like them. I'm only trying to meet the people of Tienn. Nicolar and his crew can make things happen. They could be useful if we need them."

She squirmed. "There are other sorts of people we could connect with."

"Who?" His eyebrow raised. "Like those roughnecks at the mine? Are they going to 'open the doors' of this city for us?"

She put a hand on her hip. "There are good men at that mine. Not a lot of them, but there are some. And I'll have you know the mine has the potential to open a lot of doors."

Lia pulled her hand out of her pocket.

Danik's eyes widened. "You already earned one argen for, what . . . two days' work?"

Lia chuckled, then shook her head. "This is nothing. This is a small bonus from that piece I told you about yesterday, but *today* . . ." She grinned. "I found another."

"More baltham?"

She nodded, then formed a ball with her hands.

Danik's eyes grew even larger. "That big?"

Her smile grew. "It was *huge*! It's gonna be worth . . . I don't even know how much—the owner will find out on Finday."

"What will you get?"

"My bonus should be . . . probably five sol, maybe up to ten."

Danik's jaw dropped. "Ten sol!"

"We'll see."

"Is that why," he motioned to her face, "you look like a line of carriages ran you over. Is that what it takes?"

"Eh . . . someone tried to kill me, but it wasn't as easy as they expected."

Danik's attention drifted, his eyes lighting up. "We can live like royalty—buy whatever we want."

"And we don't have to *steal*," Lia added.

Danik nodded.

Exhaustion washed over her. She wrinkled her forehead, the crust of dirt and sweat reminding her how filthy she was.

"Come downstairs," Danik said, standing and waving her toward the door. "Get to know the crew. I'm sure you'll grow to like them."

She shook her head. "I wish I could take a bath."

Danik perked up. "The tub is still full. I used it earlier."

Her eyes narrowed. "While I was earning money, nearly dying in the mine, you were here soaking in the tub?"

He shrugged. "I had to make sure it worked." He gestured toward the street. "There's a shop across the way that delivers hot water. I'll have them bring in a couple of fresh buckets to heat it back up."

She nodded. "Thanks."

A SIGH ESCAPED Lia's mouth as she lowered her body into the tub. The water crept up her skin until she dunked her head under. While not hot, it was warm enough. She ran her hands through her hair, loosening the tangles and rinsing out the crusty portions before she reemerged, tossing her hair behind her.

Vertical slats of wooden boards held together by metal bands formed a large circle for the tub. She leaned her head back against the edge and allowed her body to float. Only her toes touched the bottom.

The heat and sweat of the day faded into the distance. The worry about suffocating and dying dimmed. Lia closed her eyes and pictured herself in a palace, attended by servants, able to soak in a private bath whenever she desired. *I could get used to this. I wonder if Father and Mother ever have time to—* Her thoughts jarred. *Mother.*

She'd been so busy that she'd forgotten what happened.

The image of Chelci bleeding out on the wall fixed in her mind. She splashed water on her face, but the memory wouldn't fade —her mother staring disapprovingly, her father yelling in a rage, blaming her for everything.

They wanted me to be like them. They didn't care what I wanted or who I was. Lia's jaw fixed. Her blood heated. *They kicked out Raiyn. They kicked out Danik. They don't deserve to have me.*

She grabbed the soap next to the tub and vigorously scrubbed her body. Caked dirt rubbed off her neck and arms. She lifted her legs out of the water and cleaned them one at a time. She used a brush to scrub her backside. The water grew opaque, tinted with brown.

While she cleaned, she repeated to herself that her parents didn't care who she was. They didn't listen. With nothing else to distract her, a nagging question tugged at her. *Who am I? What do I want?*

Raiyn came to mind. She pictured his shaggy, black hair and his earnest smile. *What's he doing now? I hope he landed on his feet.* Training him made her feel alive and purposeful. She missed the early one-on-one training sessions and the genuine way he responded to everything they did.

A crash and a round of laughter sounded through the floor. *I hope Danik isn't down there showing off again.*

Her mind shifted to the baltham she discovered. *If my bonus is as large as I hope, Ben's going to be set now.* She smiled.

A stumbling sound drew her attention to the door. Someone's heavy footsteps clunked down the hall.

"'Ere are you?" a slurred voice came through the door. *Cedric.*

The knob turned and Lia gasped. The latch rattled against the frame, the door remaining shut. She covered her chest with her arms. "Um, I'm in here," she called. "What do you need?"

"I need a bath," he yelled.

"I'm *taking* a bath, now," she replied.

"Exactly." He laughed and hiccuped. "We can help each other." The door rattled again.

"Excuse me!" she shouted. "You may *not* come in."

Pounding sounded.

"Stop it!" Lia stood and climbed out of the water. She grabbed her towel and wrapped it around her body.

The door bowed as if someone pushed from the other side. The latch groaned.

Her anger simmered. The origine was ready, and she prepared to teach the man a lesson.

"Cedric! What are you doing?"

Lia paused with her fingers on the latch. *Danik is here.* Someone was shoved in the hall. Crashing sounded through the door.

"Leave her alone," Danik said. "She's bathing."

Leaning against the door, imagining the scene in the hall, a proud smile formed on Lia's face.

"I wanted to bathe *with* her," Cedric muttered. "I'm dirty too, see?"

"She's not yours to bathe with."

"She's young and pretty. She needs a man like me!"

"Keep your hands off her," Danik warned. "Lia is mine!"

Lia's head jerked, her brows pinching together. *What?* Her heart pounded as she played his words over in her head. *What have I gotten myself into?*

Shuffling sounded and footsteps faded. Lia leaned against the door, her hair dripping onto the floor. She strained her ear for any sign when a soft rap sounded. She jumped back.

"Lia. Are you all right?"

Her heart thumped, conflicted over what happened. Keeping one arm around the towel, she pulled back the latch and cracked the door, peeking her head through. Danik stood in the hall. "I'm okay. Um . . . Thanks."

"Sorry about Cedric. Ignore him—he's drunk."

Lia frowned. "Yeah, sure. I could have handled him anyway."

"I'm sure you would have." He motioned down the hall. "I'm going to kick them out. You sure you're fine?"

She nodded. "I'm going to get back in for a bit. I'm fine though."

Latching the door, she lost the towel and entered the water again. She dunked her head, trying to wash away the memory of Cedric's ramblings and Danik's possessiveness. She pictured herself back at the mine, holding the chunk of rock high in the air, displaying the gray baltham for all to see. The crowd clapped and cheered. She saw herself spinning, beaming. Her parents' images formed, standing in the back of the crowd. Her arm faltered. They clapped along with the others, with reserved smiles on their faces. Lia stared while red spots grew on her mother's clothes. Chelci continued to smile as blood dripped down her tunic.

Lia gasped as she emerged. Her heart pounded. Her breath rattled. She wiped the water from her face and pushed her hair back. The water continued to drip. She wiped her eyes, but muffled sobs filled the room.

39

THE SIPHON CHAMBER

T alioth walked with sure steps through the cave, despite the darkness of the passage. He knew the tunnels well enough to walk through them blindfolded. His boots padded over smooth rock and patches of dirt. Valdok followed, keeping pace. Faint red crystals dotted the rock walls at regular intervals, their light barely enough to see by.

They rounded pillars of stone and stepped over jagged crevices. Dark passages branched off, but the men continued straight. After a turn, a large space opened where a crevasse plunged to the side. The light from the crystals stretched into the gaping darkness but couldn't touch its depths.

After a minute more of walking, two torches burned ahead. A steel door nestled into the rock face. Two men stood guard, perking up at their arrival.

"Bring him out," Talioth ordered.

Valdok stood at his side with a leather satchel slung over his shoulder.

The metal lock shrieked, and the solid door opened with a loud creak. Damp, moldy air wafted out from the dark cell as the guards entered. They returned a moment later, leading a man. The shadow knight was quiet. He didn't whimper or whine. He didn't ask what they were going to do with him. His chin lifted high, and his eyes held a fierce determination.

Talioth chuckled. *If he only knew what he's about to go through.* "String him up."

The guards looped the chain connected to his hand shackles above a hook on the wall. The man's arms stretched, his toes barely touching the ground.

"Was it Shawn?" Talioth asked, getting into the man's face and wearing a false smile. "Did I remember that right?"

Shawn's disheveled brown hair fell in front of his eyes. His jaw clenched tight, unmoving.

"I'm sorry," Talioth leaned forward, inclining his ear, "I couldn't hear you."

A wad of saliva hit him in the cheek. He sneered, wiping his face with his hand. After the flash of anger, Talioth's smile returned.

"How were your days of darkness and hunger? Did they prepare you to talk?"

Shawn didn't reply.

"Let's start with what we know. Your name is Shawn, and you are a shadow knight. Your leader's name is Veron Storm-bridge. You're young—maybe . . . twenty-four, so you've been with the Knights for six to eight years, probably. During this time, they filled your head with propaganda about doing the good of the kingdom. And even though you have these amazing skills, you can't use them for yourself—only to help others." Talioth stopped and raised his eyebrows. "How am I doing so far?"

Shawn adjusted his feet, clanking the metal links between his legs.

"You're one of the most powerful people in Terrenor, yet you take orders from someone else."

"Veron's a great man," Shawn said, pulling at the chain lengths.

"Oh, he *can* speak! How about that, Valdok?" Talioth stepped closer. "If he's so great, he must permit you to access the devion . . . right?"

Shawn flinched.

Talioth's mouth curled. "You know of it, but . . . you're not allowed to use it."

"The devion is evil!" Shawn yelled. "It fills you with corruption and selfishness!"

Talioth laughed, the booming sound bouncing down the rock passage. "Evil . . . how absurd. The Devion is *power!* Pure, unadulterated potential. This . . . Veron holds you back. He doesn't want you to tap into your full potential. He feeds you lies and nonsense about needing to seek the common good. I'll bet you don't sleep in a palace, do you? I'll bet you're not permitted to use your powers to help yourself, are you?" He rested a hand on Shawn's shoulder. "I can teach you all of this, Shawn. I can help you tap into your full potential. All I need is for you to answer two questions."

The knight seemed to mull the words over in his head. "What questions?" he asked, finally.

Talioth grinned. "First, where are the Shadow Knights located? And second, how can Veron use the origine with the shackles on his wrists."

Shawn took a deep breath. He tossed his hair back with a flick of his head and leaned in. "Veron is a great man. I follow him because I trust him. If he tells me the devion is evil, then I believe him and want nothing to do with it."

Talioth's grin morphed into a scowl.

"Secondly, the Shadow Knights are wherever you're not. No matter where you go, no matter who you ask, you will *never* find them. You can ask as many times as you like, and I won't tell you."

Talioth stared hard at the man. "It's a pity . . . for your sake." He turned and nodded to Valdok, who removed the satchel from his shoulder. "You *will* tell us what we want to know. The only question is how much will it cost you."

Shawn squirmed, his eyes flitting between the men.

"Valdok here has a talent."

A wicked grin covered the large man's face. "One I'm happy to use."

"He's good at extracting stubborn information. While you say you won't tell . . . you are wrong."

Valdok set the bag on a rock, unlatched it, and rolled it open. Metal instruments lined the inside: cutters, clamps, prods, curved devices, straight ones. The sight made Talioth shudder inside.

"You can resist him and his devices of pain if you choose, but you'll regret it. Everyone talks eventually. It's only a matter of how much you want to endure. Plus, if you don't cooperate, it's the Siphon Room for you. And no one can fight that."

The young knight's eyes flared, but his resolve didn't weaken.

"All right, Valdok, he's all yours."

Talioth turned on his heels and left up the dark tunnel. As the surrounding light dimmed, a nervous muttering grew behind him. After a moment, a scream flooded through the passage. He shook his head and smiled thinly.

Talioth paced the smooth floor of the Hub while he waited. Others gathered nearby, busying themselves in conversation. He circled the room, brooding over the next steps to take. After a while, Rosalik and Centol approached.

"Is he cooperating?" Rosalik asked.

"Valdok's been working on him for the last few hours," Talioth replied.

"If we can't find the others, how much will his power alone help?"

"I'm not sure. It's been a long time since we've siphoned one of them. It should be much more than those villagers, though."

"Which will expand the distance we can travel," Centol added. "Plus, it will be one less to draw from the power."

"Brellok grows ill," Rosalik said, her voice soft.

Talioth breathed deep. "Since when?"

"Sometime while I was gone. He's not as far along as Balakolt, but . . . he doesn't sound great."

"I'm sorry, Rosalik."

She nodded.

"Hopefully this knight will be enough," Centol said.

Talioth lifted his chin. "We will take this man's power, then we will do the same for the rest of his group. Brellok will recover, and the rest of the Marked Ones will be safe."

Rosalik wiped her nose then cleared her throat. "Do you think there's a chance of this man giving them up?"

Talioth pursed his lips. "Their leader, Veron, pumps them full of rhetoric. All this one could spout was what he'd been fed. I don't think he will turn, but who knows about the others?"

Centol nodded. "We just need to find them."

"Bromhill was a dead end for me," Rosalik said. "I'm pretty sure they're not based there. When is Gralow due back?"

"I'm surprised he's not here yet," Talioth said. "Should be anytime. He wasn't going far."

Feet padding across the smooth stone turned their heads. Valdok approached, splatters of blood covering his gray outfit.

"Any luck?" Talioth asked.

Valdok's face turned down. "He claims Veron is the only one of the Shadow Knights who can resist metal's effect."

"Sounds convenient."

"Yes, but it seems to fit. Clearly he can't, or he would have tried to escape long ago."

"Does he know why?"

Valdok shook his head. "Apparently, Veron doesn't even understand it." He chuckled. "He spends his days studying old texts to try to figure it out."

"Ha!" Talioth laughed. "The fool. What about their location?"

"He wouldn't talk. I tried everything in my power, but . . . nothing."

Talioth frowned. "Bring him to the Siphon Chamber. If torture doesn't work, surely the effect of the crystal will loosen his tongue."

TALIOTH STOOD AGAINST THE WALL, watching the pulse of the crystal in the center of the chamber. Meliand positioned herself behind the shadow knight, placing both hands on his head. Heavy chains held the man down, unnecessary, given his condition. Black-and-blue bruises covered his arms and face. One eye was swollen shut while the other peeked through a slit. Blood soaked his tattered clothing, and two of the fingers on his right hand were gone.

"Drain what you can, but keep him alive," Talioth ordered. "Then we can talk."

Meliand nodded.

The knight's body stiffened. His arms shook as the red glow of the crystal intensified. He fought to tear his gaze away, but Meliand's hands tightened. A hum grew to a deafening level, matched only by the roar from Shawn's throat. His head shook and back arched. The walls trembled as the light grew impossibly bright. Dust fell from the ceiling.

The others standing around shielded their heads. "It's too much!" someone cried. "The crystal can't handle it!"

"Don't let him die!" Talioth shouted, his words lost in the tumult.

The knight's skin glowed, and the crystal's light blinded the room.

"I can't stop it," Meliand yelled, her hands shaking as the man's head spasmed. Her words labored as she strained to keep it together. "It won't . . . let . . . go."

With a final *boom,* the knight slumped, and the glow of the room peaked. Talioth covered his eyes until the light faded. When he looked again, the knight had collapsed into a pile of shriveled skin. *It went too far.* He clenched his teeth. *We don't know where to go next.*

His attention snapped to the pulsing crystal in the center of the chamber. The throbbing light settled. The mutters around the room quieted as everyone watched the glow. It dimmed only the slightest bit until it stabilized its intensity.

Excited laugher and cheering filled the room. "That did it!" someone called out.

Talioth's eyes widened, and his mouth curled into a reserved grin. The crystal in the center, as well as the ones set in the walls and the ones around their necks retained their glow. Bright, strong, and steady, power flowed through his body. He inhaled, filling his lungs with air before breathing it out.

Meliand moved away from behind the shriveled knight. "I'm sorry. I tried to stop it, but the pull on him was too great."

Talioth stepped in. "It's all right, Meliand. We found him, and we can do it again." He looked down at his arms, sensing the power flowing through him. "But now, we have the power to go farther."

Smoke emanated from Shawn's skin as if it were the remains of a snuffed flame. The husk of a man turned his head, the slow movement creating popping and cracking sounds. He opened his mouth, but the only sounds that came out were a low hissing noise. Talioth sneered as he kicked the carcass forward. The shadow knight tumbled into the pit, disappearing into the dark abyss.

"It worked, Talioth," Valdok said, his eyes bright.

"Yes, it did."

A commotion began at the back of the room. The crowd parted as Gralow entered, his broad shoulders and shoulder-length gray hair standing out in the group. His eyes were wide as he took in the scene. "You found one?"

Talioth nodded. "I lured two to Karondir and was able to capture one. Did you find anything?"

An eager grin formed on Gralow's face. "I think so. I found someone at a tavern doing parlor tricks—things no one should be able to do."

"A shadow knight?"

"He must be. If not, then someone who has the same abilities."

"Did you approach him?"

"Not yet. I thought it best to gather more of us."

Talioth took a deep breath then blew it out. "Good." He turned and spoke to the room. "Rest up tonight. Tomorrow, we go to gather more knights—enough to sustain us indefinitely. Tomorrow, we leave for Tienn."

40

SIGHTING

Despite being recently buried alive, Lia's body felt strong as she walked the morning streets of Tienn. Building from the incredible find she had the day before, a simmering excitement flowed through her veins.

A smoky scent wrinkled her nose as she passed the last building and crested the foothills of the mountains. With each step toward the mine, the smell grew stronger, and soon, a column of gray smoke puffed into the air, blowing toward the city. Her heart sped. *What's going on?* She hurried.

When she rounded the corner by the mine, her stomach dropped. The mine itself yawned its black mouth as usual, but the office had been reduced to a pile of smoking, charred timbers. Miners gathered around, digging through rubble and tossing water onto portions that continued to smolder.

"What happened?" she yelled, jogging up.

Bones paused after flipping a burned piece of wood over with an axe. "The office burned last night."

"Clearly," she said. "But why?"

Bones shrugged.

She found Ben, knee-deep in the rubble, picking through the remains.

"How can I help?" Lia asked, making her way to him.

The owner's shoulders slumped. His face drooped as he looked in her direction. "Lia. I—I don't know."

"What caused the fire?"

He shook his head. "I don't think I left any candles or lanterns burning. I have no idea."

"Is everything gone?"

He turned back to the rubble and lifted a beam. "I'm not sure. I'm trying to get to the safe, now."

Lia's eyes grew. "The baltham?"

He nodded. A crisp black metal corner emerged after a smoking board flipped away, and Ben gasped. The side of the safe contained a gash with the metal peeled back. "No!" He crouched over it, peering into the cavity. His chin quivered, but the rest of his body remained motionless.

Lia leaned closer. The inside of the safe was bare.

"Where'd it go?" the owner shouted, his voice trembling. He kneeled beside the safe, frantically patting the inside walls. He sank back onto his haunches.

"Did the fire do that? Could it have burned up?" Lia asked.

The man didn't reply. He stared at the empty safe with slumped shoulders.

"Do you think it was stolen?"

He pursed his lips. "No one has the strength to puncture through the side of this. It must have been the fire."

No one, huh? I wonder . . . Her stomach twisted. *Surely he wouldn't have.*

Ben kicked a board. A mixture of anger and despair showed on his face. "I'm ruined." He motioned with open hands to the burned building. "I can't come back from this. I'm already behind with the bank. There's no money to rebuild, and now —" He choked up, placing his clenched fist in front of his mouth. "My family . . ." A tear fell down his cheek. "I don't know what we're going to do."

Lia stood quietly. She didn't have words to comfort the man —at least none that contained any hint of truth. Meanwhile, her gut told her something was wrong.

Lia yanked the door to their house open. Instead of the sleepy morning quiet she expected, the room brimmed with energy, and her jaw fell. Nicolar's crew spread throughout the room, with Danik standing before them. They each extended their arms, alternately swiping them through the air and standing motionless and focused.

"Don't rush it," Danik called. "You'll feel it before it's ready."

"What are you doing?" Lia shouted.

The group of thieves lost their focus. Danik turned, a wry grin on his face. "Lia, you're back early."

"Are you . . ." she leaned her head forward, "teaching them?"

He waved the question away. "Don't be silly. We were just talking about focus and control. What, um . . . happened at the mine?"

The change in topic felt abrupt. Lia narrowed her eyes. "Did you have anything to do with it?"

A thick silence followed, broken only by a sniff from Jade. Danik motioned outside. "Walk with me."

"What about my friend?" Nicolar asked.

Danik stopped in the doorway and turned back. "When's he coming by?"

"Any time now."

"And you're sure he's trustworthy?" His eyes flicked toward Lia. "As a guard."

"I do."

Danik nodded. "I'll be right back."

Lia walked stiffly, following Danik. He sauntered through the street, gazing at the shops as if window shopping. Lia's patience ran short. "Did you burn the mine office down?" she asked when no one was in earshot. "Did you take the baltham?"

Danik's feet stopped. He looked toward the air as if the sky held the answer. "I'd hardly call it an 'office.'"

Lia's blood boiled, her hand forming into a fist. "Ben Edkins is a good man!" she breathed emphatically. "He has a family, and he needed the money."

"Everyone has a family," Danik said, resuming his casual walk. "Everyone needs money, including us."

"Give it back."

"The baltham?" He screwed up his face. "No."

"You're ruining his life!"

Danik scoffed. "He did that himself, long before you came along."

Lia frowned.

"That's right. If he's in a bad spot, it's not your fault or mine. Remember, Lia, *you* were the one who found those deposits, not him. Why should he benefit from them?"

"It was—" She paused, considering the situation. The resolve in her voice weakened. "It's his mine. He employed me to work there. Anything I find is his."

"And how fair is that? You want him to make all the money from your hard work?"

"I was going to be paid *well* for my finds."

"And now you're going to be paid everything."

Lia stopped walking. She clenched her jaw and held out her hand. "Give them back."

He glanced at her open hand and chuckled. After a pause, he shook his head. "I can't. They're not here."

"What did you do?" she yelled.

Danik shrank under her outcry and glanced around the street. He lowered his voice. "Nicolar is moving them."

Lia's breath caught. "What?"

"Think about it, Lia . . . how are we going to sell them? We can't. It will get traced back to the mine, but Nicolar has connections. We'll get the money tomorrow."

"You trust him?"

Danik extended his chin and stood taller. "We're partners now—him and his crew. I hadn't told you yet."

Lia shook her head. "I don't like him *or* his crew. They give me the creeps."

Danik waved the comment away. "Don't be silly. They have the same goals as we do, and they can help us achieve them."

"Goals?" Her brows pinched together. "What goals?"

"To run this city!"

"That's not my goal. I just—" Her words cut off. *What are my goals?*

"What do you want, Lia? You want to work in a mine for the rest of your life? Do you want to eke out a mediocre life?"

She didn't have a response.

He clenched his fist and lifted it with a grin. "Or do you want to make something of yourself? Do you want people to hear your name and gape in awe of your greatness?"

"I—I don't know what I want."

Danik placed his hand on her arm. "Lia, we have these amazing abilities! We can do whatever we want, and we're no longer limited by any silly code. Why would we not use them? We can live like kings!"

Her head dropped to the street. "What about Ben?"

His brows tightened. "Who?"

"Benjamin Edkins, the owner of the mine."

"Come on, Lia!" Danik swatted his hand through the air. "Are you afraid of success?"

"No, but . . . he didn't deserve that."

Danik sighed and tapped his foot. "Fine. I'll take a chunk of the money and ensure it makes it back to him. Satisfied?"

She paused a long moment with her lips pursed. "No. But it's a good start." The tension in her body loosened.

He wrapped his arm around her shoulders and nudged her toward their home. "Now, can we return? I think if you take some time to get to know the crew, you'll grow to like them."

Lia took a deep breath and blew it out. Her insides trembled. *To be fair, I haven't given them a chance.*

Danik's arm went rigid. She looked at him, but his face fixed up the street, his eyes wide. In a flash, he looked away and pulled her toward the closest shop. "Don't look," he said.

Lia followed where he pulled her but looked out of the corner of her eye. Her breath caught. A bald man with a gray beard strode up the street. His loose tunic displayed muscled shoulders, and a deep tan covered his skin. "Xander," she breathed.

They both faced the wall. Lia strained her ears. Several unknown people passed in both directions, but Xander's heavy stride was clear. Lia and Danik turned as the sailor passed.

"What's he doing here?" Danik whispered.

Lia shook her head. "Maybe he moved away like we did?"

"Maybe he's on the run after an attempted murder of a shadow knight?"

A wave of fury rushed through her. *Mother.* The images fixed in her head: her bleeding body, her father crying, the looks on the rest of the knights' faces. Finally, Veron's last words *—we're better off without you—*played in her mind. She gritted her teeth, trying to block out the memory. *No,* she thought, forcing the idea into her head, *I didn't endanger her. Xander did.*

He continued up the street several buildings until he stopped. Lia gasped. The bald sailor reached out his hand and knocked on the door to their home.

"What's he doing at our place?" Lia muttered through her teeth.

Danik's mouth hung open, but he didn't answer.

After a moment, Nicolar opened the door and shook hands while clapping the man on the shoulder.

"Xander must be the man Nicolar invited."

"What?" Lia said, too loud. They both ducked their heads. Her voice dropped to a hiss. "You can't seriously let him into our home as part of this . . . crew or whatever it is."

"Of course not. I had no idea it was him."

Lia peeked again as Nicolar craned his neck into the street, looking in both directions. She spun away. "What are you going to do?"

Danik took a deep breath then shook his head. "I can't go back there, now. We'll have to wait him out."

They stood in silence in their hiding place for several minutes until the bald man finally left. He returned back up the street.

They kept their faces hidden until his heavy footsteps passed behind them again. "I'm following him," Lia said after he was out of earshot.

Danik came too. They hung back, pressing to the side of the street.

Xander moved, seemingly oblivious to his tail. After crossing half the city along the main street, he turned up a side alley. Lia peeked around the corner. The bald man opened the door of a single-story dilapidated building with a thatched roof. She shrank back as he glanced over his shoulder then disappeared inside.

"You think that's where he's staying?" Danik asked.

She scanned the alley, taking in the buildings and windows. At the far end of the street, an elderly man tottered in their direction, using a cane to steady his legs. A woman brushed by them, turning the corner and carrying a basket of grain against her hip.

"Yeah, I do," Lia said with a nod, her hand clenching into a fist. "He deserves to be held accountable."

"What do you want to do?"

"I want to do to him what he did to my mother. I want to watch as he bleeds out, and I want him to know I was the one who killed him." Her teeth ground together. "Let's come back tonight."

"You ready?" Danik whispered, cutting through the still night.

Lia inhaled, her chest puffing. She looked down at the thatched house from the roof of the stone building across the street. She felt exposed without her Shadow Knights cloak, but she was still just as deadly.

"The light's been out for an hour. The street looks asleep."

Lia's hand twitched. Her insides felt jittery as she stared at the house. Feelings swirled in her mind: rage toward the man who nearly killed her mother, regret at not being there to defend her, and even uncertainty at what she intended to do. *I've killed people before. Why does this seem harder?*

"Lia?"

Her whispered name snapped her attention to Danik. She nodded. "Let's go."

Lia dropped first. She landed on the street and used the origine to absorb the fall. Danik landed just behind. They slunk to the house and leaned on either side of the door. She tested the handle. It turned. A soft push ended with a sharp resistance.

Danik cocked his head, and Lia mouthed, "Latched."

Letting go of the handle, they hurried around the side of the house. Faded blue shutters framed a window. As expected, they didn't move when Lia tested them. Working a sliver of metal between them, a latch lifted, allowing the shutters to pivot.

Lia poked her head in. No lights shone. No sounds greeted her. Grabbing the eaves at the edge of the roof, she slung her legs in, then wriggled her body after. Inside the house, she crouched and pulled a dagger from her sleeve. Her breaths stopped. Her pulse thudded in her ears. Moonlight rolled through the window, splashing onto the floor. A faint breathing sound came from somewhere, but a chipped table with stained legs blocked her view of the room.

Danik slid in a moment later, and they both stood. A rudimentary kitchen lay on one side of the room. Pots lay askew on the counter, and a smell filled the air—turnfoil root and sage. Her nose wrinkled. A cracked door lay in the center of the room with a dark space beyond. *Probably a bedroom*, she thought. On the opposite side of the space, two chairs faced each other. One had a torn cushion, and the other contained a man—a bald man with a gray beard and closed eyes. The breathing noise came from his ajar mouth.

Lia's heart pounded as she crossed the room. She held her dagger tight in her clammy fist. Danik stepped beside her, holding a knife of his own. Their eyes met, and Lia nodded.

Danik stepped forward and held his knife underneath the beard to the man's throat. "Don't make a sound," Danik said, his voice firm.

Xander's eyelids fluttered. With a start, he stiffened. His hands grasped the arms of his chair. His chin stretched, and his bare feet splayed forward.

Lia took a step closer, leaning forward so the man could see her. "Remember me," she said quietly.

His eyes grew, and he managed a tight nod.

"You visited the Shadow Knights center last week. Why?"

Xander's eyes flitted to Danik, who relaxed the tension of the dagger on his throat. "I-I was there for you," he whispered. His face hardened. "For you both."

"And yet you attacked my mother."

He only responded with a sneer.

"Now my father hates me . . . because of you."

A mocking laugh answered her. "What do you intend to do?"

"I want you to feel what she did," Lia said, her voice low. Danik readjusted his dagger to position it over the man's chest. "And I wanted you to know it was me."

"Daddy?" a high, wavering voice pierced the room.

Lia spun. A girl, no more than nine, stood in the doorway, her hand propped on the frame. She held the hem of her nightshirt, her hand shaking.

"Are you all right, Daddy? What's happening?" The girl covered her mouth while she coughed.

"Go back to your mother, sweetie. Daddy's fine." His voice shook. "Close the door behind you."

"No, stop!" Danik said, keeping the dagger pinned to Xander's chest. "Don't move."

The girl froze.

"Please," Xander said. "She's sick. Leave her alone."

Lia felt as if someone had sucked the air from her lungs. Her mouth moved, but she couldn't form words. She stared at the girl with her straight-brown hair and couldn't help but see herself.

"What is this?" Lia breathed, turning to the bald man. "You have a family?"

Xander nodded. "My eldest have grown and gone, but Charlotte was our surprise."

"But you live in Felting?"

The sailor shook his head. "My family's always been here. I only go there for work.

"Daddy, do you want me to get Mommy?" Charlotte asked.

"No!" Xander said, sucking in air as Danik's knife pressed tighter against him. He forced a laugh. "These are friends of mine. We're just talking."

"My cough is doing better," Charlotte said. "I think the tea you made helped."

That's the turnfoil root, Lia thought.

"Leave her out of this," Xander pleaded. "Please."

"No," Danik growled. "She stays so she can witness what you did to Chelci."

"Danik," Lia said, her eyes wide, her head shaking. "This isn't right. Not like this."

"What? Because he has a family, he doesn't deserve consequences. Wake up, Lia! Everyone has a family."

"It was *my* mother. I don't want this anymore. Let him go!"

"It wasn't just you he wronged. He answers to the Shadow Knights, and I'm here to deliver justice!"

Danik's arm tensed. His body moved to deliver the killing blow.

"Danik, no!" Lia was too late to stop him. Instead, she turned to block the girl's sight.

A sickening thrust of a knife sounded from the chair as Lia wrapped Charlotte into her body. A man's scream hit her back. Lia spun the girl and pushed her back through the door. "Go to your mother." She didn't wait for a response but closed the door with a slam.

"That's what you get for messing with the Shadow Knights," Danik taunted.

Lia turned as Xander fell from his chair. His arms and legs splayed onto the floor, and a spasm rolled through his body. A red pool grew on the rug.

"Let's go," Danik said, striding through the kitchen. He kicked the front door with a powered blast that knocked the door off its hinges and sent it tumbling into the street.

Lia followed in a stupor. Their walk turned into a run, twisting back through the city. Hard steps jarred her body, but her mind couldn't stop picturing the girl. *And now the pain starts fresh for her.* A tear fell down her cheek until she wiped it away.

41

RESCUER

Lia lay in bed, staring at the ceiling while light poured into the room. She'd been awake all day but couldn't bring herself to get up. Her heart felt jittery, unsure of anything. When she was back in Felting, running away from everything she knew seemed exciting, but the feeling had long faded.

Running into Xander the night before left her shaken. *I wanted the man dead*, she thought. *But not how it happened.* A thought crossed her mind. *Would it have been any different if I'd killed him on the street? It would have felt different.*

The change in Danik over the week they'd been gone bothered her. They used to be so similar—having fun and getting into trouble together, but he'd changed ever since they left Felting. *Maybe I shouldn't have left.* She pictured the Shadow Knights Academy, where she'd grown up: her room, training in the courtyard, playing games and eating in the common room. A smile came to her face. *I miss that. I miss Dayna's strictness. I miss Bridgette, and how she always had the right answer. I miss Mason.* She chuckled. *Mason . . . following me around like a puppy.*

The image of her yelling at her father jolted her back to

reality. Her jaw clenched. *It was my fault. I killed my brother. I'm the reason Mother almost died.* Tears pooled at the corners of her eyes. *Father will never forgive me.* She wiped her tears away. *I don't deserve to be forgiven.*

A tapping at her door turned her head. "Yes?"

Danik's voice drifted through the solid wood. "Lia . . . are you all right?"

Her anger flared. She sat up and brought her legs over the side. "I'm fine—just feeling . . . under the weather."

"Are you sure I can't bring you something? The guys brought over some boar. It's good. Maybe some meat would do you well."

Lia's stomach turned at the thought of Nicolar's men. "No. Thank you."

"Also, I, uh . . . got that money we talked about—from the baltham. You want to see it? It's pretty impressive."

She gritted her teeth. *Money that belongs to Ben and his family.* "No," she called back.

"All right. Well . . . the boar will be downstairs if you change your mind. We're . . . um, heading out soon. We won't be back until late."

Lia frowned. *Heading out for what?* She didn't reply, but his footsteps left after a moment.

A voice whispered from the window. "Lia!"

She jumped from the bed, gasping. A silhouetted head peeked in the second-story window. She leaned forward, her eyes squinting. "Mason?"

A smile grew on the figure's face. "I can't believe I found you! Can you, uh, help me in?"

"What are you doing here?" Lia asked, keeping her voice down as she hurried to the window. She grabbed his arm and helped him wriggle the rest of his body through. He fell onto the floor with a thump.

"Are you . . . trapped?" Mason asked, looking around the

room. "Are you safe?"

Lia knit her brown together. "Trapped? No. What are you talking about?"

Mason made it to his feet and looked her up and down. "You're all right? You're not hurt?"

"Mason, I'm fine. How did you find me?"

A look of relief washed over him. He sighed, his shoulders relaxing. "Raiyn had a Dream."

Lia's eyes widened. "Really? A Dream?"

Mason nodded. "He saw you here." He glanced around the room again, then looked out the window, pointing at the tower. "I've been searching Tienn for second-story windows that faced the tower. Thankfully, yours was open. You should have seen some of the alarmed looks I got."

"Why did you come? What did he Dream?"

His face fell. "You were imprisoned, and you—" He paused, his forehead wrinkling. "You were dying."

Lia gasped. She stared at Mason, blinking her eyes. "I-I don't understand. This was from Raiyn?"

"He's been staying in Felting. I met up with him to make sure he was all right. The other day, he Dreamed you were in this room, and you were in trouble."

"So where is he?"

"We split up." He gestured out the window. "All he knew to go by was the tower. He's on his way to Tarving now to check there. I came here."

"When was this supposed to happen . . . the part about me dying?"

Mason shrugged. "He didn't know. Just that you would need help."

Lia chuckled, part of her mouth curling. "So you came."

He smiled back. "Yeah. Look, I know, it has to be tough to hear, but I don't think you're safe here. What is this place?"

"It's . . . well . . . Danik and I share it."

Mason's smile turned into a scowl.

"And there are these others . . . a gang of thieves as best as I can label them. Danik's become friends with them. They're around all the time."

"You've got to get out of here," Mason implored. "If what Raiyn saw is true, then you're in danger. Come back with me."

Lia frowned. "I . . . I can't go back there. My father hates me, and—"

"He doesn't hate you."

Lia's mouth hung loose.

"He was upset that night," Mason continued. "He regretted what he said, and he misses you."

She closed her jaw, the words swirling in her head. "I don't believe you."

"It's true. You're a ray of sunshine in our lives. We *all* miss you, Lia."

She noted the emphasis on the word *all*. After a long pause, she shook her head. "I can't face it again. My father was right—it *was* my fault. I don't deserve to be a shadow knight."

Mason sighed, then looked around the room. "How are things here . . . with *him*."

Lia swallowed the lump in her throat. "It's . . ." Her arm shook. She held it to her side. "He's changed. He's not the same carefree, fun Danik I've always known. These people he's gotten in with . . . They're no good."

"Come back with me, Lia."

She opened her mouth to reject the idea but stopped. She bit her lip and turned to the door. "He'd be mad if I left."

"Who cares?" Mason said. "If he's getting in with people who are bad, you don't want to have any part of it."

After a long pause, she nodded. "All right. I'll come."

Mason beamed.

"Danik is leaving with the others. Once they're gone, I—"

A quick knock preceded the doorknob clicking. Danik

opened the door and poked his head through. The sword on his hip clattered against the frame, and his forehead wrinkled.

Lia and Mason froze.

"Mason? What are you— How'd you get here?"

Lia and Mason exchanged petrified looks. Lia stuttered as she spoke. "H-he … um …" Her mind raced to think of a viable explanation.

"I got her letter," Mason blurted.

Lia sighed. "That's right. I sent him a letter when we arrived."

Danik's eyes shifted between the two. "You … wrote him?" His incredulous tone matched his face.

"I didn't get to say goodbye, so I wrote him a letter. I mentioned where we were and invited him to visit."

Mason laughed nervously. "And I couldn't wait, so I came to check on her."

Danik tilted his head. Lia could see his mind spinning. "But how did you get *up* here?"

Mason's eyes flitted to Lia. "Um … I just came up the stairs."

Danik's eyes narrowed. He pointed to the wall behind him. "Those stairs?"

"That's right." Mason shifted his feet.

"I didn't see you. None of us saw you."

"I, uh … snuck by." Another hesitant laugh escaped from Mason. "I thought it would be fun to surprise her."

Danik looked back and forth between the two while a tense silence filled the room. "What's going on here?" His question was hard and accusatory.

"Danik," Lia said, "what's the matter? Why are you acting like this?"

He pointed at Mason. "You're trying to take her back, aren't you?"

Lia rested her hand on his arm. "Danik, he just came to talk."

He sloughed off her hand and pulled his sword.

"Danik! What are you doing?" Lia shouted.

Mason pulled his own sword, both young men staring daggers at each other, facing off in the small space.

"Put those away, both of you!"

"Admit it, Mason. You came here to take her away!"

"I did! So what?" he shouted back. "She's missed by everyone!"

"She's missed, but I'm not. Right? Well, you can't take her. She's mine!"

Lia inhaled sharply. She stared at Danik. "I'm not *yours!*"

"Let her make her own choice, Danik," Mason said, his sword rising higher.

Danik laughed. "Like she would ever choose *you* over me."

"Guys, stop!" Lia shouted. "I'm not *choosing* anyone." She took a step back to move farther from the bared steel.

Danik pivoted to his left, and Mason moved counter to him.

"Get out of here, Mason," Danik growled, pointing the tip of his blade toward the door. "You're not welcome."

"I'll leave when I'm sure Lia's safe."

"Safe!" Danik exploded in laughter. "You think she needs your protecting?" He turned his sword toward Lia, taunting with the tip. She backed into the wall, her eyes wide. "You think I'm going to go crazy and hurt her?"

Mason stepped forward, his arm taut and sword ready to strike. "Leave her alone!"

"Or what?" Danik snapped. "What are you going to do?"

With a look of fury, Mason inhaled to snap back, but the words never came. His body jerked, and a strangled gasp escaped. Limbs went rigid, and his back arched. His mouth opened and a throaty yell forced its way out.

"What's wrong?" Lia asked.

Mason's legs stuttered. He stared with a vacant expression before falling to his knees.

"Mason!" she moved to him.

Like a tree gaining momentum as it toppled, Mason fell face-first to the floorboards. A shiny green dagger handle stuck into his back, and Jade stood in the doorway.

"No!" Lia screamed. She fell to her knees by him. "What did you do?"

Jade shrugged. "I protected Danik," she said in a slippery voice.

"He wasn't going to hurt him!" Lia yanked the dagger from Mason's back, eliciting a moan from him. Jade stepped aside as she flung the bloody weapon into the hall, where it clattered to the ground.

"He looked pretty serious," Danik said.

"Danik!" she screamed, pressing her palm against the wound. "This is *Mason*, your friend!"

"He was never my friend."

She glared at him. "Help me get his shirt off!"

Danik huffed and took the clean dagger from Jade. He sliced the back of Mason's tunic and folded back the fabric. "Let's see it."

The wound bled, but the incision was tight. As they watched, the cut closed.

"Ah, he'll be fine." Danik said, standing. "Nothing a little origine can't heal." He turned to Lia. "I want him gone by the time we get back."

Lia's mouth dropped. "He can't travel! Not like this! Even with the origine, he needs time to recover."

Danik sighed. "Fine. He can stay the night, but he's gone first thing." He nodded toward Jade. "Let's go." The two of them left the room, their footsteps fading down the hall.

"Mason," Lia said, gently shaking his shoulder. "Are you all right?

A moan answered her. He lifted an arm and attempted to

push his body over. Lia helped, rolling him gently. He winced as his back hit the ground. "Help me up," he whispered.

Lia pulled at his shoulders and helped him to a sitting position. His chest heaved as he gulped in breaths. His head looked like it could barely stay held up. "Are you healed?" she asked.

Mason coughed. He covered his mouth. When he pulled his hand back, it glistened bright red. "I still hurt." A raspy sound emanated from his mouth as exhaled. He winced again, arching his back.

"Use more!" Lia pleaded. "It must have punctured your lung. Can you—" she stopped, her mouth gaping. "The green dagger."

"What?" Mason asked, his voice weak.

"S-She poisons it." Lia stared toward the door.

"I feel it." He grimaced.

Lia snapped into action. "You've got to use more to heal. You can do this, Mason!"

He waved his head from side to side. "I'm spent, Lia."

"No!" she cried, her sight blurry with tears. "You must be able to do something."

The rattle in his voice increased until he exploded in another round of coughing. Blood snuck past his hand and splattered onto Lia's shirt.

"Mason. I'm so sorry," she said. "I should never have left. I shouldn't be with these people. If I hadn't run away, you would never be here."

"It's okay, Lia." He reached for her hand and gave it a weak squeeze.

Lia ran her other hand across his face, pushing his hair back. She sniffed back tears. "Mason . . ."

His eyes, soft and tender, locked with hers.

"Thank you for always being kind to me. I didn't deserve it, but you were my friend anyway."

He managed a faint smile. He opened his mouth but faltered. Lia leaned in to hear.

"Everyone deserves it, Lia," he whispered.

The words struck her. A tingle ran up her spine. She nodded, considering how to reply when his eyes lost their focus. His chest stopped moving. Mason was gone.

Lia closed her eyes, pressing them together while tears fell down her cheeks.

Mason's dead because of me, just like my brother. My parents will be even angrier.

Something Mason had called her tickled her mind. *A ray of sunshine.* A memory from the recesses of her mind popped into her head: her father cupping his hand tenderly against her cheek on her eighth birthday and calling her, "My Little Sunshine."

I haven't thought of that in years. That's strange. Her tears paused.

Another image surfaced. She was ten and had just finished a run with her father. He pushed her sweaty hair back off her face and smiled at her. "Great job," he said. "I'm proud of you, Little Sunshine."

A flood of past events rushed into her head: joining her father on watch for the first time, when she cooked a meal for the entire group of knights, a night where a storm kept her awake in bed. In each memory, her father beamed a proud-parent smile at her. She remembered his gentle touch and his affectionate words when he called her by her nickname. She could picture the way lines creased around his eyes as he smiled.

I'm his Little Sunshine.

When Lia was young, she used to watch the east in the early morning, waiting for the moment when the first rays of the sun peeked over the mountain range. Her father gave her the nickname because of how she giggled and celebrated the morning light.

The memory of the time just before her brother's death came next. Her sinuses cleared when the lucid recollection dispelled the fable she'd told herself for years. After they hugged her brother in the courtyard, her parents didn't yell at her. They didn't scowl at her as she trounced off to the river.

They hugged me, too. Mother gave me a kiss on the forehead, and Father beamed as he told me to have fun. A gasp escaped from her lips. *Then he told me he loved me.*

It was as if scales had fallen off her mind. After Morgan's death, she had walled off her memories, and over time, a jaded truth had replaced the affectionate moments that marked her childhood.

They did love me. A deep regret filled her gut followed by anger toward Danik, Jade, and the others. She sniffed and wiped her face. *I'm leaving,* she thought.

She found the sack she'd used to travel there and gathered the few clothes she owned, stuffing them in. A warm tunic she'd brought but never used scratched her as she jammed it in the bag. *What's that?* A letter fell to the floor. She stared down, her heart jumping at the word *Lia* written across the top.

As if it were a dangerous object, she bent slowly to pick it up. It was a simple, folded piece of paper. She lifted the flap and gasped. *Mother!* It was a note from Chelci, tucked away in her tunic. Her hand trembled. She sat on the bed and rested it in her lap to keep the note from shaking.

My dearest Julia,

I'm sorry I disappoint you sometimes. It's difficult being a mother, and I often feel like I have no idea what I'm doing. I may not show it enough, but I'm incredibly proud of the work you did with Raiyn. Over the last several weeks, you've impressed me in many ways. I'm sorry things didn't work out with him. You're right. He seems kind and respectful, and he likely would make a great shadow knight. I wish we could have let him stay. I know you don't agree with the decision your father made, but I want you to know it wasn't an easy one for him.

Today, you said you wish you could escape your blood. I thought that many times when I was younger, so I understand what you're feeling. I never knew your namesake—your grandmother, Julia. She died when your father was born, but I heard stories from your grandfather. He beamed when he spoke of her—how she enjoyed doing what no one expected and how she lit up any room she was in. I smile when I think of you, in the same way William did when he spoke of her.

Today you said you hate me. While I can't change how you feel about me, I can express how I feel about you. I love you, Lia. From the moment you were born, not a moment goes by when I haven't been happy that you were my daughter. Years ago, after your brother died, I may not have expressed it well. To be clear, what happened that day was not your fault. Neither I nor your father blame you for Morgan's death. Life happens with or without our influence. We can't control it all, but we can make the most of the pieces. There's nothing you could do that could stop my love for you. No matter what. Hear me: No matter what.

- CHELCI

TEARS STREAMED DOWN Lia's face, dripping on the letter. She choked on racking sobs that echoed in the empty room. Her body slid off the edge of the bed and lowered to the floor. She wrapped her arms around herself, clutching the paper to her chest.

The memory of her mother's injured body slumped against

the wall ran through her mind, but the words in the letter pushed it away. *She loved me . . . no matter what.* A smile grew. She leaned her head against the mattress, sniffing and wiping at her face.

Renewed in her desire to leave, she stood. *I can't stay another day, no matter how much Danik wants me here. But before I leave, there's something I need to do.*

She pushed open the door and poked her head out. The house was quiet while she snuck down the hall. The knob to Danik's room turned, but a lock kept it closed. The keyhole taunted her. Origine built, tingling her legs before she gave it a swift kick. The frame splintered around the knob, and the remains of the door pivoted inward.

She hurried to the desk in his room and opened the drawer. A smirk covered her face as she counted out thirty-two gold sol. Her heart pounded. It was more money than most people would ever see. *And it's not Danik's.*

42

JOINING FORCES

The sun had just fallen behind the buildings, tossing long shadows through the streets. Lia made her way through the city, keeping a wary eye out for Danik or the others. She retraced their steps from the previous night until the busted door of Xander's house made her pause.

She looked around. Some old men sat on a bench talking. A woman swept the stoop in front of another house. The home with the busted door was quiet.

She walked to the side, acting as if the building held no interest to her. The window they had entered the night before was open. Lia walked past without breaking stride and tossed a pouch in through the window. It thunked when it hit the floor, and someone called out in surprise. Her feet picked up, and she ran, leaving no time for the occupants to notice her. She continued running until she'd rounded a few corners, leaving the house far behind.

The length of Ben Edkins' house suggested a few rooms inside, but the thatched roof sagged, and plaster chipped off the walls. A candle flickered through a window. Lia crept to it and peered through the pane. Ben sat at a table in the center of the room with his head in his hands. His wife, Mary, rubbed his back and said something Lia couldn't hear. His daughter, Lily, stirred something in a pot over the fire. All three faces were long, stretched, and worried.

She ducked under the window and placed a larger pouch on the ground in front of the door. It pained her to take her hand away from the heavy object. *It's the right thing,* she reassured herself. Taking a deep breath, she knocked twice with a firm hand, then ran. She glanced back as she rounded the nearest corner. Ben emerged, peering hard at the leather pouch on the ground. Lia grinned as she left the scene behind. *Twenty gold sol should get them right back on their feet.*

Between the mine owner and Xander's family, Lia left herself five sol and Danik nothing. The thought of the empty drawer at the house brought a sweat to her brow. *What if he comes back early? What if he sees Mason's body and my bags?* She cut through an abandoned building to take a more direct route. When she was about to turn down a back alley, movement caught her eye. She stopped, taking even breaths and peering around a crumbled wall to get a better view.

The building ahead had long since fallen down. The stone walls still standing contained cracks and moss. Wooden beams rotted, discarded to the side. In between the walls, a large space opened up—space for several men to move . . . and train.

"Wait for the tingle in your gut. That means it's ready," Danik said, standing with his back to a wall and facing the others. A lantern hung from a peg, lighting up the area.

Lia's heart pounded. *He is teaching them the origine!*

Nicolar and his team spread through the abandoned space. Several focused with their eyes closed. Some held swords, and others clenched their arms in front of them.

"I feel it!" Cedric said. The man bent over and wrapped his

arms around a huge chunk of broken stone. He lifted it into the air in one fast motion while laughing, high pitched and giddy.

"Me too," Nicolar added.

Jade waved daggers before her, the weapons turning into a blur. She didn't speak, but a wicked grin formed.

"Good!" Danik called, pointing at them. "You've got it!"

"I don't feel anything," Donte muttered.

Broderick groaned. "Me neither."

"Give it time. Once you learn to find it, it will become easy," Danik said.

Lia's mind told her to run, but her legs forced her to stay. Not wanting to be noticed, she jumped, grabbing the top of the crumbled wall. She found a perch hidden in the darkness above that allowed a clear view.

Nicolar cleared his throat. "Say again . . . how is this different from—what was it called? The origine?"

Lia's head cocked. Her breath caught in her throat.

"The origine is what the Shadow Knights teach. It's focused around the good of mankind and never doing something for your own benefit. The devion uses the same type of energy, but it's much more powerful. It lasts longer, and you can use it for anything you want."

Lia's heart pounded. *Danik, no!*

"And the Shadow Knights don't use it?" Nicolar asked.

"Most barely know it even exists." Danik laughed. "Their leader says it's evil, so everyone is afraid of it. If they knew how much power it holds, they would change their mind. I only learned about it earlier this suether."

Cedric's form turned into a blur that moved back and forth along the length of the room several times. When he stopped, he cried in delight. "This is amazing!"

"Watch the energy use, though," Danik warned. "Your body has to recover from what you spend."

Cedric held up his hand in front of him and stared at it.

"Yeah, I feel tired."

Lia's eyes were wide. *His first time with movement like that should exhaust him!*

Cedric hopped over a chunk of wall and moved back to his position. "It's not bad though."

"Okay, now I'm feeling something," Donte said, holding his limbs out from his body and looking over himself.

"The origine takes many weeks to learn," Danik said, "sometimes years. Although anyone can learn it, only a few have the natural ability to grow proficient. The devion, however, is much, much easier."

"So, what is your vision?" Nicolar asked, "for our group?"

The gang all looked at where Danik stood. Lia held her breath, afraid of what she might hear.

"We begin here in Tienn." Danik paced through the midst of the crew. "With these abilities, we can do anything. We take what we want. We live where we want. People will do whatever we command. Eventually, our skills will develop and—" He paused. "And we'll decide from there."

"You're thinking Felting, right?" Nicolar said.

Danik shrugged with a mischievous grin.

"What about the Shadow Knights?"

Danik's grin faltered. "We'll have to deal with them, but we're not ready for that yet."

Lia's mind raced. *Father, Gavin, Dayna, Bridgette, the others.* She struggled to breathe. *Surely Danik wouldn't . . .* She stopped herself from finishing the thought.

"I'd like to hear more about these Shadow Knights," an unfamiliar voice said.

Lia's head jerked toward the dark outskirts of the room where the lantern's light didn't reach, but several red glowing dots reflected.

"Who's there?" Danik called.

A man in a gray cloak stepped from the gloom. His blue eyes shone in the light of the lantern while his long, gray hair seemed to mix with his thick beard. In a moment, several others appeared behind him, spreading out. On the opposite side of the room, more stepped forward, forming a tight box around the thieves.

A black spot marked the man's throat. *What is that?* Lia thought, leaning forward and squinting. Her eyes darted through the crowd. They all had the same stained marks and red crystals hanging from their necks. *These are the people who took Shawn!*

"We seek the Shadow Knights," the man said. "Did you say they were in Felting?"

Danik raised his chin and stared down his nose. "Who's asking?"

The leader took another step forward, smiling. "My name is Talioth."

Lia's eyes grew. *That's him!* The origine readied itself, simmering inside.

"We are the Marked Ones, and we come from . . . nearby. We need to find the Shadow Knights, and it sounds like you know where they are."

"What's your business with them?" Danik asked.

Talioth stared for a long moment. Tension radiated all the way to Lia's perch.

"It sounds to me like you have a problem with the Knights," Talioth said. "You want to 'deal with them' but aren't capable of it."

Nicolar pulled his sword. "We're capable of plenty," he said, his words a growl. In a blink, he appeared next to Talioth, holding his sword to his gray-shirted chest with a smirk. "You don't want to test us."

Gasps sounded from the marked ones while Talioth's eyes grew. The red crystals brightened as the people in grey drew swords of their own. Talioth swatted the sword away, shattering the blade using only his hands. Nicolar staggered backward, his confidence gone.

"You're the one from Karondir," Danik said, stepping forward. "You took Shawn."

Talioth smiled, raising an eyebrow. "Ah, yes . . . Shawn. He was a pleasant guest during his short time with us."

"They *are* the Shadow Knights," the man in gray next to Talioth said.

Danik's eyebrow rose.

"Now, all of you will go on a trip with us." Talioth's crystal grew even brighter.

The tingle in Lia's gut vanished and emptiness filled her. She fought to keep her panting breath quiet. Her father's story made sense. *They can take away the origine!*

Talioth pulled metal cuffs from a pocket, then his body blurred. He moved into the room, but Danik moved with him. Lia watched with wide eyes as a rapid skirmish of dust and steel resolved after a few seconds. Talioth and Danik both stared at each other, panting. Danik held a sword, and Talioth a long, curved knife with jagged spines.

"We are *not* the Shadow Knights," Danik said.

"How did you do that?" Talioth asked before glancing down to check his glowing crystal.

Another marked one stepped forward. "They're not using the origine," he breathed.

Danik's eyes jumped between the men. "You're not taking us!" he said, his arm clenched and sword held taut.

Talioth took a step back and lowered his weapon. "Was that . . . devion?"

Danik glanced at Nicolar, then back to Talioth. "So what if it was?"

Talioth held up his palms, faced out, his mouth curling at one side. "Please accept my apology. No, we don't want to take you. We use the same power." The bright glow of the crystals faded to a muted light.

Danik took a hesitant step forward, looking at the man at Talioth's side. "You use the devion?"

Talioth nodded.

"What do you want with the Knights?"

"We need them," the other man said, "to take them back to the mountains."

"Centol!" Talioth barked.

The other man shrank back.

"If I tell you where they are, what do you intend to do with them?" Danik asked, his eyebrows arched.

"Danik, don't do it," Lia whispered. Her stomach churned. The tingle had returned as the light dimmed, but a nauseous feeling left her wanting to retch.

Talioth stood straight. "If you help us find them, we will take them away. We can make sure they never return." He inclined his head forward. "Is that something that serves your interests?"

Danik pursed his lips until a grin grew. His head nodded. "I believe we can help each other."

Lia's blood felt like fire. *How dare he turn on them!* She stopped herself as she prepared to drop from her perch. Her instinct told her to fight, but restraint forced her to use sense. *I need to warn the Knights!*

She turned to leave. Grit from the stone rubbed under her feet, and a rock broke loose. Her breath caught. She watched as the loose stone tumbled from the top of the wall, heading in slow motion toward the ground. Rather than wait to be caught, being free from the crystal's power, she used the origine to flee. She leaped from the wall, jumping clear of the building before the rock alerted anyone. When she hit the ground, she continued in a run, taking the straightest path back to the house.

The door slammed open at her rough push. She headed to the kitchen, grabbing a sack and stuffing some bread and dried meat inside. After setting it by the door, Lia ran upstairs. The sight of Mason's bloody corpse turned her stomach, but she choked back the feeling. She hefted her sack of clothes over her shoulder, then looked at Mason's body. *I can't leave him in Tienn. He should be buried with the Knights.* Amplifying her strength, she grabbed his limp arm and heaved his body over her shoulder.

As she trudged down the stairs, she formed her plan. *I can buy a horse to ride to Felting, but first, I'll carry him down the street and stash my things where Danik won't find them.*

She picked up the bag of food with her free hand, then turned the knob to pull open the door to the house.

Slam!

A club hit her in the face. Searing pain tore through her body. Her vision turned to white. Lia stumbled backward, dropping the two bags. Mason's body became too unwieldy, and she fell to the ground, his corpse flopping to the floor.

She rubbed her face. When her vision focused again, her stomach dropped.

"Where do you think you're going?" Danik asked, holding a club.

The gang of thieves spread to the sides. Jade bared her teeth along with her daggers, and Nicolar held a sword.

Danik checked her dropped bags. "We decide to make new lives. We run away together. And just when things are coming together, you want to leave?"

Lia's heart raced, glancing between them.

"Were you going to Felting? Going to warn them—those people who *hate* you?"

"They don't hate me," she yelled back. She tensed her

muscles, ready to spring to her feet and fight until something grabbed her arm. "Wha—?" A metal cuff clicked into place around her wrist. The tingling power faded as she turned to see Cedric sneering beside her. She pulled against him, but her arm caught. "Let me go!"

Danik nudged Mason's body with his foot, a curious look on his face. "Did he die?"

Lia glared at him. "Yes"—she nodded at Jade— "she killed him."

Danik paused a moment, his lips pursed. "Pity," he said, turning away. His gaze fell on Lia while a softness shone in his eyes.

Come on Danik, have some decency, she thought.

He turned to Nicolar and nodded. "Deal with her."

Lia tensed. She looked between Nicolar and Danik, ready to kick and scream until a heavy object hit the back of her head. Her vision flashed, then went dark.

HER HEAD POUNDED EVEN before she opened her eyes. It took a moment for her vision to clear. After several blinks, her room came into focus.

"Danik!" Jade called from the doorway, angling her head down the hall.

Lia was in her room, sitting against the wall. A flickering candle sat on the table next to her bed. Both arms wrapped around her chest, pulled tight against her body. Her hands were out of sight, pulled behind her by metal restraints. She leaned forward, and chains rattled as her movement arrested. A gag stuffed into her mouth, tied around her head. She tried to speak, but only a muffled mess came out.

"There you are," Danik said, passing Jade and entering the room.

Lia narrowed her eyes and pressed against the wall to get as far away as possible.

Danik crouched before her. "I've been waiting to say goodbye. We're about to leave." He pulled a large coin pouch from his pocket—the one Lia had earlier. Leaning forward, he pulled on the gag. Her jaw ached as it stretched until the fabric slid away. "Where is the rest of this?" he asked.

She glared back but didn't answer.

He got in her face. "*Where* is the rest of this?"

"It's gone," she replied.

"Where?"

She chuckled. "I gave it away."

His face turned sour.

"Where are you going?" Lia asked.

Danik took a deep breath and stood. "We have things to do."

"With the Marked Ones?"

His eyes narrowed.

"You're going to Felting to betray the people who gave you everything. You're going to kill the Shadow Knights."

"I am not. I don't intend to do anything with the Knights."

Lia cocked her head. "But you'll allow Talioth to do whatever he wants."

Danik's jaw clenched. He stared for a long moment. "As much as I'd like you with me, I can't have you stopping me, either."

"Are you going to kill me?"

Danik took a deep breath. "I couldn't kill you, but I can't have you coming after me." He stood and backed away, a hint of regret flashing across his face. "Goodbye, Lia."

The words sounded hollow and final. Lia's stomach lurched, and her breath grew shallow. Danik turned to Jade and nodded before exiting into the hall. Jade sauntered forward.

"So, you're going to do it?" Lia asked, with an empty feeling in her gut.

"Danik was clear," Jade said, crouching and raising the gag back over her mouth. The fabric stretched her jaw. "He doesn't want to be around when you die."

Lia's mind whirred.

"You haven't liked me since we met. That's all right. I haven't liked you either." A twinkle showed in Jade's eye as she pulled her blue dagger from its sheath. "I've decided you get to die a slow, agonizing death."

A searing pain registered in Lia's side. She screamed through the gag, the muffled noise filling her ears. She tried to suck in air, but a sharp pain filled her chest.

Jade pulled the dagger away, the blade coated in red that dripped down the handle. She wiped the weapon across Lia's pants then backed out of the room. She blew a kiss before closing the door behind her with a click.

Lia moaned. Short of breath, her sight grew blurry. She tried to breathe, but the labored effort only increased her pain. She pulled at the restraints, but her arms wouldn't budge. She strained to the side to get a view. Her torn shirt stained red. A pool of blood grew on the floor. A dizzy feeling washed over her. She closed her eyes and focused. *Come on, origine, where are you? If Father can do it, why can't I?* She strained, clenching her muscles and seeking the power, but nothing came. After a moment of holding her breath and flexing, she gasped and relaxed her head against the wall.

A door closed somewhere in the house, and she jerked open her eyes. She strained to hear something—anything—but nothing made a sound. *I'm alone and bleeding to death with a punctured lung.* Her heart pounded. Lia tested her gag. She attempted to pull it away with her shoulder, but the knot was too tight. She tried to yell, but the sound was too quiet.

Her mind turned to Raiyn. *He's halfway to Tarving by now. Once he gets there and doesn't find me, he could turn around and come to Tienn. A day or two to get there, another four back to Felting, then another two to get here. If I could last—* Her mind refused to calculate the number. *I can't live that long.*

43

DIMINISHING HOPE

The faded page crinkled as Veron turned it, the smell of aged parchment clinging to his nose. He ran his finger down the next sheet, scanning with a permanent frown on his face. His eyes ached from hours straining in the low light. With a sigh, he flipped the book shut and erupted in a frustrated groan. *Shawn is out there, and I have no idea where to look!* His desperation seemed to grow with each failed attempt to find something.

Veron grasped the back of his neck and rolled his head, slowly working the muscles. The lantern on the table flickered. He glanced at the oil reservoir. *Nearly dry. Have I been here that long?* He stood and grabbed an oil container with a long, thin spout. Opening the door to the lantern, he poured the oil into the bottom, filling the basin.

The King's Library took three entire levels of the southern-most tower of Felting Castle. A circle of bookshelves lined the walls, spread between six oval-shaped windows. Started hundreds of years earlier, the library grew significantly during the previous reign of King Wesley. Everything written in Terrenor on politics, history, economics, or a variety of other subjects resided there. Rolled-up desk-sized maps filled an entire quarter of the room. There was even a section for fiction, a pastime growing in popularity as the kingdom grew increasingly literate. Above the three main levels, a spiral staircase led to a smaller loft where journals of famous individuals rested with books on the sciences and the natural world.

Bright stars shone through the closest window. A light breeze passed through the room, flowing to the opening on the opposite side. Veron grabbed the next volume in his stack and fell into his chair. He opened *The Strange Among the Natural*, a thin book that promised answers to mysterious phenomena in Terrenor. The title on the faded cover was barely visible. The binding of the book warped with tears along the spine.

The first chapter made him groan—*Defending Yourself from the Dead*. He scanned the pages, flipping as fast as he could read the headlines. The next chapter was on Dreams and where they came from. His flipping slowed. He lingered on the words, his interest turning to skepticism. "Your mind knows what your body will one day manifest," he muttered. A quick head shake led to rapid flipping to the next section.

Veron paused at the third chapter. *Tapping into Your Power.* He tilted his head. *Could this be talking about the origine?* The exact term didn't appear, but much of the content was similar. The chapter spoke of summoning the body's power in a rush of energy. It even used an analogy of a well to explain the energy source. His pulse sped, but frustration took over as the description grew vague. When he flipped a page, the end of the chapter made him groan. *Communicating with Tree Frogs* stared at him from the next section.

He flipped through the rest of the book, but no other sections stood out. He closed it with a *thump*.

"Nothing good in that one?"

The voice made him spin. King Darcius mounted the last few steps, leaning on the railing.

"Your Majesty." Veron offered a quick bow. "You surprised me. Um, no, nothing of use. It hinted at the origine for a bit but had no details."

"What are you searching for?"

Veron leaned back in his chair and sighed, looking at the stack of dusty books resting on his table. "Anything on that mysterious guy with the stained neck: where he's from, how he blocks the origine, stuff like that."

Darcius pressed down on the table while he lowered himself into a chair.

"How are you feeling?"

The king grimaced, wobbling his hand from side-to-side. "Not great. My bones hurt from an ache deep inside."

"Is there anything you can take to relieve it?"

"Oh yes," Darcius chuckled, "you should see me when I haven't taken anything. It's all right though." He waved his hand, as if dismissing the topic. "Any change with Chelci?"

Veron shook his head. "Not much new. Her color has improved, but no signs of waking yet."

The king hung his head, pausing a moment. "So, what about this mysterious man from Karondir? It's been, what, two weeks? Do you expect to see him again?"

Veron took a deep breath. "All he cared about was finding the Shadow Knights. There aren't many people out there who know where we are. Kings, barons, ambassadors—they all know to come to Felting when they need help, but it would be tough for him to get to any of them. We work hard to keep our location quiet. But Shawn—Talioth intended to torture him to find out."

"Do you think he talked?"

Veron sighed. "I don't know. Pain is a powerful motivator, but it would take a lot for Shawn to give us up. We've talked about leaving the center as a precaution, but I'm worried about moving Chelci. As soon as she wakes, we plan to. But if that takes much longer . . ." His thoughts trailed off. "We've used three guards a night for the last two weeks, but that's a challenge, being that there are only seven of us."

Darcius raised an eyebrow. "Only seven? Could you use some royal guards to help?"

Veron shook his head. "Thank you, but I'd rather not raise any attention. Plus, if Talioth does show, with his ability, I'm not sure the number of guards we have will really matter. Yeah, only seven, now. We were at thirteen for a while, before Raiyn was dismissed. Chelci's still out. Shawn's taken. Danik and Lia are gone, and Mason disappeared a couple of days ago."

"Disappeared? That's odd. You don't think those people found him, do you?"

Veron shook his head. "I hope not. No one knows where he went, but my guess is he went after Lia. He always had a thing for her and took it hard when she left."

The king took in a deep breath, his face falling. "No further word on her, I presume?"

Veron's mouth cracked, but he paused. His bottom lip quivered as his chest clenched. His eyes blurred. "I—" He stopped himself, his throat thick with emotion. He wiped his eyes, but tears streamed down. "It was my fault."

Darcius set his hand on Veron's arm. "Hey, it wasn't your fault she left."

"It was," Veron blubbered. "I-I pushed her away. I forced her to be what I wanted instead of who she was. I blamed her for the attack on Chelci."

"Didn't you say she skipped her guard duty?"

Veron nodded. "But she didn't stab her. I was angry. I shouted things I didn't mean. I-I wish I could take them back." Veron wiped his eyes with both hands.

"You have time to make it right."

"Do I?" Veron lowered his hands. "She's gone. Someone hunts us. And you're—" He motioned to the king but stopped.

"And I'm dying," Darcius finished. "It's all right. You can say it."

"I'm sorry. This probably seems petty compared to what you're going through."

The king moved his head to catch Veron's eyes. "There is nothing I care about more in this world than the well-being of you, Chelci, and my granddaughter. It is *not* petty."

"Well, I hope I get a chance to make things right with her ... before it's too late."

LIA'S EYES fluttered open as a sharp pain twinged her side. She attempted a deep breath to bring relief to her lungs, but it only made the pain worse. The rough wall grated against the back of her head. Her arms had lost their feeling, stretched around her with the shackles. The room tilted in her vision. It took great effort to keep her eyelids open. She didn't know how long it had been since Danik left. *Minutes? Hours? Days?* The candle on the table continued to burn, melted down nearly to its base. Lia's shoulders slumped. *No time at all.*

The pool of blood had grown. It seeped across the floor, showing a light film across the surface. A steady throb infused her side, with twinges traveling down her leg. Her head lolled. She tried to focus, but the room continued to spin.

I've got to get out of this!

She twisted her head, checking everywhere she could see. Hopes of a metal pin to pick a lock ended in disappointment. She kicked the end of the bed. The wooden frame jostled but gave her no hopeful ideas. The diminishing candle was the only reachable item that contained any hope of usefulness.

Lia stretched her legs as far as they could reach, touching the leg of the table with the tip of her boot. *This is probably a bad idea, but I don't know what else to try.* She curled her toe and pulled the table. Wood scraped against wood as the table moved. Her heart surged. Soon, she wrapped her entire foot around the table leg and pulled harder. The table jumped, causing the candle to bounce. *Don't go out!*

The chunk of wax leaned. Lia held her breath as it jostled back and forth until the candle fell. It rolled off the backside of the table and dropped to the floor, landing on the faded rug to the side of the bed.

No!

The flame remained lit despite the drop, but it lay on its side. Lia tried to pull the rug with her feet, but the ancient floor covering wouldn't budge. The flame spread. It jumped from the candle to the fabric. She gasped. Her hope of using the flame to help turned to fear.

The rug burned quickly, creeping toward the wooden frame of the bed. Lia stamped what she could reach with her foot. The effort snuffed out the closest flames, but the fire continued to move. It soon jumped to the legs of the bed and slowly spread along the frame until it reached the wall.

She pulled against her restraints, the effort searing her nerve endings with pain, but she wasn't able to do anything.

The heat in the room grew stifling. She turned her head away from the flames, trying to shield her face and hoping the blaze would somehow disappear.

The roar grew as the fire spread, licking against the far wall and rounding the corner. Lia watched in horror as the fire crept along the wall, growing closer and hotter every second.

She pulled against her restraints again, but nothing changed. Sweat dripped off her face. She breathed in ragged bursts. A lungful of smoke sent her reeling with a coughing fit, causing the wound in her side to spasm with pain.

This is it, she thought. *I ran away to make my own life, and now I die, stabbed and abandoned in a fire of my own making.* The roar of the flames grew deafening. She leaned her body as far as she could away from the encroaching peril, but the distance didn't help.

A crash at the door caused her to jerk her head up. A figure wrapped in a blanket jumped through a wall of fire, landing in the center of her room.

Lia's mind reeled. Heat and smoke combined with the loss of blood left her disoriented and weak. The room spun, the body seeming to tilt. The figure of blankets hurried to her and leaned over. "Who are you?" she croaked, the words inaudible over the tumult.

Her arms jerked, the pressure from the restraints lessening at once. Her body slumped then became weightless, lifted by the figure to drape over their shoulder. A blanket wrapped over her head as they faced the flaming doorway again. Darkness enveloped her, but she felt the sudden movement and jarring steps as they rushed forward. After a run down the stairs, they burst outside. The cool night air rushed to greet her as the blanket around her fell. After crossing the street and gaining a safe distance, the person set her on the ground.

The movement had refreshed the pain in her side and chest. Her entire body ached. She felt as if she would suffocate. Her sight was blurry and indistinct. She still couldn't make out the person who had carried her. Pressure lightened on her right wrist. Her mind struggled to process the events. When her other wrist freed from its shackle, the figure spoke.

"Heal the wound," a man said. The voice sounded distant and muddled.

Heal the wound? What does he mean? She tried to make sense of the words. *I don't understand. How am I supposed to—* Clarity flooded her as she pinpointed the tingling sensation growing in her body. *The origine!*

Lia pulled from the energy source. Her body was weak, depleted from its regular strength and needing a great deal of recovery. Her side prickled. She pushed the power into the wound, not letting go. Her limbs trembled from the effort. She sensed her insides knitting together. The bloody wound on her side tightened, forming a clean scar. With a gasp, she was done.

Lia slumped, gasping for breath. The pain of the wound was gone. Her arms were free. She was free. Lia looked up. The body of blankets unwrapped itself. Thick, black hair topped a young man's head. A scruffy beard framed a smile she knew well. "Raiyn! How did you get here?"

"Are you all right?" Raiyn leaned over to inspect her side. "It looks good. How does it feel?"

"I-I'm fine." Her chest heaved as she tried to regain her energy.

"Did Mason make it here?"

Tears sprang to Lia's face. She gave a tight nod. "They killed him and left me for dead."

"What?" Raiyn's jaw hung. "Who did?"

"Danik and a group he's with. You arrived just in time."

A growl rumbled in Raiyn's throat. His face hardened. "What happened to Danik?"

Lia shook her head. "He's grown darker and more selfish. All he cares about now is power and money."

"He always gave me a bad feeling."

"What about you?" Lia said. "Mason said you went to Tarving. You couldn't have come back already. How'd you arrive so soon?"

"Did he tell you about the Dream I had?"

Lia nodded.

"We split up. I started toward Tarving, but not even a half day there, I remembered something. I recalled traveling through the city with my mother when I was young. I could picture the tower, but I also remembered the Tarphan motto across the top. *Fayyre par soi. Fayyre par tous.*"

"Do it for one. Do it for all," Lia translated.

"In my Dream, there was no writing, so I figured it had to be Tienn."

"I'm glad you remembered that."

A loud crumbling sound turned them around as something inside the house collapsed. The walls remained standing, but flames reached out through the roof. Bystanders gathered in the street, keeping their distance and shielding their eyes.

"I guess I'm finished with that place now," Lia said, ending with a laugh. She turned to Raiyn. His tender eyes looked back. "Thank you for coming for me."

He smiled. "You're welcome."

"I'm sorry that my father kicked you out. So, you really are . . . Bale's son?"

Raiyn's jaw set. After a moment, he nodded. "I can't control who my parents are. I wish I could. I don't want to be anything like him."

"I believe you."

"So, where did Danik go?"

"I almost forgot." She gathered herself to her feet. The street spun. She extended her arms for balance, and Raiyn grabbed her hand, helping her steady herself. "Thanks." She breathed in, her vision settling. "You remember that guy Veron met in Karondir? Talioth?"

Raiyn nodded.

"He's here with a bunch of others like him. They call themselves the Marked Ones." She glanced around the street, making sure they weren't lurking nearby. "We need to get to Felting as soon as possible."

"Why?" Raiyn asked. "What are they going to do?"

"They're going to kill the Shadow Knights."

44

ROYAL PLANS

Six rustling torches surrounded the room, tossing shadows and flickering light against the walls. The sky past the balcony faded from a deep blue to a faint red. Scanning the oval table, the king noted the eager eyes of his advisors and high lords staring back. The empty chair where Veron usually sat left him feeling vulnerable. The Shadow Master always seemed to have his side and shared wise words that eclipsed the others in the room.

"This should be it," Darcius said, prompting the other heads to turn to the empty seat.

"Is Veron sick?" High Lord Bilton asked.

"It's probably blue fever," High Lord Miligan said.

"No," the king answered. "We got word to him, but he has other priorities at the moment."

High Lord Hillegass's eyebrow raised. "More important than the king's business?"

Darcius sighed. "Veron has my full support. I encourage you to extend him the same courtesy." He tapped his hands on the long table, the impact bouncing about the high ceilings. "Now . . . What is our first business of the day?"

Quentin Cotterell raised a hand. "Your Majesty, are you still intent on retiring at the end of the season?"

Darcius turned to the advisor at his side and nodded. He covered his mouth while forcing out a weak cough. The effort emphasized the necessity.

"In that case, should we talk about our candidates for the crown, now?"

"Yes, that would be great. Do you have a list?" Darcius noticed the high lords of defense and trade sit up straighter and lift their chins.

"Yes, Your Majesty. We have the list down to three candidates: our own high lords, Geoffrey Bilton and Stanley Hillegass, and the head of the merchants guild, Christopher Culbert."

"Ah yes, Christopher. He's a shrewd one," Darcius said. He turned to the others. "Geoffrey and Stanley, would you mind leaving us, so we can speak for a bit?"

Both men wore smiles of respect and excitement. "Of course," they both said in unison. The two men rose and left out the large double doors, which closed behind them.

The room grew quiet. Everyone turned to the king, waiting for him to speak.

"Don't look at me." Darcius laughed. "I'm not the one choosing."

"But we value your input, Your Majesty," Quentin said.

The king nodded. He slid his seat back and stood, pushing off the armrests of his chair. Once up, he meandered around the table. "Bilton is a clear leader. He's managed the defense of Feldor for as long as I can remember. He's respected by the army and the people of the city. At times pompous and arrogant, his faults have mellowed over the years."

A few mutters of agreement sounded around the table as heads nodded.

"Hillegass is newer to leadership, but no less worthy. He has experience in trade and finance and has learned a lot about people from his wife who runs the charity drive in the Red Quarter. He's pragmatic and listens to reason, but some argue that he has trouble deciding."

After a full loop around the table, Darcius paused, tapping his chin.

"What do you think about Culbert?" High Lord Stokes asked.

Darcius resumed walking. "He knows the needs of merchants. Businesses love him. They've grown strong and well organized under his leadership." He paused.

Stokes leaned forward. "But..."

"But I worry whether his focus will be on businesses or on the people of Feldor."

Windridge raised a finger. "You think he won't care about people?"

"I know he'll care about *some* people," the king said. "Specifically, the ones that make him money and keep him in power. I worry about whether he'll care for *all* the people."

Muttering filled the room, and several heads nodded.

GAVIN PACED the wall surrounding the Shadow Knights compound. His eyes scanned the streets, looking for anything that seemed out of the ordinary. The night contained a chill, unseasonably cold for late suether. The Shadow Knights cloak hung loosely around him. His sword hung from his belt while his hand rested on the hilt.

His pacing brought him to the far left side of the wall, where Bridgette stood in position. "Nothing?" he asked.

She shook her head, her long strands of blonde hair waving from the motion. A strung bow rested over her shoulder, and a quiver with arrow feathers stuck up on the opposite side. She yawned, covering her mouth. "I wish we had more knights.

Three on guard duty is tough with so few. This is the second night in a row for me."

"Get some rest tomorrow, once day breaks. If you have trouble staying alert, pace or jog in place to get the blood flowing."

"Are we sure this is quite necessary?" Bridgette asked. "Will three people help that much more than two if we can't use the origine?"

"I don't know. If what Veron says is true and they attack us .. ." He chose to not finish. "Just stay alert."

Gavin turned and paced in the other direction. His feet made no sound as he crossed the well-worn stone path. Faint chatter bubbled up from the hallway leading into the court-yard, likely Ruby, Bradley, and Salina in the common room. After turning the corner at the far end of the wall, he met Dayna's stern face.

"You shouldn't be so loud," she whispered. "This is watch, not social hour."

"I was checking in with her," Gavin replied in a hushed voice. "She's young. I wanted to make sure she's handling things all right."

"Is she?"

"She's fine." The wind whipped over the wall, rustling the loose fringe of his cloak. "I wish Veron were here."

Dayna nodded. "I do too. I don't know that he's going to find anything useful in that library. I want to find Shawn as much as anyone but—" She stopped, eyes wide and jaw dropped.

"What is it?" Gavin spun then gasped.

Chelci stood at the top of the stairs. Her hair fluttered in the wind, and her clothes rippled. A pink color had returned to her face, but she swayed precariously, unsteady and weak.

"Chelci," Gavin breathed, a broad grin forming. "You're up."

Chelci offered a weak smile. "What happened?" she said, rubbing her chest where the injury had been. "I remember the wound, but it's healed now. How long have I been out? Where's Veron? Where's Lia?"

Gavin came alongside her and steadied her arm. "A lot has happened since you've been out. We should—" He stopped, tensing.

Dayna's brow wrinkled. "What is it?"

He released Chelci and stepped toward the edge, peering into the dark street. Nothing moved. He strained his ears, but nothing registered. "I thought . . ." He pointed. "By the far corner."

He saw it again, and his eyes widened. He sucked in a sharp intake of breath. His muscles clenched, and he pulled his sword, taking a cautious step backward then pointing to Chelci. "Get her to safety. I'll alert the others." He turned and leaped off the wall.

VERON CLOSED the thick tome with a *thud* and dropped it on the towering stack of rejected potential resources. A puff of dust wafted in the air. He sighed, scanning the library. His back and neck ached from sitting in the chair for so long. He needed to move and stretch. The lantern on the table was nearly out of oil, and he didn't have it in him to research through the time another refill would gain. *If there's anything useful here, I think I would have found it by now. I should have gone to the advisors meeting instead.* Veron stood with a sense of defeat weighing on him.

A chill breeze wafted through the window, making him shiver. He picked up his cloak and threw it over his shoulders. His sword, Farrathan, lay against a shelf, resting in its sheath. He worked it through his arms, the weight of the weapon resting against his back. Before he left the room, the view out the window caught his eye. He stepped toward it.

Past the city, over the river, the rolling hills of Feldor

extended into the countryside. The sky along the horizon retained a faint bit of light. The lighter shade of blue faded into a darker hue then to a near pitch black high in the sky. Lanterns lit along some streets of Felting. Many windows were dark, but some contained a faint glow where candles extended the evening for the families inside.

He turned back to the table with a sigh and picked up the books he'd read. One by one, he set them back on the shelves from where he'd found them. With each book he placed, his annoyance grew. *Lack of information. Lack of answers. Lack of help.* He shoved the last book too hard. It clunked against the back of the shelf, and a slight crack grew at the edge of the bookshelf.

Veron paused and leaned closer with his brows pinched together. He ran his finger along the crack. Prying with his nails, he pulled at the edge. The bookshelf fought him. He pulled harder, and it slowly pivoted, groaning and creaking. The heavy shelf scraped against the dusty floor, and the crack grew. Content with the progress, Veron stopped, breathing heavily from the effort.

He grabbed the lantern off the table and held it before the new opening. A cavity lay beyond the bookshelf. Cobwebs and dust filled the space, and the stale smell of a forgotten passage wafted before him. In the back of the compartment, a stack of leather-bound books rested against the wall, hidden from the light of day for as long as the shelf had remained closed. Judging from the difficulty of opening the compartment, Veron guessed that had been a while. He leaned forward, dusting past spiderwebs, and picked up the stack of three books.

The lantern clanked as he set it back down. He turned the volumes over in his hands. *Why would someone hide books like this?*

The first book split along the spine. The brown leather was so old that it cracked as he peeled back the cover. *The Atrocities of Norshand Rulers* was barely visible on the title page with a date of 208 written down. Veron whistled. "Three hundred years ago," he breathed. 208 was just before the Shadow Knights formed—when Norshand ruled Terrenor. *I can see why this book might have needed to be hidden*, he thought.

The second book, a faded green, looked to be in better shape. Its title was still visible on the outside—*A Case for Women Lords*. Veron smiled. A lot of the women he knew were better suited for positions of leadership than the selfish, lug-headed men. Thankfully, Felting had progressed past archaic gender limitations many years before, but Veron could see why the book might have drawn controversy at the time.

The final book was smaller. Red leather wrapped around with no writing on the outside. Its condition looked to be stable with no visible cracks or tears in the exterior. He lifted the cover, and a gasp escaped his mouth. He held the book with two hands, balancing it open. His hands shook, causing the page to waver. He leaned closer, reading the title again to make sure he saw it correctly. *History of the Origine: Rise of the Devion.*

He flipped the pages rapidly and stopped at a hand drawn map. The illustration detailed a mountain range and an area surrounding it. Dots and lines connected what looked like cities, but the names were faded or unfamiliar. Veron's eyes grew. A star marked a point in the heart of the mountain range.

A gust tore through the window, rustling the faded, delicate pages. A corner from the map cracked and tore, fluttering to the floor. Veron clenched his jaw. He closed the book and set it down on the table before turning to the window.

He stepped forward and grasped the handle of the ancient glass and metal frame. Before he pulled, he looked down Rampart Way. The street passing by the castle was dark. Veron traced the route until he found the unlit section where the Shadow Knights center lay. *I'm going to finally get some answers,* he thought with a grin.

Suddenly, a prickle grew up the back of his neck. He inhaled, his hand still gripping the handle of the window. *What is that?*

He leaned forward, his eyes straining. In the street, a faint red glow moved toward the facility. His breath caught. "Could that be . . ." Black shapes obscured the glow until one of them turned, showing a glowing red object hanging from their neck in the center of their chest.

Veron gasped. His insides felt watery, and his arm shook. His legs wobbled as he backed away. After turning, he sprinted to the stairs, using the origine to move down them as quickly as possible, leaving the forgotten book resting on the table.

"Again, I'm not the one to decide," King Darcius said, "but I think he would do a fine job as king."

The four High Lords nodded around the table while the king's two advisors sat quietly. "Are we all agreed, then?" High Lord Stokes asked.

The others around the table muttered in affirmation.

A pang of regret mixed with relief as Darcius pictured himself leaving his position. *It's time,* he reassured himself. He looked at the guards stationed by the doors. "Please find Bilton and Hillegass. We're ready for them now."

The guards nodded and stepped outside.

"Have you given thought to what you'd like to do to honor your retirement?" Quentin asked. "A citywide celebration? Perhaps we can invite people from the corners of Feldor and throw a grand party?"

Darcius shook his hand. "Please, no. I don't need a grand recognition. A party like that would cost too much. A small ceremony would be fine."

The doors opened, and the guards returned with Geoffrey Bilton and Stanley Hillegass.

"Geoffrey, Stanley, come in, please." The king gestured to the seats around the table.

The high lords returned to their chairs. Hillegass held his hands together, adjusting and moving them as if he couldn't find a natural position. Bilton's chin lifted, deep breaths moving his chest.

"The high lords have decided," Darcius said before nodding to Stokes.

The High Lord of Commerce cleared his throat, looking between the two candidates. "Yes, we have. We've decided what we think is best for the country."

"The best for the country . . . Ha!" a fresh voice called from the balcony. "More like . . . what's best for you."

Darcius jerked his head. A young man wearing dark leather rounded the nearest column, carrying a sword and staring at him. "Who are you?" the king asked.

A smirk grew on the young man's face as five other men and a woman with daggers and slicked black hair emerged from the dark balcony. Each held a weapon and a fierce look on their faces.

"Halt!" a guard called. Two from outside the door entered the room, and the four guards ran to intercept. Their swords rang, and their boots clumped as they positioned themselves between the king and the intruders. "You are not authorized to be here," the guard said. "Lay down your weapons or we will take them by force!"

The young man chuckled. The others with him formed a V-shape behind him. He lifted his sword, stopping several feet from the guards. He took a deep breath while pausing. "Are you sure you wish to do this?"

"Lay down your sword!" the guard shouted.

The man cocked his head. "Very well, then."

The others along the V moved in a blur. If Darcius had blinked, he would have missed it. Hideous cries filled the room as the guards' bodies filled with swords and daggers at the same moment. They fell to the ground, their gray-and-blue Feldorian uniforms staining red from their own blood. The young man in front hadn't moved a muscle.

The room exploded with noise. High lords and advisors jumped to their feet, chairs falling over and scraping on the stone. Suzanne Quigley's high-pitched scream was silenced by a dagger to the neck from the woman with black hair who moved across the room in a fraction of a second. The lords ran for the door, but a man appeared there, waving his sword and causing everyone to freeze.

Silence returned to the room while the king's heart pounded. He glanced around, looking for a way out, but based on their speed, there was no hope.

"You asked who I was," the young man said once everyone had stopped moving. "My name is Danik Bannister, and we've met before."

Darcius tilted his head.

"You spent so much time fawning over Veron that you never got to know the rest of us."

The king's eyes grew. "You're shadow knights?"

"Ha!" Danik roared. "I was once, but I left them behind."

"Danik," Darcius said, rolling the name over his tongue. "I do remember. You're the one who Veron . . ."

"Expelled?" Danik finished, his face growing red. "Kicked to the curb like a bit of garbage? Yes, he kicked me out, and it was his loss." He motioned to the others with him. "But now, *we* are much more than the Shadow Knights will ever be. They've had their time in the sun. Now it is *our* time."

Darcius held his ground as Danik advanced. He glanced at the others. The high lords stood frozen. Quentin stared down at his fellow advisor, Suzanne, whose body spasmed on the floor while a pool of blood grew around her. A sword waved in his face, drawing his eyes back to Danik.

"What's to happen with us?" Darcius asked.

"You'll all die," the woman with the slicked-back hair growled.

The king's muscles tightened, ready to run, but Danik's weapon pressed against his neck.

Darcius raised his chin. "Please," he whispered. "I'm ready to die."

Danik flinched, but his sword remained steady against the king's throat.

"But spare the others."

Danik's face softened. Darcius could picture the young man's mind churning, considering the benefits of retaining their services versus eliminating them. The cold metal against his neck remained frozen in place. Danik glanced around the room, then nodded. "They can live."

The king swallowed and took a deep breath. He leaned his head against the wall and closed his eyes. Whimpering sounded from across the room. The highlights of Darcius' life rushed through his head. *Becoming High Lord of Commerce. Jackson's and Chelci's births. Befriending Veron. Ascending to the throne.* A smile tugged at his face as he thought of the state of Feldor and the people helped during his reign. His shoulders relaxed. Maintaining a smile and filled with a sense of accomplishment, he nodded, keeping his eyes closed. He exhaled as the blade did its work.

Veron exited the winding staircase, running at full speed. The door to the Advisors Council meeting lay ahead, a slight crack permitting a sliver of light to spill out. *Where are the guards?* he wondered. He longed to continue sprinting toward the Shadow Knights but decided, if the council was still in session, he could petition them for help.

Veron yanked the handle of the heavy wooden door and

thrust himself into the room. "Your Majesty!" he yelled, panting. "In the library, I saw—" His stomach jumped. He grasped the door, clenching it tightly.

The high lords stared at him, their eyes wide. Tears ran down Marie Windridge's face, and Magnus Hampton's arms shook as he held the back of a chair. Slumped to the floor, King Darcius' body lay unmoving. His lifeless eyes stared at nothing. Blood ran down his tunic, dripping to the stone floor. A young man with a stained sword stood over the king, his head turned toward the door. Veron locked eyes with the young man, and his jaw dropped.

"Danik! What have you done?" His heart pounded. His ragged breath clung to his dry throat.

Danik stepped away from the king and moved toward the rest of his gang. He held his sword out straight. Despite the waver in the blade, his posture was straight, and he held his chin high. The gang of men and a woman gathered around him, holding their own weapons ready.

"It's time for a change in Feldor," Danik said, his jaw tight.

"But—" Veron scanned the room, noting the terror on the high lords' faces. "The king . . . he—"

"He's gone. Now *we* rule this land."

Snapping out of his stupor, Veron pulled Farrathan. The ruby in the hilt caught the light of a lantern and flashed across his face. He clenched his jaw and stepped forward.

"I don't think you want to do that, Veron," Danik said.

Veron ran into the room, leaping over the oval table. He hit the ground with his sword raised. A mighty clash rang in the air as the two knights collided. Veron pulled the origine, trying to incapacitate his opponent quickly, but Danik was a move ahead. He knocked the sword away, but Danik spun back into place. Veron tried to kick him down, but a deft step kept his opponent clear.

After several failed attempts on Veron's part, Danik turned

on the offensive. The returned attacks were brutally hard and fast. Even using the origine, Veron could barely keep up. Danik smiled as he pushed the Shadow Master toward the wall. Veron spun to the side, giving himself space to breathe. While he rested, a man sporting a messy goatee and shaggy brown hair joined the woman holding daggers and approached. Moving as fast as Danik had, they attacked in unison.

Veron paled. He fended off blow after blow, barely keeping ahead of their brutal assault. Outmatched, he retreated by leaping back over the table. "Are they . . . trained?" he blurted, gasping for breath.

"In the origine?" Danik asked, not even appearing out of breath. A smirk grew on his face. "Something like that."

The woman rubbed her two daggers together as she came around the table. The metallic grating rang through the silence.

"Leave us be, Veron. I won't hurt the rest. What you need to worry about right now is your precious Shadow Knights."

Veron's head jerked, the memory of the glowing light approaching the training center returning in a rush. His pulse thumped in his ears.

"Did you bring them here?" He breathed.

"The Marked Ones?" A wicked smile grew on Danik's face. "Like I said, I think your knights need you more than these people do."

Veron's eyes jumped to the high lords. He longed to run, but his legs wouldn't allow his body to leave.

"It's all right, Veron," High Lord Bilton said, nodding toward the door. "Go to them. Darcius is gone, but they won't hurt us."

Stokes and Hillegass also nodded. Veron stepped toward the door. He looked at Danik when he reached the threshold. "This isn't done," he threatened, pointing his sword at the young man. Before waiting for a response, Veron turned and ran.

45

DISTRACTION FROM DEATH

Talioth strode down the street. The other eight surrounded him, focused and ready. Despite his confidence, his stomach churned. *We need this to work. The stakes are too high for failure.* The wall of the Shadow Knights center rose into the air like a dark fortress ahead. He nodded. The others knew what to do.

Valdok rushed the door with two trailing him. His shoulder collided with the wood, splintering the barrier. Centol led four others over the wall. They leaped together, their bodies flying with a smooth efficiency. Fierce roars from the attackers shattered the night's silence. Down the street, the glow of Gralow's necklace disappeared into the house that held the secret entrance.

Talioth followed Valdok through the main center's doorway. He swept through the dark hallway, passing small rooms with barely enough space for a bed. He paused at a large room with tables. A lit candle sat on the counter. Chunks of half-eaten bread lay on the table while a smattering of playing cards spread haphazardly. Rosalik hurried through the room, peering under tables and behind the counter. She looked at Talioth and shook her head. They continued down the hallway and spilled into a dirt courtyard where Centol and his crew already gathered.

"Check upstairs," Centol shouted, pointing his sword up the external staircase. A man and woman with glowing red crystals ran up and disappeared into the building.

"Talioth! Look here!" Valdok waved to him from an opening in the wall where a torch burned brightly.

Talioth plucked the torch from its holder and joined him. The dark room tucked into the wall was an armory packed with every weapon imaginable. He ran his hand along the handles of the swords hanging on the wall and grinned. "This is it."

"But where are they?" Valdok asked.

Gralow jogged into the courtyard from the far hallway. "The secret tunnel is clear," he called.

"Nothing up here, sir," the upstairs pair reported from the top of the steps.

"Are you sure?" Centol questioned. They nodded.

Beside the armory, a sparse smithing shop lay quiet. The forge was cold, and the space was empty.

Valdok jogged to the last door along the courtyard. His hand didn't move as he tried to turn the knob. "It's locked!"

Talioth's mouth curled at the edge. The marked ones moved in unison to surround the door, each raising a weapon. At a signal, Valdok rammed the door, the effort shattering the wood and leaving a mangled mess. He yanked on the knob and the remains of the door fell to the dirt. A puff of dust flew into the air, but the group was silent, their shoulders slumping. A closet stared back.

Talioth walked forward. A thick book with a dark cover and gilded edges rested on a shelf. The hairs on his neck stood on end. He extended his arm and lifted the book from the shelf. *Chronology of the Shadow Knights.* He smirked, a soft chuckle escaping. "They think they know so much. What a waste of paper." He held the book away from his body and positioned the torch at its corner. The flame grew, leaping to the dry pages and progressing across the face of the book. He dropped it. Fire covered the object, turning the pages into charred flakes.

"They have to be here somewhere," Talioth said, turning to the others.

"Unless Danik lied," Centol said.

Talioth shook his head. "He didn't lie." He looked around the courtyard, nodding his head. "This is it. I *feel* it. I feel . . . *them.*"

He moved slowly, crossing the courtyard, and returned to the weapons room. His senses tingled as he held the torch up. The room shimmered, the light of the flame bouncing off the metal swords, daggers, and axe blades. Something called to him. *They're close.* His eyes dropped to the ground, and he took a step back. In the corner, a faint line in the dirt formed a straight edge and made a corner before it blended in with the rest of the ground. The grip on his sword tightened.

He nodded to Valdok. The man creeped forward, bending down to lift the camouflaged covering. Talioth held his sword up. His crystal glowed strong. His body tensed, ready for action.

"I'm here!" a voice called from behind. "I'm the one you want!"

Talioth spun on his heels. He lifted the torch, and a reserved grin covered his face. The man from Karondir stood in the center of the courtyard. "Veron," he said, dragging out the name as he spoke. "It's good to see you again."

"DID DANIK LEAD YOU HERE?" Veron asked, trying to determine if they'd found the secret compartment where the others would be hiding. *Hopefully, they'll only take me and not find them.*

"It seems you and he aren't on the best of terms," Talioth said, his voice raspy and deep. "He was quite helpful to us."

Veron flinched. "Well, you found me, but I'm afraid I'm all that's left."

Talioth chuckled, glancing back toward the weapons room. "I don't think that's the case."

"It's true. Danik—" Veron paused, searching for the right words. "—left with several of our knights. We had to kick out some others, and you took Shawn. Now, it's just me." He searched for the origine, but—like in Karondir—the power was nowhere to be found. The glowing crystals worn by the seven intruders taunted him. Veron dropped his sword into the dirt and held up his hands. "Take me. Do whatever you want. I know I can't beat you."

Talioth nodded to a woman, who produced a set of shackles. She crouched at his legs. Veron flinched as she clasped the restraints around his ankles. Immediately after, the bright crystals dimmed from several of the marked ones.

"No!" Talioth warned, the glow returning. "Don't let your guard down with this one. He's an alloshifter."

Veron's breath escaped him, and his eyes flashed. *What?*

A grin tugged at Talioth's face. "You don't know that term, alloshifter, do you? You can resist the metal, but . . . you don't know why or how." He raised an eyebrow, stepping forward. "Do you want to know?"

Veron's eyes grew. He raised his chin, quiet for a long moment.

"I can teach you. There's power you've not yet tapped into. If you join us, your world will be opened."

Veron's heart pounded. *I've searched for it for years. Do these people have the answers?* The memory of what he knew of them hardened him against the temptation. "I've seen what you do," he growled. "You kill. You take. I heard what you did in Rynor to that village. You think only of yourselves and nothing for the good of anyone else."

"No one else matters," Talioth said, his jaw tight.

Veron's eyes narrowed. "I would never join you."

Talioth sighed and shook his head. "Very well." He turned to the others. "Get the rest of them."

Veron's throat caught. *Do they know the others are there?*

Fierce yells emanated from the weapons room. Six shadow knights wearing black cloaks and brandishing swords, knives, and a bow ran into the light of the courtyard.

"No!" Veron yelled, his sacrifice squandered.

The marked ones spread out, surrounding the group. The glow from their crystals doubled in intensity. Talioth laughed, pulling his wicked-looking curved knife. The knights' movements were sluggish and awkward. They attempted to use the power they always relied on, but it was nowhere to be found. Veron could do nothing but watch.

They swung their swords, but the marked ones stayed several steps ahead. Blades met with nothing but air. Bradley's sword shattered from a vicious blow by a war hammer. They casually plucked arrows shot from Salina's bow from the air. Bridgette jumped with a flying kick toward another attacker's chest, but he slid to the side, allowing her to tumble to the dirt. Another man laughed as he ran circles around Gavin, who desperately swung his sword.

Another knight emerged from the armory, and Veron's breath caught. *Chelci! She's awake!* His wife raised a sword, stumbling toward the marked ones. "Chelci! No!" he yelled, his words drowned in the chaos of the fight.

She stumbled forward, weak and unsteady, but with a look of determination on her face. One futile swing toward a man in gray ended with her splayed on the ground and her sword knocked from her hands.

"Chelci," Veron muttered to himself, tears bursting into his eyes.

Her head raised, and she looked around. Their eyes connected, and Veron's heart fluttered. A reluctant smile stared back at him until she mouthed, *I love you*, in his direction.

"I love you, too," he whispered.

"That's enough," Talioth shouted. "Chain them up."

The marked ones became blurred shapes, moving through the courtyard with speed the knights couldn't match. One after another, the knights' weapons fell as shackles appeared on their arms and legs. Veron hung his head.

"Eight of them," Talioth said, nodding. "Perfect. This will last us years."

The knights jerked their arms, useless in their chains. Veron's heart ached.

The marked ones' crystals dimmed, and Veron's breath caught. A glimmer of hope blossomed. *They're not used to dealing with . . . whatever I am.* He reached deep inside, searching for the origine. Its presence was faint, but it hummed deep inside him. He crouched, pulled at the power, and grasped the metal links with his hands. Keeping an eye on the group, he pulled. Filled with strength, but controlling the power, a faint *clink* reached his ears as the links broke. The bands remained around his ankles, but the link between them was gone.

While the marked ones rustled the other seven together, Veron slunk low to the ground. He picked up Farrathan from the dirt and hustled on his tiptoes toward the nearest attacker. Fighting the effect of the metal, he pulled through the resistance to strengthen his arms and quicken his movement. His sword reared back, preparing for a killing stroke. He pulled even harder.

As he was about to unleash a flurry of violence, the origine disappeared. His sword drooped and legs stumbled. Two men with glowing red crystals around their necks appeared before him with swords held against his chest. Veron groaned, exhaustion overwhelming him.

Talioth cursed. "We can't forget about him!"

Veron sucked in air. The points of the swords pressed into his chest with each heaving breath. His pulse raced.

The woman who shackled him crouched by his legs, lifting the broken links. "What should I do with this?" She looked at Talioth. "Use a fresh set?"

Talioth ran a hand across the back of his neck and stared.

"He's too dangerous to take to the caverns," a bulky man with dark hair said. "We can't constantly subdue him."

"We don't *need* all of them," another whispered.

Veron shuffled his feet. He looked past the men to the knights, bound and held at sword point. Chelci's hair fell down her face, brushed with dirt but free from fear. Gavin's eyes met his. His face was long, filled with sorrow.

Talioth nodded. "I agree. We can't take him with us . . . but we can't leave him here." He turned to the bulky man. "Valdok, siphon him here."

The other man nodded. "How much should I take?"

Talioth's jaw was tight. His words were barely audible. "Everything."

"No!" Gavin shouted. One of the marked ones jabbed an elbow into his face, knocking him to the ground.

The men around Veron pressed their swords harder against his skin, grabbing each arm with their other hands. He pulled against them, but their strength was far beyond anything he could muster. He reached inside for the origine, but the glowing crystals taunted him. Nothing. His pulse raced.

The man named Valdok approached. His smirk turned Veron's stomach. "If you hold still, this will hurt less," the man said.

Veron jerked against the arms holding him.

Valdok extended his arm, resting it against Veron's chest. The crystal around his neck pulsed, a faint humming filling the air.

Veron's body stiffened. Every muscle seemed to stretch taut at once. His head tried to shake, but he clenched his jaw and held it tight. His chest felt as if it were being torn open from the inside. He held back a scream. His skin lit with pinpricks of light through his pores. *What are they doing to me?* His mind raced. He pulled again, but the men held him fast. *I can't take much more of this!* The humming grew deafening. The pulsing glow from the crystal became impossibly bright. The walls around the courtyard rumbled. Excruciating pain touched every part of his body.

A roar grew. *Something new*, Veron thought, his mind murky and slow. *What is that?* Despite the blinding light, he opened his eyes a slit. Valdok's body trembled, facing him with his arm extended. The other marked ones and shadow knights all turned away, covering their eyes. *It almost sounds like—*

A rush of wind blew his hair back, and a blur sliced through Valdok's arm. The portion of the limb close to Veron dropped, lifeless. Valdok screamed, falling to the ground and clutching his stump of an arm.

The strain on Veron's body fled. The two men holding him both cried out, and the grip on his arms loosened. He collapsed. His body was spent, drained of any energy he could muster. He fell to his knees, struggling to keep upright. After two deep breaths, he lifted his head. Valdok wailed, his body curled on the ground with blood spraying to the dirt. The two guards who had held him lay twitching on the ground. One showed his exposed neck where a deep red gash marred the skin. *What happened?*

Two bodies stepped in front of him. One was a young woman. Straight, brown hair fell down her neck. Her lean arms flexed as she held a sword in front of her. Light from the torch caught the side of her face, and Veron gasped. "Lia!" he croaked.

She glanced over her shoulder, a rueful smile on her lips.

Tears welled in his eyes. His chest tightened again, but it was pride that caused him to ache.

"You want him? You'll have to come through me!" Lia shouted toward the others.

"And me, too!" the other body yelled.

Veron looked at the young man with the black hair. It took a moment to place him in the dim light, but his eyes grew when it clicked. *Raiyn!*

Lia held up a sword, and Raiyn carried an axe, their bodies blocking him.

Veron tried to stand, but attempting to move his leg sent a wave of dizziness through him. His head felt light, and his vision spun. *What did he do to me?* Lia shouted something, but he couldn't discern it. Unable to keep himself upright, he lay down. When his head hit the dirt, he closed his eyes, and his mind went black.

46

REDEMPTION

The six remaining marked ones surrounded the shadow knights, holding swords. The sight of her friends in chains broke Lia's heart. Bridgette, Dayna, Gavin, and the others stared back at her, their faces turned down.

Mother!

Chelci stood with them, her body slumped and appearing weak.

"Run," Bridgette mouthed.

Lia shook her head. The glowing crystals surrounding her confirmed what she already knew. The origine was not accessible.

"Who are you?" Talioth asked.

The man whose arm she had chopped in half stopped yelling. The blood remained on his shirt, but the exposed wound near his elbow had closed. Breathing heavily, the muscled man stood, lifting his sword with his good hand and backing away.

How is he not wiped out after a healing like that?

His eyes pierced hers. His face held a simmering rage while

his chest heaved.

"Let them go!" Lia shouted.

Laughter bounced back from the marked ones. "I think not," Talioth said. "Again, who are you?"

She puffed out her chest. "Lia Stormbridge." She motioned behind her. "This is my father, and those are my brothers and sisters of the Shadow Knights. Let them go."

"And I'm Raiyn Crabtree." Raiyn lifted a battle-axe that had been discarded in the dirt courtyard. "We will defend them with our lives."

A deafening silence filled the courtyard, interrupted only by the flicker of the torch.

"Come on," one of the men said. "We have seven already. Let's leave them."

Talioth nodded.

"No!" the one missing an arm shouted, his face twisted in fury. "They deserve to pay!"

"Fine," Talioth said. "Killing them will free up the power."

Lia swallowed hard as four of the marked ones closed in.

"No!" the man shouted again, holding up his good arm toward Lia. "*I* want them."

"Are you good to fight, Valdok?" Talioth asked.

"I'm fine! I wouldn't even need the devion to finish them."

"No, Lia!" Gavin shouted. "It's hopeless. Run!"

"Gag them!" Talioth shouted over his shoulder before nodding at Valdok. "They're yours. Be quick about it."

The others backed off. Valdok ripped off the remains of his bloody shirt and tossed it to the ground. His hairy chest rippled with muscles. He twirled his sword in his remaining hand as if it were a natural extension of his arm.

Lia glanced at Raiyn, who nodded. "You won't be able to use the origine," she whispered.

"I know. It's all right. You and me together. We can do this."

Her father lay on the dirt, passed out from exhaustion. She sighed and approached Valdok.

The red crystal around the man's neck glowed brightly, taunting her. He danced to his left then to his right, swinging his sword in a blurred motion to show off his speed. He moved so fast, Lia could barely follow him with her eyes.

Raiyn moved around to the opposite side, placing Valdok between them. His axe held before him with both hands. Lia nodded, adopting horn stance with her sword.

Valdok moved to keep both in his sights and flashed a wicked grin. Lia tracked him as he moved. From pure instinct, her sword pivoted and body turned. Something struck her weapon with a brutality she was not prepared for. The grip rattled in her hand, but she managed to keep her fingers around it.

After the single attempt on her, the man lunged for Raiyn, who was already moving in response to the strike on Lia. The blade just missed his side.

Valdok's body materialized again between them. He glanced at each, his brow furrowed after the failed attempt to take them in a single effort.

"Nice try, Valdok," one of the marked ones taunted. A handful of chuckles followed, turning the one-armed fighter's face into a mask of rage.

He roared as he lunged at Lia. His sword flashed and arm worked side to side.

Lia backed up. Half guessing and half moving where her body naturally flowed, she fended off five strikes in lightning succession but the sixth caught her on the arm, tearing a gash. She yelled, but the adrenaline pumping through her helped her ignore the pain. A swing at her head collided with the wall behind her after she ducked. Stones exploded into dust, and crumbling rocks fell to the ground. She spun out of the way.

Valdok turned and rushed toward her. He raised his sword

to attack, and Lia froze. Her body told her to move or block, but her limbs couldn't respond quickly enough. When the sword was about to descend upon her, a sweeping blade entered her vision from the side. Raiyn swung his axe toward the undefended chest of the man.

At the last moment, Valdok's eyes shifted, and his hands dropped. His sword pivoted and blocked Raiyn's attack. He followed with an elbow to the face, throwing Raiyn backward, clutching his nose.

Lia watched in horror as her friend stumbled, the marked one's sword slicing toward his stomach. She opened her mouth to yell, but it all happened too fast. The long blade caught Raiyn in the side just above his hip.

Raiyn groaned, spinning and falling to the ground, clutching his side. He remained on his knees, facing away from the fight. With a sneer, Valdok rushed to him, raising his sword in a killing blow.

"No!" Lia yelled. Her arm throbbed, blood staining her shirt.

Valdok hesitated, glancing over his shoulder with his chest heaving. The time gave her a chance to close the distance and attack.

She struck as hard and fast as she could, forcing him to fend off her blows. His parries were smooth, but his troubled eyes gave her a confidence she hadn't previously felt.

Valdok moved backward, easily fending her off, but after a moment, the speed of his arm seemed to slow. Her flicker of hope grew. Lia pressed in harder, forcing him farther away from Raiyn. Valdok's brow furrowed, and his moves grew frantic. After an awkward parry, his chest lay exposed. Her muscles twitched as fast as she could manage, and she jabbed at his chest. The whites of his eyes showed as the tip of her sword reached his flesh, tearing a gash over his ribs.

Lia's hope surged while Valdok stumbled away. She rushed

to Raiyn and crouched. Blood ran down his hip where his hand covered his side. "Can you heal?" she asked.

He shook his head. Sweat dripped down his pale face, his ragged breath uneven.

Lia gritted her teeth and stood, turning back to Valdok. The marked one hunched over, breathing heavily. Sweat dripped down his torso, glistening in the torchlight. He didn't even cover the wound. The black-and-red gash was narrow but looked deep. As she watched, her stomach lurched. The wound closed. First it changed color to a faint red, then the tear mended itself. After a few seconds, the gash she made didn't appear to have ever been there at all.

Valdok continued to pant, but his deep laugh chilled her bones. "That was . . . good," he said between breaths, "but, maybe, I should begin over here."

What does he— Lia blanched as the man turned around. Veron lay on the ground behind him. *No!* Raw emotion welled up in her, fighting to take over her senses.

"Say goodbye to your father," Valdok said, raising his sword with his one arm.

The space was too far. If she could use the origine, she could close the distance, but without, it was impossible. Something tapped her leg. Raiyn extended a dagger with a trembling arm. She grabbed the knife, the cool grip solid in her hand. The weight was perfect. She spun to Valdok. The man reared up, lifting on his toes. He aimed for Veron's exposed neck.

Lia cocked her arm and tossed the dagger. She had no origine to strengthen her—no extra senses to help her aim. She threw with as much force as she could muster, hoping the effort would be enough. The blade twirled through the air, flipping end-over-end. Valdok's massive shoulder moved, his weapon high in the air ready to drop. Just before it descended, the dagger's blade found its mark. Lia gasped as the tip buried itself into the base of the man's neck, at his spine.

Valdok's body jerked. His sword dropped, clattering on the dirt. He spun as he fell, his eyes glancing toward her one last time. He hit the ground with a puff of dust and remained motionless.

Lia stood. She faced the remaining six marked ones and readied her sword. Blood dripped from her arm to the dirt of the courtyard. She ignored the wound and fought to hide the exhaustion inside. "Who's next?" she said, her low voice eerily calm.

The others glanced between themselves, their faces hesitant.

"We can take them," one whispered.

"You go first," another said.

No one moved.

"We have plenty," Talioth said after a pause. "Carry the prisoners. We leave the rest."

The marked ones moved in a flurry, picking up the shackled shadow knights and tossing them over their shoulders. Bridgette's blonde hair waved nearly to the ground. Muffled sounds came from Gavin's upside-down head. He kicked his legs in every direction until a punch landed on his side, quieting him. Using their stored power, the marked ones ran toward the hallway to flee the courtyard.

Lia wanted to run after them. She wanted to save her mother and the others, but her legs wouldn't move. Her last view before they disappeared into the dark hallway was of her mother's face. Hanging over one of the attackers' shoulders, Chelci twisted to look in her direction. A peaceful look reflected back. In an instant, the regret and guilt Lia had felt toward her mother vanished, replaced by love and acceptance.

She ran after the group, but their enhanced power and speed was far beyond her. They were long gone by the time she exited through the front door of the building. "I'm sorry, Mother," she whispered to the air, picturing her mother's and her fellow knights' helpless faces somewhere in the night. *Fellow knights*, she thought. *I'm one of them.*

She jogged back to the courtyard, moving first to Raiyn. "How's your wound?" she asked. "Can you heal yet?" She searched inside herself for the origine and exhaled in relief when the familiar tingle returned.

Raiyn nodded. Sitting on the dirt and leaning against the wall, he winced as he closed his eyes. The wound at his hip healed. After holding his breath, he exhaled. "Oh, that's better. I thought I was in trouble for a minute." He moved to sit forward, then stopped. "Whoa!"

"Take it easy," Lia said. "Lay back. Give yourself time to rest."

Raiyn nodded. "Just give me a bit."

Lia stood and ran to where Veron remained on the ground. Three dead bodies lay strewn around him. She crouched and rested a hand on his shoulder. "Father?" She trembled. "Father, are you there?"

Metal clanked as the cuffs on his legs rubbed together. Still, he didn't wake. She ran to the smithing room and grabbed an awl and a hammer before returning. After a minute of pounding the awl into the anklets' pins, she removed both shackles then shook her father again.

Veron's eyelids fluttered and finally opened. "Lia," he breathed.

She smiled, relief rushing through her. "Are you all right? Are you injured?"

He lifted to a sitting position and glanced over his body. "I ache all over, but . . . I don't see any injuries."

"They took Mother and the other knights," Lia said. "I'm sorry. I tried to follow, but . . ."

"But it's difficult without the power."

Lia nodded. "The glowing people are gone, now though.

The power is back. Use the origine to make sure you're not injured." She pointed to his feet. "I took off the anklets."

"Thank you." Veron's eyes focused across the courtyard. He took steady breaths until his forehead wrinkled.

Something is wrong, Lia thought. "What is it?"

He shook his head and paused. "There's nothing there," he said, his voice shaking.

Lia cocked her head.

"The origine," Veron clarified. "It's not there."

Lia spun around, expecting to find a glowing red crystal from a marked one dangling over her, but no one was there. She tested it herself, the power ready and eager to be used. She turned back to him, checking each side. "Do you have metal anywhere else?"

Veron gave a tight shake of his head and pursed his lips. He was silent for a long moment. "They took it."

"What do you mean?"

"The origine. They took it from me."

"How can they do that?"

"Whatever he did with his hand and that crystal—when you arrived. It . . . *took* something from me."

Lia shook. She'd never seen her father so uncertain. "Can you get it back?"

"I don't know. I feel . . . empty."

She rested her hand on his arm. "I'm so sorry, Father."

"I thought I had lost it before, many years ago. But it returned." A faint smile grew as he looked into her eyes. "I can find it again."

With a sinking feeling, she remembered rushing out of Tienn. "Danik's here, too. He told the Marked Ones where we are."

Veron's face fell. He dropped his chin to his chest.

"You were right about him, Father. I should have listened to you. He's embraced the devion as his power, and he trained a group of others."

Veron nodded. "I know."

Lia pinched her brows together. "How do you know?"

"I saw him," he looked up, "right after he killed your grandfather."

The words twisted her gut, and the air felt sucked from her lungs.

"King Darcius is dead. Danik and his new gang have taken control and will force the high lords to do their will with the devion."

"We can stop them," Lia said, glancing across the courtyard to where Raiyn struggled to his feet. "Us three, we can do it."

"You mean, you two?" Veron asked, pressing his hand against his knee as he stood. "Unless I can find the origine again, I won't be much help."

"Count me in," Raiyn said.

"Raiyn," Veron said. "Thank you for coming. I wouldn't be alive without you both."

"He saved my life, too, Father," Lia added. "Danik turned on me, and I would have died if it weren't for him."

"It was nothing," the young man said, blushing and waving the attention away.

"I was wrong about you, Raiyn," Veron said. "I judged you based on your father and couldn't see the person you were. You're the definition of what it means to be a shadow knight."

A broad smile grew on Raiyn's face. "Thank you, sir."

"I also need to apologize to you."

Lia turned to her father, shocked to find him staring at her. "To me?"

Veron nodded, facing her. "I pushed you away. I tried to force you into what I wanted and never took the time to understand the person you were. I—" A glisten formed at the corner of his eyes. "I said some awful things."

Lia swallowed, her heartbeat speeding.

"I've thought about nothing else since you left, and I wish I could take them back."

"It's fine, Father, you don't have to—"

"I do! I need to get this out." He wiped his eyes, then stepped closer, resting his hands on her arms. "The attack on Chelci was not your fault."

Lia tensed, the sudden wave of emotion overwhelming her. Her teeth clenched to keep from crying.

"Had you been there, you may have both been hurt. Those men were the ones responsible. I was angry and scared, and I lashed out at you, the one person I needed to protect. Also, your brother . . ."

Lia inhaled.

"Morgan's death was an accident. I've always known that, and I've *never* thought you responsible. Again, I was foolish and careless with my words. I wanted you to hurt because I was hurting." He squeezed her arm tenderly. "I'm so sorry about everything."

"I'm sorry, too," Lia said, choking on tears. "You've given me so much and done nothing but try to help me be my best. I resented it. I put up a wall and refused to listen or even recognize the ways you loved me. I thought I wanted to be free from it all. I thought being on my own and doing whatever I wanted would be what I needed, but as soon as I left here, I wanted to be back. I missed you and Mother. I missed the Knights."

She stepped forward, opening her arms. Veron returned the gesture, and they wrapped their arms around each other. Lia pulled against his back, tears flowing. Veron's chest jerked as he sobbed. The strength and warmth of his body allowed her to drift away. The fear of attack and of dying faded. Her purposeless feelings dissipated. Acceptance and love of a father filled her heart. "I love you," she whispered.

"I love you, too," he replied.

When they pulled apart, father and daughter both wiped their eyes. Lia laughed, a hollow, nervous sound. "Sorry. I'm not used to crying like that."

He chuckled. "Neither am I."

Raiyn took a step closer, and Lia turned to him. "You sure you're all right?" she asked.

He nodded. "I feel good."

"Me too," Veron added.

Lia looked around the courtyard. "I don't think we can stay here anymore."

Veron nodded. "The Marked Ones know where we are, and so does Danik."

"How do you two feel about tracking?" Lia asked.

Veron smiled. "A group that size . . . They're bound to leave a trail."

"I'm in," Raiyn said with a nod.

Lia stood up straight. "Mother needs us. Let's grab some food, weapons, and supplies, then see if we can get our knights back."

STANDING in the king's bedroom, Danik's face hurt from grinning. He had spent the last hour walking through the castle, marveling at the size and number of the rooms. The bedroom was the grandest of them all. The gilded bed frame and purple curtains gave the space a regal feel. Windows looked out toward the mostly dark city. Holding a lantern in one hand, he ran the other along the mahogany trim of the wall.

Who would have believed I'd end up here? he thought with a smirk. *The Shadow Knights taught me, but never gave me a chance to rise like this.*

After killing the king, the high lords took surprisingly little convincing to swear allegiance. Threats of death and promises of power kept them in line, and with their support, the transfer of power would be simple.

A knock rattled the door.

"Come in."

The door opened, and Nicolar stuck his head through.

"What'd you find?"

"Three bodies."

"Shadow knights?"

Nicolar shook his head. "Marked ones."

Danik's eyebrows pinched together.

"One was missing an arm. We disposed of the bodies, but there was more blood in the courtyard."

"What of the knights?"

"They wanted them alive, so . . . It looks like they took them."

"With those crystals, it should have been easy. I can't believe they took down three of them." Danik paused a moment in thought then waved his hand. "Thank you, Nicolar. You can go."

The thief ducked back through the door and closed it behind him.

A pang of regret ran through Danik. *Veron and the others taught me what I know. Now they're captured or possibly killed.* The power of the Marked Ones troubled him, but as long as they focused on the Shadow Knights, he was content to let them do as they wished.

Nicolar and his crew are the ones I should concern myself with. The gang of thieves had proven to be quick studies in learning the devion. *They're quick to violence and could turn on me in an instant if I let them. I just need to keep them happy.*

The memory of Jade entering the room in Tienn to dispose of Lia came into his mind. *Lia.* His face fell. *I wish you had stayed with me. We could have ruled Feldor together. We would have been unstoppable.*

He flexed his muscles. *Power.* It flowed through him like a raging river. The origine paled in comparison to what he felt with the devion. *I'm stronger, faster, and can fight longer. The Knights were fools to prevent this.*

He stopped in front of a mirror. He held the lantern up higher to shine light on his face. His skin looked a touch paler than he expected. He rubbed it, trying to get the blood flowing. *I'm just tired. I need some sleep.*

As he turned from the mirror, something caught his eye. He stopped. His pulse sped, thumping in his ears. He took a hesitant step forward, lifting the lantern with a shaky arm. The whites of his eyes showed as he stared at his reflection.

He lifted his free hand, moving it to his neck. His fingers grazed the skin, moving across his throat. A rough section tickled the tips of his fingers. He pressed harder. The skin was taut and scabbing.

He yanked his hand away, his heart pounding. Danik angled his body to the side and lifted the lantern higher. His breath left him. On his neck, a small section stood out. The oval shape was unmistakable. A dark stain grew at the base of his throat.

THE EPIC STORY of the Shadow Knights continues in Shadow of Sacrifice. Preorder it today!

"I THOUGHT my dad's first three Shadow books were doggaly great, but this one . . . (Yowls in delight) . . . this is incredible! I'm trying to tell everyone I can cause Dad says it's the best way to help spread the word. Can you all do me a favor? Can you tell people by leaving a review online?" - Charlie

PLEASE LEAVE an honest review on Amazon or wherever you got the book from. Do it for Charlie.

Get a FREE prequel novella to the Shadow Knights series - Shadow Knights: Origine - by signing up for my mailing list at www.subscribepage.com/michaelwebbnovels or scan this QR code

ACKNOWLEDGMENTS

Writing books is unique in its ability to be both terrifying and rewarding at the same time. The reason I put myself through the hundreds of hours of work and nerve-racking vulnerability that comes with publishing books is because of you. YOU are why I write. Thank you for taking the time to read the story I crafted. There is nothing more encouraging than hearing from you and knowing that my story made an impact on your life. I want to thank a few people specifically for their help in creating Shadow of Betrayal...

Joe Solari: Thank you for donating your time to talk with me through my books and publishing process. You were the main reason I came back to the Shadow Knights and set out to write this next-generation trilogy.

Beta readers: You were all AMAZING! This was the largest crew I'd used yet, and every one of you were critical in helping. Thank you...Tara, Nicholas, Manton, David, Andreas, Aden, Eli, Johnny, Debbie, Laura, Don, Keith, Riya, Hayley, Dick, Brian, Tammy, and Sandra.

Jeff Brown: Thank you for continuing to create jaw-droppingly beautiful illustrations that bring the story to life visually. Your covers are second-to-none, and I'm so appreciative of your work.

Everyone who read and loved the first trilogy: Thank you for giving my books a chance! And thank you for telling your friends. Your enthusiasm for the Shadow Knights motivated me to explore what the next chapter in their saga looked like.

Julia: Thank you for being proud of me and continuing to let me spend time writing my crazy stories.